DISCARD

Confessions
of a
Five-Chambered Heart:
25 Tales of Weird Romance

Confessions
of a
Five-Chambered Heart:
25 Tales of
Weird Romance

CAITLÍN R. KIERNAN

Subterranean Press • 2012

Proofreading by Sonya Taaffe and Kathryn A. Pollnac.

First Edition

ISBN
978-1-59606-473-7

Subterranean Press
PO Box 190106
Burton, MI 48519

www.subterraneanpress.com
www.caitlinkiernan.com

Table of Contents

*Pour tous ceux que j'ai baisés un jour
(au sens propre, au figuré, ou autre).*

For Henry Darger and his beloved Vivian Girls

Love is about craving for transformation. And all transformation, all movement, happens because life turns into death.

Angus Fraser and Lynne Stopkewich,
Kissed (1996)

"Anyway, that's the proper function of art, isn't it?" I ask you. "To unsettle us?"

Caitlín R. Kiernan,
"Lullaby of Partition and Reunion" (2008)

I cannot pretend that I felt any regret,
Cause each broken heart will eventually mend,
As the blood runs red down the needle and thread.
"Someday you will be loved."

Death Cab For Cutie,
"Someday You Will Be Loved" (2005)

Introduction
Sexing the Weird

It's the taste of sea spray, of salt dried on my lips. That precise taste, licked away hours after I've left the shore. And it's swimming a hundred yards out from land, over water that grows deeper and deeper below you, and it's having no idea what is moving about beneath you. It's this frisson, that fleeting or prolonged shudder. Fear that is not *only* fear, but that is equal parts pleasure and awe. I suspect this is what some people mean when they say *God*, or *god*, or *gods*, but rarely do those words appeal to me. Rather, the bleached skeleton of a gull in the dunes, or the feel of greenbriers against my skin. Lying alone in a room so dark that my eyes have no hope of discerning any genuine light, and so begin to create their own desperate whirls and flickers. It's the taste of my blood, or anyone else's, a kiss becomes a nip, a razor opening the skin of my shoulder to expose the crimson sea that flows inside me. It's the thought of being consumed, willingly or by some grim seduction, slowly becoming one with some other, consciousness preserved or lost to digestive dissolution. Let us entertain the thought that what I am trying to communicate could be summed up by saying, simply, imagine gripping daemonic horns, those of a ram or gazelle or some other member of the Antilopinae (oh, and Pan comes immediately to mind, that sacred, rutting son of gods), and then the thrust from *without*, from without to *within*, and all the impossible things that might follow.

All these things are but the barest glimpse of what I mean when I speak of *weird erotica*, which comprises the bulk of the book in your hands. The intrusion – often by invitation – of the Outside into that most intimate and ancient act.

And the *Outside* is the *Unknown,* and, as Lovecraft tells us (Lovecraft who only *seems* a prude until one realizes how preoccupied so many of his stories are with sex, very weird sex, indeed, no matter what dim view he took), "The oldest and strongest emotion of mankind is fear, and the oldest and strongest kind of fear is fear of the unknown." And what can be more unknown than Death? And what is Death but our penultimate encounter with the Unknown (despite those who choose to delude themselves, and so believe otherwise)? And now, now, sex and death – recall the French phrase for the orgasm, *la petite mort,* the small death – and we are almost to the abovementioned moment of frisson. There is an association between sex and death that may be as old as the consciousness of human beings, or that may predate our species and have first been felt by our australopithecine forbearers. In our mind, and I would argue in any objective sense that may exist *beyond* our minds, sex and death are merely two sides of a coin. Better yet, yin yang, only seeming to exist in opposition, but all the while intimately interconnected. And oh this sounds so preposterously cliché I want to erase it and write something else. But, often, that which is cliché is so because it's profoundly fucking true. Sex is the author of death, and without death, without the clearing away of old life, there will be no further sex. The *Unknown* begets the little death, granting that gift, then delivers it again into that "strongest kind of fear."

Undique enim ad inferos tantundem viæ est.

And this one I walk does not deny the certainty of death, nor of life, nor of the Unknown, nor of the Outside, nor of the strongest kind of fear and the undeniable link between all these things. Integral. Intertwined. I'm following – and not necessarily by *choice,* excepting I've refused self-denial – the paths of Ovid, de Sade, Swinburne, von Sacher-Masoch, Crowley, *Le Jardin des supplices,* Mapplethorpe, Wilde, Dorian Cleavenger, Giger, and here there is suddenly great frustration at naming so many males, so add Sappho, Angela Carter, Dion Arbus, Octavia Butler, Patricia Piccinini's parahumans, Kiki Smith, Veruschka von Lehndorff, Karen Finley, Charlotte Roche, Diamanda Galás, Anaïs Nin, and the perplexing mess that is Anne Rice. And I almost forgot *Le Théâtre du Grand-Guignol.* Yet few of these artists go even half far enough into the territories I've set myself to exploring. Oh, and I'm risking the insufferable *pretension* of name-dropping (bolstering the legitimacy of my work by making reference to more renowned artists), and how can I have named only *one* musician while I was at it?

Ah, well.

Well.

It is a well, you know. I dip into it again and again and again. In my "real" life and in my fictions and in all the interstitial spaces bridging these. So, as one who draws deeply from that well, endlessly, I may fairly be accused of committing a confession via these introductory comments. Of lowering my guard, baring my "soul." Choose your apothegm. In Olden Days, the Recent Past, even into this enlightened Twenty-First Century A.D., and even tomorrow, I would be/have been/am labeled a pervert, indecent, a degenerate, polymorphously perverse, a sinner, a sicko, a pornographer, depraved, and debauched. And only for stating truths that others so frequently shy away from admitting. We paint and spin tales and sing all our fantasies, violating the fabric of decent, factual *Reality* at every turn. Human beings tear down the crushing weight of their life prisons and erect blasphemous surrogates, and I dare say blasphemous because, in times not so very far past, the tamest of fantasies were deemed unhealthy to the mind of man (especially the minds of the children of men; legal persecution against sellers of comic books and manga spring at first to mind, and, in the same vein, the *de facto* censorship of New York Magistrate Charles F. Murphy's Comics Code Authority, and also Fredric Wertham's *Seduction of the Innocent*). So, yes. I freely admit that I respond to myself, my highest power, and lock denial of desire outside (not to be mistaken with the *Outside*). As do all those other fantasists so much less concerned with sex, or concerned not at all with sex, or even prudish in thinking themselves different from me not by degrees but by kind (to mangle the words of Charles Darwin, who gave me great insight into the mutability of flesh).

I go to the well. My perverse well of words.

I swim in those deep waters far from shore, not knowing what swims beneath me, and what might rise at any moment. *As a fantasist*, I do this thing. I grip the horns of horned and rutting creatures. I do not allow my ears to be plugged with beeswax against the songs of sirens. I delight at restraint and the pricking of my skin and the act of restraining, and a thousand imaginary monstrous lovers, a dozen lashes and countless other tortures, mutations and transfigurations (of mind and body), welcome alien violations, negations of gender, and we might go on like this quite a terribly long time. I think not many writers of the weird have ventured into these warpings of the world (and, no, not for a moment, do I count as comrades those recently teeming writers of "paranormal romance" and "shifter fiction," for rarely do they accomplish anything more dangerous than dressing the safe and normative up in wolf's clothing; these authors, and their readers, are merely *tourists*). I think that, but I may well be wrong. And if so, I stand corrected, and would wish someone to point me to those authors. You'd be doing me a kindness.

In exchange for my showing you the path down to the sea.

Which I am about to do.

Or, I should say, I am about to do again. I've been doing this for years stacked upon years now, haven't I? It may be I have cultivated an infamy, spawned an ill reputation, which I'd call an occupational hazard. For those who embrace the frisson, that fleeting or prolonged shudder. For those who show their darkest dreams and experiences to others (not to be mistaken with the *Other*), thereby opening themselves to accusations of corruption. But this is what fantasy does. Fantasy corrupts reality, as does dream. You can leave out all shameless mention genitals, the satyrs, of mermaids, of frog toes and tentacles, and fine, fine, fine, but this, I conclude, does not change a thing.

Death and sex, these are among the cornerstones of reality.

Pain and pleasure.

Fear of the Unknown.

Love of the Unknown, commingled with *eros* and *philia*. Desire without boundaries, no safe words, and I hardly care if this sort of thing *is not for everybody*. I steadfastly agree it's for more than are willing to admit. But, the rest of you, take my hand, and let's swim out past where our feet can touch the bottom.

Caitlín R. Kiernan
3 December 2011
Providence, Rhode Island

The Wolf Who Cried Girl

She has lost count of exactly how many times winter and summer have traded places since the woman came upon her in the woods and took away her pelt. The woman also took her claws and her teeth and everything else that had made this girl a wolf. So complete was the theft that there are days now when she can hardly remember the way it was before, when she went about on four legs, instead of only two, when she had no need of words, but knew, instead, a near-infinite vocabulary of smells and tastes and subtler sounds than mere language can convey. She was sleeping when the woman found her, and the girl who was then a wolf dreamed of eyes the color of moss and spruce branches and dreamed, too, the sudden, wrenching pain of being divided from oneself. She awoke naked on the snow, truly naked for the first time in her life, and lay gasping beneath the watchful, star-stained sky as the green-eyed woman wrapped herself in stolen fur, then loped away into the night on another's paws.

In the morning, the girl's pack found her shivering in a rocky place, and they snarled and bared their fangs at the helpless, pale-skinned thing the woman had left behind. They understood, in their dim and certain way, the crime that had transpired in the night, how it was that a wolf could lose its skin to a human being. Wolves have never needed religion to fear such demons, and they have never needed folktales to pass that fear from mother to cub. Confused and frightened and faintly mourning the loss of the wolf she had been, the pack skulked away and left her alone in the rocky place, though she cried out after them, fashioning ugly, aching noises with her new tongue and vocal cords. They ignored her pleas for help, unable to recognize them as such and too afraid that the demon might come back for yet another change of skin.

Later in the day, having grown somewhat bolder, the wolves permitted her to take a few mouthfuls from a half-frozen elk carcass. And while she struggled to chew the meat with jaws wholly insufficient to the task, the pack sniffed her ass and licked at her sex, trying to discover some vestige of her former self. But they only succeeded in recalling the fullness of their fear, and soon they had nothing for the naked girl but bristling coats and black lips curled back to expose threatful, nipping incisors and canines. And so she left them, forever, and wandered down from the mountains and forests to the steel and glass and concrete city of men.

For a time, the girl was made to live in cages, of one sort or another, and she was given pills and pricked with needles that made it even more difficult to remember what she had once been. She was forced into the peculiar, ill-fitting, mismatched pelts men and women wear because they long ago forgot how to grow their own. She was taught to bathe in soapy, hot water, because all the scents of her body had become shameful and offensive. With every passing day, she was, bit by bit, more a human girl and less the wolf she'd been born. And when she at last stopped biting and howling, when she had learned a few words, and how to dress herself, and that there was only one proper place to piss and defecate, she was turned out of the cages and hospital beds and back into the streets.

In this city, here in the lee of the mountains, she lives off whatever scraps she finds discarded and rotting in trashcans and dumpsters. Sometimes, she's lucky and catches a stray cat, or a rat, or a pigeon, the city's stingy wildlife, and so there's meat that has not been charred or boiled. There's warm blood and bones to crack open for their marrow. She sleeps in the empty concrete and brick shells of abandoned or disused buildings, of which there is no shortage. She does her best to stay clear of all the other women and men who have been driven away from the vast, murmuring pack of humanity, the ragged castaways whom the girl at first mistook for other wolves robbed of their true shapes by other demons. But she has long-since learned her mistake, and they are almost always as wary of her as are the rest. Perhaps, she thinks, the outsider's senses are somewhat keener than those of the ones who live always inside their neatly stacked cages and their rolling, roaring caves, and who constantly scrub at themselves, dulling their noses and ears and eyes with perfume and noise.

She was born a wolf, and even now there is some lingering shred of her lupine birth that the shape-stealing demon and the city people have not managed to pry from her. She is certain that they *would* have, if they could only have found it, if they'd suspected there was anything left to take from her. She imagines that shred is like some small burrowing animal, dug in too deeply for even the most determined claws to ever extract from the sanctuary of its hole. But it is enough that there are nights when she finds her way up rickety fire escapes or deserted stairwells to the rooftops where she has only the omnipresent glare of electric lights to half obscure the moon and stars and the far-away mountains. If she is sure no one is watching her, that she is alone with the sky and the horizon, then she strips away all the filthy, alien raiments from her body and squats naked on tin and masonry and tar-shingle. She goes down on all fours again, though her anatomy is no longer suited to a quadruped's gait.

She throws back her head, matted ginger tresses falling away to reveal bright eyes like moss and spruce boughs, and the cry that escapes her throat is not a howl so much as it is a wordless, keening threnody. It is the nearest thing to a howl of which she is now capable, and hearing such a strange and utterly inconsolable ululation, the men and women and children of the city lie awake in their beds, listening, breathlessly waiting to see if the cry will come again and maybe nearer than before, maybe right outside their windows. The girl who was a wolf wails her sorrow at the moon, and, in that instant, all those who hear her cry flinch or cringe or shut their eyes tight as the refuge of civilization seems suddenly to melt away around them. All at once, the Pleistocene was only yesterday, at best, and will surely come again tomorrow. Ancient, unconscious memories buried a million years in the deepest neocortical convolutions lurch slowly towards recognition. Shades are drawn and locks are double and triple checked; countless fretful dreams of humdrum inconvenience and workaday disaster are traded for nightmares of running in dark places and hungry red eyes and gnashing saber teeth. And maybe in the morning, there will be a rash of phone calls to the police and animal control and to anyone else who might help to reassert the promises of this modern century and remind these people when *and* where they are. Hearing the girl, a pious few mutter prayers, but they pray to a fatherly god of light and love and justice, a god of right and wrong, for men no longer recall the names of those dark, amoral spirits who once were summoned to stand between firelight and slavering jaws.

On the rooftop, the green-eyed, ginger-haired girl, who was not born a girl of any sort, rocks back on her naked haunches, and she barks and yowls until her throat has gone raw and there are only tears. She wets herself and moans and scratches in vain at her own body with short, brittle fingernails, as though she might tear away this obscuring flesh and discover her true form secreted just underneath. There will be bruises and scabby welts in the morning, but her clothes will hide most of them, and hardly anyone ever pauses to consider the wounds the city's dispossessed inflict upon themselves. Finally, exhausted and trembling, she finds some place out of the worst of the wind and curls up there to wait for daylight. Drifting in and out of wakefulness, she has her own sour dreams to contend with.

For a time, she is wandering the hospital cages again, those endless white caverns lit by tiny suns that blind her, yet shed no warmth. At last, she finds a hole in a wall of the cavern, and when she looks out upon a high and winter-bound meadow, she sees the corpses of all her pack strewn about there, a dozen lifeless bodies disemboweled and stripped clean of their hides, limp crimson smears stark against the fresh snow, become only carrion now left behind for starving ravens and coyotes. And she can also see the footprints of women and men, the tracks of the skinwalkers who have done this thing. Their laughter rises and falls, buoyed triumphant on swirling, icy gusts or drifting down from the hazy blue-grey sky, and they sing her a song that is all rattling bones and thunder.

Older than the one who spins the World,
We are free.
Not enslaved by the likeness of Mother or Father,
We are free.
Unencumbered, unafraid, ever undying,
We are free.

And she turns away from the window, then, back to the nurses and their pills in paper cups. She is begging them to help her to forget that she was ever anything but a human girl. She is promising them that she can learn to use a fork and to shit where she's told and to look at people when they speak to her. *Only let me forget*, she pleads. *Only let me forget and never remember myself again.* But they frown at her and say she clearly isn't any better at all, because there was never anything to be forgotten.

She opens her eyes, and it's day again, and there is a young man squatting beside her on the roof, brushing the tangled strands of hair back from her face. The girl who is no longer a wolf bares her teeth and snarls at him before she remembers how short and dull her teeth have grown and how little threat is left in her voice. Still, it is enough that he immediately pulls his hand away, and enough, too, that the man's expression changes, his curiosity and concern dabbed now around the edges by surprise and wariness.

"I didn't mean to scare you," he says, then glances at his hand as though checking to be certain that all five fingers are still where they ought to be. "But you must be freezing," and as if to prove the point, his breath fogs. "You're going to get pneumonia or frostbite or – "

"I'm not cold," she says, though she is, in fact, very, very cold, and the girl sits up, scooting a little farther from the man. There's a brick wall at her back now, and nowhere left to go.

"Do you have a home?" he asks. "Someplace to get in out of the weather for a bit? Do you have someone to take care of you?"

"I am awake," she says, and he slowly nods his head.

"Yes, you're awake. But it's very *cold* out here, and we need to get you inside, maybe get some coffee or soup in you. Maybe a strong cup of tea if you don't like coffee."

She wrinkles her dry nose, remembering the bitter black water called *coffee*. Then she hugs herself and glances up at the January sky. There are no clouds, no sign of snow, and she cannot hear the skinwalkers singing. But she is sure they must still be watching her, and so she looks quickly down at the toes of the man's boots.

"Where are your clothes?" he asks, and she shrugs, not because she doesn't understand him or does not know the answer, but because right now she'd rather be cold and naked than wrapped up in those tattered false pelts. This hairless skin is terrible enough, and when she sees the cuts and abrasions on her arms and breasts, her belly and thighs and long hind legs, she is only sorry that she has not done herself more serious damage.

The man removes his own coat and cautiously takes a step towards her. "Here," he says, "please, take this," and he drapes it around her shoulders. It itches, and the suede leather smells faintly of some long-dead thing, but she doesn't shake it off.

"We really do need to get inside," he tells her, "before someone else sees you and decides to call the police." And when he offers his hand, she accepts it, rising slowly to her feet. The man leads her across the rooftop and in through an open window. He shuts and locks it behind them, and then she follows him down a long hallway and a flight of stairs to his apartment one floor below and on the other side of the building. He talks, and she listens. She understands most of what he says, enough to know that he was out all night the night before, and that he often comes up to the roof in the morning.

"The view," he says, though the girl has not asked him to explain. He closes the apartment door and turns the deadbolt, then smiles and adds, "Most days, you can see all the way to the mountains from up there. That's one reason I rented this place."

She has to pee, and so he shows her where the bathroom is, then goes to make them each a cup of tea, leaving her alone. And when she's finished, and her bladder no longer aches, the girl who was born a wolf stands before the mirror mounted above the sink with its shiny silver faucet and its knob marked H and its knob marked C. The girl watching her from the glass was also born a wolf, and she also wears nothing but the young man's suede jacket. Her body has all the same inconsequential wounds. But the girl has long since come to comprehend the nature of mirrors – that she is only seeing herself reflected there and not another. It isn't so different from sunlight off a pond or a slow-running stream, only made so much clearer, so much stiller, the image never marred by a ripple or the movements of a curious fish or turtle rising to the surface. She puts a finger to her chapped lips, as though warning herself not to speak, and the girl in the glass does likewise, and their eyes are the greenest things that she's ever seen. She flushes the toilet, turns off the bathroom light, and then goes out to drink the steaming cup of tea the man has made for her. She dislikes the taste, though not so much as she dislikes the taste of coffee, and at least it makes her warm inside.

"No," the man tells her, answering a question she hasn't asked. "As it happens, I wasn't born here. I came to the city a few years back, looking for work and wanting to be near the mountains, wanting to photograph – " He pauses, staring back at the odd, soft-spoken girl sitting across the counter from him, shamelessly naked except for his jacket, holding her empty cup and watching him intently.

"It's easier, I think, if you see for yourself," he says, and so he shows her to the room that he calls his studio. There are a great many odd things there the girl cannot understand, though he tries to explain them to her. But mostly, there are images pinned upon the walls with thumbtacks or held inside black aluminum frames or kept safe between plastic archival sleeves in thick photo albums. She has seen this trick before, too, and knows that it's something like a mirror. Unlike the objects seen through a mirror, however, these images do not move, but appear inscrutably suspended in time. He shows her alpine meadows strewn with the bright blooms of columbine, lupin, and butterweed, and deep glacial lakes stained the color of polished turquoise by the constant influx of rock flour. There are photographs of jagged, snow-dusted peaks stark against the palest blue skies, and photographs of the ghostly white trunks of aspen groves, their leaves gone gold with autumn. There are elk and black bears, otters and mink and a badger, moose and mule deer, and one shot of a lynx crouched in the limbs of a ponderosa pine. And finally, he produces an album filled only with photos of wolves. She does not say a word, but only stares down at the familiar amber eyes and the lolling tongues as the man turns the pages and explains that he is especially proud of this one shot of a pack moving in a line across the snow, alpha wolf at the lead and the scraggly omega trailing out behind the rest.

She closes her eyes, so that she will no longer have to see the photographs. And he wants to know if something's wrong, if it's anything he's said or done, and she can only shake her head and mutter entirely unconvincing assurances that she is fine. Then she asks to be excused and returns alone to the bathroom, where she sits on the edge of the tub, weeping and shaking and digging her nails into her palms until they leave behind red crescents and draw the tiniest bit of blood.

And later, after he makes her French toast with powdered sugar and pours her a glass of milk, the man asks her to stay with him, if she has nowhere else to go. And because she *hasn't* anywhere else to go, excepting the streets, and alleyways, and the homeless shelters when she's feeling very brave, she says yes. But the girl knows that isn't the only reason that she's agreed. Now that she has seen and held the album filled with his photographs of wolves, she cannot bear the thought of never being able to hold it again. She is lying on his sofa, warm beneath a woolen blanket, wondering if he would try to stop her if she simply decided to take the album and leave, when she falls asleep. She dreams, but this time there are no hospital nightmares or singing skinwalkers waiting for her.

When she awakens, the sun is already setting, and the threadbare clothes she left scattered all about the roof the night before have been washed and dried and are lying folded neatly on the floor beside the sofa. The man is sitting at the kitchen table, tinkering with the innards of one of his big cameras, and he doesn't stop and turn to watch as she dresses. "Thank you," she says and buttons her grey corduroys, then pulls the raveling yellow sweater on over her head.

"No bother at all," he says. "It was laundry day, anyhow. But you're welcome, regardless. You know, I was just thinking, I don't even know your name."

She sits back down on the sofa, and almost replies that wolves don't have names, that wolves do not *need* names. But she's not a wolf, anymore, and girls *do* have names. In the hospital, one of the doctors had called her Anastasia, though she'd never understood why.

"You don't have to tell me, if you'd rather not," the man says. "Or maybe you could tell me some other time, if you wish. It's entirely up to you."

"Anastasia," she answers. "My name is Anastasia," and that makes him smile.

"Then I am glad to know you, Anastasia," he says. "And I'm very glad you didn't freeze to death on the roof." Then he goes back to working on his camera, and she sits staring out the window, watching as twilight turns to dusk and dusk turns to night.

The night is filled with the ugly, clamorous sounds of the city, which, more often than not, and even after so many years, she still finds inexplicable and alarming. Footsteps falling hard on cement and asphalt; the angry, argumentative shouts and the cries of pain; the laughter and taunting catcalls; the hot screech of automobile tires and the blat of automobile horns. The long hiss of a bus' air-brakes, a barking dog, and the rattling cacophony of an upturned garbage can. All of it to keep her on edge, to keep her startled and constantly looking over her shoulder, even here, in the relative safety and comfort of his apartment. The man does not object when she takes the clean sheets and blankets and pillows he has laid out for her on the sofa and makes an untidy nest of them beneath a table in one corner of the room. And he also does not object when, shortly before dawn, she wakes from another nightmare and leaves her nest to join him in his bed. That is the first time they have sex, and there is only a moment's awkwardness when she whimpers softly and then bares her throat to him, before rising on hands and knees and offering him her ass. These might be peculiar overtures to a man who was never a wolf and never will be, but he's a quick study and catches on soon enough.

Afterwards, when they are finished, he whispers, "I have questions." She lies next to him, feeling at once satiated and ill at ease, watching the sunrise leaking through the slats of the white Levolor blinds that cover his bedroom window. "But I don't have to ask them, not now or ever, if you'd prefer that I didn't."

"I am lost," she says, hoping she'll not have to say anything more, and not taking her eyes off the window as the world outside and inside grows brighter by scant degrees.

"That much I'd pretty well figured out on my own. I've never met anyone who seemed so entirely lost as you. But, there's something else, Anastasia."

"And I am not a sane woman," she says, remembering all the things the doctors and nurses told her before they finally sent her out to live on the streets. "You should know that. I'm delusional, and likely schizophrenic." There is enough sunlight now that she has to squint to keep from looking away from the window.

"Are you on any sort of medication?" he asks, and she shakes her head. He doesn't ask why not.

"I am a wolf," she tells him, then gives up and closes her eyes, because the sun has started making them smart and water, and she doesn't want him to think she's crying. "I was a wolf when I was born. I was not born a girl."

For a while, he says nothing else, and she lies there watching the orange-white afterimages dancing about behind her eyelids. *This is when he will make me leave,* she thinks. *This is when he will lead me back up to the rooftop and lock the window so I can never come back inside.* The thought only makes her a little sad, because she's known it was coming all along.

"Is that why you believe you're crazy?" he asks, instead.

"You have been very kind," she says without opening her eyes. "If you want me to leave now, I wouldn't blame you. I promise I won't be offended."

"You never even asked my name."

"Names are new to me," she replies.

"And yours isn't really Anastasia?" he asks.

"It's the only name anyone has ever given me," she replies, then adds, "Wolves do not need names."

"I have to go to work," he says. "I have a wedding to shoot today, and it's not the sort of thing I can afford to cancel. Will you still be here when I come home?"

She does not immediately recognize the tingling sensation in her chest and belly as relief, and it's possible she has never *felt* human relief. But the girl who was not always a girl nods her head, and she says yes, I will be here, because you haven't told me to leave, and I have nowhere else to go.

"I hope," he says, "that you'll still be here because I *want* you to be here. I hope that counts for something with you."

"Possibly," she says, answering him as honestly as she can, and then he kisses her lightly on the left cheek and gets out of bed. She lies there, listening to the noises he makes showering and having breakfast and getting dressed, and before he has gone, she has drifted back to sleep. In her dreams, she is in the mountains again, chasing rabbits and chipmunks and voles through the litter of a forest floor. It isn't winter, but maybe early spring, and she isn't a wolf, either. She brings down one of the rabbits just before it reaches its tunnel in a jumble of rocks and fallen spruce boughs. Even without her wolf's teeth, she kills it quickly with a single crushing bite to the back of its skull, then lies down to eat amid the dead leaves and moss, the fern and harebells.

"If they catch you here, you must know they'll surely kill you," says the green-eyed demon who stole her skin, and when the girl looks up, the thief is standing on a boulder not very far away. She wears the wolf pelt, forelegs tied tightly about her throat and shoulders and the hind legs cinched around her waist, the bushy tail hanging between her thighs. To most eyes, whether wolf or human, she would seem no more or less than any wolf.

The girl sits up, her dead rabbit and all its delicious smells forgotten, and she stares directly at the demon wrapped in her fur. "I was born here," she says. "Even after what you have done to me, this is still my home."

"Do you think so?" the skinwalker laughs, flashing a glimpse of its stolen teeth, and that's when the girl notices the wolves standing not far behind the green-eyed woman. "Do you think they will ever have you back, bitch, looking like *that*?" and the demon motions towards the girl.

"They know me," the girl says. "I am of them, and I will always be of them."

"They do not even recall the smell of you," the demon tells her, and then she sits down on the boulder as the wolves come nearer. They are all painfully thin, ribsy and half-starved as though this is the longest night of winter and the world is locked in snow and ice. A large male steps forward and stands next to the demon, it's ears held erect and it's lips curled back in a warning snarl.

"You have allowed yourself to be bedded by a man," the skinwalker says. "You have given yourself to him freely. The magic is complete," and her voice swells, become the wind through tall trees, and the dry slither of a venomous snake along the forest floor, and the roar of an avalanche rushing forward to bury everything caught in its path.

"Can you not *see* me?" the girl who is no longer a wolf asks the wolf who has never been anything else. "Can you not *smell* me? Has she truly taken everything I ever was?"

"Were I *you*, child, I'd start running," says the demon, and, at that, the wolf standing with the woman growls and bounds towards the girl, and the rest of the pack follows close behind him. She hears herself scream and turns to run, but finds that the forest has vanished, if it were ever there, and now she can see nothing but the gaudy, sharp-edged sprawl of the city, waiting to take her back. Knowing that the wolves will not follow, and knowing, too, the imperative of their empty stomachs, she lets it have her. And when she opens her eyes, there are only the white walls of the man's bedroom, the slightly musky smell of the sheets where they fucked, and the late morning sun shining in through the blinds. She lies still, listening to her heart beating and staring up at the ceiling, pretending that she cannot still hear the hungry, pursuing wolves or the green-eyed woman's hard, victorious laughter.

Desiring no more of sleep or nightmares, she passes the afternoon exploring the man's apartment. She does not bother with her clothing, as the dry, hot air blowing from gaps in the floor is sufficient to keep her warm. Like most human contrivances, the rooms and all their various contents strike her equal parts delightful, mystifying, and unnerving. She spends half an hour trying to discern the whys and hows of the telephone, before giving up and eating an assortment of things from the refrigerator. It is late afternoon before she finds her way back to the man's studio, and still he has not returned home. She is beginning to wonder if he ever will, or if perhaps he has found some other cave somewhere, and now this one will belong to her. She sits on the floor and stares at the photographs on the wall, but doesn't go near the cameras. They must be very dangerous things, if they can capture these moments, these slivers of the world, and freeze them forever. It must not be so very different from what the skinwalkers do, and she wonders at all the holes the man has left where the trees and animals and mountains in his photographs once were. And does he kill the things that he captures, or does he merely imprison them? She resolves that she will ask him, if the man ever does return, but then the girl decides maybe it will be better if she doesn't. It might be better, she thinks, not to know. She looks through all his photo albums again, spending the most time on the book that is filled entirely with images of wolves. Staring at the pictures behind their plastic sleeves, she realizes that all wolves have come to look the same to her, aside from obvious variations in their coats and size, and she remembers what the demon said to her about the magic being complete now. Most times, she cannot even tell the males from the females.

Her belly rumbles softly, and the girl who is beginning to suspect that her name has always been Anastasia, that she is only delusional and forgot somehow, is thinking about going back to the icebox. But then she notices the tall wooden cabinet standing alone in one corner of the studio. It has not been locked against her, and when she opens it and peers inside, she discovers the white-grey pelt of a large wolf, rolled up into a tight bundle. At first, she is too afraid to even touch it. Her hunger forgotten, she sits back down on the floor, though still within easy reach of the pelt, which has been stored on the cabinet's lowest shelf.

You have allowed yourself to be bedded by a man, the skinwalker told her in the dream, but now she understands that he is something more than a man, and something less, as well. And she also understands why he came to her on the rooftop, when all other men avoid her, and why it is he led her into his cave and took her as a mate. What the green-eyed woman began, this man has finished.

"Do they know what you are, any of them?" she asks aloud, and her own voice startles her. She glances back towards the entrance to the studio, the open door leading out into the hallway. But there is no one there, no one to have spoken except her, and so she turns again to the tall cabinet. A few minutes later, she finds the courage to reach inside and remove the stolen wolf pelt. She presses it gently to her face, to her nostrils and lips and the tears streaking her cheeks. When she sniffs at the thick fur, she is not surprised that it hardly smells like a wolf, anymore. On the street, there is the wail of an ambulance or fire engine, an awful, hurting wail not so unlike the noise swelling inside her. When the siren has passed, the girl unfolds the pelt and spreads it out across the floor, smoothing it flat. She lies down on it, weeping and wishing that she'd never noticed the cabinet, that she'd never opened it and looked inside. And she rubs herself furiously against the pelt and then pisses on it in a futile effort to drive away the bland, sweet stink of mankind. If she ever was a wolf, she is not one now, and she only succeeds in working the odor of humanity deeper into the hide. She opens her mouth and despair spills from her like vomit, and she howls as best as any woman may ever expect to howl.

I hope that you'll still be here because I want you to be here, he said. *I hope that counts for something with you.*

You have given yourself to him freely, said the demon in the woods.

When there are no tears left, and her throat is too sore to make even the pathetic sound that is not a howl, she lies still and silent for a time. She listens to her heart and to the dry, hot air sighing from the holes in the floor. She listens to the muffled din drifting up from the street below, to the babble of men and women and their machines. And then she stands and drapes the wolf's pelt about her shoulders, even though she knows this pelt is not her own. Remembering the demon, she loops the forelegs together around her throat so that the hide won't slip off and fall in a heap to the floor.

Were she to stand before a mirror, she would see reflected there the perfect image of the skinwalker who took away her true form. In the placid, unrippling glass, she would encounter again those same moss- and spruce-green eyes staring out at her. Because the magic is complete now, the curse consummated and absolute, and she would gaze into that same inexorable determination that greeted her when she awoke to find herself flayed and gasping beneath the star-haunted mountain sky.

But there are no mirrors on the way back to the kitchen. She finds a sharp carving knife there, a stainless-steel surrogate for the teeth and claws the demon stripped from her. And then the girl who was born a wolf, but who knows that she will one day die only a human woman, sits down on the man's sofa, facing the door, and waits to see if he will return.

The Bed of Appetite

I say Wolf, for all wolves are not of the same sort; there is one kind with an amenable disposition – neither noisy, nor hateful, nor angry, but tame, obliging and gentle, following the young maids in the streets, even into their homes.

Charles Perrault (1697)

"Such big teeth," I say, and your laugh is the quietest sort of which you are ever capable. Only the cobwebs shudder at the sound; only the curtains rustle. That is almost the sound of my heart in the presence of you, the easy brush of velvet against the windowpane. I am writing, and you are sitting naked at the foot of the bed, watching me and listening to the scritch of my pen across paper. I have learned to write while you watch, and I have learned to pause for your questions, and I have learned to explain myself and my ridiculous stories in words that will not make you scowl and brush it all aside with a dismissive wave of your right or left hand. I have learned how to forestall the contemptuous rolling of your grey eyes.

"And such big eyes," I say, and this time you do not laugh, but only shrug your thin shoulders and nod.

"So, then, what is it this time?" you ask, pointing at my paper, pretending that you are actually interested when I have long since learned to know better. But I have also learned not to argue, for you are not the sort who asks questions which are then permitted to go unanswered. Whether you are authentically curious or have even the least bit of enthusiasm is completely immaterial to your desire to have an answer. You despise incomplete equations, you have said.

"It's a love story," I say, and this time when you laugh, it is the splintery sort of laughter that makes the air wince and the candle-light grow very slightly dimmer for a moment or two. "It's not like I am entirely inexperienced," I add, expecting more laughter and more flinching night, but this time you only smile and lean towards me and ask, "So it's autobiographical?"

"Such long, long claws," I reply, and you stop smiling and look down at your hands, checking to see whether they are only paws again. It is November, the nights of the full Hunter's Moon, and so you are never quite confident of your mercurial anatomy's disposition.

"It's not an autobiography," I continue. "It is a love story for cannibals, and for someone who loves a cannibal."

"So it *is* an autobiography."

"Do you want to hear this or not?" I ask, risking impatience, and you shrug and lick at your palm in the most indifferent manner possible. But I put my pen away, my pen and the notebook, and then roll over onto my right side so that I don't have to crane my neck and peer over my shoulder in order to watch you.

"Two women are in love, and one of them is a cannibal," I begin, and you make no sign that you're still paying attention or have even heard me. "The other, she wishes to be consumed, that her lover will at last be fulfilled. But the cannibal, she does not desire the *death* of her inamorata, despite her desperate *need* to consume. So, I am writing a story about how long these two women can conspire to prolong death, how much can be cut away and yet the object of the cannibal's affection remain alive and conscious."

You stop licking your hand and look up at me. "So it *is* an autobiography," you say again.

I sigh and shut my eyes, because sometimes it hurts too much to see you. "Maybe it's a metaphor," I reply. "Anyway, whatever it is, I am writing it."

"And how much of the cannibal's lover is left?" you want to know, and I keep my eyes closed, not so naïve and knowing too well the way *yours* seem to glint when you pose a question like that.

"I have been doing research," I say, "because I want it to be plausible. The cannibal is a skilled surgeon."

"How convenient."

"The cannibal's lover – whose name is not particularly important – has already given up her legs, her arms, her breasts and buttocks, her right eye, a kidney – "

"You *are* a depraved little bastard," you smile again and lean back into the nest of pillows. "How did I ever manage to find such a depraved little bastard."

"Oh, I'm sure I was not yet this way when you found me," I lie, finally looking at you again, because I know it's a lie, and I would rather lie to your face. "I was a babe in the woods. You were the crucible of my perversion. You were my moral undoing."

"Always," you say and glance towards the ceiling or some mythic heaven you are perpetually trying to forget. "Do they still fuck, your cannibal lesbian and her vivisected inamorata?"

"It's getting quite difficult, as you can well imagine – but yes, they still fuck. That's part of the challenge, you see, that they remain lovers as long as is possible."

You spread your legs a little, showing me that undecided sex, that mutable orchid growing wet and the slightest bit erect. I want to cup it in my hands and feel your sharp nails against my scalp while I lick away your excitement. But I do not move, because I have not yet been precisely invited.

"Does she share?" you ask, and for a second I'm not certain what you mean, and so you have to ask again. "The cannibal," you sigh. "Does she share these delicacies with her lover? Does the one who is being so slowly devoured at least know the taste of her own sacrifices?"

"Yes," I say. "The cannibal insists. Otherwise, she says it would be selfish. The act would be incomplete, if she did not share this largesse with her benefactor. And the cannibal is not a selfish woman."

You nod and then glance down at your smooth, flat chest, at the place where your nipples would be, if you were merely a human male or female. "Still, it can't possibly last very much longer, can it?"

"I don't imagine so. The cannibal is about to take her lover's left lung, I think. She will stew it with crushed garlic and parsley. Then, perhaps, she will begin on the large muscles of the abdomen – the pectoralis major and the trapezius and so forth – the remaining obliques, as it were."

"And what of the bones," you ask, and now, to my surprise, I hear a note of inquisitiveness that is more than perfunctory, something more than going through the motions.

"Well, it would be a pity to waste the bones," I reply, and when you speak, the candles flicker once more. "The cannibal is a conscientious woman, after all. She splits and broils the long bones for their marrow, of course, and she is fashioning a sort of shrine with the rest."

"A reliquary," you whisper. "That's a nice touch."

"Thank you," I say quietly, almost blushing, always too easily flattered and very much more so when the compliments come from you. For you are not the sort given to casual praise, but rather the sort to hold back even the most heartfelt of commendations, lest the world begin to think you something different than what you are. Or, perhaps, for fear the world might begin to guess anything at all about your nature. Myself, I have so little use for the world, and less use still for the world's ill-considered opinions, and, compared with the simple fact of you, I am no more than a raindrop set against the sea's most unfathomable abyss. I cannot even comprehend your apparent concern with appearances.

"Would you read it to me?" you ask, lazily teasing between thumb and forefinger what might at first glance be mistaken for your penis. "If I asked nicely, would you let me hear your story."

"But it isn't finished," I say, and in hardly an instant my delight has become anxiety. Because it *isn't* finished, and you have never before asked me to read you anything I've written, and suddenly it all seems so contrived and trite and superficially grotesque, all the things I've committed to those pages. "In truth, it's barely even properly started, really."

"But you just said you don't imagine it can continue very much longer, this anthrophagous tryst you've concocted, so how can you be so terribly far from the end? The poor woman must already be nearing expiration, and here you tell me you're about to take a lung."

"She was a medical student," I say, hoping that if I offer a few more details you will be satisfied and so forget, or let slide, your request to hear me read. "The cannibal's lover, I mean. That's how they met. She frequently attended lectures on human physiology and pathology, and also demonstrations given by the surgeon. The student – who would soon, of course become the lover – had excruciating dreams in which *she* was the cadaver lying motionless and exposed on the surgeon's table, flayed raw before the eyes of her classmates. In her dreams, she felt all those eyes on her, and the scalpel blade, and the dexterous hands of the surgeon. One thing led to another – "

"As they say," you sigh, interrupting me. "Dear, you only need answer, 'No, I don't wish to read you my story.' It was not an *order*. At least, I do not *believe* I phrased it as an order. Perhaps, in my excitement – " And here you pause and stop teasing yourself long enough to find a more comfortable position in among the pillows. " – maybe, I sounded too eager. I merely thought you might welcome an audience for a change, for the words themselves, in the order you have placed them, rather than squeezing them into summaries and approximations."

"I think if I really wanted an audience, I'd probably try to find a publisher."

You take a very deep breath and then exhale so slowly that breathing out seems to last almost forever. "Unless, love, you are too afraid, or too intimidated at the thought of criticism or rejection." Here you smile a third time, and tonight your teeth would put a starving hyena to shame.

"I'm not afraid," I say, telling you another lie, though I cannot say for certain if you know this one for what it is. "I do not write for anyone but me. And I only share my stories with you because you ask."

"Fair enough," you say. "I did ask. I asked because you are always so awfully intent, so diligent at your work. But I find it admirable, that you do not crave an audience, that you have no *need* of listeners or of readers or of printed volumes to find satisfaction. That you do this simply because it pleases you to do so."

"It keeps me busy," I reply, "when you're out. When I am alone."

You watch me silently for a time, your fingers still busy with the elaborate folds and creases and protuberances of your genitalia (though you are engaged in nothing so deliberate or directed towards an end as the act of masturbation). In the candlelight, the shadows conceal so much, and it is difficult to be sure where your long fingers end and those most secret regions of the temple of your body begin. There is the undeniable, wet gleam and the erection to signify your arousal, but I am left to wonder if I will be the instrument of resolution, or if tonight you will seek out some other means of release. And, too, I must wonder if the sight of my own body was sufficient stimulation, or if it was my story, or some union of the two.

"Does she have regrets?" you ask me. "The cannibal's lover? Now that it has gone this far, that she been so diminished and her death is within sight, is she sorry?"

"No," I say, and doubtless I respond too quickly. "She is not sorry. She only regrets there is so little time remaining, that she did not have more to offer."

"She had what any woman would have had."

"Yes. But she fears now it was not enough, and that when it's done, their courtship, the banquet, when it is finished, she will have been inadequate to the surgeon's needs."

"But not possibly more or less inadequate than *any* woman willing to acquiesce to the preconditions of such a necessarily transitory relationship."

I frown and watch the candles instead of watching you, trying now to ignore my own nagging erection. "You make it sound so dry, so cold." And you assure me this is not your intent. I can smell you now, that musky sweetness leaking from the cleft below your stunted phallus, the saltiness of your sweat, your breath which always stinks slightly of old blood and carrion. "These women love one another," I say.

"So, you insist it is more than need, more than lust or a maniac hunger?"

"My, Grandmother, what big ears you have."

I glance back to your face to see that familiar expression that says maybe *this* is the night when you have inevitably grown tired of me. Maybe this is the night you will no longer indulge my impertinence, because, after all, I am only a depraved little bastard and there are a thousand more where I came from. The world is lousy with depraved little bastards – or bitches, depending on your mood. The bored, exasperated expression that reminds me that you will never tell me how much you love me, because you have probably never loved anything, not in that frail, careless way that human beings love one another. There are plenty enough nights when I see that look in your wide eyes the color of polished granite and absolutely *know* that I would be relieved to find we had come to *our* conclusion, that I had nothing left in my flensed soul for you to cut away and stew with shallots and baby potatoes and rosemary and a bit of fennel.

"No," you say. "Not tonight. If I killed you tonight, how would I ever find out how your love story ends?"

"Oh, see, I think you know exactly how it will end," I tell you, and you shrug and go back to lazily playing with yourself.

"It is enough that I am confident," you tell me, "that you will find the ending, or that it will somehow find you. That you and the ending will find one another. I do not remember you ever leaving one of your little tales unfinished. That would be indecent, and though you may well be depraved, my sweet, I have always sensed a nasty streak of decency about you."

And then you *do* invite me, and as is usually the case, there is no need for clumsy words, for language which might be misunderstood. You deliver the invitation by means of some voiceless communion a hundred million years older even than the coming of mankind into the decaying, time-haunted world. You call me, and I have never yet failed to answer, and soon my tongue has better things to do than tell you stories for which I have not yet discovered endings.

I have always been the sort who sleeps after sex, and so I have been dozing, drifting in that calm and utterly satiated space between orgasm and groggy wakefulness, that sleep which might almost recall the perfect amniotic peace of the womb. I do not dream here, and I am not plagued by the self-awareness that, in the old mythologies, drove the damned from this or that Eden and forever consigned them to the wastes that sprawled beyond the gates of Paradise. It is not a deep sleep, but rather like a stone skipping one, two, three, four times across still, dark waters, and yet, inevitably, consciousness returns with the utmost slowness, by imperceptible degrees. And, for a time, I am staring at candlelight without the knowledge that I am staring at anything at all. But then you speak, and I am lost in the chaos of myself again.

"Why are your hips so hairy, Grandmother?" you whisper, pressing your cool, wet nose against my cheek, and I cannot yet recall the correct reply. I can only be annoyed at how unfair it is to be asking me such a question, when I am still blinking and disoriented from the ignorant bliss of that post-coital slumber.

Then it comes to me, and I hear myself answer, "Because I wore my corset too tight." I only dimly wonder at how our usual roles have been reversed, certain that there will be some suitable explanation when you are ready to explain yourself and not before. And without turning to see, I can hear your smile, so similar to the noise aluminum foil makes when crumpled in the hand.

"Grandmother, why are your knuckles so hairy?" you ask, nuzzling playfully at my left ear.

And though my hands are hardly the least bit hairy, I reply, "From wearing too many rings on my fingers."

"Dear heart, I thought that you would sleep until dawn," you say, and this is when it occurs to me that I cannot move my legs or my arms, and I turn my head away from the candles to stare into the more genuinely molten pools of your paradoxically freezing-scalding grey eyes.

"I'm tied," I say, and you nod, as though I need the confirmation.

"There was hardly time enough for the alternative," you respond. "The sun will be up soon."

"*Why* am I tied?" I ask, and I want to laugh, even if I have not quite decided what is funny.

"Grandmother," you say, "this wine is very red." And I do laugh now, because you have begun lapping delicately at my temple and your long, rough tongue flicks across my left eyelid.

"Drink and keep quiet," I tell you, struggling to sound appropriately gruff and reproachful, trying to remember how *you* would deliver these lines to me, had the night not turned topsy-turvy. "It is your grandmother's blood."

"Yes," you whisper. "Yes, it is, indeed. Love, I read your story while you were sleeping. I hope that you don't mind me having taken such a terrible, audacious liberty."

And, just as I have learned to write while you watch, just as I have learned that you despise unanswered questions, so too have I learned when to hold back the truth even though you will have no doubt that I am lying.

"No," I say, allowing the anger and the murky, sudden sense of violation I feel to wash through me and quickly fade, as I would do with anything which is of no use whatsoever. "I hope you did not find my handwriting too totally illegible."

"I think I know how it ends now," you whisper and lap at my face again.

"Is that why I'm tied up?" I ask, and I can feel the nylon ropes at my ankles and knees, at my wrists, which have been firmly bound behind my back so that my arms have gone numb and cold. Your ingenious, expert knots, and I know that wrestling with my bonds will only make them draw that much tighter, until they bite into my flesh. Not that you would mind the welts.

"I sat here, while you slept," you say, not even bothering to brush my question aside, negating it with no effort or acknowledgement at all. "I sat and read these pages, and it occurred to me, dear heart, that the cannibal in your story truly *does* love the woman she is so slowly devouring."

"I believe I'd told you that already."

"Then perhaps I failed to comprehend. I needed to read it for myself, to fully appreciate the cannibal's devotion."

Somewhere far away there is the keening wail of a police car's siren, and I close my eyes, wishing now that I were still asleep and dreaming nothing at all. But then you place a hand beneath my head and lift it slightly, taking care that your short, curved claws will not tear at my scalp or the back of my neck. "I have been very busy," you say.

And, opening my eyes, I see now that you have been very busy, indeed. Gazing down the length of my bare torso, past the limp droop of my own sex, I see that you have wrapped both my legs in blankets, shrouding them in such a way that, in the flickering candlelight, I am greeted by the impression that I have no legs at all, the illusion of a double transfemoral amputation, and I do not need to ask to know that you have done the same with my arms all the way up to my shoulder blades. While I dozed, you have made of me an immobile, swaddled simulacrum of the cannibal's lover, as you worked out the ending to a story that was not yours to end.

"What I found," you say, "is that the cannibal suffers a sort of epiphany." And now you gently return my head to its place upon my pillow. "To quote James Joyce, 'By an epiphany he meant a sudden spiritual manifestation, whether in the vulgarity of speech or of gesture or in a memorable phase of the mind itself.'"

"*Ulysses?*" I ask reflexively, not particularly interested in the provenance of the quote, having never cared very much for Mr. Joyce's writing.

You are propped up now on your right elbow, watching me. You frown and scowl, the way any good professor might when faced with an indolent schoolboy. "No," you say. "It's from *Stephen Hero*," and you explain how this was the manuscript that Joyce abandoned in 1905, then later successfully reworked into *A Portrait of the Artist as a Young Man*. "The cannibal is about to cut out her lover's tongue, even though she knows this means that she will also be excising her lovers *voice*, and that she will also be robbing her lover of the ability to share their feasts, to *taste* the flesh her lover is surrendering."

"It is *my* story," I say, delivering the words with more deliberateness than I usually hazard with you. "It is not *yours* to finish. I had not planned for her to take her lover's tongue, not until the very end, and I had not planned for her to suffer an epiphany."

You watch me for a time, then, and I cannot even begin to read the thoughts trapped in back of those seething granite irises. One might just as well try to guess the thoughts of a cat or a serpent or a tree. When some number of minutes have come and gone, you flare your wide black nostrils and cock your head to one side.

"Grandmother," you whisper, "you have such a very big mouth."

And I reply, "That comes from eating children."

"So it does," you say. "Sometimes, we must open our jaws very, very wide to swallow even small things."

"The cannibal has an epiphany," I whisper, shaping each word as though it were spun from glass or built of segments stolen from the most fragile insect's shell. "She comes to understand that her love for the girl transcends her compulsion to devour – "

" – and that in the absence of her lover," you continue for me, handling the words with far less care, "she would be left empty. An emptiness that no amount of gluttony would ever assuage. Surely, now you see how it could end no other way?"

"You have a finer sense of irony than I will ever have," I say, conceding the point, and then I sigh and frown as though this sentiment is somehow undesigning, as if it has arisen from an epiphany of my own rather than from baser instincts of self-preservation. But we have been playing these games for years, you and I, and you do not mind my masks, but ask only that I wear them well.

"Are you too horribly uncomfortable, my dear?" you ask, and I shake my head, accepting the discomfort as I would accept any necessary evil, knowing it is finite, like your whims. "I needed to see you like this, to make you a surrogate of the cannibal's lover, so that I might begin to understand. You know that I will never be half the storyteller you've become, for I must always resort to such crude devices to find a conclusion."

"It is not so marvelous a talent that you should feel deprived," I say and shut my eyes against the growing ache in my shoulders and the vacant chill where my arms should be. Beside me, you're silent and still for a time, and I lie there, waiting, listening, wondering halfheartedly if this might be the night when your infatuation has inexorably run its course, and wondering again, as well, if I will be disappointed or relieved if that proves to be the case.

And then you ask me, "Shall I tell you how it ends?"

"What comes after the epiphany, you mean?"

"Yes. That is, the consequences of the epiphany."

"How else will I ever know?" I reply, and, even with my eyes shut, I see now that this is not the night (or the final hour before dawn) when at last I feel your teeth close about my throat, clamping down upon and collapsing my windpipe and severing my carotid artery and jugular veins, spilling oxygenated and deoxygenated blood alike. I will live to see the sun at least one more day, and it does not surprise me, knowing this, that I feel nothing much at all.

"Open your eyes," you tell me, though not unkindly, and so I do. "*Ma mère-grand, que vous avez de grands yeux,*" you smile, and the darkness all around our bed shudders, but does not withdraw.

"*C'est pour mieux te voir, mon enfant,*" I answer in my turn.

"Yes, that's better," you say, your smile becoming a wide grin to flash the razor gate of crooked incisors and yellowed canines and the untenanted spaces where premolars should be. At this instant, the paling dregs of night lingering or caged inside the room would roll back, retreating like ocean waves from slaty Jurassic shingle or white quartz sands, if it but knew how to withdraw without the age-old push of sunrise.

And then you are speaking again, telling me exactly how my story ends, and I concentrate on the interplay of your tongue and lips and teeth and palate and larynx and all the things this easy dance of flesh reveals.

"The surgeon – the *cannibal* surgeon – lays aside her clamps and scalpel, and she stares deeply into her lover's one remaining eye. All the universe is cradled within that eye, which is the soft green of moss after a spring rain. And she says, 'No, I cannot take your voice away.' Before her confused lover can respond, the cannibal says to her, 'I see now that there is more to me than appetite, and more to you than the capacity for surrender. Already, I have taken more than I deserve, and I will take no more, not now or ever.'"

"So," I say. "She loses her nerve."

"You are not listening very closely, *mon enfant*. No, in this moment the cannibal *finds* her nerve, or her resolve, or her balance, or self-restraint, or whatever you wish to name it. She discovers, looking at what she has *made* of her lover, that her love is greater than her lust. Do you not understand? You *said* it was a love story."

"Yes, I did."

"In this moment, the cannibal finds a compassion that outweighs her lover's need to sacrifice, and also her own perverse trophic desires. She promises that she will forevermore take care of her lover, and that they will have a long life together, and that she will do everything in her power to atone for the weaknesses of her mind and body. 'I will make you comfortable,' she says. 'You will not ever want for anything that I can give you.' But her lover, reduced by their many long months of feasting, is horrified – literally and wholly horrified to the innermost core of her being – and she begs the cannibal to please, *please* continue, swearing that she cannot possibly live like this, not as the broken abomination they have together made of her. She swears that she would take her own life, if all their gormandizing had not robbed her of that ability.

"'But *look* at me!' the cannibal's lover cries out. 'I am hideous. I am a monster!'

"But the cannibal kisses her and wipes away her tears and assures the girl that she is even more beautiful now than on the first day they met. Every single scar, every amputation, every morsel they have shared between them, she tells her lover, has only served to perfect her. Before she was, at most, what any woman might be. 'And where is the glory in that?' she asks her lover. 'Where is the beauty or the splendor in being no more than the progeny of insensible, uncalculating Nature?'"

And then you fall silent, looking suddenly very pleased with yourself. I watch your grey eyes and slowly nod my head. "Is there more?" I ask.

"No," you reply. "There is no need of any more than that. How could this ending possibly be rendered any more impeccable?"

"Are you going to untie me before you sleep?" I ask, no longer particularly interested in how my story – which, I know, is no *longer* mine – has or hasn't ended. The muscles between my shoulder blades and down the length of my back have begun to knot and cramp. I need to piss, and would prefer not to do so in the bed. But it would not be completely unlike you to leave me this way until the sun has risen and set and you have some further need of me.

You nod, but your eyes are watching the window and the first faint rays of morning leaking in through the fabric. "So, I've found you at last, you old sinner," you say, your voice gone as dry as an autumn wind and as cold as a mid-winter's sun. "I've been looking for you for a long time."

Subterraneus

Below the streets, and *then* below all that lies below the streets – basements and sewers, cellars and subway tunnels, lines for gas and water and electricity, cable television, the crawlways dug two hundred years ago by smugglers and pirates and those whose motives have been entirely forgotten. Below asphalt and grey concrete and moldering brick and sedimentary bedrock so honeycombed and hollowed that it's surely a miracle the earth does not simply collapse beneath the combined weight of skyscrapers and automobiles and however many millions of human beings come and go overhead. Here, then, below all that lies below, is this ancient void carved not by the labor of picks, nor dynamite, nor machines, but by the hands (if we may call such appendages hands) of the ones who so long ago forsook the sun and moon that both are now little more than doubtful half-remembrances. The weathered limestone walls glow faintly with the chartreuse light of phosphorescent fungi, at least a dozen species of various grotesque shapes, found nowhere in the world but this cavern, aligned with the Ascomycota and Basidiomycota, yet likely to remain forever unknown to prying, categorizing science.

And those who come here now, those few who find their way down, they come by choice, each and every one of them. None are ever *brought* here. None are lured, and none are shown the way. None are ever dragged kicking and screaming like the victims in some B-grade horror film. A month might pass between visitations, or a decade. The ones who keep this pit are patient and have long since learned to wait, relying upon providence and happenstance and whatever incomprehensible drive does, on occasion, lead one from above to seek them out.

She was half dead, by the time she found them, and now she is at best only half again that alive. Her name is Beryl, by chance – or not by chance – and for three years has she seen this deep place in dreams, for three years has she heard their voices and seen their faces. She hangs now suspended a few feet above the mire and stinking, motionless water that is their burrow. She did not resist when they came to her with the steel hooks and chains, because she'd seen all that in dreams, as well. As the antique hand winch – itself a marvel of rust and Colonial-era ironwork – was turned and the chains slowly grew taut, she did not cry out. When at last Beryl's naked, shivering body was lifted from the squelching mud, she did not scream, though the pain was more than anything that she'd ever anticipated. The pain was never in her dreams of them, but she can now believe it nothing more than some splinter of the reward for her perseverance. *This*, she thinks, *is no more and no less than what was always meant to be.*

They crouch directly beneath her, gazing up with famished, thankful eyes, eyes black as inkwells. There is already blood, drawn by the hooks piercing the skin of her calves and buttocks, back and shoulders, and it dribbles across their upturned faces like rain upon the parched faces of men and women who have survived a drought of ages. It is only the first, teasing drops before the storm, however, and they sit together in the mud with mouths open wide and their long tongues lolling to capture every drop spilled. Later, there can be waste, when the deluge begins in earnest. Later, the blood can pool, congealing in the ooze and spattered wantonly across the fungal walls.

Aside from the winch and chains and hooks, they have little in the way of tools. Their claws are sufficient to their modest needs. But there is one item, and if their memories were less undone by time and the slow madness that has come upon them across the centuries, they would recall how this one thing came to them, washed up on a rocky Massachusetts beach and discovered by a man whose name was once Zebidiah If-Christ-had-not-died-for-thee-thou-hadst-been-damned Wilmarth. All their names have long since been forgotten, for what need have they of names? The artefact found lying among sand and whelks, kelp and wave-polished bits of pink Cape Ann granite, is kept on a high ledge in the burrow, wrapped in a mildewed bit of burlap sackcloth. It bears some resemblance to a surgeon's scalpel, but no more than it resembles a buttonhook or the high whorl of a snail's shell. In 1789, Wilmarth showed the peculiar object to a scholar of archae-ological studies at Harvard's Peabody Museum, but the man was unable to determine it's age or origin or even the material from which it had been crafted. For, at times, it seemed most certainly made from hammered bronze, while at others, and under certain wavelengths of light, it took on the characteristics of cobalt-stained glass of a sort known from excavations in Egypt and Eastern Asia dating back to the mid second millennium BC.

Suspended above them, Beryl hovers somewhere between the thresholds of ecstasy and shock, feeling almost as weight-less as though her body were buoyed up by water. Her breath has become strenuous and uneven, and she is sweating now despite the chill air. Her long hair, an indifferent and unremarkable shade of blonde, dangles lank about her face and shoulders, and she keeps her eyes shut, because it seems impolite to watch them, when they have accorded her such an honour. Even when she finally feels their strange seeking hands upon her, even then, out of respect, she does not open her eyes.

They might yet reject me, she thinks, though the thought is dimmed and made indistinct by the swelling, throbbing pain and by exhaustion and the bright sizzle of the adrenaline and endor-phins coursing through her bloodstream and brain. *They may still see fit to pull me down and turn me out to either find my way back or die alone in the darkness.* She cannot know that this isn't true, that though they are patient creatures accustomed to interminable waits, they have never once rejected a soul who has successfully navigated the labyrinth and so found the long, winding path down to them.

Wilmarth's beach-found treasure has been taken from its place of pride, and the one among them who found it, but who is no *longer* Wilmarth, removes the oddly mercurial object from its filthy shroud and holds it up for all of them to see. The instrument glints dully in the feeble yellow-green light suffusing this cavity in the world's bowels, and they all turn to see, momentarily distracted from Beryl and her gifts. This is as close as ever they come to awe or reverence, these rare glimpses of the thing that is neither a scalpel nor a buttonhook, that is neither bronze nor blue Egyptian glass. From their withered vocal cords come the most gentle utterances left to them, sounds which to Beryl's ears seem hardly more than the final, strangling gasps of drowning men and women. But she knows, too, that it is not for her to judge the beauty or fearsomeness of these voices, and she is merely grateful to the dark gods of her secret pantheon that she has lived long enough to hear them at all.

The same one among these creatures who first touched the object holds it high above his head, left arm extended far as his atrophied reach will allow, and immediately all the others slither or hop or scuttle to one side or the other, clearing a path to Beryl's suspended body. One by one by one, the crowd grows silent, ceasing their guttural exaltations, and she knows that at last her terrible journey is almost done. In her dreams, she has seen this moment half a hundred times, and Beryl does not need to open her eyes to know the gleeful, voracious expression on the slack-jawed face of the muttering thing advancing on her, or the way the instrument gripped fiercely in its hand has begun to writhe and twist from side to side, as though it has come alive and urgently seeks to escape its captor. She has only to wait, as they have waited for *her*, and she is confident the wait will not be a long one. The creature picks its way forward through the morass of mud and shit and piss-tainted water, moving with as much speed and agility as its twisted limbs are capable.

And then, *here*, the familiar is passed straightaway, and Beryl's understanding of exactly what awaits her grows abruptly less definite, since it is from *this* instant on that her dreams have often varied and contradicted one another. For the first time, she fears something more than dismissal. For the first time since she has entered this chamber, she fears the unknown, however many or however few seconds still lie ahead of her and whatever they do or do not hold in store. From here, she can doubt herself, as she has not yet seen – even in dreams – what is to come, and so she cannot begin to guess whether she is equal to those ordeals.

The oyster-skinned creature who was once a man called Zebidiah If-Christ-had-not-died-for-thee-thou-hadst-been-damned Wilmarth squats below her, so near that she can feel his every hot, foul breath against her face. And suddenly faith is no longer sufficient, and the woman from Above opens her eyes and stares down into the face of the one who will be her executioner. There is an unexpected and indescribable softness in his black eyes, a compassion she would never have anticipated, for what and who is she to find mercy among such as they? But there it is, unmistakable, regardless of her presumptions. A cast to that ruined and perfected face that she cannot mistake for deceit or only cruel misdirection. This empathy is genuine as her devotion to the pit dwellers, and finally she can allow herself to weep – not from the ravages of pain or dread or any shortcomings of her soul, but from relief and a duty to acknowledge the courtesy in her master's face.

Perhaps it is no more than her exhausted imagination, but Beryl seems to "hear" a raw and grinding voice speaking directly within her mind. *Nothing which will be done here is done without your acquiescence,* it whispers. *No liberties will be taken. This is the Law, and the Law is eternal and inviolable.* And then the voice withdraws, and the creature's face, by slow degrees, drains of its commiseration. Beryl nods, though she knows that the nod is irrelevant to what comes next, and the creature's thin, pale lips stretch themselves wide in a ragged sort of grimace, exposing its crooked fangs and bucked incisors set firmly into rotten gums. But Beryl's cloudy half-consciousness grasps the necessity of this exchange, that there may be no misunderstandings, and that her sacrifice will be untarnished by any equivocation.

The wasted thing squatting in the mud shows her the instrument, sent to them by the sea, lost therein for five hundred million years after it fell from the stars, adrift in the near-vacuum of interstellar space a billion years before that, snagged by Earth's insistent gravity, it fell, streaming incandescent gases. It has witnessed the demise of the trilobites and of the giant sea scorpions, has lain in benthic silt beneath the eel-like shadows of reptilian leviathans and watched on as the heretical grandfathers of the great whales abandoned land and returned to the oceans. Seeing it, Beryl knows that it has always hungered for her, just as it has hungered for all who have come before and who will come afterwards. It is beautiful and glorious and undeniable. It is a stray mote from the collective and insentient will of the Cosmos, the shard from an angel's broken sword, a bit of refuse spewed across the event horizon of a white hole. It wriggles eagerly in the hand of the misshapen subterranean being who is not its keeper, but only its servant, and only that until its indisputable will chooses another.

Recollecting some diminished and useless appetite, the creature that was once Wilmarth raises the gnarled and taloned hook of its right hand and tries clumsily to caress Beryl's exposed breasts, her belly and thighs, the matted thatch of her pubic hair, and she does not resist him. But the instrument clutched in his other hand shrieks its protest and begins to smolder. Beryl catches a whiff of seared flesh, and the creature stops fondling her.

"I am ready," she says, speaking now for no one but herself, an affirmation to close a life that never could have led her anywhere *but* here, below the streets, and *then* below all that lies below the streets. And the oyster-skinned creature blinks his ebony eyes, and without further pomp or ceremony, he slits her open, sternum to crotch, and now comes the rich red flood and fleeting mitigation for their thirst, and all the greedy mouths rush in to drink their well-deserved fill.

The Collector of Bones

From the rainy February street and the taxi, the collector of bones leads the boy through the lobby of the apartment building to the elevator, and hardly a word passes between them as cables and gears haul them all the way up to the fifteenth floor. The collector of bones is not a young woman, but she also is not a poor woman, and has long since discovered that she can have her pick of the hookers and hustlers who sell themselves on the streets of the city. Money talks, and meat listens and eagerly responds. This boy, twenty or twenty-one, but certainly no *older* than twenty-one, this one she picked up at Twelfth Street between Second and Third Avenues, and sure he's a junky, but his addiction only makes the meat that much more eager. That much more vulnerable. The elevator smells like melting snow and stale cigarette smoke, like her perfume and the boy's unwashed body, and each time they pass a floor, a hidden bell somewhere dings loudly, and every time it dings, the boy flinches. He must be so very new at this, the collector of bones thinks to herself, to be so jumpy, and that thought is the first thing all night that's made her smile. The bell dings again, and the doors slide open, and she's glad that there's no one waiting to ride down to the lobby.

"This is our stop," she says to the boy, and so he flinches again. "Everyone ashore who's going ashore." And she tells him to relax, that she's not quite the Big Bad Wolf or the witch who tried to eat Hansel and Gretel. The boy smiles his nervous smile, and she almost asks him if its heroin or crack or something else. From the look of him, she thinks it's probably heroin, but she's always thought it impolite to pry.

Her apartment is all the way down at one end of the long hall-way, on the north side of the building, next to the window that has been painted shut and so no longer actually leads out to the rickety fire escape beyond. The boy wipes at his nose while she unlocks the door, and she asks him if he has a cold, and he tells her no, that it's just his sinuses, that he's had bad sinuses all his life.

"Well," she says, "you can't be too careful with colds, not in this sort of weather, and not when someone spends as much time out of doors as you must." Then they're inside, and she offers him tea or coffee, and he frowns, so she offers him something strong, instead. He takes a brandy, and it hardly matters that it isn't good brandy.

After she has handed him the glass, and after he's taken the first hesitant sip, she asks for his damp coat, which he surrenders without a fuss. It stinks, she thinks, like some ugly little terrier sort of dog that's gotten caught in a downpour, and she hangs it on a brass hook near the door where it'll only drip on the avo-cado-colored ceramic tiles near the threshold and not on the rugs or the hardwood floors. The boy stands near a bookshelf, sipping at his brandy and, she supposes, glancing at the titles printed on the spines.

Forming the wrong impression, she thinks, and by now he's probably at least half convinced himself she's some sort of serial killer. One among that slim eight percent of American mass mur-derers with vaginas, possibly, and here, poor thing, he's been unlucky enough to stumble upon her. It amuses her, that he might be thinking this; flinchy or not, he isn't likely to lose his nerve and run, not now, not one hurting as bad as this one's obviously hurting, not one who needs his fix *that* badly. She stands just a few feet away, watching him, deciding whether to tease or maybe ask, instead, where he's from and how he wound up turning tricks on the streets of Manhattan. She decides to tease him, because it's been a while since she's had one this jumpy, and if she's wrong and worse comes to worse, if he turns rabbit, it's not too late in the evening to find another.

"So," she smiles, "which sort do you think I'll be? An angel of death, perhaps, intent upon ending the suffering of my victims? Or simply a sexual predator?"

The boy turns away from the bookshelf so quickly that he almost spills his drink. "What?" he asks and blinks at her, and she thinks that his bleary eyes are the same color as unpolished emeralds.

"Or maybe I'm something new," she continues, only half ashamed at his reaction. "Or my motives are entirely too difficult to discern, so I don't fit neatly into the categories created by FBI profilers and psychiatrists."

"I wasn't thinking that," he says. "I wasn't thinking that at all."

"Sure you were," the collector of bones smirks at the sniffling, skinny boy. "But that's okay. Misconceptions are easy to come by, and I've long since learned to take them in stride. Water off a duck's rump and so forth and so on." She points to his glass. "Then again, maybe I put arsenic in the brandy," she says.

"Yeah, and maybe you just get your kicks scaring people," he snaps back, surprising her, and the collector of bones is impressed enough to laugh, having grown accustomed to prostitutes with considerably less pluck and more street-smart trepidation. "Maybe *that's* your kink, lady."

"Oh, for fuck's sake, child. Don't start in calling me *lady*. So, I might not be a serial killer, but I'm sure as hell no *lady*. If you're pissed and want to insult me, just cut to the chase and tell me that I'm a dried-up old hag. At least then you'll be half right."

"I know you didn't bring me here to kill me," he says unconvincingly, and takes another sip of brandy.

"How's that? I mean, how can you be so sure?" she asks, pressing her luck again. And there, she thinks, that's my *true* perversity, and the collector of bones savors the uncertainty, the slightest possibility he'll turn tail and head back to the elevator, back down to the slushy sidewalk and someone who won't ask for anything more than a twenty-dollar blow job.

"Just a hunch," the boy replies, trying hard to smirk back at her, but not quite pulling it off. "I get hunches. My grandmother used to tell me I was psychic like that."

"Did she?" asks the collector of bones. "Did she, indeed?" and the boy nods his head and finishes the brandy in a single gulp, wincing slightly at the way the liquor burns his throat.

"Sometimes my dreams come true," he says, handing her his empty glass, and when she offers him another, he says sure, why not.

"Here I pay for a common streetwalker, and I get a bona-fide clairvoyant. That's got to be some sort of bargain. Maybe I should start playing the lottery."

The boy sniffs and wipes his nose again, glancing around the apartment while she pours him more of the cheap brandy. "Doesn't much look like you're the sort who needs to," he says.

"I do all right," she tells him, handing the glass back to the boy. "But you won't ask at what, because that's none of your business, and I wouldn't tell you, anyway."

"I'd guess you married well, and the fucker died and left you everything. If I *were* to guess, but since it's none of my business, I won't."

The collector of bones screws the cap back onto the brandy bottle and sets it aside. "Don't go and get so drunk you'll be useless," she warns him.

The boy shrugs his shoulders, and he says, "Oh, I can hold my own." So she laughs at him again, and this time he makes a face like she really *has* hurt his feelings. "Never mind," the collector of bones tells the boy, and then she asks him to get undressed, and she slips out of her skirt and blouse and stockings while he watches. She gives him a condom, and then they spend half an hour fucking on the sofa, and she comes twice, which is better than usual. Most times, she doesn't come at all, though she's never yet blamed any of the whores for her own limitations. Afterwards, he asks for another drink, and this time she gives him the bottle, what's left of the bottle, and tells him to finish it.

They sit naked together on the sofa, him drinking brandy and her watching him getting drunk, and it isn't long before he asks why she offered him three times what he usually gets just to fuck.

"You're not done quite yet," she replies, and then she stands and walks across the room to the bookshelf, and she pretends that he's watching her because he likes what he sees and not because he's wondering what comes next. She opens a small box carved from sandalwood – something she bought on a business trip to Indonesia half a lifetime ago. Inside is a key strung on a faded length of silk ribbon the color of cranberries. She takes it out and closes the box again, and then the collector of bones turns back to the boy and holds the key up so it catches the dim light and she's certain that he can see it.

"What's that?" he asks, slurring just a little now.

"It's a key," she says unhelpfully.

"I can *see* it's a goddamn key," he mutters and starts picking at the foil label on the brandy bottle. "What I'm asking is what it's a key *to?*"

"The key to the reason I'm paying you so much," and then she says for him to follow her, not to bother with his clothes, just follow her. The boy sighs and shakes his head, but he does as he's told. Money talks, and the flesh listens. She leads him down a short hall to a door that looks in no way different from any of the other doors in the apartment, except, of course, that she's made sure he knows that it's the door that fits the key from the little box. And that makes it the sort of door to be regarded with caution, the sort of door, for example, from a Charles Perrault fairytale about a man with a blue beard and a young wife too curious for her own good.

"Have you ever heard of an ossuary?" she asks the boy as she unlocks the door, as the door swings slowly open, and he says no, he's never heard of an ossuary. The room is dark, but there's a switch on the wall by the door, and she flips it, which saves her the trouble of explaining to the whore what an ossuary is and isn't. All he has to do is look at the thousands of bones covering nearly every inch of the room, the walls and the ceiling and the floor, all of it clearly illuminated now by tasteful incandescent tracklighting to reveal shades of tortoiseshell and ivory, cream and ginger, innumerable greys and browns.

"Fuck," he whispers.

"No, we did that already," she says, because she's tired and it's too easy and she can't help herself. She watches the boy's eyes as he studies the intricate arrangements of ribs and femora, humeri and countless vertebrae.

"You did this?" he asks.

"Yes," she replies. "I did this. Well, technically, I still am doing this. A work in progress, as they are wont to say. Truthfully, I'm not sure that it will ever be finished. Or that I'll know if it is. Finished, I mean."

The boy steps into the room without being told to do so, and his unpolished-emerald eyes are wide, and his mouth is hanging open just a bit.

"It is really somewhat amateurish, I'm afraid," she says, because false modesty is one of those things that has never particularly bothered the collector of bones. "Now, if you want to be impressed, you should see the Sedlec Ossuary in Czechoslovakia. Well, it was still called Czechoslovakia when I was there in 1987. Anyway, there's an enormous chandelier hanging in the vault, and they say it contains at least one of every bone in the human body."

"All these bones are *human?*" he asks, taking another couple of steps forward, and she gently pushes the door closed behind them. The latch clicks, but he doesn't notice. "Jesus fuck, lady, where the hell does anyone get this many human bones?"

She almost reminds the boy how she requested he not call her *lady*, but decides to let it go, because her ego's really not as frail as that. "Well, no," she says, instead. "They're not all human. When I started, I didn't want to limit myself," and she points to a pair of scapulae mounted nearby, wired with their glenoid cavities set end to end so that the effect is rather like the wings of an enormous ivory butterfly. "Those two came from a sort of camel called a dromedary. *This,*" and she motions towards a massive tusked jawbone set just above the scapulae, "this is the mandible of a hippopotamus. There are more than three hundred species represented here, all told, mammals, birds, fish, and reptiles."

"And people," he says, not quite whispering.

"Yes, child, *and* people. That was covered under mammals. Don't be so goddamn squeamish. There are more than six and a half billion people in the world, and do you know how many of them die every day?" She doesn't wait for him to say he doesn't. "About one hundred and fifty million, which is something like two per second. Say roughly half the population of the United States, every day, and the adult human body has an average of two hundred and eight bones. So, that's something like thirty-one billion bones a day that are no longer needed by their former owners. Now, is it really such a big deal if a few of them wind up in here?"

The boy just stares at her for a moment or two, then shrugs again and blinks drunkenly before he goes back to examining her meticulous patterns and groupings. There's a narrow path snaking between the heaps and jackstraw sculptures, leading farther in.

"The human bones," she says, before he asks, "have come mostly from suppliers in China and Africa. There are a few here from India that I picked up from collectors who acquired them before India banned the export of human skeletons. And yes, I assure you it's all perfectly legal. And none of the animal bones come from endangered species, for that matter. A few are actually fossil, some mammoth bones from Siberia and Alaska, and there's some dinosaur material from Canada, Wyoming, Montana, and Mongolia, but these are mostly extant species."

"Extant?"

"Still living today," she says. "Not extinct."

The boy nods again, squinting at a complicated roseate of weasel, skunk, and rodent skulls. "So, you paid me all that extra money to see…*this*?"

"No," the collector of bones says, and she slips the cranberry ribbon over her head, so that the key dangles in the space between her bare breasts. "I'm afraid you're going to have to work just a *little* harder than that to earn your bonus, kiddo."

"What? You want me to fuck you again, in here?"

"No. That's not what I had in mind, either. I want to photograph you, that's all," and then the boy starts to touch the snout of a beaver skull, but she stops him, her hand encircling his thin wrist and guiding it away. "Look, but don't touch, unless I *say* touch."

"You want to take my picture," he says. "That's all?"

"Are you disappointed?" she asks. "You're not *afraid* of being photographed, are you?"

"No, and no," he replies, frowning. "I was asking, that's all. I figured it'd be more…more involved, more intimate." And then he starts to say something more, but stops himself.

"More intimate? Don't you think that photographs can be intimate? Especially nude photographs, when the subject is so completely…" The collector of bones pauses a moment, searching for the right word and finally settling on *accessible*.

"That's not the sort of intimate I meant. I've never posed for anyone before." He's stopped inspecting the beaver skull and has moved along to an assortment of leg bones, mostly tibiae and fibulae and most of them taken from various sorts of deer and ante-lope. The bones have been set into a thin layer of plaster of Paris and aligned to form a sort of spiraling sunburst formation, with the smallest bones at the center and the largest forming the perimeter.

"It won't take long," she says, as if she hasn't already paid him more than he was likely to make all night.

"Lady, you're an odd one," the boy sighs, and she nods and agrees with him, because she hardly sees what's to be gained by denying anything so obvious.

"So, you're cool with this, my taking your picture?"

"Hey," the boy says, raising the nearly empty bottle of brandy as if he means to toast her, "whatever floats your boat."

"You really should be more careful what you offer," she tells him, but he's drunk enough now that her words fail to register as either a joke or a warning. And then the collector of bones takes the boy by the hand and leads him past a rough ziggurat fashioned from human skulls and the skulls of horses and cows and goats. Just beyond the ziggurat, where she's hidden a window under-neath plywood and more gypsum plaster and yet another sunburst (this one built primarily from the remains of coyotes), there is a low dais supporting a chair built almost entirely from the thigh bones and ribs of dead men and women, its seat and back uphol-stered with cerise velvet. She asks him to sit, and he does so with only a moment's hesitation. She steps back and stares at the boy for a minute or two, then turns to a pair of elk antlers nailed to the wall and removes one of the necklaces of python and anaconda and rattlesnake vertebrae hanging there. She drapes it about his neck and takes the now empty brandy bottle with its tattered label from his hands. He doesn't protest on either account, but only glances down at the necklace resting against his bare and hairless chest, and then back up at her.

"Can I touch them?" he asks, and she tells him yes, that he can. The way the boy delicately fingers the snake vertebrae, one at a time, exploring all the sharp angles and the flat, smooth surfaces, reminds her of someone praying the rosary. She's about to turn away again, to retrieve her camera bag and tripod from their hiding place within a hollow mound of pig bones, when the boy says, "There's something I remember from high school, just some poetry. But I'll recite it for you, if you want to hear it. No extra charge."

"Poetry?" she asks, realizing just how drunk he is, all the liquor on top of whatever else he might have taken before she found him. "What sort of poetry?"

"William Shakespeare," he replies. "I think I remember it all, if you want to listen. But if you don't, that's okay, too."

"Of course," she says, curious now and amused at her own lack of impatience. "I would love to hear you recite Shakespeare for me. At no extra charge."

And at that, the boy sits up a little straighter and stops fidgeting with the necklace. He squints and blinks a few times, then makes a show of clearing his throat, and the collector of bones realizes that he has an erection.

"I can't remember which play it's from," he says. "Just something I liked enough to memorize," and she tells him that it doesn't really matter. The boy laughs very softly to himself, and when he speaks, his voice seems clearer and more confident than it has been all night.

...and, when he shall die,
Take him and cut him out in little stars,
And he will make the face of heaven so fine
That all the world will be in love with night
And pay no worship to the garish sun.

And then he laughs again, and she claps, and she tells him that the lines come from *Romeo and Juliet*, Act V, Scene II, Juliet with her nurse in the Capulet's orchard.

"Well, fuck, there you go. I always was a bit of a fag," he says, and she tells him how much she has always loved that particular passage, which is true.

"Yeah, like I said before, my grandmother used to say I was sort of psychic, so I guess I must have known that, right?"

"Yes. I suppose so," the collector of bones replies, and then she stoops to retrieve her camera bag while the whore halfheartedly begins to fondle himself.

Beatification

She lies naked on the long, low table carved from slate half a hundred years ago. And around and above her, the smoky, fragrant air has filled almost to bursting with the muttering, intoxicated clamor of all those who have come this night to worship her, all those whom she soon will serve. They are naked, too, every one of them, these ecstatic men and women, and their bodies sway to drumbeats and the trill of ivory flutes and to other still stranger music that can only be heard *inside* their heads. Their feet pound the dusty wooden floor of the attic, and she listens, trying to catch the rhythm of the dance, if there is a rhythm to be discerned, and the pretty eunuch kneeling beside her on the table smiles and kisses her again. The walls of the high old house at the edge of the sea are washed by alternating tides of firelight and shadow, a wild and restless chiaroscuro that might just as easily pass for shades of Hell or Heaven.

"You're not afraid?" the eunuch asks her, and she shakes her head very, very slowly.

"I am not afraid," she whispers.

"No pain," he sighs, and the woman lying on the slate table stops watching the walls, then, and lets her eyes wander back to his.

"No pain," she smiles, though it is only the slightest possible of smiles, and someone who has not spent weeks learning her subtlest mannerisms might have missed it or mistaken it for another expression entirely. But the eunuch has spent all those days and nights studying her and tending to her needs, and it doesn't escape his notice.

"No pain," he says again, "but there is great pleasure, yes?" And now she nods and grins so that anyone would know her smile for a smile.

The table is cluttered with an array bowls and bottles and jars, a granite mortar and pestle, whisks and basting brushes, colanders, measuring cups and spoons – ceramic and glass and stainless steel to contain everything that is required. There are generous bouquets of herbs, both dried and fresh – basil, cinnamon, nutmeg and mace, bay, cumin, coriander, licorice and anise, tarragon and wild thyme and sage. There are onions and leeks and fat bulbs of garlic, lemons and key limes, the speckled eggs of quails, pomegranates grown in faraway Azerbaijan and rose hips picked that same morning from the dunes near the house. There is extra-virgin, cold-pressed olive oil, vinegars fermented from apples, dates, raisins, and malt, and there is an assortment of wines and liquors. There are neat mounds of salt from Bolivia and Senegal and Spain. No expense has been spared, no detail overlooked, and it is unlikely that any banquet has ever been assembled with more deliberation and exacting care.

"They have all come to see *you*, my dear," the eunuch says, and then he goes back to massaging her bare belly and breasts with the pungent mixture of oil and spice that he has prepared while the others drank and danced, fucked and howled their wordless bacchanal to the New England skies and whatever dark, half-forgotten gods might or might not be listening.

"To *see* me," she whispers, still smiling, and her eyes drift back to the frenzied interplay of light and shadow swarming across the attic's walls and ceiling rafters.

"You are such a *wondrous* sight," the eunuch says. "A very special thing to behold, and none of us are ungrateful for so precious an opportunity."

The pale woman lying naked on the table has violet eyes, and her long hair is almost as colorless and fine as corn silk. There is a small scar on her chin, from when she was seven and took a tumble on her bicycle. There is a faint scatter of freckles across both shoulders, but not a single one to be found anywhere else on her body.

"You are almost, *almost* perfect," the eunuch says, rubbing a bit of oil deeper into her left nipple. "You are *special*, and we might well wait a thousand years before another such as you comes along." Then he sits back on his heels, wiping his hands clean on a towel, and he admires her glistening, milk-white skin and those eyes like nuggets of hard Christmas candy. "You must not for a moment think us ungrateful, or believe that we are taking your gifts for granted."

She nods, but her gaze remains fixed on the ceiling and walls. "I am also grateful," she replies, and he listens, expecting something more, desiring something more, revelation or confession. But there are only those six syllables, and then she blinks once, and smiles for him again.

At sunset, before she was taken from her cell in the basement of the old house, the woman was shaved with a pearl-handled straight razor, and the mound of her sex, the gentle rise of the *mons Veneris*, is nearly smooth as the day she was born. She has been fully dilated, and her vagina is held open by the metal jaws of an antique speculum of the type first constructed by the French physician Philippe Ricord in 1834. The eunuch glances at her face, relieved to see such complete peace there, certain now that the cocktail of iv-drip opiates and hypnotism has done its job, and whatever the violet-eyed woman feels – whatever caress or wound or violation – can only be interpreted by her brain as pleasurable sensations.

"We will not live long enough to ever again see anything even *half* so beautiful as you," he says, reaching into a large wooden bowl heaped with peeled garlic cloves and whole yellow chanterelles, diced shitakes, peppercorns, and ripe cranberries. He takes a single handful, and while she watches the shadowplay thrown across rotting boards and peeling wallpaper strips, he begins to stuff her with the ingredients from the wooden bowl. She moans a welcoming sort of moan at his familiar touch, and so he reaches for a second handful, and then a third, packing in as much as she can contain. Soon, her moans and gentle gasps are not a response to the eunuch's hands on and inside her, but to the growing sense of *fullness* between her legs.

"I can hear the sea," she tells the eunuch, realizing that the dancers aren't moving to a rhythm dictated by the drummers or the flutes, but to the crash of waves slamming themselves against the rocky shore. The woman lying on the table laughs, feeling foolish that she did not recognize the source of that cadence from the very beginning – each icy line of breakers shattered in foam and spray, energy and momentum that has traveled halfway across the Atlantic, perhaps, finally spent and dissipated before the sea rushes back upon itself, marshalling an inexhaustible strength for another assault upon the exposed and weathered bones of the continent. And then she whispers, dredging a bit of poetry from her drowsy, meandering thoughts, "It's melancholy, long, withdrawing roar, retreating to the breath of the night wind…"

The eunuch pauses to wipe his hands again, after removing the speculum and setting it aside. He asks her, "It isn't really so melancholy, is it? Not when you start to comprehend what it is she's saying to us, the sea, what she has *always* been saying since we were only single-celled things, twitching in her Proterozoic womb?"

"No," the woman replies. "You're right. It isn't melancholy. I was just remembering, that's all. The words just came to me."

"Words will do that, unless you're very mindful," the eunuch says, and then he has to hunt about a moment before locating the surgical needle, partly hidden beneath half a green bell pepper. The needle is already threaded, and, for the third time, he says, "No pain."

"No pain," she assures him. "I have gone where it can't find me, not ever again."

"Yes," he tells her. "Yes, you have. And any one of us would give everything this night to take your place, if it were only our place to take. You are blessed, and soon you will fill us with all the blessings of Mother Hydra."

"Soon," she says, and then he leans over her and pierces her right labium majorum with the tip of the needle, pushing the steel easily into and through the soft fold of flesh, then drawing the length of catgut after it. Her blood paints the straw-colored thread a wet shade of crimson that is almost black, but the woman doesn't cry out or flinch. A moment later, the needle cleanly punctures the left labium, and the eunuch snips the thread and ties the suture off tightly with a triple throw knot. It's a procedure he has performed more often than he can now recall – several times each year, and some years more than others – and his hands move quickly, without hesitation, certain in their work.

"Closing the door," she murmurs.

"Yes," he says. "Just as I explained, closing the door and locking it behind me, that nothing will be lost."

"Even as our Mother slammed closed the doors of the ocean," she sighs, repeating one of the eunuch's litanies. She memorized most of them, waiting in her basement cell below the high old house, not because he expected her to, but because it helped the time go faster. "Closed and sealed," she continues, "against all incursions, and against any who would defile the absolute night of the Abyss, against man and demons, against time and the storms that lash at the heart of the world."

As the eunuch stitches her shut, some of the women and men have stopped their dancing and come to stand at the edge of the cluttered slate table. The smell of her blood has commingled with the animal stinks of sweat and sex and with the aromatic smoke rising in grey gouts from smoldering brass censers strung up over-head – frankincense and myrrh, blood and perspiration, copal and juniper, spilled semen and leaking vaginal secretions. When some among the dancers press their fingers gently against the bleed-ing, sutured flesh, the eunuch does not try to stop them. Nothing should be wasted, and he works around their eager, groping fin-gers, pausing now and then to watch as they lick precious drops of the violet-eyed woman from their fingertips.

"Only a taste," he cautions, then ties off the twenty-seventh stitch. "Only an intimation of what is to come."

"Yes. Only a *taste*," she whispers and laughs again, struggling to remember the rest of the litany, trying to think through the deli-cious throb and ache spreading out from her crotch. The eunuch has taken care to leave the head of her clitoris exposed, and she lets her left hand wander down to it. It is slick with oil and blood, with her own juices and those from the mixture stuffed into her distended vagina and cervix; delicately, she pinches the erect glans between thumb and index finger. She shuts her eyes, wanting to hear nothing now but the surf against the granite headlands. The voice of the goddess speaking across aeons, in this moment calling out to her and no one else.

"Below the thunders of the upper deep," she says, slowly strok-ing her clit as she recites the lines. "Far, far beneath in the abys-sal sea, her ancient, dreamless, uninvaded sleep…faintest sunlights flee about her shadowy sides; above her swell huge sponges of mil-lennial growth and height. And far away into the sickly light…

and far away..." But she trails off, quite sure that she's gotten it wrong, completely wrong, and this is some other prayer or poem or incantation, and one that she is not even remembering the right way round.

"It doesn't matter," the eunuch says, as though all her thoughts have been laid bare to him, and for all she knows they have. "Whatever words you have to offer, she will be flattered."

And then, because there is more bleeding than usual, more than a mere taste for greedy, impatient fingers, he stops suturing just long enough to select a small blue and white china bowl from the jumble of utensils and dishes and bottles. He places it beneath her, to catch the trickle that has become a steady stream, and soon the floral pattern decorating the bottom of the bowl is lost to the life leaking from her body. For a moment, he watches her masturbate, marveling at the tiny spur of her clitoris and her pale, bloodstained fingertips.

"Any words will suffice," he reminds her. "Any words that feel right to you," and he picks up the needle and catgut again, and listens to her patchwork reverence and supplication while *she* listens to the sea. The dancers swirl madly around them, tracing careless eddies in the smoke trapped there beneath the steeply pitched roof of the house, and the moon watches on, jealous, but much too far away to give voice to her jealousy.

Untitled Grotesque

They come to this place as infrequently as once or twice a year, though there are surely those among them who would make the pilgrimage weekly were that an option. But such gems as are here displayed are few and far between, and in a market such as this it is a simple given that demand will always far exceed supply. They come from half a hundred cities, half a dozen countries, and they sit silently together, rarely speaking above a muted whisper. They sit on the hard wooden benches in the darkness, and each alone and all together they stare into the stark white spar of electric light spilling from the rafters and pooling on the boards of the tiny circular stage. No photography or audio recording of any sort is ever permitted here, and there are no exceptions, and for these women and these men the threat of exile from future gatherings is all that is required to enforce the prohibition. What is seen here and heard here is intended to be fleeting, the rarest delicacies made even more so because they may only be preserved by fleeting, fading, fallible memory.

It has no right name, this playhouse, though to some among its patrons it is known as the Well, a fitting appellation as it is little more than a wide shaft sunk deep into the soft sand and clay strata below the city. The walls are lined round about with bricks laid in precise vertically staggered bonds by the hands of Colonial masons, and what purpose the pit might have originally served has long since been forgotten. Entry is gained through the rear of an antique shop, by way of a locked door painted several shades of green. Behind the door there is a hallway that ends in a second green door, and behind that door are stairs leading down to an enormous basement. The basement is crammed and cluttered

63

with crates and broken furniture and the iron skeletons of wasted machineries, and the winding labyrinth leading to the trapdoor by which one may reach the subbasement might as well be guarded by Pasipha's bull-headed son. The path is never precisely the same, though most would swear that nothing ever seems to have been moved from the time before. By contrast, the subbasement is empty of everything save ages of accumulated dust and darkness, rats and the rubbery grey mushrooms that seem to need only the damp and the cold, stale air to thrive. Set into one corner is a cast-iron grate, six-sided and notched in such a way that it may only be displaced by a pry bar shaped just so, and beneath the grate is the steel ladder leading down, finally, into the Well.

The air stinks of mold and, yet more faintly, of rot, and there are numerous shallow pools along the periphery where the ground-water seeping in through the ancient masonry accumulates. Here and there, the high walls have been shored against their even-tual, inevitable collapse with a mismatched assortment of wooden braces and steel girders, some dating back to the decade before the War Between the States.

There is no declared dress code, but most come more or less formally attired. Masks are not permitted, any more than are pho-tographs or tape recorders, for part of the price of admission is the bearing of one's face to all the others who have come down to this pit hungry and anxious and wide-eyed. And somewhere there is a great leather-bound volume in which everyone who has ever sat here has inscribed his or her name with the nib of a pen long rumored to have been used in the signing of the Treaty of Versailles. Alcohol is not allowed, nor is smoking or the use of any other stimulant or nar-cotic; sobriety is requisite, for these exhibitions are too uncommon and too terrible and too wondrous by far to be squandered on those who cannot bear the experience clear-headed and self-possessed.

The audience completely encircles the dingy stage, which slowly revolves, left to right, by means of an unseen clockwork apparatus so that all will be permitted a good view. Binoculars and opera glasses may be employed, and access to the first row is determined weeks beforehand by a lottery.

There is still one additional requirement of this audience that bears mentioning here, the criterion by which those who would occupy these benches are sorted from the merely casually curious and the only superficially perverse. Each member of this audience is him- or herself a freak, not by any accident of genetics or birth or subsequent mishap, but through a conscious choice. And though none of them could ever begin to approach the profoundness of the deformities and calamities of human anatomy which they assemble to witness and to lust over, the commitment must be significant and irreversible. So, for example, we find here the lawyer who gave up all the toes on both feet, and the librarian whose tongue has been surgically excised, and the silk-skinned young woman who wears an expensive auburn wig because all the hair on her body, head to toe, has been permanently removed by means of electrolysis. Here is a man who must most days bind his perfectly formed breasts, and the young heterosexual couple who have become impossible, discrepant Siamese twins, and the former prostitute who has allowed almost every square inch of her skin to be tattooed with graphic depictions of the least savory scenes found in the works of the Marquis de Sade. No two are alike among these elective aberrations, for they must also always reflect the endless variety of malformation and corporeal blasphemy needed to satiate their shared hungers.

This is the place, and these are the rules, and this is the grand congregation of voyeurs. And tonight is no different from the hundreds of gatherings that have preceded it, except that each one is unique. There is no master or mistress of ceremonies, and the players – there are two tonight – have already taken their places. Somewhere in the shadows an old phonograph begins to play, Act II of Puccini's *Madama Butterfly* released from scratched and brittle vinyl grooves by the grace of a diamond-tipped stylus. And now, for the most part, the murmurs and the nervous shuffling of feet ends, and, with no more fanfare than this, the pageant begins.

But first, these two, seated side by side in the second row because neither one was lucky in the lottery for first-row seats. The thin blond man, the head of his penis bifurcated five years ago that he might attend the gatherings, and, on his left, the red-headed woman whose ears have been carved to delicate points and whose upper lip has been split and her nose flattened so that she bears some slight resemblance to a cat. This is his seventh time through the green back door of the antique shop and down the rabbit hole, while it is only her third. In that other, distant world, the one which could only just begin to imagine the necessity of the Well, much less the possibility of its existence, he designs computer games, and she is a novelist of mediocre, mid-list mystery novels. Both are past their fortieth birthday now, but, in the strictest sense of the word, both are still virgins, which is not to imply that either is in any sense innocent. Innocence, were it ever permitted entry, would not long survive amid the appetites and indulgences of this place. And though neither is innocent, each remains saddled with a lingering, incongruent naïveté, which might best be described as *expectation*.

He wears a practical grey gabardine suit that smells slightly of dry-cleaning fluid, a silk necktie dyed a deep carnelian red. She is dressed all in fine white satin, as though in stubborn defiance of the native soot and grime of the pit, and of the journey to and from the pit. Her short nails have been lacquered almost the same deep red as his tie, and her long hair has been pulled back into a simple ponytail held up with white silk ribbon. He does not dare take his eyes from the stage, but she, the bolder of this pair, spares the briefest of sidewise glances at his face, his brown eyes, and his hands folded together neatly on his lap.

"Did you receive the letters?" she asks, and then she has to whisper the question a second time because he has not replied, and she thinks perhaps, in the excitement of what is to come, he did not hear. "Did you receive my letters?"

"Of course," he says, and squints at the bright stage. "Of course, I got them."

"But you didn't write me back?"

"No," he answers, sitting up just a little straighter. "I didn't write back."

And when almost a full thirty seconds has passed without his volunteering an explanation or excuse for his silence, she takes a deep breath and asks him why. He licks at his lips and shrugs.

"I have been busy," he whispers. "Busier than usual," though he hasn't. In truth, he has not even read her letters, which he keeps unopened in a bureau drawer, bundled together with a bit of twine.

"Oh," she says, trying to not to sound surprised or disappointed, but sounding a little of both.

"I'm sorry, but I have been so very busy. The deadlines have been murder."

"I understand," she tells him, even if she doesn't understand at all. "Well, at least I know they were not lost in the mail. I always worry, whenever I send a letter, that it might wind up being delivered to the wrong address, or might be mislaid by someone at the post office and never be delivered anywhere at all."

"How many of them did you send?" he asks her, and she replies that there have been four since the last time they were here. That was not quite ten months ago, a bitter January night. He wore the same grey suit then, though his tie was the orange of a tangerine's peel.

"Well, I have all four," he says. "You really shouldn't worry so much. I don't think I've ever had a letter go missing, not that I can recall."

"It happens," she assures him. "Every year, fifty-seven million pieces of undeliverable mail end up in dead-letter offices. They mostly burn the letters. They don't even try to find out who wrote them."

"Fifty-seven million undelivered letters?" he asks skeptically. "Are you sure?"

"It's not just letters," she whispers. "It's all sorts of things, parcels and letters and whatever else people happen to mail, but I imagine quite of lot of it is letters."

"Still, fifty-seven million."

"There were only four letters," she says again. "So, you received them all? The last was only about five weeks back, I think."

The man nods for her and blinks, and now his hands are not merely folded in his lap, but clenched together so tightly that his knuckles and the ends of his well-manicured fingers have begun to go white and later there will be crescent-shaped welts from his nails.

"If it worries you so much, maybe you should send emails, instead," he tells her, though he treasures the four unread letters, which smell of expensive stationary and more faintly of lavender, and he can hardly stand the thought that she might take his advice and then there will never be another for him to add to the bundle.

"I always makes photocopies before I mail them," she responds. "I have photocopies of almost every letter I have ever sent. That way, if one doesn't reach you, I can always send a photocopy."

"Well, like I said, I got them all. If there were only the four."

"And the article I clipped from the newspaper, you have that too, then? You read it?"

"Of course," he lies, knotting his hands together even more tightly than before, left squeezing right and right squeezing left, his palm gone sweaty and slick.

"As soon as I read about the murders, I knew that you'd want to see the piece. I knew that if anyone could fully appreciate their significance, it would be you. But I don't know if you read the papers, or even watch the news on television, so I thought I'd best send you a copy."

"Yes, that was very thoughtful of you," the man with the bifurcated penis says, and then the phonograph begins playing *Madama Butterfly,* and if the cat-faced woman wants to ask him anything else, she'll have to wait until after the exhibition is finished. She looks at the man once more, then sighs softly to herself and stares past the luckier people seated in front of her at the two figures on the stage. Only moments remain until it begins, whatever *it* is to be, and now the full weight of their expectation presses down upon this woman and the man seated on her left, these two who haven't learned that the Well is not a means to some greater pleasure or some more magnificent, more recondite secret. That knowledge will come to them in the fullness of time, as it eventually comes to every member of the audience, for this subterranean theater has never claimed to be anything more than an end unto itself, a yawning cul-de-sac which has no more to offer than their eyes can see or their straining ears can hope to apprehend.

Nailed in the brilliant beam of the spotlight, the evening's attractions stand side by side, hand in hand, on the slowly rotating stage; the naked girl and boy who have come all the way from the Louisiana bayous or the Mexican desert or a Bangkok brothel, depending which version of the story you've been told.

They are not twins or even brother and sister, though clothed just so, one might easily enough pass for the other. She is a year his senior, now only a few weeks from her twenty-second birthday, and already they have been on the road together for more than half a decade. Few have ever bothered with the futile argument that they are not beautiful. Their hair is long and straight and the lustrous black of mink, and their skin is the color of a cup of coffee that's mostly only cream and sugar. Their eyes are dark and guarded, and tonight the girl and the boy do not look out into the staring, impatient crowd of freaks gathered in the Well, but, instead, watch the dusty boards and their own bare feet, keeping their heads down and waiting for the music that is their cue. They are here to be seen, not to see, and experience has long since taught them how much easier it is to sleep without dreams of the bottomless longing and despite and emptiness that stains the faces of the assembled onlookers. In the end, all their audiences are the same, always; every city and every country might as well be no more than different nights endured beneath a single roof.

When the phonograph begins to play and the musty air is filled with the strains of an opera recorded fifty years before they were born, the girl releases the boy's hand, and, reluctantly, she takes a step back from him. He raises his head and watches her for a moment, almost smiling, because he knows their separation will be brief. She nods once, then spreads her arms wide and takes several very deep breaths, hyperventilating like a swimmer preparing for a deep and prolonged dive.

And then she is speaking to him – gently, reassuringly – though her lips do not move, but rather speaking directly to his mind in the secret vernacular that they have always shared and have come to believe must be some small compensation for the peculiarities of their physiology, and for their tiresome, meandering, nomadic lives, and, too, for the burden of all these eyes upon them.

Are you ready? she asks, though not in so many words, and he replies that he is. The boy kneels upon the stage, on the thin woolen blanket that has been provided for them, and the girl gazes upwards towards the sagging rafters hidden in shadow, somewhere far overhead. The boy is turned towards the audience, his head bowed and his back set to the girl, and now both their almond bodies glisten with an oily sheen of sweat.

I love you, he tells her, as he has always done before their demonstrations begin, and behind his chocolate eyes he can feel her smile, that private, incorporeal smile never meant for anyone else but him, hidden from view and from any possibility of exploitation. Something that is theirs and theirs alone, like the unspoken words that pass between them. She exhales loudly, and some in the crowd will later swear that they heard her laughing, too, though others will disagree. The boy leans forward, supporting himself now with his hands and strong arms as well as his knees, bracing himself for what's to come.

The girl's body shudders, as though she has already found the orgasm that some might well imagine will be the culmination of their performance. Her pink tongue slips across the gate of her teeth, past her lips, and it lingers there as both her hands descend across her hard, flat belly and to her crotch, which she keeps shaved smooth. There is a small tattoo an inch or so below her navel, and those with the best seats may discern the indelible symbol worked into her skin. Later, there will be confusion and even heated discussions over the identity of the tattoo, and over its purpose, whether it has been placed as a protective talisman or as an invocation or solicitation to wicked, unnamable gods. The truth is almost always a disappointment, disclosure more often than not a letdown, and only the boy and girl need comprehend it is no more than a private joke between them.

She has begun to massage the edges of her vagina, her fingertips tracing those familiar, sensitive contours, and now her tongue retreats before she bites down hard on her lower lip.

We should leave them like this, the boy smirks, almost breaking her concentration. *These sad, deluded mutilations, these goddamn poseurs, it would serve them right, every last one of them.*

Why don't you shut up, she laughs, though no one in the Well can hear her but the kneeling boy. And now the girl's short, unpolished nails press expertly into the flesh of her labia majora, and the thin, hymen-like membrane sealing her shut splits open, and those with front row seats can plainly see the sudden gout of blood. There is no pain, but she knows that they *want* pain, so she twists her face into an agonized grimace and moans loudly enough that most of the crowd can hear her over the Puccini. Inside her body, coiled snug within the lightless warmth of her womb, that quirk of her soul's tenement stirs awake.

Not much longer now, she tells the boy, and he grits his teeth in anticipation and watches the dark spatters of sweat that have dripped from his chin and forehead and hair onto the thirsty boards of the stage. *It is drinking me,* he thinks, *the stage is drinking me.* And though the thought was not intended for the girl, it pleases her and earns for him a silent snicker.

Oh, I will drink you, little bird, she says. *I will drink so deeply you will be a Saharan wasteland when I am done.* But she is also thinking something else, of tiresome, old unanswerable questions buried within the grey convolutions of her brain so that the boy cannot hear them. *What is it they need of me? What is it they have come to find? What do they mean to take away, and what will then be left?*

They can take nothing but what I show them, and then they have to carry away only the insufficient memory.

When the sleek purplish tip of the hidden organ or appendage emerges from the folds of her labia, there are audible gasps from the audience. The girl encircles it with her left thumb and middle finger, and the spotlight glimmers wetly off that taut iridescent shaft. But before the watchers can mistake her for some common hermaphrodite, the head of the shaft swells slightly and the foreskin opens to reveal minute rows of needle-like teeth. At least, they look more like teeth than anything else, and so the girl has always *thought* of them as teeth. Another three or four inches of the shaft glides eagerly, effortlessly out from between her legs, through the caressing ring of her thumb and finger, and she shuts her eyes and takes another deep breath.

And as though it has become now a single creature, some colonial aggregation of simpler cells thinking and moving as one beast, the audience leans nearer the stage. Without gazing into all those watchful, salivating eyes, the girl and the boy understand that the crowd can be teased just so long and not a minute longer. For this precious, obscene spectacle, and for all those who have come before on other nights, and those that will follow after this night, the gapers and gawkers have made oddities of themselves.

They have surrendered to another will, believing themselves supplicants, believing desire the equal to devotion, believing that their personal sacrifices have brought them somehow nearer to the purity of those marked from birth by prenatal misadventures, by the precise vagaries of genetic recombination and the whimsy of mutagens and *in utero* cataclysms. But the boy and girl know that even the most drastically altered of this company would barely be fit for a cheap sideshow tent, and the gulf between all these token crucifixions and genuine martyrdom is deeper and wider than any haloed baptismal river.

Almost a full foot of the glistening organ has escaped from the girl's vagina, and now it writhes in her hands like a serpent or eel, a ballet of lewd convolutions and contortions, and she bends her knees slightly, slightly thrusting her pelvis towards the boy's ass. *Are you ready?* she asks him, and he silently reminds her that he is always ready, that the promise of this coupling pulls him from one dreary day to the next. She whispers something then, whispering aloud by the mundane conspiracy of tongue and palate and larynx, verbs and nouns, some assurance of love that he does not need, because all he needs now or ever is her inside him. There is no greater intimacy waiting anywhere to be found, not for these two, and she watches as the pulsating, vertical slit where his anus should be widens to receive her. She enters without another word, spoken or unspoken, and it only seems an act of violence to those who have been damned to merely observe. Once more, they would be disappointed by the truth. He closes himself firmly around her, and now the girl also sinks to her knees, consumed in ecstasy, lost in this congress which is always over far too soon. She is crying now, as he leans forward and backwards again and again, accepting inch after inch of her womb's gift, and hardly anyone in the crowd fails to notice the flaccid, disinterested droop of the boy's penis as he grinds himself against her. Silently, gasping, she reminds the boy to pace himself, that they've been paid for a full half hour, and it would not do to rush to the exhibition's climax prematurely.

And far above the pit, above the subbasement and the basement labyrinth and the two green doors, in the immaculately furnished attic of the antique shop, seven men and seven women and seven others who prefer to keep matters of gender fluid and undefined sit together on claret velvet cushions or in chairs upholstered with the tanned skins of unborn calves. On the walls hang three enormous flat-screen LCD video monitors, and these twenty-one watchers sip their cocktails and laugh amongst themselves and puff cigars or cigarettes or delicately flavored imported tobaccos from great bronze hookahs. Each of the three screens shows a portion of the gathering, the wide eyes and attentive, unflinching faces of those who have been granted access to the Well. At no point do any of the closed-circuit cameras hidden all around the edges of the revolving stage swivel to reveal the girl and the boy. For here, in the attic parlor, are passions and proclivities far more subtle. They would say far more *refined*, were anyone ever to ask. They would point out that when Roman emperors loosed lions and tigers, leopards and starving wolves from the depths of the hypogeum upon the Colosseum's innumerable victims, the mob was not watching the animals.

This is their puppet show, as it has always been, and these days they trade DVDs and VHS tapes and QuickTime files of the ordeals endured by the members of the audience far below, exacting, step-by-step documentaries of those many elective transformations, and then the twenty-one assemble here to watch and consider and compare observations. They find potential voyeurs, and they arrange their various alterations, and they also supply "the bait," all those warped and misbegotten things the puppets come to see. It is a simple and efficient ecosystem, and everyone is fed that which they crave, and if there are deceptions, they are only the deceptions of camouflage and predation common to all robust biological systems.

"Ah," one of the men whispers, setting his Scotch and water aside and pointing to one of the screens. "That one, there. Isn't she exquisite?"

And the remaining twenty take note of the cat-faced woman seated next to the man in the grey gabardine suit. She is no longer watching the stage, but staring instead at a small-caliber handgun cradled in her lap.

"Do you think she has the courage this time?" one of the women asks, and the attic is filled with laughter.

Flotsam

The moon is three nights past full, and I sit here alone at the edge of the low dunes while the tide goes out again. That moon, so high and cold and thoroughly disinterested, one great all-seeing, uncaring eye slowly beginning to close in the lazy, inevitable wink of lunar cycles. There's a warm late summer breeze rustling through the green tangle of dog roses and poison ivy, cordgrass and sea lavender, back towards the brackish expanse of Green Hill Pond. And Block Island Sound stretches out before me, restless and muttering beneath the moonlight, describing time and the night with the rhythmic language of troughs and cresting waves and breakers. I come here when she calls, which is more often than it used to be. I come here, and maybe there are others she awakens, on other nights, but, if so, I have never seen them for myself. I drive down from Charlestown, always stopping somewhere along the way for a few bottles of beer, a pack of cigarettes, following her voice and carefully minding the gauntlet of traffic signals and stops signs. I never play the radio. On these nights, there's room in me for no song but the one she sings, and it pulls me east and south towards the sea. By the time I cross the iron, concrete, and asphalt bridge where Green Hill and Ninigret ponds are connected through the narrowest of confluences, the song is the only momentum I need. All else has become distraction, annoyance, if I listen, and I freely admit there have been nights I've stopped there on the bridge. I've pulled over and stood gazing out across the soughing marshes, contemplating the life I lived before. She has left me my will intact – or so she swears – and I will say that it seems as though, in those rare moments of hesitation, my license to turn back, to simply *stop listening*, is right there before me. I only need the courage to turn away. I linger near my idling truck, hands shaking, smelling the stink of my own anxious sweat (which smells not so very different from the ponds and the sea), smelling the night, and I can *almost* comprehend the restraint and abnegation that would be required to turn around and drive home again. I have never yet done so, and I don't believe I ever shall. It is not my will. So, tonight I sit here at the edge of the dunes, beneath the indifferent moon as the tide slides steadily away down the berm, here and there exposing a few stranded jellyfish and an unlucky, gasping cod. Never yet has she asked me to come any nearer to the water than this. I think that's part of our peculiar symbiosis: she leads *me* down to the sea, but I am the magnet that pulls *her* up from the depths where she sleeps away the days, wrapped safe from the hungry sun, shrouded in veils of silt and darkness. Half a mile out, there's the wreckage of the *Caoimhe Colleen*, a trawler that went down during a gale, back in '75. She sleeps in the wheelhouse, most days, coiled up snug as any eel, tight as an oyster in its shell. I don't know where the sea hid her before the trawler sank; I've never thought to ask. It hardly seems to matter. I do, however, know that once, many years ago, she still slept on the land, keeping to one boneyard or another like any good cliché. I know she spent a decade haunting Stonington Cemetery, and the local teenagers still swap ghost stories that must have begun with her. And I know, too, that, farther back, she once rested among caskets locked safe inside a marble vault at Swan Point in Providence. It was there that she first thought of the water, and so traded the mausoleum for the succor of the muddy Seekonk River. The only time I ever asked her why – why the water, why the sea – she leaned close, laughing, and whispered, "You really have no notion how delightful it will be, when they take us up and throw us, with the lobsters, out to sea." Her laughter makes the night flinch, and sometimes I imagine it is harder than diamonds, that laugh. She loves Lewis Carroll, and there have been evenings I've gone to her when every word from her lips is something remembered from "Jabberwocky" or "The Walrus and the Carpenter." When she bothers to speak at all, and there certainly are enough nights when we have no need of mere words for this necessary exchange. And now I realize that I have been woolgathering, partway drunk on convenience-store beer and drawing circles within circles in the sand. There was a noise, or, rather, there was the most minute alteration in the familiar sonic tapestry of the beach, the wind, the night, so I look up, and there she is, walking out of the waves towards me. She trails some dim bluish phosphorescence, something borrowed from dinoflagellates and tiny shrimp, only by accident or because she thinks it suits her. Beneath all the valleys and mountains and dry basaltic maria of the waning moon, she glistens. Not for me, but this is of no consequence whatsoever. I have never imagined myself at the center of anything, nor asked the paths of stars to bear some relevance to my own existence. She glistens, and it is sufficient that I am permitted to bear witness. For a while – I can never say how long – she stands over me, dripping and murmuring about the gravity of appetite and all the epochs that have come and are yet to come. Or this is only my straining imagination, and, instead, she mutters a bit of "The Lobster Quadrille," or there is not *any* shape or sense to her voice. Or there is not *even* her voice. For the song requires so much from her, and there is no need to keep singing when I am sitting at her feet. She kneels before me in the sand, though I must be clear that she is not kneeling *to* me. If she has ever deigned to play supplicant to any god or goddess, any demon or angel or pagan numen, it is a secret known to her and her alone. For my part, I like to think she has never prayed and never will. She kneels before me in the sand, naked save the limp strands of knotted wrack and ribbon weed woven into her black hair and hanging down about her shoulders and breasts, the sharp scatter of barnacles like freckles across her cheeks and belly, the anemone she has allowed to take hold in the cleft between her legs. One day, one evening, I know, she will become a garden, and no longer will she need sing across the nights to insomniacs and mad men, suicides and lonely women. If she does not forsake the sea, it will, in distant centuries, make her well and truly its own. She will be nourished not with the warm blood of creatures that walk beneath blue skies, but by the photosynthesis of kelp and pink leaf, by sponges and colonies of encrusting bryozoans straining the murky sound for zooplankton and detritus. She will wear lady-crab garlands and sand-dollar brooches. These visions she has passed along to me, over the months and years, and I think they are a sort of comfort to her, the possibility of an end to untold ages of predation, an end which she accepts with the resignation of one who has been so long in agony and understands that death is, at least, release. She will not end, as my human consciousness will one day end, for that luxury was stolen from her long ago, but she might yet be permitted in this sea change to *fade*, diminishing as all unperverted Nature diminishes. She kneels in the sand before me (which is only to say in *front* of me), her eyes the still hearts of hurricanes, and then she smiles the smile I have driven through the South County night to see. She leans forward, kissing me, and so I taste salt and estuary sediment and, beyond that muddy, saline veneer, the harsher flavors that I know are truly her own. Maybe she is speaking now, words hardly even breathed they fall so softly on my ears. Maybe she is thanking me for following the song again, or maybe she is merely reciting Lewis Carroll. Maybe she is describing some careless, wanton conclusion to our meetings, a crimson abandon that would leave my body torn apart and strewn among the dunes. But it's all the same, really, as I am hers to do with as she will, no strings attached, no farthest limits to my devotion; I made that promise the first night and have not yet regretted it. Her tongue, rough as any cat's, probes eagerly past my lips, and now she is pushing me down into the sand. She is the weight of all my joys and disappointments, the bitter weight of *living*, bearing down upon me. She rises from the ocean and delivers to me the merciless press of fifty or sixty pounds per square inch, and with a single inhalation she could collapse my fragile lungs. *Her sighs and cries would rend the skies for her lover that was drowned.* And when the kiss has finally ended (for, like a hall of mirrors, it only *seems* to go on forever), I show her my throat, my paltry, insufficient offering. She trills enthusiastic approval, though, so never mind my own insecurities and misgivings in this moment. We cannot ever know the minds of the gods we serve, and we cannot second-guess their approval or disdain. *O Mother, even a dullard becomes a poet who meditates upon thee raimented with space,* and at best I am a dullard as the terrible, exquisite crucible of her mouth opens so wide and her long eyeeteeth flash the moonlight like pearls. *Creatrix of the three worlds, whose waist is beautiful with a girdle made of numbers of dead men's arms,* *and who on the breast of a corpse...*and I do not flinch or cry out or attempt to pull away as those fangs honed hundreds of years before my inconsequential birth divide skin and fascia and muscle to find the hot stream of my carotid artery. I do not turn away from the pain, but embrace it, as she is embracing me in her long white arms. The pain is one part of my penance, one part of my reward, a sliver of agony to last me until the next time, which I understand, as always, may never come. She clamps her jaws tight about me, and in this instant we may almost be as one, the embanked river spilling itself out into the boundless sea, and yes, yes, I am but a dullard, at *best*, and this is not poetry at all, Shri Kalika Devi, Morrigan – virgin Ana, mother Babd, great crone Macha, Queen of all the Phantoms Circe, Nerthus, Al-'Uzzuā, al-Manāt, al-Lāt, Demeter: the devouring, loving, enveloping, consuming mother who draws witches to their sabat bonfires and men to sacred crematoria and priestesses to shrines in secret groves surrounding bottomless, serpent-haunted pools. The circle drawn about a stone to render it a mystery, and my mind reels and is all but lost in this ecstasy that I am well aware is not *my* ecstasy, but hers and hers alone. I am, at most, vicarious. Dullard. Grateful, weeping dullard on a beach with the summer sea pulling back towards the fullest extent of low tide as she feeds. You do not satiate that hunger, but only placate it. She could devour the world and not be filled. Her thirst is as profound and abyssal as the "hole" proceeding a star's collapse, and I am damned and blessed to circle this event horizon forevermore, until she is done with me. Let me pray here for death, which is the same prayer I would utter for life, being and unbeing, and the blood that escapes her greedy, sucking lips trickles down my throat and chest and spatters like ink across the brown-sugar sand. I close my eyes, that shrinking moon, the single eye of all goddesses, glaring down at me. I will not, even now, forget those few lines memorized from the Saktisangama Tantra – *...there is not, nor has been, nor will be any holy place like unto a woman...* – but these are only a lunatic's ramblings, an idiot grasping at straws, and a dullard worshiping at the alabaster feet of the incomprehensible universe. I close my eyes, and the night falls away, and the sea is forgotten, and she is only my dream of purity and taint. She folds me open, and folds me shut, and when I awaken, shivering, in the morning to the giggle and screech of the gulls and the roar of the tide coming up again, I shall say my wicked, heathen prayers, and imagine her sleeping in the ruin of the *Caoimhe Colleen,* and already I will have begun waiting all over again.

Concerning Attrition
and Severance

You may call this place a *room*, in the sense that it is "a space that is or may be occupied," and may fairly be described as "an area separated by walls and partitions from other similar parts of the structure or building in which it is located." So, call it a room, and the authors of dictionaries may, at least, be placated and satisfied with your pronouncement. And yet, none of those who come here have entered by way of a door or window or any other such contrivance of three-dimensional architecture. Some have been here so long there remains no recollection of their arrival. Some were fashioned to exist nowhere else, and others have arrived, by unfathomable agencies, only in the last fraction of a second. The ceiling, floor, and walls appear to be no more than dusty slabs of poured concrete, and the darkness of this place is broken only by the flicker of a few clusters of pillar candles placed here and there, beacons shining in the gloom like the bioluminescent organs of abyssal anglerfish or gulper eels. In the end, the candles' glow serves only to underscore the tyranny of this darkness, and they are permitted more as a lark than through any sincere desire for illumination. Those who occupy this space (making it a room), if they have need of eyes, they have eyes which have little or no need of the vagaries of the "visible" spectrum. And they need not be named, either, these occupants, though, inevitably, they have been gifted by men with innumerable names. Those women and men who fear the dark have named them, again and again, in acts of grand and masterful futility, as humanity often seeks, through nomenclature, to subjugate that which it fears. But those names are never spoken here, unless it is in jest (akin to the placing of the aforementioned candles).

There are furnishings and various other accoutrements and instruments scattered about, though accurate descriptions of many of these objects would escape a mind accustomed to more mundane Euclidean geometries. But, because the occupants here are only the most devoted species of collectors and practitioners, drawing their devices of pain and supplication from very *many* planes of existence, others of these objects shall undoubtedly appear more conventional, more familiar, to human eyes. There are curtains, or veils, of some indeterminable, diaphanous material strung from the high ceilings and reaching down almost to the floor, and these draperies stir with unaccountable breezes, or stray sighs. And, sometimes, they drip, as well, spattering that dusty floor with all the four humours of classical medicine – sanguine, choleric, phlegmatic, and melancholic. And, on one side of this room, placed flush against one wall, there is a point of focus and activity, which, for the sake of convenience, we shall name a *stage*. The stage is raised some distance above the level of the floor, that all might have an unobstructed view, and access is gained by way of a low flight of stairs.

In this room, upon this stage, a scenario is unfolding, the latest in a functionally infinite set of conceivable scenarios begun ages before this particular moment. A tall woman stands before a kneeling woman (and here, again, a word – *woman* – is chosen more with regard to convenience than to accuracy, and for want of some more applicable, more prosaic noun). The woman who stands wears skin as perfectly white as any block of Parian marble, and she is attired in a curious sort of costume, a dress that seems borrowed, in equal parts, from the retinue of Marie Antoinette and the brothels of 1890s Montmartre. A pair of pince-nez spectacles with smoked lenses sit upon the bridge of her nose, and about her neck hangs a finely wrought silver chain, and on the chain is affixed a pendant containing a single exquisite step-cut ruby. In her right hand, she holds a pearl-handled straight razor, folded open, and the steel blade glimmers red and wet. Her compatriot in this moment wears a skin that is merely pale, and this second woman is entirely naked, save a ruby necklace identical to that worn by the first. The second woman's arms are raised high above her head and her wrists lashed together and then bound with rough jute cord to a wooden post set into the stage.

During the years 1888 to 1891, the white-skinned woman stalked the filthy, crowded streets and alleyways of London's poverty-blighted East End, and her insatiable razor (a being in and of itself, perhaps) was glutted on the wantons and harlots of Whitechapel and Spitalfields. She recites their names like a holy litany or a checklist of heroic deeds, all their names and the places where she left their mutilated corpses to be found – Mary Ann "Polly" Nichols at Durward Street, Catherine Eddowes at Mitre Square, Elizabeth Stride at Berner Street, Martha Tabram at George Yard, Mary Jane "Ginger" Kelly at No. 13 Miller's Court, and so on and so forth. She memorized the epistles that she penned to the detectives of Scotland Yard and to the press, as well as many of those written by various of her imitators and copycats, and, on some occasions (though obviously not *this* occasion), it is sufficient merely to recite those letters, and the audience will find itself briefly satiated. The mad exploits of "Saucy Jack," as she styled herself in those hectic years; she'll pause, now and then, to sing out a "fare thee well, my fairy Fay," recalling Christmas of 1887 and a prostitute whose name she didn't take the time to learn.

Thus far, the bound and kneeling woman has suffered only superficial lacerations to her face and back and buttocks, paper-cut signatures marking the most casual flicks of the white woman's blade. But the crowd is getting hungry, and that hunger breeds impatience. So the time has come to set aside this schoolyard teasing and commit some more memorable mischief. There was a slight, earlier, whether real or imagined, an insult to the white woman's person committed by the one who is now trussed before her. And here, in this place we may call a *room*, this vicious show of skill and control counts as remuneration. The white woman reaches down to clutch the ruby pendant draped about her victim's neck, and she gives the silver chain the slightest tug before she speaks.

"You wear my tear," she says, speaking hardly above a whisper, then releases the pendant so that it dangles once again between the other woman's breasts. "Now, I will taste a few of yours, I think." And then, speaking louder, the white woman addresses all the Others.

"I can take anything of hers I wish, for she is mine. Bound to me. And I *desire* to take her life."

And, having so spoken, the white woman is pleased by the shining sliver of fear sparking somewhere behind the bound woman's eyes. The white woman smiles, and the audience murmurs and waits and does all those things which make it something we may (not quite arbitrarily) call an audience.

"Yesterday," the white woman continues, "that's what I *would* have done. But now...now I'll have to settle for a little less."

Somewhere among those avid, solicitous watchers, who have here been designated an "audience," a third woman smiles, pleased by what she hears. If beings such as these ever had need of mothers, then she might fairly be thought the mother of the white woman on the stage, or, at least, the author of her current molecular configuration and metaphysical condition. In fact, let us use the phrase *Mater Puerorum*, following the work of the Persian alchemist and philosopher Abu Bakr Muhammad ibn Zakariya Rāzi (865–925 AD). This third woman – also marble white, but incalculably older and more puissant than the one whom we may, strictly for the purpose of this narrative, consider to be her daughter – has set forth the conditions of the scenario at hand. Though the white woman on stage is, by the fluctuating rules of this place, permitted satisfaction for any insult or trespass, tonight she must *also* exhibit, for all assembled to witness, the virtues of restraint and self-abnegation, a quality for which she is not especially (and, truthfully, not even remotely) renowned.

"The word, tonight, is *Control*," says the white woman, delivering those last two syllables like a gut punch, like a falling star, and the audience laughs among itself. The white woman ignores them and speaks now directly to the one kneeling before her. "And, it occurs to me, belatedly, that I should set forth a number, placing a limit upon myself and how many times I may strike. And so the number shall be *ten*, for the number ten has always pleased me." And now the white woman recites ten examples of the significance of the number ten, nothing that they do not all know, of course, but there is ritual to be observed. She ticks them off on the porcelain fingers of her left hand, citing: the Judeo-Christian Decalogue, the tenth concerning the coveting of a neighbor's wife or ass or house or what have you; the ten incarnations of the Hindi supreme deity Vishnu; the tenth sephiroth of the Tree of Life, Malkuth, which, according to the Qabalah, completes the decad and leads, then, back to god; Pythagoras' contention that ten is the perfect number, tireless and comprehending all harmonic and arithmetic proportions; the precise sum of carbon atoms present in the alkaline hydrocarbon decane; the ten plagues visited upon Egypt, as recorded in Exodus; the atomic number of the element neon; Gui, the tenth celestial stem in Chinese astrology; the claim that ten is the smallest of the infinite string of noncototients; and, finally, the Ten Lost Tribes of Israel.

"And already," says the white woman, "I have delivered three of my ten strokes," and she points to the seeping cuts on the kneeling woman's body. "Which leaves me only seven remaining. And not *even* seven, for to show more fully my devotion to this *thing* – control – I shall hold back my tenth stroke, and we can, perhaps, count this a demonstration of mercy, as well." And that last bit elicits a hearty round of laughter from the audience, for they know the white woman too well, and so know that she is, and always shall be, incapable of mercy.

"So," says the white woman to her supplicant, "six to go, and I would have you count them out for me aloud, lest I forget my place and fail this...lesson."

The kneeling woman nods.

The razor flicks, almost too fast to be followed by these eyes and not-eyes, and it draws a deep gash across the kneeling woman's forehead, and soon blood is flowing down into her eyes, blinding her.

"Four," she says, dutifully, and everyone can plainly hear the dread nestled in her voice, the certainty that, even with only five strokes remaining to her tormentor, and even given the temperate nature of the first four strokes, there is yet the threat of inconceivable harm.

"Would it not be somewhat more entertaining," says the carmine-skinned "man" who, in this moment, serves as consort to the white woman's *Mater Puerorum*, "if you, perchance, made her *want* these castigations?" He yawns then, sounding more than slightly bored.

Hearing this, the white woman on stage affects a dramatic frown, the very mask of Tragedy, and then she knots the fingers of her left hand in the kneeling woman's auburn hair. The white woman forces her supplicant's head back, her chin up, so that she must now squint through the haze of her own blood into the face of her harrier (the bound woman, for all her faults, knows better than to close her eyes).

"Do you hear the clamoring mob?" the white woman asks. "They want you to *want* it. And, always, *must* we amuse and satisfy that bloody, fucking mob, yes?"

The kneeling woman doesn't reply, knowing all her cues and that this is not one of them.

"Bread and circuses," the white woman sighs, and then she disentangles her fingers from the kneeling woman's hair, and in a considerable rustle of stiff crinolines, she sits down upon the stage beside her victim. She draws the pad on an index finger across that freely bleeding brow, then licks her finger clean.

"Sweet, almost," she says. "If one has a *taste* for fool. Me, I wish my fool to become *more* than a fool." And then, with no prefacing remark or forewarning, she flicks the steel blade down and cleanly slices away the kneeling woman's left nipple. She screams for the first time since the exhibition began.

And now there is a half-hearted smattering of applause from the audience, a grudging rumble of approval, and, in the darkness, the white woman's *Mater Puerorum* smiles again and nips at the shoulder of her carmine-skinned escort, nipping with incisors and eyeteeth that would put any predator from any world to shame.

"So nice to see an accomplished artist at work, don't you think?" she asks, expecting no reply and receiving none.

On stage, the white woman sits contemplating the severed pink button of flesh as the cavernous room echoes and then devours both the scream and the sound of applause.

"Now, was that four?" she asks. "Or was that five? I fear I have quiet entirely lost track. I might have to start over again – "

"*Five,*" the bound and kneeling woman gasps.

"Are you *sure*? Five already?"

"Yes, yes, five. It *was* five, I swear."

"Five. A hallowed number. Then that leaves me only four, correct?"

"Yes," the kneeling woman says, struggling to nod her head, and blood and sweat drips from her brow, falling like rain across the concrete.

"Very well, then," the white woman replies, sounding slightly disappointed. "Now, please, be so kind as to open your mouth for me."

"Five," the kneeling woman says, uttering the word for the fourth time and, in so doing, earning gales of laughter from the watchers pressing in about the edges of the stage, that voracious, taunting organism of many individuals which we have called only an audience.

"Open...your...mouth," the white woman says again, and in a tone that leaves no doubt she has tired of asking and will not bother to ask again. The bound woman's eyes flash shock and confusion, but she does as she's been told.

"Good girl," purrs the white-skinned woman, and she slips the nipple past quivering lips and into the open mouth, pushing it beneath the tongue of her victim.

"Now, be careful. I'd not want you to swallow that. And, make no mistake, I will slice your throat if you do something silly like spit it out." And then, whispering a whisper so low that she's sure the audience cannot hear her, she adds, "Ear to fucking ear." The kneeling woman nods, a curt, perfunctory nod, and she tries not to dwell on exactly what has been placed beneath her tongue, and failing, she tries not to gag.

There is a new round of discontented mutterings from the audience, for any given act of savagery can only slake its thirst for just so long, and now that period of time has expired. Well aware how quickly the worm may turn (though, it should be noted, there are no worms in this place we call a room), how readily painter can find herself a canvas, the white woman tightens her grip upon the razor and slides it between the thighs of the kneeling, bound, and only pale (but growing ever paler) woman. The razor does not yet touch her flesh, but lingers, millimeters from her sex, indecisive or merely teasing, merely drawing out the moment, stalling the unavoidable.

"Now, my sweet," the white woman says, "a quick riddle to amuse our friends. Tell me, is my blade facing *up*, or is it, instead, facing *down?*"

The kneeling woman's lips part slightly, and her eyes, which have become muddy and glazed with the burden of exhaustion and pain, abruptly grow both clearer and wider, swelling with new fear.

"*Tell* me. Tell me *quick*. They're all waiting on your answer." And when moments pass and still no answer is delivered, nothing but that uncertain, frightened stare, the white woman growls, "Tell me *now!*"

When the woman bound to the post speaks, she takes great care that the severed nipple does not slip from beneath her tongue. "Up," she says, not *knowing*, but making her best educated guess based on the reputation of the white woman, this creature who was once Saucy Jack, and who, more than a century before the Whitechapel mystery, prowled murderous on all fours through the forests and vales of the Margeride Mountains of France, nameless, but earning for herself the epithet *La bête du Gévaudan*. And some one hundred and fifty years before the ravages at Gévaudan, she was known – in at least one worldline – as the Hungarian Countess Báthory Erzsébet, before finally growing tired of that game and the endless mutilation and slaughter of peasant girls and the daughters of the lower gentry who had been sent to learn courtly etiquette in her gynaeceum at Castle Csejte.

"Are you quite *sure* of that?" the white woman asks.

"Yes," the kneeling woman replies. "Yes, *up*."

And, at first, the white woman only smiles, but then the smile breaks apart into ugly gales of laughter, and she kisses her victim's forehead and then her left cheek and, finally, her trembling lips.

"Yes!" the white woman proclaims. "You are such a perfectly *brilliant* fool, my doll. Up! Of *course*, it's up!" And with that, she slams the blade heavenward, slicing deep into the labial folds and vagina of the kneeling woman.

We do not need to note the screams, nor describe their specific attributes. Her screams are a given.

Shivering now, held upright only by the ropes about her wrists and sliding quickly into shock, she whispers "Six," and the white woman nods approvingly, then yanks back on the mother of pearl-inlayed handle, pulling her razor free.

We need not note the screams.

"A wicked shame…it was not…down," the white woman sighs breathlessly, grinning and intoxicated by the violence of her handi-work. The audience, once again won over and approving, offers up wolf whistles and shouts of "Brava!" and more applause. And the walls of this black space that we here call a *room* seem to shift and settle ever so slightly, so that dust sifts down from above, and the diaphanous curtains undulate in a sudden, fetid gust of displaced air.

The white woman stares at her razor for some length of time, feeling the wind from those inconstant walls and recalling a thousand other cuts, and then she pauses to lap at the kneeling woman's tears, thereby making good on her promise. She brushes the kneeling woman's sweaty, blood-slick hair back from her eyes.

"Do not worry," the white woman says. "Maybe I'll even stitch it closed for you later. But…first, we must finish the task at hand, what we have started, for it is the worst sort of sin to leave a story unfinished, or so I have come to believe."

"Six," the kneeling woman says again, her voice hardly more than a ragged sigh.

"Yes, dear, six – but *only* five, my sweet. Which leaves yet three remaining. You can *handle* three, can't you?" And then, quickly, before there is time for a reply, the white woman's blade – that sixth finger of her right hand, and also one of the many puppeteers who mind the strings of her will – hacks through the left ear of the kneeling woman.

We need not note the screams.

Someone in the audience calls out, "Come now! That one was old when van Gogh did it!" And the white woman snarls and tosses the flap of cartilage and skin in the general direction of the complaining voice.

"Seven," she says, and never mind the possibility that they might think this somehow a show of weakness, not demanding the count from her supplicant. "And that leaves two."

"Well, at least she can fucking count," the carmine-skinned man mutters to the white woman's *Mater Puerorum*, and, nearby, someone else chuckles softly to him- or her- or itself.

"You haven't gone and swallowed that nipple, have you?" the white woman asks, and it seems to take the better part of an hour for the bound and kneeling woman to shake her head *no*.

"Good, good. I think it might look pretty, pickled and floating in a jar of formalin. But, moving along to my second from last stroke..." and now the white woman seizes her victim's right hand, taking care to select the middle finger from the rest, and she immediately begins to force it backwards. "You insulted me," she says. "You challenged me. You dared to even *suggest* I was something less than what I am."

The middle finger pops loudly, dislocating at the knuckle, but there is no scream this time. The kneeling woman merely shudders, her pain-wracked body convulsing once before it is still again. And, as though incensed by the empty place the scream should have filled, the white woman growls and bares her long canines.

"I have murdered *stars* in my time," she growls. "I have scorched worlds, and you would dare to *doubt* me?"

When the dislocated finger has been forced so far that it rests flat against the back of the bound woman's hand, the razor flicks again, slicing the finger free at the violated joint.

"We shall call that eight," the white woman hisses, and "Eight," her victim whispers, replying unexpectedly.

And now the white woman peering out through the windows of her tinted pince-nez – this one who is no longer Jack the Ripper nor *La bête* nor the Countess Bathory, and who is not, in this instant, driving a healthy yellow star to premature supernova – she permits herself the luxury of forgetting all those watching on. What happens next will be for her and her alone and the rest be damned (though, as it happens, simple, unobtainable damnation probably would come as a relief to the lot of them). She reaches down to the thatch of the bound woman's pubic hair, and easily slips the detached finger into her – blood making such an excellent lubricant – then works it in and out, in and out, time after time after time.

"You *doubted* me," she says again. "Now, as they say, you can fuck yourself, sweet." She laughs, and though all the Others also laugh at her joke, at her wit and cleverness, she doesn't hear them. She shoves the finger in a final time, pushing it all the way to the opening of the cervix and leaving it there.

"Don't you let that slip out," the white woman whispers and laughs again. Then she asks how many that makes, and how many she has remaining before she has taken her full measure of satisfaction. And because the lesson is Control, she waits in an affected mimicry of patience for the reply, and around her the curtains rustle intrigue and secrets and lies. And this indefinable space we have defined waits, also, as do the indefinable beings who have herein been designated Audience. All this time, all this pain and fury, all this void and unplumbed darkness, poised forever upon an invisible fulcrum. And then the answer comes, as it must, and the white woman lifts her razor again.

Rappaccini's Dragon
(Murder Ballad No. 5)

Flower and maiden were different and yet the same,
and fraught with some strange peril in either shape.
Nathaniel Hawthorne (1844)

1.

The young man's work would be so much simpler if he were merely desirous his own death. A minute dose from any number of the glass vials or stoppered bottles in his possession, and the matter of his life would be quickly, and, if he so chose, painlessly concluded. Suicide, he knows well enough, is rarely farther away than the reach of his arm, or the distance from any given point to the spacious, but stuffy, room situated in one corner of the old greenhouse, the room that he's converted into his apothecary, his laboratory, his grand mephitical cabinet. But his own death is *not* his goal, though accomplishment of that goal will likely, in time, *mean* his death. And the young man, whose name is Daniel, has long since made peace with this inevitability. If the end of his miserable life is the price of justice, than it is a price he is willing to pay.

And on any given night, during the course of the last year, he may be found sitting alone at the cluttered table cobbled together from salvaged scraps of plywood and nails. He sits on his stool and reads aloud from Cassarett and Doull's *Toxicology: The Basic Science of Poisons* or the monthly journal of the Society of Toxicology, from M. D. Ellis' *Dangerous Plants, Snakes, Arthropods, and Marine Life* or perhaps Haddad, Shannon, and Winchester's *Clinical Management of Poisoning and Drug Overdose*. He sits here, and he reads, and he makes his meticulous notes and calculations, or he busies himself with the menagerie of banded kraits, Gaboon vipers, mambas, rattlesnakes, black-widow spiders, brightly colored dart frogs, Ethiopian deathstalker scorpions, caterpillars of the *Lonomia obliqua* moth, and Tasmanian inchman ants, those and two dozen other highly venomous terrestrial taxa. All must be properly fed and cared for, and, too, all must be milked. There are aquaria, as well, ten and twenty-five gallon tanks containing zebrafish, stonefish, weeverfish, blue-ringed octopi, various species of sea urchins, box jellies, and cone snails.

Beyond his laboratory, the old greenhouse itself is a cornucopia of virulent leaves and blossoms, roots and berries. There are pots and pallet boxes of nightshade, columbine, Jack-in-the-pulpit, buttercup, foxglove, monkshood, baneberry, bloodroot, bleeding heart, rock poppy, mandrake, and several varieties of *Rhododendron* and *Iris*. The young man named Daniel is especially proud of his success growing numerous forms of wild fungi, a collection which includes, but is by no means limited to, *Amanita* mushrooms, Ink Copernicus (only toxic when consumed in conjunction with alcoholic beverages), and the False Morel, *Gyromitra esculenta*. This is his bountiful *Jardin d'Éden*, his *edinu*, and every carefully chosen stalk is a cultivar of the original Tree of Conscience.

Only a handful of deadly animals and plants have eluded his acquisition, for one reason or another. The slow loris, for example, though its toxin is not particularly dangerous, he has savored the irony of employing in his endeavors a poisonous primate. He has also failed to acquire any other genus of venomous mammal, such as the insectivorous *Solenodon* of Cuba and Haiti, or a duck-billed platypus, or even one of the three relatively common sorts of poisonous shrews. But Daniel tries (though often in vain) not to let himself fret overly on these few missing bits of his garden, for he is keenly aware that the most lavish sort of overkill was surpassed quite some time ago.

It has, now, become more than anything else a question of distillation, combination, recombination, concentration, refinement, formulation, and so forth, and, too, the vexing and perilous problem of finding the absolute tolerance of his own regrettably fragile corpus. So, he labors here with pipettes and flasks, centrifuge and test tubes, hypodermic needles and stereomicroscopy. No mean task, no walk in the park, and already there have been a number of near-fatal mistakes. But from each one of these has he learned more of the necessity of patience. And, to be sure, the young man fears nothing now so much as futility and failure, that a single inattentive or reckless moment could ruin it all. And so he proceeds at the pace his work demands, always keeping desire at his back, that it might drive him forward, but never take the lead and spell disaster.

On this night, near the end of summer, he takes up a dried bit of fly agaric and works at it with mortar and pestle, and, now and again, he glances over his shoulder to see the pallid shafts of moonlight falling across the long, straight rows of his garden.

2.

It begins *here*, let's say, on some other night, nowhere near the end of summer, but in some interminable month of gales and ice and frostbitten windowpanes. It begins before the assemblage of Daniel's garden, for few fairy tales are ever truthful in asserting that "Once upon a time…" is the genuine start of the story at hand. Little Red Riding Hood must have had a history of straying from the path and talking to wolves. We are never told through what alchemy or dark art the poor miller's daughter came to be able to spin straw into gold. And what event, exactly, was the author of the Queen's longing for a child "as white as snow, as red as blood, and as black as the wood of the embroidery frame?" There is always the beginning before the beginning, as all beginnings are, by degrees and necessarily, arbitrary. Prick any seemingly straightforward narrative, and it will, soon enough, hemorrhage infinite regression, the events contained therein falling back upon themselves like neatly arranged lines of wooden dominos. Not a hungry wolf, nor a spinning wheel, nor a distracted royal finger stabbed while embroidering, but a thousand prefacing occurrences, too inconvenient and indirect to be related in simple childhood fables. But, that said, we will begin *here*, on this cold and moonless night.

There was a party, an especial sort of party for those with especial predilections. It was, in fact, the sort of party that Daniel and his twin – whom will not herein be named – frequented, for purposes having more to do with their own predilections than the money that men and women at these gatherings sometimes gave them in exchange for their company, their services, or nothing more than their stray thoughts. The twins were never poor, their mother having died and left to them a small, but sufficient, fortune deriving from the family's granite quarries far away in Massachusetts, and also from holdings in diamond mines in Russia and Botswana. Fortunately, it was a small fortune that demanded very little of their actual attention, for neither possessed much in the way of business acumen. Their finances were managed by an aged and odd sort of fellow named Stebbins, and more than once he had waved his monthly fees in exchange for a few hours alone with the twins.

On the night of this particular party, both Daniel and his brother had drunk more than was their custom, and well before dawn, they'd left, accompanying an admittedly peculiar heterosexual couple dressed all in white leather and white silk and the man and woman both wearing white nail polish and white lipstick. They called for a car, and the limousine ferried the four of them uptown to a loft with hardwood floors and redbrick walls hung with an assortment of paintings by someone named Albert Perrault, whom the white couple explained had recently been killed in a motorcycle accident in France. The painting depicted various black-a-vised and only vaguely defined grotesqueries, all of which made Daniel uneasy to look at for very long, and so he didn't. The furniture was upholstered in white leather, and the kitchen tiles were the same immaculate, snowy hue, as were the bedroom walls and bedspreads and satin drapes.

There were more drinks, and there were tabs of ecstasy, and then Daniel was tied to a white-enameled chair with lengths of nylon rope the color of cream. This was nothing unusual, in and of itself, and even the gag, with its white silicone ball, had sounded no alarms. The party, as noted already, catered to those with certain needs, and this was only the latest variation on a scene that the twins had played out numerous times before. The chair sat at the foot of that long white bed, where the man and woman took turns with his brother, while Daniel could only watch, aching for some release, or his turn upon the mattress, and forced to look upon the Perrault hung above the headboard. The canvas was enormous, and almost its entire surface had been painted the same charcoal grey. There was a figure at the center, which had looked to Daniel like a satyr, perhaps, and he thought, possibly, that the satyr was crouched beneath a tree, but it was hard to tell, as the painter's style strayed to and fro between impressionism and the abstract.

And it was after his twin's second orgasm, once the man and woman had each fucked him repeatedly and with a ferocity that had seemed to match, somehow, the murky threat of that grey painting above them, that the woman had produced a small syringe. Daniel's brother was lying on his belly, wrapped snug in the ivory folds of those cum-soaked sheets, laughing at some scrap of profanity the man had whispered in his ear. Later, all the misdirection would be clear, but, in that moment, Daniel only felt his own neglected desire, the distracting, deafening throb of his erection. The woman jabbed the needle into his brother's left thigh, and the convulsions began within only a few seconds. It was neither a pretty nor a painless death, though it was, at least, relatively quick. Indeed, his twin was dead before Daniel had fully begun to comprehend *what* he was seeing. He could not scream or cry out for mercy or help – the ball gag saw to that – and had to make do with muffled howls and curses. And when his brother's paroxysms ceased, Daniel shut his eyes tightly, that he would not have to watch what the man and woman did to the corpse.

And then he must have passed out, succumbing to the combined effects of shock and fury, alcohol and the tab of MDMA, because there were dreams. He stood alone in a charcoal pasture beneath the boughs of a charcoal tree, and the satyr played its pipes for Daniel and told a story of the beautiful nymph he had once loved, but who had spurned its love, and so the satyr had torn her to pieces and scattered the remains across this same charcoal field. The satyr offered to take him as its eromenos, and one question lingered on Daniel's lips, too fearsome to be spoken – *And what if I should decline?*

And sometime later, after sunrise, he awoke hung-over on a park bench, thoughtfully bundled up in a white chinchilla coat.

Daniel discovered a typed letter in the left-hand pocked of the coat, folded and sealed inside a white envelope, written in ink from a crimson typewriter ribbon explaining, quite convincingly, how any attempt to prove the man and woman's culpability in the death of his brother would not only prove futile, but would surely be met with the occasion of his own death. Daniel sat there for more than an hour, surrounded by the winter and the city, the bleak landscape of leafless branches and black ice and newly fallen snow, manhole covers steaming on the street and the exhaust of all the yellow taxis rushing by. For a time, he held out hope that he was dreaming still, and the satyr would appear, in due course, to kindly lead him back through the charcoal painting to the bedroom where his brother still lived. He looked for hoof prints in the snow, and sniffed the air for its musky, goatish scent. In the end, he gave up and hailed one of the taxis, which drove him to Penn Station, where he took a train out of the city. It was almost dark by the time Daniel found his way home again, and this, then, is what we shall consider a more suitable beginning to the tale.

Other beginnings, all equally suitable and equally legitimate as starting points, might be detailed here, but the catalog would quickly grow tiresome, and the reader might lose interest and wander away. And so, regrettably, this affair must be relayed with discretion. There are some who say that one of the sacred duties of the storyteller is to divide reality, history, fallacy, myth, fiction, fact, and parable into discrete and easily processed units, sparing the ear and eye and mind all manner of indigestion. You may choose the garden, or you may choose the party, or you may imagine those earlier beginnings for yourselves.

3.

Scotch-taped to one wall of Daniel's cluttered greenhouse workshop is a page torn from a 1932 edition of Robert Burton's *The Anatomy of Melancholy* (1621), pulled from the portion of that voluminous and obsessively subdivided manuscript titled "Bad Diet a cause. Quality of Meats." A single sentence has been marked over with a neon-yellow highlighter, and it reads,

"Mithridates by often use, which Pliny wonders at, was able to drink poison; and a maid, as Curtius records, sent to Alexander from King Porus, was brought up with poison from her infancy." (The First Partition, Section 2, Member 2, Subsection 1). Daniel chanced across the passage almost a year after his brother's death, and, to quote Charles Darwin, "...from so simple a beginning..." was born Daniel's scheme. In that single sentence from a book published the better part of four centuries ago, he found direction, and so began the gathering together of his fatal garden and menagerie, not to mention a vast cabinet of deleterious minerals, elements, chemical compounds, and microbes. Daniel soon discovered that this theme of incrementally tainted women delivered as a sort of passively assassinous gift could be traced back to the early Middle Ages and the *Purnanas* or *Suhrit-Sammitas*, said, by the faithful, to have been compiled by Vyāsa Rishi, the Krishna Dvaipayana, at the close of the Hindu Dvapara Yuga.

No matter the source, it is the *fact* of the inspiration here that matters, those few words that set Daniel on this path, that gave him some hope, however expensive it might prove, of avenging the murder of his brother. And, too, there is the private detective retained to locate, identify, and keep tabs on the couple in Manhattan. By now, Daniel has five thick files on them, exacting profiles of their habits and history, and he has cause to believe his twin was not their first or their last victim. The detective, who has been paid, and paid well, to maintain the utmost discretion and secrecy, has linked them to disappearances of young men and women from Virginia to Massachusetts, Richmond to Boston, over a period of nine years. There appears to have been two victims since the death of Daniel's brother. But he has not allowed these facts to rush him towards the pair's reckoning, and he will feel no guilt for not having saved the lost he never knew. His twin is burden enough, and he will take on no more. Still, there is a map taped to the wall alongside the page from *The Anatomy of Melancholy*, and there are pins with colored heads to mark each murder committed by the two. They are not his responsibility, all those other deaths, but they are a useful reminder.

This morning, May turning to June, he draws into a three-tenth's cc syringe half a milliliter of a drought concocted from the venom of a burrowing asp, .8 micrograms of quicksilver (specifically, mercuric chloride), and a drop of neurotoxin taken from the telson of a fat-tailed scorpion from the vast salt pan of Chott el Djerid, north of the Grand Erg Oriental of Tunisia. This is a new formula, and though he has run numerous computer simulations and tested it on rabbits and white mice, there is never any knowing, with certainty, the consequences in a human subject, especially one whose body has already been saturated with so many poisonous compounds. Daniel makes a fist and injects himself in the left arm, just above the bend of his elbow. He quickly jots a few notes, recording the time, his blood pressure and body temperature, and then retires to a sofa in the house adjacent to his workshop to wait out the coming sickness and to list what he can of the effects of the compound. He knows, in truth, there is very little reason for compiling such subjective details of his self-poisonings. He will live, or he will die, and very little else is important here. But the conceit that this is somehow a scientific undertaking helps to keep him focused through the pain and sickness and delirium, sometimes. And, sometimes, it does not.

Very often, during his "treatments" (as he thinks of them), there are hallucinations and wild fever dreams. So, Daniel has hired a nurse who watches over him on these days and nights, that he will not in his frenzied thrashings do himself some irreparable harm, thereby ruining all his work and allowing the predatory couple's spree to continue, unchecked.

And as this morning gives way to afternoon, and the pain and nausea wraps him in its razor folds, she sits nearby, watching, attentive should some intervention be required. And at last he sets his clipboard and pen aside, and surrenders to the tarantella rhythm of the pollutants coursing through his veins.

And *this* time, the visions come fast and hard, more brilliant and more lucid than is usual, most likely owing (he will later hypothesize) to some quirk of the scorpion's toxin, to its precise arrangement of tiny proteins and the potassium and sodium cations. He closes his eyes, and the world spills around him like rivers of flame and ice floes and the displaced sediment and volcanic ash and scalding incandescent gases of pyroclastic flows. And, for a time, he walks those grey fields again with Albert Perrault's Pan, the grass crunching like frost beneath his bare feet and the satyr's hooves. The mold-tinted sky is low and velvety, and the air around them stinks of turpentine and linseed oil. The grey fields end, finally, at a precipice, and if there is some opposite side to this chasm, it is so far away that sight of it is lost in the distance and the scattered light of the painted world. He looks down, even though the satyr told him not to, and the blackness there roils and curls back upon itself, as alive as the serpents in Daniel's workshop, and incalculably more treacherous.

"Orpheus wouldn't listen, either," says the satyr, "and that poor bastard's still wandering about in there somewhere."

"No," Daniel replies. "Orpheus found his way out. That's the way the story goes. He found his way out of the underworld, but... he looked back and so lost Eurydice."

"Ah, now. Is *that* the way they're telling it these days?" And the satyr laughs and stares up at that sagging, moldy, zinc-tinged sky.

"On her wedding day," Daniel replies, wishing he could look away from the chasm, "Eurydice was pursued by Aristaeus, and she came upon a snake that bit her. And she died," and then he says something about Virgil's *Georgics* and hexametric verse, and he cites Hansel and Gretel and Lot's wife as examples of the dangers of looking back, but the satyr isn't listening.

"The son of Calliope and Oeagrus was hardly more than a silly little faggot, him and that goddamned lyre. Not so different from that brother of yours – or you – really. I figure the punk pretty much got what was coming to him, the day he met up with those Thracian Maenads. That was Ovid, by the way, not your sainted Mr. Virgil."

"But," Daniel protests, "you *just* said he's still down there, wandering and lost."

The satyr sighs and spits over the precipice. "Don't you go putting words in *my* mouth, boy. I said he was still there, somewhere, but I never said he was *lost*."

"But if he died in Thrace – "

"You make me tired, boy," the satyr says, tugging at its wiry beard, and soon he loses interest in Daniel and vanishes into the shadows of the painted world. And so Daniel stands alone at the place where land ends, there at the edge of a canvas, and he wonders if Hades and Persephone would ever take mercy on him. And if they *did*, he wonders if he could then walk those winding, labyrinthine paths leading back to this field that Perrault painted, before his motorcycle accident, back to this limbo created for the one who delights *all* the gods. Back to the enormous painting hung above the bed where his twin died, the twin and surely others, and where the killers still sleep.

There are storms near dawn, shortly after the delirium and agony release Daniel to consciousness and the nurse's care. He sits propped up on the sofa, still drenched in corrupted sweat, still dizzy and ill. He sips a hot cup of tea she has made for him and watches the lightning, feeling the reverberation of thunderclaps deep in his chest. He sits and thinks of the gift sent to Alexander by the Indian giant, Raja Puru, the maiden "brought up with poison from her infancy."

4.

And now it is three days, three nights from midsummer's eve. No matter all the tests and notes, all his exacting attention to detail, the nurse and the detective and the hundreds of exotic toxins and venoms obtained from all around the globe, and the many long months of suffering endured as Daniel gradually made his body like unto that of the young woman "brought up with poison from her infancy" and then sent away to Alexander by Raja Puru – in the end it came down to a simple matter of chance and probability, and also, maybe, the whim of half-forgotten deities. Using the detective as a courier, he sent a hand-written letter to the couple who had murdered his brother. Along with a set of nude photos Daniel had taken of himself (using the vanity mirror in his bedroom and a Polaroid). The detective delivered the following letter, by hand:

> Dear Sir and Madam,
> Possibly, from the enclosed photographs, you will remember me. But possibly not. Some time ago now, you killed my identical twin brother and, for reasons I can

only begin to surmise, left me alive. Though I suspect I should be grateful for whatever mercy or caprice spared my life, the truth is that you took half of my soul that night. My days since have not been worth living, and yet I confess I am weak and find myself without the courage to commit suicide. So, I'm offering to you the opportunity to finish what you started, by whatever means you may deem appropriate. I am not afraid of death or pain, only of being left alive and alone. I pray you will find this offer agreeable, and know that the gentleman who delivered this package will bring me your reply. You will find his contact information on the attached card. I leave it to you to choose the date and time and place, should I be so fortunate that my offer appeals to the both of you.

Sincerely,

Daniel

Taking his vision of Pan as an omen, following the delivery of this letter, Daniel made an offering to the three Moirae, having constructed a modest stone alter behind his greenhouse. Though, in the end, his preparations left him too ill to get around without a wheelchair, he made what he deemed a generous blood sacrifice of his nurse, calling upon the three bearded daughters of Zeus and Themis – the ladies Clotho, Atropos, and Lachesis – to tilt the scales in his favor. The detective helped with the ritual, in exchange for having been willed Daniel's estate and what remained of his inheritance. Shortly thereafter, an answer came from Manhattan, typed in red ink upon the whitest possible stationary imaginable, perfectly matching the note that Daniel had discovered in the pocket of the chinchilla coat. The terms were, in fact, acceptable, and a date and a time and a place were set. All non-negotiable. Take it or leave it, and at once Daniel sent the detective away from Connecticut to New York to deliver word that the arrangements were entirely unobjectionable. June 17th, 11:35 p.m. sharp, their loft on the Upper West Side. Daniel took the train down, and there was a driver and limo waiting for him at Pennsylvania Station. On the way to their flat, he sips vodka and watches the lights of Manhattan glittering like the stars of an alien sky beyond the tinted windows. He took two white tablets of oxycodone hydrochloride and three dextroamphetamine capsules on the train, something against the pain and fatigue, against his failing kidneys and liver, against the charcoal-grey fog the satyr had left in his head. Before leaving home, he'd done his best with powder and rouge, trying to hide the ravages of his experiments. He will explain to them that his diminished condition is the result of alcoholism, mourning, and drug addiction, and hope that they believe the story.

Three nights before midsummer's eve.

If the white couple (he in an alabaster suit of Egyptian cotton, she attired in a dress of eggshell sateen) doubt the story, they kept those doubts to themselves. The driver pushed Daniel's wheelchair to the elevator, and then down the long hallway to their door. There is precious little small talk, and Daniel can smell their eagerness, their hungry urgency, as surely as he can smell his own sweat and the vase of callalilies on a bedside table. He grew the same species in his own greenhouse, admiring the fact that every part of the plant is fatal if ingested. The blossoms are snowy white, of course. The painting by Albert Perrault still hangs like an ashen blotch above the bed.

The man and woman are kindly and polite, and even offer to show Daniel pictures that they took of his brother before disposing of the corpse. He declines, and soon the three of them are naked together in the wide white bed. Together and apart, the man and woman explore every crevice and orifice of Daniel's flesh, delivering and accepting lingering kisses, working at his dick until the man's mouth and the woman's vagina are filled with cum. She demonstrates a fondness for the act of anilingus, forcing her tongue repeatedly in and out of his asshole. And Daniel tries to think only of this fortunate opportunity, that the Fates have smiled upon him. He feels the couple's loathsome caresses and violations, but those sensations seem to reach him from at least another lifetime, or a dream of grey grass, or across a considerable distance.

"So sweet," she says, and "So much better even than your pretty brother," he says. The woman whispers how she wishes they could keep him alive, keep him forever, and the man reminds her how many other delights the world yet holds for them, and this night is only a transient pleasure.

"So very easy to forget," she says. It has been maybe twenty or thirty minutes since he lay down upon their silk sheets, and Daniel notes that the woman has gone pale and is slurring her words. He notes a similar paleness in her husband, and offers mute gratitude to the satyr squatting there beneath the charcoal tree, hanging there above the bed. Another five minutes, and the man is vomiting and the woman has begun to shiver uncontrollably.

Their deaths are neither pretty nor painless.

He props himself up against the headboard and watches as they writhe and moan and shit themselves, as blood flows from their nostrils and from underneath their fingernails. He smiles when they mutter weak appeals for help and mercy. The woman goes into convulsions first, and Daniel has the pleasure of seeing the fear in the man's cloudy eyes as she thrashes upon the varnished hardwood floor.

"So sweet," Daniel whispers, smiling, and when they have both stopped moving, he realizes that it has begun to rain. He lies down in the cool, sex-stained sheets and rests, watching the night fade to a wet dawn and soggy morning light almost as sooty as the satyr's painted universe. Sometime later, he drifts into the last dreams he will have before his corrupted physiology finally ceases to function. He walks the stony, briar-strewn labyrinths leading down and down through lightness tunnels and ebony hallways and inconceivable subterranean galleries to the shadowy abode of Hades and Persephone. Daniel has no trouble with the ferryman, nor in locating the gates, for they have been left open in expectation of his imminent arrival. His brother is waiting there, and together they seek the waters of Lethe and the blessed forgetfulness of that conclusive drowning.

For Robin Hazen, who suggested the title of this story.

Unter den Augen des Mondes

Only rarely is she awake at daybreak or at late morning or afternoon. But in those infrequent hours when she finds herself staring past the bars of her cage at the dusty shaft of light leaking in through a basement window, the werewolf almost remembers how it began. How she came to be here. Who she might have been before. There are iron bars bolted across the window, as well, and so the light makes a checkered shadow on the earthen floor. She squints and distrusts the light, for all the things it would have her remember, memories she suspects are only lies told by the sun that she might forget the moon and so, too, forget herself. This illumination is much too plain, she knows, too obvious, and she whimpers and turns her face away, wishing her dim wishes for sleep and dreams and the night. There are two dominions in the heavens, the Kingdom of the Sun and the Kingdom of the Moon, and long ago now did she cast her lot with the latter. The sun would tell her it was not an irrevocable decision, but the werewolf knows better. The sun promises green fields, where she walks upright beneath blue skies. It promises yellow flowers and bees and warmth across her upturned cheeks. It promises one body, instead of the two she inhabits, a single state of being never countermanded by the violence of metamorphosis. But she knows it lies, the sun, the flaming, devouring sun. She huddles in a corner of her cage, curled into the folds of filthy blankets, cowering as far from the checkered wash of light as she may. The werewolf whispers to herself one of the stories the moon has taught her, and in this story the moon is named Selene, and the sun – named Helios – is her brother, as is the dawn, Eos. The moon loves a mortal man named Endymion, and he is so beautiful and so pleases her that the moon asks Zeus to gift Endymion with eternal sleep that they would never again be parted by the cruel day. The werewolf tells herself that story, as the light moves across the dirt floor, and she tells others, too, of the wolves who chase the sun's chariot across the sky, and of the great Egyptian serpent, Apophis, who swims deep rivers and strives always to swallow the sun. These are *her* stories, this mismatched, patchwork mythology to comfort a scalded soul on those rare occasions when she is so unfortunate as to awaken before the balm of dusk. She tells herself these tales, fables fingered like prayer beads, familiar, worn so smooth, and she tries hard not to hear the deceitful white-hot tongue of that blinding star. And more rarely still, there are the terrible days when the pale man comes down his creaking basement steps and purposefully wakes her. With an old broom handle, he roughly jabs her in the ribs, spoiling dreams, and she tumbles out across milky constellation rivers and moonless midwinters to the stink of mold and dust and her own shit. To the sour reek of *him*, which is the reek of sunlight, for she has long since come to understand that the pale man is a servant of the Kingdom of the Sun. He keeps her always locked inside this cage so that his god will be pleased and smile its molten approval. The man sits safely out of reach on a metal folding chair, and he drinks his whisky and smokes his cigarettes and prods her roughly with the broom handle. He talks, sometimes, though she knows enough to understand these are not the man's own words, for in ages past the sun entered him, and it burned him until nothing more than a hollow shell remained. Now, when he speaks, it is the sun's voice, and the words sear her ears as surely as the light sears her eyes. He asks, "How long's it been now, puppy?" or "Wouldn't it feel good to run free again, out there beneath that twinkling bitch-whore sky you call your mistress?" But seldomly does she answer with anything more than a snarl or a low, warning growl. The werewolf knows perfectly well she is being taunted with rhetoric, that these questions are not meant to be answered. There was a time when she offered up replies, against the moon's advice, hoping to satisfy the hollow, pale man. But when she spoke, he only jabbed her that much harder with the broom handle and refused to feed her for nights and nights afterwards. "You are *an animal*," he would sneer. "A filthy animal, and it is unseemly when animals deign to speak. It is an insult to the Order of the World." She knows better, for with her ears the werewolf listens to the gentle songs of owls and whippoorwills, eavesdrops on the chittering of bats, the busy conversations of hunting coyotes and the raccoons snuffling about the garbage cans. She knows the languages of crickets and katydids, and understands that the sun and all its agents loathe this multitude of voices that speak only when their backs are turned. "Crazy as a fucking loon," the pale man laughs and taps his stick against the hard dirt floor. He laughs a lot, and she thinks that's probably so he won't remember how the sun slid down his throat and made, at most, a papery husk of him, only a convenient mouth to spew fire and anger and the heat that comes with fire, only a puppet stuffed with soot and cinders to wield a broken broom handle. "What did *she* ever do for you, anyway?" he asks. "What did she *ever* do, puppy, but warp you and lead you astray and drive you insane? Seems to me, you've been worshipping in the wrong goddamn churches." But she only sits back on her haunches and watches him through the bars, watching with the brilliant amber eyes that were her reward on that first night the moon kissed her and she realized she was meant to return the kiss. There was a grove of apple trees, an orchard long neglected and claimed by wild grapes, honeysuckle, and the pricking vines of greenbriers. And the moon, two nights past full, found her hiding in the crisscross shadow of the branches, and whispered that they had always, always been lovers. The werewolf wept and tried to hide herself beneath the carpet of fallen, rotting leaves, because she thought it was another trick. All her life had been comprised of tricks, wicked tricks of one sort or the other. There had been many men and women, in almost equal measure, who said that they loved her, and yet she had never once felt loved. *And why*, she asked the moon, *should you be any different?* The moon replied, but not with words, as words are too easily doubted and vows too easily broken. The moon replied by giving her a second skin, a pelt, sharp claws and sharper teeth, and that night she ran on all fours beneath the forest's concealing limbs, all the way down to the rocky place where the land falls away to the sea. She opened her new, quick jaws and sang ancient, thankful, reverent songs for the moon. That night, the werewolf caught and killed a rabbit, and what she didn't eat, she buried for later. She pissed on the trunks and gnarled roots of oaks and hemlocks and maples, leaving her invisible, inkless signature scattered about for any other wolves to note, should they happen across it. She searched tirelessly for them, those other wolves, that night and on many nights thereafter, not yet comprehending that men had long since slaughtered and driven away the wolves that had once haunted those woods. *That is why I have made you, daughter, lover, confidant,* the moon whispered from the star-dabbed sky. Hearing this, the werewolf felt disappointment and an awful, aching loneliness, but she also, finally, felt loved, and knew she was *not* alone. "Are you *listening* to me, bitch?" the man asks, and jabs her again with his broom handle. "Puppy, has she so addled your poor bitch brains that you can't even tell when someone's *talking* to you?" But the day is almost done, so that now the checkered pattern on the floor has slipped all the way across the hard-packed dirt to the far eastern end of the basement. She knows the dance – sun east to west, sunlight through the barred window west to east – and she watches on, relieved as those skewed, divided squares of white light grow ever fainter and are steadily consumed by patient, waiting shadows. Already, the sky above her will be going countless shades of purple and indigo, bruising to match those ugly marks the hollow man has inscribed upon her ribs and shoulders and thighs. And, of course, *he* knows it, too, that the moon will be up soon, that the sun is going down, deserting him as the earth spins round about. When he speaks again there is a seething desperation in his voice. He sounds cheated. He sounds the smallest bit less certain, and so the werewolf knows that the soot inside him is already growing cold and heavy. "It hardly matters," he tells her. "Ten hours, then you're mine again, if I want you. Truth be told, I've half a mind to go upstairs and get my shotgun, put an end to this abomination, once and for all. Would she want you then, I wonder, full of buckshot and buried six feet down below the turnips and cucumbers?" And, even though she knows the price for daring to talk, she answers the man in his own clumsy tongue. "You will not kill me, ghost, for in death you may not torment me, and buried six feet down, below the turnips and the cucumbers, your master would never again burn me. He might burn what's left of *you*, though, for robbing him of me." She waits a moment, watching his face and the embers in his eyes as he raises the broom handle. "Even by daylight," she whispers, "you are a coward." She makes no sound when he strikes her, does not yelp or scream or beg for mercy he does not have to give. She lies still, tasting her own blood, knowing that *he* knows that everything she's said is true. Three times he brings the broken handle down across her head and shoulders, and he has passed now beyond the power of coherent speech and can only roar like the beast he will never have the freedom to be. The fourth time that he strikes the werewolf, catching her smartly across the face just above her left eyebrow, a consoling nothingness surges up to wash over and through her, unconsciousness interceding, stealing his punching bag away. And for a while, then, there is neither pain nor fear, neither contempt nor regret, and when she opens her eyes again, silvery moonlight lies in its own checkered pattern across the basement floor. And she hurts, yes. She hurts like hell, but still not so badly that she's ungrateful to be awake. A far worse thing it would have been if she'd *not* come to before dawn, and the night had passed her painlessly by. She lies motionless in her blankets and the soiled straw the man sometimes bothers to rake out and change with clean straw. She lies there and gently murmurs through split and swollen lips all the names she has ever learned for the moon, and from her eccentric, ecliptic orbit, across more than two hundred thousand miles of near vacuum, the moon replies with benediction. It is an old war, the struggle between the Kingdom of the Moon and the Kingdom of the Sun, and the werewolf knows that there have been prisoners and casualties beyond reckoning. And she knows, as well, that her captivity is not her mistress' will, but, rather, her sorrow. Unlike the sun, the moon asks for no sacrifices, no immolated flesh, no blood spilled in anything but the immemorial joy of life and death. The moon would have long since freed the werewolf, were that an option, if her light but had the power to dissolve iron bars or shatter steel padlocks. The moon would have strangled and frozen the sun's sour puppet in his sleep, if she were that manner of goddess. But she is not, and the werewolf has never asked for anything that cannot be granted. She does not blame the moon, and she does not blame herself. The man's trap was clever and baited well, and that night she was hungry enough to risk the snare. She lies in her cage, blinking only when she must, and allows her soul to slowly fill with that wan, redeeming glow, trying not the think upon the open fields or the tree-lined labyrinths where she has not run for more than a year and may never run again. Instead, she imagines a day when the man will come too close, the day when his fury will overcome his caution, the day when she will spring from this pen and drag him down. She stares deeply into the moonlight pooled on the basement floor, and sees his blood splashed across the dirt walls, his throat held fast between in her jaws. She imagines him dead, and her padding quietly, warily, up the creaky stairs to the house above, and then, at last, back out into the world. She even permits herself the fantasy of a time when the Kingdom of the Moon defeats the Kingdom of the Sun, and the vanished wolves return. And then, recalling a few lines of poetry from the life before she was anything but a human woman, before she was blessed and loved, the werewolf, changing only a single syllable, whispers, "…and *she* will make the face of heaven so fine that all the world will be in love with night and pay no worship to the garish sun." And the moon shines brightly down, and somewhere out beyond the basement an owl swoops down upon a careless mouse, and the mouse screams, and, in her welded cage, the werewolf smiles, and waits.

The Melusine (1898)

1.

In this blistering, midsummer month of bloatflies and thunder without so much as a drop of rain, the traveling show rolls into the great smoky burg spread out at the foot of the Chippewan Mountains. By some legerdemain unknown to the people of the city, the carnival's prairie schooners and Bollée carriages declare its name in letters five-stories high – Othniel Z. Bracken's Transportable Marvels – shaped from out nothing but the billowing clouds of red dust raised by those rolling broad steel and vulcanized rims. The traveling show arrives at midday, as if to spite the high white eye of the summer sun glinting off tin roofs and factory windows and the acetate-aluminum envelopes of the zeppelins moored at Arapahoe Station. "Only mad dogs and Englishmen," as the saying goes, but apparently also this rattling, clanking hullabaloo of steam organs and barkers and pounding bass drums.

And the townspeople, confused and taken off their guard, peer from the sweltering shadows of their homes, from shop windows, from all those places where shade offers some negligible shelter from the July sky. They gaze in wonder, annoyance, or simple, speechless bafflement at this unexpected parade spilling along East Evens Avenue, led by an assortment of automaton mastodons, living elephants and rhinoceri, and a dozen white and prancing Percheron's with braided manes. There are twirling, summersaulting women on the horses' backs, scantily clad after the fashion of Arabian harem girls; from the distance of only a few feet, it's difficult to tell if these acrobats are mechanical or the real thing.

Soon, there is an impromptu assortment of street urchins and drunkards trailing alongside the parade, coming as near as they dare to wheels and stamping hooves and stomping brass feet, and clowns with gaudy faces toss candy and squibs from the wagons, delighting the ragged children and frustrating the drunks, who might have wished for just a little more. And a man in a long black duster, his face half as red as ripe cherries, stands on a wooden platform mounted precariously atop one of the schooners. He bellows a command through a shining silver speaking-trumpet, and at once a flock of clockwork doves erupt from some hidden recess to flutter and cavort beneath the merciless sun.

"A long, long way have we come!" he shouts, the trumpet magnifying his voice until it can be plainly heard even above the noise of the parade and the clatter of the ironworks two streets over. "From the Cossack-haunted steppes of Siberia to the deadly forests of French Equatorial Africa, from the celestial palaces of the Qing Dynasty to the farthest wild shores of both polar climes, we arrive, bearing the perplexing fruits of our intrepid journeys!"

The barker pauses, taking a breath or pausing for effect or both, and from his high perch he watches the peering, upturned faces, the thousand flavors of skepticism and dismay, anticipation and surprise. The clockwork doves circle him again, then suddenly retreat into whatever cage released them a few moments before.

"Yes! It's true!" he continues, wielding the trumpet the way, two decades earlier, before the Great Depredations, a buffalo hunter would have wielded his Spencer repeating spark rifle. "In these very wagons, the treasures of the wide, wide world, the secrets of the globe that have so entertained crowned pates and bewildered men of science and philosophy! Here, presented for each and every one among you to look upon and draw your own conclusions!"

And now, there is a hesitant smattering of applause, a handful of wolf whistles and catcalls, and the barker leans out over the railing of his platform, risking a dreadful tumble (or so it surely seems).

"And lest any there among ye lot think us mere profiteers and scalawags," he bellows through the speaking trumpet, "unscrupulous purveyors of humbuggery or chicanery, let me please *assure* you otherwise! A *small* return, yes, yes, astonishments for a most nominal and reasonable fee, *only* to cover our not-inconsiderable expenses in wending our way about the fearsome world. *But,* by the sacred horns of Moses, *not one copper more!*" And at this, on cue, or by providence, one of the elephants splinters the already cacophonous air with a trumpeting of her own. There is laughter from the onlookers, and the tension breaks, and some of the hesitant skepticism dissolves. The barker grins his wide grin, knowing half the battle's as good as won (and making a mental note to reward that particular elephant later on), and he sets the silver megaphone against his lips again.

"For, indeed, it is to the *betterment* and general *erudition* of all mankind – even savages in their mud huts and wigwams, that the men and women of Othniel Z. Bracken's Transportable Marvels have devoted themselves!" And though, at this point, he knows it's unnecessary, the barker adds the customary, "Come *one*! Come *all*! Come and *see*! Come and be *astounded*!" Then the agreeable elephant raises her trunk and lets out a blast that would have shamed even the troops of Jehoshuah, in his blaring seven-day march about the walls of ill-fated Jericho. The animal's cry echoes down the slatternly, riveted canyon of thoroughfares and alleyways. Below the chandeliered ceiling of the Grand Chagrin, the dancers and sporting girls stop flirting and fanning themselves. In basements and backrooms, rapscallions and reprobates pause at their games of *crapaud* and poker, at the cutting of purse strings and throats. The air thrums and crackles, transformed, as if by the sizzling tendrils of an electrical storm. The choking, obscuring cloud of red dust streams out behind the wagons and automobiles.

And the barker, almost whispering through his trumpet, ends his soliloquy with a tipping of his tall black top hat, a bow, and, finally, a single, pregnant word – "Miracles..." – and the show rolls on, triumphant, through the smoky, industrious city.

2.

At the southernmost edge of the city, just before the crooked, tumbledown shacks of Collier's Row, in the lee of the towering gob piles stripped of their lustrous anthracitic treasures, the carnival has unfolded across the dusty, disused cavalry training grounds. Like an inconceivable bird fashioned all of canvas and tent poles, the show has spread itself wide, unfurling beneath the vast western sky. And by dusk, there are what seems veritable miles of Chinese lanterns and gas lamps and Edison carbon-filament bulbs strung gaily, gaudily, here and yon. You might think, spying down upon the city from the windy crevice of Genesse Pass or Kittredge Point, that all the stars of Heaven had been lured down to Earth, to light these delirious festivities. All those who can have come, and the air is filled with laughter and conversation, and it smells of sawdust and confections, incense and the exotic dung of at least a hundred species of animals.

Here are aisle after aisle of flapping, painted broadsides depicting the most fearsome and obscene and unlikely beings. And a gigantic, revolving iron wheel crafted by G. W. G. Ferris & Co. of Pittsburgh, Pennsylvania, and just one thin Liberty dime buys a ten-minute ride in its rocking, colorful gondolas. There's a musical carousel fitted with all manner of saddled clockwork beasts – horses, humped camels, giraffes, a pair of snarling iguanodons, roaring lions, and even an ostrich. All around the cavalry grounds, there are fire-eaters and fakirs, tattooed women and a legion of wind-up Roman Praetorians, unicyclists and jugglers and a trio of sword-swallowing Malays not content with swords, but, contrarily, busy swallowing Nantucket harpoons and living rattlesnakes (headfirst, naturally). And rising lofty and somehow yet more unreal above all this orchestrated madness and phantasmagoria stands the great main tent, a red, white, and blue octagon fringed with golden tassels and the twinkle of ten thousand artificial fireflies.

Her name is Cala – Cala Monroe Weatherall – this tall, freckled, straw-haired woman who has come alone to answer the barker's battle cry, and, also, a more urgent, secret cry. All day, every day but Sundays, she sees to the production of valves at Jackson-Merritt Manufacturing, steel valves designed and tooled to the most exacting specifications for such august clients as the Colorado and Northern Kansas Railway, the new Colorado Central Railroad, and the Front Range and West Coast divisions of the Gesellschaft zur Förderung der Luftschiffahrt. Cala Weatherall is a learned woman of industry and science, a rationalist and an engineer with a hard-earned diploma on her office wall, received a decade earlier from the Missouri School of Mines and Metalliferous Arts. Unmarried and generally disinterested in such flitting, womanly pursuits as matrimony and men, hers is a life of math and precision, of slide rules and difference engines, logarithms and trigonometric functions. She does her small (and well-paid) part to keep the trains running and the zeppelins aloft, and she sees no shame or sin in the pride she feels at her modest accomplishments in an arena still dominated by men.

But, this night is not any usual night for Miss Cala Weatherall, who rarely spares even the strayest thought for such oddities and amusements as those offered up by Othniel Z. Bracken's Transportable Marvels. Any other night, if asked, she might have laughed or snorted and dismissed the whole, seedy affair as only so much brummagem, silly distractions best left to those *without* the responsibilities she shoulders every single day, excepting Sundays (and even then, she usually works from her room at Jane Smithson's boarding house on the lower end of Downing Street). Last night, however, and for each of the three proceeding nights, she's had a dream, a dream so vivid and bizarre that she might *almost* name it a nightmare. But Cala doesn't *have* nightmares, and, for that matter, she only rarely ever remembers her dreams upon waking. But *this* dream, this dream spoke of the imminent coming of a traveling show, and of many, many other things, besides. Though she sets no store in the fashionable delusions of spiritualism, mysticism, and theosophy promulgated by the likes of Madame Helena Blavatsky and the Hermetic Order of the Golden Dawn – charlatans and liars and fools, every one – she *has* had this dream, this dream that was *almost* a nightmare, if there had not been such beauty and longing to it. And so, uneasy and reluctant, embarrassed at herself, she has come to the old cavalry training grounds, to the traveling show, to face this rutting coincidence and be done with it, once and for always.

So, this is how she finds herself outside the sideshow tent, heavy canvas painted in a garish riot of blues and greens, whites and greys, as though some impossible Artesian well leading all the way to the sea has sprung up, suddenly from this very spot. Above the entrance is a wooden placard that reads, *Poseidon's Abyss Revealed!* In her dream, there was this selfsame tent, or one near enough to raise goose bumps on her arms. And there was a placard, too, though she is not able to recollect the lettering she saw there. She pays her fifteen cents to the black man outside the tent flap – the "talker" in his scuffed-up bowler and red suspenders, busy enticing the crowd with promises of the mysteries that lie within, the *arcanum arcanorum* of the Seven Seas and any number of lakes, fjords, fens, wells, bogs, rivers, and the most desolate of swamps. Another man pushes open the flap for her, and a stream of cool air rushes out into the muggy summer night. Air so cold and damp it seems to seep forth and wrap itself about her, air that smells of low-tide along an Oregonian shore or icy slime dredged from the supposedly lifeless bottom of the Atlantic.

"Good evening, Miss," the second man – an Oriental – says, beckoning her inside. And then he winks and adds in a whisper, "She'll be glad to see you've come."

Cala Weatherall almost turns back then, at the man's peculiar confidence and, too, at the memory of that chill, dank smell from her dream. But now there's someone very close behind her, pushing, hurrying her forward, some other rube who's paid his money and is chomping at the bit to look upon whatever hoaxes and half truths the carnies keep hidden in this place.

"Please, sir," she grumbles. "No shoving, *please*," but then she's inside the tent, and when Cala Weatherall glances over her left shoulder, the fellow's attention has already been seized by a desiccated "Feejee mermaid," and by the dim gaslight she can read the plaque mounted below the pathetic, shriveled thing – "Formerly of Phineas T. BARNUM'S AMERICAN MUSEUM, prior to that Grand Institution's DESTRUCTION on the night 8 October 1871, a CASUALTY of the GREAT CHICAGO and PESHTIGO FIRESTORM, following this Earth's COLLISION with parts of the Comet BIELA." And for a moment, Cala Weatherall forgets the dream and her trepidations, and she almost steps over to explain to the man that this purported "mermaid" is no more than the upper portion of a monkey sewn onto the rear portions of a fish, the seams concealed, no doubt, with putty or papier-mâché. And, while she's at it, also inform him that no reputable scientist anywhere accepts that the terrible fires in Chicago and Peshtigo were in any way connected, one to the other, much less the result of a collision with any ethereal object.

But then she hears a loud splash, and turning about, squinting into the gloom of the tent, through murk interrupted only by the unsteady light of the gas jets, her eyes fall upon a tremendous, roughly rectilinear slab of white marble. Stepping nearer, she sees that it's surface is inscribed with all manner of pictogrammes or hieroglyphics. This time, the accompanying plaque reads, "IRREFUTABLE PROOF of the ANCIENT & SUBMERGED realm of LOST LEMURIA, dredged by BRAVE SEAMEN off the coast of PERU, from a depth of more than 2100 FATHOMS!" Cala shakes her head ruefully, noting that the glyphs are a nonsensical hodge-podge, vaguely resembling something Egyptian, and that the chisel marks appear quite fresh. There is certainly no evidence that this stone was ever long subjected to the rigors of the sea's abyssopelagic plains or hadopelagic trenches. She laughs to herself and *at* herself, laughing at having paid good, hard-earned coin and to have come this far, suckered in with all the others. The anxiety borne of her dreams, and the coincidence of the traveling show's arrival, and the existence of this sideshow tent begin to release their hold upon her, and she laughs again, louder than before, and shakes her head at the blatant forgery.

"I should ask for a refund of the price of admission," she mutters. Then, rather more loudly, so that anyone else nearby might hear, she says, "You should *all* ask for your money back." And, to herself, Cala adds, "I should notify the law, that's what I *should* do."

Increasingly embarrassed that she, even for one moment, feared her vivid dreams were anything more tangible than any dream, or the arrival of the carnival any more than a coincidence, she walks past a number of other "exhibits" arranged beneath the tent. There is a fossilized whale vertebra, almost big as a pickle barrel, of the sort long known to anatomists and students of bygone eras as *Basilosaurus cetoides*, generally found by cotton farmers while plowing their fields in Alabama and Mississippi. Here, though, the backbone is claimed to have come from the GREAT AMERICAN SEA SERPENT "HYDRARCHOS," sighted in Gloucester, Massachusetts in 1817, and, earlier, in the cold waters off Cape Ann in 1639. Farther along, past the vertebra and any number of peculiar fishes and invertebrata floating in corked jars of formaldehyde, and protected inside a locked display case, is something like a golden tiara or crown, tall towards the front, and with a very pronounced and curiously irregular periphery, as if designed for a freakishly elliptical skull. Adorned with an assortment of geometrical and marine designs, the tiara's plaque reports that it was recovered from a now-extinct cannibal tribe on some undisclosed location in "the South Seas." And all this time, there are other men and women (though mostly men), and occasionally she speaks to one of them, explaining the more likely identity or origin of some specimen or artefact. Cala Weatherall has never thought that a lack of education or of a well-nurtured intellect should be an excuse for gullibility. From time to time, her whispered explanations (whispered, for several people have dared to *shush* her) are interrupted by sudden splashing sounds, like water sloshing about in a container of some sort, or the tail of an otter or beaver slapping the surface of a pond. And that sound is something else from her four-times recurrent dream, the dream which was emphatically not a nightmare, and even as the sound seems to draw her forward through the ill-lit maze of this rough and mismatched collection, she pushes her *conscious* awareness of the splashing away, away and down.

"If they are all fakes," one man asks her, "why hasn't someone put a stop to this?"

"Likely as not, Sir," she replies, ignoring another of the sudden swashing noises, "whoever runs this racket paid off the relevant authorities well ahead of time, to prevent just such an interruption of commerce."

The man furrows his brow and cocks one bushy brown eyebrow, at least appearing to look shocked at what she's just said. "My word, woman," he scowls. "We *elect* these people. Our taxes pay their salaries. We must surely not be quite so cynical as all that." And then the man goes back to examining the barnacle-encrusted iron anchor supposed to have come from the *Argo* of Grecian myth. She patiently explained to the gentleman that the barnacles are of a genus not found anywhere in the Mediterranean, though quite common along the western coasts of Mexico, but the man only harrumphed and said something rude about women no longer knowing their proper place. Cala let it go, as she's heard far worse in her days, and is accustomed and, to a degree, dulled to the narrow opinions of such men.

"I only *thought* – mistakenly, I will concede – that you'd want to know the truth of the matter," she murmurs, and quickly steps past the *Argo* anchor exhibit and through yet another curtain, this one comprised of innumerable small glass beads the colour of sea foam and thunderstorms, strung along dangling lengths of silk twine. This area seems even colder than those previous sections of the labyrinth, but somewhat brighter, too, and she pauses, waiting for her eyes to adjust to the unexpected glare. The air here is markedly more dank, and smells particularly, almost overwhelmingly, briny. So strong is the odor, Cala might be standing at the very edge of the sea. Around her, the canvas walls are washed with a reflected, coruscating light, and in only a few seconds more she sees the source of both the saltwater smell and the constantly shifting rays playing across the tent's walls. At first, squinting at and into the enormous aquarium standing before her – thick glass and a rusty cast-iron framework, a chugging pump to keep the water oxygenated and filtered of detritus – she expects to see nothing more remarkable than a pair of trained seals or, possibly instead, some grim variety of devilfish or giant squid to appall and startle these people who have never known the ocean and its inhabitants.

But the tank does not contain trained seals.

Nor an octopus or squid.

For a time, Cala stands quite still, staring, disbelieving the evidence of her own eyes, willing herself not to draw any obvious conclusions or connections with the dreams, for too frequently are we deceived by that which seems so perfectly obvious to our senses. The thing in the tank, she reasons, must certainly be an automaton, an admirably cunning clockwork, impermeable to moisture, but not so unlike the mastodons and doves in the afternoon's parade along East Evens Avenue. The acquisition of such a device is clearly not beyond the resources of the carnival, and if it *is* only mechanical, then there remains but the niggling issue of coincidence to address. Despite her pounding heart and the sweat slicking her palms and upper lip, she is very near to dismissing it, this absurd fairy-tale chimera peering back at her from the aquarium, its head and shoulders held above the slopping surface, the rest coiled below the waterline. But then it opens its mouth and speaks, and that voice is so exquisite, and so familiar, that Cala

Weatherall believes that she might well scream, and never mind who would hear or what they would think.

"So long, girl," the thing in the tank sighs, its voice rolling, tumbling, rushing through the tent like breakers before an incoming tide. "So very, very long have I waited for this night, hauled across time and these death-dry lands, through arid wilderness and the smoldering, unseeing cities of men."

"No," Cala says, but the word is not meant as a response, only as a personal statement of her disbelief, spoken aloud for her own benefit. There is still no reason, beyond the coincidence of her recurring dream, to suppose the thing in the tank is not a hoax, and that its voice does not originate, for instance, from a woman sequestered somewhere behind the tank. She speaks into a small brass horn attached to a length of tubing, and her voice emerges from the mechanized rubber lips of the melusine.

"They *said* that you would be the Skeptic," the thing responds, not knowing that Cala was not speaking to it (for what sane woman *talks* to an automaton).

"They," Cala says, repeating what the thing has said, though still not speaking *to* it.

"My dear sisters," it replies, "Palatyne and Melior. They each, in turn, warned that, in the end, all my searching would yield only so much dubiety and fleer."

"I have seen many a clever puppet show," Cala says, and this time she realizes that she is answering the thing in the tank. "I did not always see the strings or the puppeteers, but I never doubted the performers were only marionettes."

"You do not strike me as the sort to attend a puppet show," the melusine replies. "Which is a shame, I think."

Cala Weatherall glances uneasily back the way she's come, and there's the curtain of glass beads, still swaying slightly, softly clicking and clacking against each other. She looks back at the aquarium tank, still clinging as ferociously to her disbelief as any caterwauling Baptist minister ever clung to his King James Bible. The thing in the tank has the appearance of a very pale and beautiful woman from the hips up. Its skin has a disquieting iridescent quality, almost opalescent in this light. Its perfectly wrought hands have no nails, but end in sharp, recurved, and chitinous claws at the tip of each long finger, and its eyes are the yellow of the yolk from a chicken's egg. Its small breasts are shamelessly bare, though Cala notes that it has no visible nipples, and so she wonders, absently, at the utility of breasts so ill-equipped for nursing. A sculptor's fancy or accidental imperfection, and likely nothing more. She dares to take one step nearer, seeking some other flaw in the design. The melusine's long straight hair hangs in sodden strands about its mother-of-pearl shoulders, black as a freshly-exposed vein of coal. Only, on closer inspection, there are what appear to be dozens of fleshy tendrils writhing within those sable tresses, no bigger around than a lead pencil. It's sharp teeth flash when it mimics speech, and they are almost identical to those of certain lamniform sharks known to ichthyologists as sand tigers, row upon row anchored in gums the bruised colour of ripening elderberries.

"I know your lonely nights, Cala," the melusine tells her. "I have watched you, at your window, envying the couples passing by."

"Enough," Cala replies angrily, for there are limits to what any woman must endure, even in well-meaning jest, and this jest has long since transcended the boundaries of propriety. "I do not know how you people learned my name," she says, not speaking to the thing in the tank, but to whatever unseen person speaks its lines. "Though I doubt it was so very difficult. You must have numerous marks each time you enter a new town."

"And we know your dreams?" the melusine asks, as its scaly, serpentine tails coil and uncoil beneath that human torso. It cocks its head to one side, waiting for an answer, and the small flukes at the ends of its tails slap the surface of the water. "Pray thee, tell how it is we might accomplish that feat?"

For the span of several heart beats, Cala does not reply, transfixed not only by the power of the thing's question, but by the rhythmic, almost hypnotic, *smack* of those silvery-green flukes. *Yes*, she thinks. *Hypnosis, mesmerism, autosuggestion, these must be part of the deception. Turning my own mind against me to achieve this effect.*

"Yes," the melusine says. "Hypnosis, mesmerism, autosuggestion, these must be part of the deception. Turning my own mind against me to achieve this effect."

Cala Weatherall gasps, and takes another step towards the tank. "It cannot be," she says.

"Why?" asks the thing in the tank. "Because you have not been taught that it is so? I have not come so far, across gulfs of time and space, merely to deceive a lonely, dissatisfied woman. What bitter daemon has taken hold of the world of men that it no longer trusts its own eyes and its own ears?"

"It is an enlightened age," Cala says, but her voice is hardly audible now, a half whisper as she steps still nearer to the aquarium tank. "Not an age of ignorance and superstition. Not...an age of sirens and mermaids and sea monsters."

"And neither is it an age in which a woman who is brilliant and enterprising, but whose heart does not seek a *man*, can hope for the balm of love or even of a soul mate's companionship? Did you also sell your heart, Cala Weatherall, when you sold off your imagination? Is there remaining now no way ever that I may comfort thee?"

"It simply is not *possible*," Cala whispers, meaning only the existence of this creature, and not to answer its question. And she realizes, if only distantly, that she has begun to weep, and whether from sympathy or mockery, the melusine has begun to weep as well.

"You must be brilliant, indeed, if your mind contains a catalog of all those things possible, and all those things that are not."

"They were dreams. *Only* dreams. I have never even dared to *hope*."

"A mighty daemon, indeed, that it leads a woman to fear even the meager solace of hope."

And now Cala is standing so near the tank that she might easily extend a hand to reach out and touch the melusine's strange, restless hair and pearly skin. And she sees, for the first time, a small and tarnished brass plaque bolted to the tank, which reads simply *Le Fontaine de Soif.*

"It *is* so, is it not?" the melusine asks, seeing that Cala's read the plaque on the aquarium. "You are so terribly thirsty, like a woman lost and wandering in an endless desert." And then the creature ventures the faintest of smiles, and one glistening arm slides out over the rim of the tank towards her.

"It *is* so," Cala confesses to the beast. "I am so alone. I am so lost, so terribly alone. And you...*you* are more beautiful times

ten than anything I have ever looked upon with waking eyes."
She starts to take the melusine's hand, recalling again details of
her vivid dreams – the wordless embraces in lightless, submerged
halls formed of coral and the carved ribs of leviathans. Already, she
knows the taste of the melusine's thin pink lips, the feel of those
vicious teeth upon her skin, the unspeakable pleasure of the faerie's mouth and hands and those appendages for which men have
not ever devised names upon her and probing deeply within her.

"It is such a small thing, belief," the melusine tells her. "It is
no more than taking my hand."

And then, in the last fraction of an instant before Cala *does*
accept that proffered hand, there is a violent hissing, and a loud *pop*,
and all at once the smell of ozone and hot metal, of shattered gears
and melting polymers fills the air inside the tent, pushing back the
salty, primordial smells of the ocean and of birth and death and
love. The thing in the tank shudders and then goes limp, and steam
begins to rise from the water in the aquarium. Somewhere nearby,
she hears a woman, a woman with a voice like the melusine's, cursing, and a man begins to shout. Cala lets her arm drop to her side,
and her eyes linger only a few seconds longer on the ruined automaton, before she turns and silently makes her way out of the tent
and back out into the muggy summer night and the hullabaloo of
Othniel Z. Bracken's Transportable Marvels. The next day, after
a few hours of fitful sleep, she will discover the jimmied lock on
her dresser drawer and the missing diary wherein she recorded all
her secret thoughts and desires and dreams. And there will remain
unanswered questions, but she will not ever ask them. There is too
much work to be done, a job that fifty men, fifty men easy, would
be happy to take if she were to fail. There are calculations to make
and orders to be filled, and if in the empty stretches of her nights,
she sometimes finds herself far below the churning surface of the
sea, beloved and belonging in those sunken corridors, these are
things she keeps forever to herself and never again commits to the
fickle confidences of ink and paper.

Fecunditatem
(Murder Ballad No. 6)

In my dreams, we go down to the still waters together, though, of course, this is not how it happened. Not in this waking world. But in dreams, we walk hand-in-hand across the wide plowed fields. Some years there is tall corn, and other years there are fat orange pumpkins on snaking vines. In the autumn moonlight, the rich soil beneath our bare feet is dark as chocolate, and you lead the way, and I listen while you talk. Always was I the student, always the one who followed and never the leader, my eager Anactoria to your patient Sappho. You have shown me all your secret places, the mysteries and confidences of both your body and the land. You lead me on and on across those fields, and also along the hidden trails through the woods that lie to the north of the Old Bulgarmarsh Road. In my dreams, you speak frequently of the Eleionomae, or Heleionomae, those nymphs who held to the fens and boggy places of the world. Or, in other moods, on nights when there are clouds to dim the moon, you offer me tales of Peg Powler or the grindylows, grimmer spirits luring naughty children to their rightful drownings. You are a deep well, and have no end of stories. No matter how many times I've heard them before, the glamour of your voice always weaves them into something new, making, by arts unknown to me, unfamiliar lays of threadbare ballads.

With that cocoa earth soft and alive beneath our feet, and the Full Hunter's Moon watching over all, you tell me, for example, of the suicide who, by the death of her choosing, becomes a *rusalka*. In the waning hours of some Ukrainian night, her eyes flash iridescent green with fairy fire, and she sits upon the shore of the river that she haunts and sings her pretty songs to lure foolish, lustful men into her arms. If she wants them, they go to her, even as I am helpless to do other than follow you. There is great wisdom, you say, in recognizing the piper, and peace in the dance, and I laugh and look up to see the outline of an owl against the star-specked sky. You tell me not to look, to cover my eyes, but the warning comes too late, and I have already seen the silhouette of that huge funerary bird.

That grim harbinger of Lilith, searching our field for mice and voles and careless rabbits, for dreamers who do not avert their eyes. I know those sickle talons, how they tear the evening apart, how they tear my skin and pull me from one dream to another. Also, I have a scrap of paper on which you copied a few lines from *Walden* – "I rejoice that there are owls...They represent the stark twilight and unsatisfied thoughts which all have. All day the sun has shone on the surface of some savage swamp, where the single spruce stands hung with usnea lichens, and small hawks circulate above, and the chicadee lisps amid the evergreens, and the partridge and rabbit skulk beneath; but now a more dismal and fitting day dawns, and a different race of creatures awakes to express the meaning of Nature there."

The room where I sleep is littered with such quotations, the confetti of your thoughts. You would not keep a proper notebook or diary, though you never told me why. I never asked. I sleep here amid the thoughts you found and stole from others.

The dream will change, most nights, as dreams are wont to do (even without the intrusion of owls). The fields vanish, and take the moon with them. Now there is the harsher light of the bulb above our bathroom sink, and you lying naked in a tub of warm and steaming water. I am sitting on the cast-iron rim, and I lean down and kiss your lips. You taste like life, I think, and your breath is sweet. Your tongue flicks across your teeth, over my lips, and I pull away.

"It would be a very simple thing," you say again. "You're certainly strong enough to hold me under."

"But I would miss you," I protest. "I would be alone."

"Always thinking of yourself," you laugh.

But then I *am* pushing you down, and it *is* easy, one hand on your head and another laid firmly between your breasts. In the first few moments, you are surprised and begin to struggle. But then you grow calm, a calm I read as resignation and curiosity, and your hazel-green eyes open wide to watch me from beneath the water.

"It's a game," you whisper in my right ear. "It's only a game."

I turn my head, hoping for even the briefest glimpse of you. But, for a very long time, there's only the open bathroom window, and beyond the sash, a full moon shines down on fields of ripe pumpkins.

"Six Indians," you say, as we pick our way between the neat rows. "They felled the unfortunate Zoeth Howland on a March night in 1676. He was on his way to a Quaker meeting, because, you see, he was a Quaker."

This is not one of your usual tales. There will be no sirens here, and I want to tell you that I'd rather not hear it, that's it's not the sort of ghost story I fancy. *Tell me about the nymphs, instead*, I want to say, but I don't. I'm not a dullard. I know better than to break the spell, once the incantation is begun.

"The Narragansetts ambushed him, and then tossed the poor man's mutilated body into the stream. Afterwards, the waters ran crimson with his blood, and it became known as Sinning Flesh Brook. Over the years, though, that became Sin and Flesh Brook."

"What was Howland's sin?" I ask.

"I am afraid, dear, that you'd have to ask those Narragansetts," you reply, and now we have come to the easternmost edge of the field. We stand together on the banks of the very brook where Zoeth Howland's body was discovered by his horrified Christian brethren. We linger here a short while, and then, without a word to indicate your intent, you turn south. I follow, inevitably I follow. And before long we have come to the swampy place where the brook drains into a nameless pond. The chilly night is not silent, but replete with the songs of frogs, and crickets, and of whippoorwills. I can hear a rowdy chorus of dogs barking at the farmhouse a few hundred yards to our southwest, and a breeze stirs and rustles the tall grass blades and goldenrod, the ragweed and the dry stalks of cattails. These are all accustomed, welcoming noises, and the chorus puts me at ease, helping me to dwell on other things than your tale of the murdered Quaker.

My hands – certainly strong enough – holding you down in the tub, and the silvery stream of bubbles leaking from your nose and mouth.

"You are bleeding," I say, amazed at the sight, "but you are only bleeding air."

The fat moon gazes down on us, neither approving nor disapproving. We stand there at the edge of that wide expanse of unflowing water, looking out across the cold and glistening tract of mud, and you squeeze my hand very tightly. Almost so tightly that it hurts.

"I would lie here forever," you say, and then tell me again of the kindly, perpetual shadows cast by floating mats of duckweed and water lilies. You talk of sacred groves of filamentous green algae, the apocrypha of turtles, the arcanum of newts, and how you would know everything forgotten and forsaken during hundreds of millions of years of terrestrial evolution. You speak of the womb, the *first* womb, and tiny silver bubbles trail from out your nostrils.

"I only want to go home," you say. "I only want to find my way back."

The screeching owl passes overhead again, or this is another owl entirely. It hardly matters which. I catch the fire in its terrible, glowing eyes. I catch fire. And, in its claws, the dream shreds again around me. So, now I am kneeling in the mud, and with both my hands I dig your bed. My fingers tangle in roots and disturb the affairs of worms and grubs. And you lie somewhere nearby, still and oddly silent, so I am left to do the talking. We are, neither of us, clothed, and in the moonlight your skin shimmers like mother-of-pearl, while mine seems dull and black as charcoal. It isn't, but the dream makes it so. Neither is this the way these events transpired, not exactly, and so it is safe for me to dream this dream of laying you to rest.

"Tonight, since you're so awfully quiet, I will tell *you* a story, my love," I say and smile, scooping out another double handful of muck from the widening, deepening hole. Digging, I have sunk in now up to my thighs, and the intimate caress of the marsh is not entirely unpleasant. I do my best to recount the tale of Hermaphroditus and the nymph Salmacis. It has always been one of your favorites, and so long as there are no vengeful Narragansett Indians and no slain Quakers, it suits me, also. I am well enough aware that I am mangling the beautiful dactylic hexameter of Ovid, and I am well enough aware how you would scowl at my sloppy recitation, if you were awake and *could* scowl.

Now, undressed upon the bank he stood,
And clasped his sides, and leaped into the flood.
His lovely limbs the silvery waves divided,
Appearing even more lovely through the tide;
As lilies trapped inside a crystal case
Take on the a glossy luster of the glass.
"He's mine, he's all my own," the Naiad cried,
And threw off all, and after him she flew.
And she fastened onto him as he swam,
And held him close, and wrapped about his limbs.

"You're doing better than you think," you tell me, leaning down to inspect an especially large pumpkin. "You don't give yourself enough credit."

In the tub, you have stopped bleeding air, and have finally stopped thrashing wildly about; the floor and walls are soaked. I am soaked, and my hair is dripping, but that was to be expected, wasn't it; my own part in this baptism, if you will. Your hazel-green eyes are still open, and I wish I could see whatever it is that you must see so clearly now, no longer shackled by the burden of living only from one breath to the next.

"Please," you say, and look up at me. "Go on. I'm listening. You were just getting to the good part."

I nod, but for a moment I am too fascinated by the intricate collage of moments swirling about me, so many competing, incompatible pasts superimposed upon one another. I could very easily become lost in that spiraling maze of images and events. It would not be so bad, to linger always in so many days and nights that might have been, and all of them witnessed simultaneously.

"I'm waiting," you say again, and go back to inspecting the pumpkin at your feet. "Salmacis held him close, and wrapped about his limbs."

"That's not really right," I replied. "I know that I'm getting it wrong."

"You're getting it right enough."

"I wish the owls were not listening," I say, and you glare at me over your right shoulder.

"Don't be so shy," you tell me. "Come on. What happens next."

The hole in the mud is almost wide enough to contain you, and I begin to concentrate on getting the edges as even as I can. It seems to me it should be made neat, the bed where you will sleep. But every time I try to smooth out a side or make a corner conform more closely to ninety degrees, the mud shows me it has ideas of its own, surrendering to gravity and sloughing and sliding back into its natural asymmetry. The marshy place at the end of Sin and Flesh Brook couldn't care less for right angles; it is doing me a favor simply by permitting you this sanctuary.

And then I am talking once more, and I've begun to wonder how I will ever get your body out of the tub.

The more the boy resisted, the more he was coy,
The tighter the Naiad clung to him.
She kissed the struggling boy.
Like the wriggling snake snatched on high
In an eagle's claws, hissing in the sky,
Around the foe his twirling tail he flings,
And twisted her legs, and writhed about her wings.

Then, lying on the floor of our bedroom, you roll over to read me another of your innumerable quotations, those slips of paper like gutted fortune cookies. I listen. I always listen. It is something from Swinburne: *Love, is it love or sleep or shadow or light / That lies between thine eyelids and thine eyes?*

You were always reading me Swinburne. I have a manila envelope filled with your quotations and sealed with a glob of crimson wax. I will place it beneath you, here in the marsh at the end of the brook where Zoeth Howland was ambushed and met his untimely, messy end, three hundred and thirty two years ago.

The restless boy still obstinately strove
To free himself, and still he refused her love.
Amid his limbs she kept her own entwined,
"And why, coy youth," she cried, "why so unkind?
Oh may the Gods thus keep us ever joined!
Oh may we never, never part again!"

And here I pause, staring a long moment into that amniotic gouge laid open before me. Womb. Cunt. Grave. All these and many, many other things besides. I am sweating despite the chilly night, even though my fingers have grown numb from the cold ooze. Already, a few inches of water have collected at the bottom, seeping up and also seeping through the sagging walls of the hole.

"Should I go on?" I ask, though I'm uncertain if I am asking you, or asking the owls, or asking the voyeur moon.

"No turning back now," you say, scribbling another line of Swinburne on another slip of paper, staining your fingers with sepia ink.

"I mean the story," I say, in case you'd misunderstood. "Should I continue with the tale of the rape of Hermaphroditus, or have I said too much already?"

"You truly think it was a rape?" you ask, licking at the ink on your fingertips. "He didn't have to enter the pool, after all, and it *was* Salmacis' pool. In fact, if one favors symbolism over a literal interpretation, you might say the boy was the one initiated coitus."

"I have always leaned towards the literal," I admit, and you grin, showing teeth gone the color of old ivory set into gums the color of indigo berries.

"What happens next?" you ask.

And now I am certain that there is more than one owl, that there are, in fact, at least a dozen, battening at the sky and perched in the limbs of what few small trees grow at the edge of the marsh. Those birds are also listening, also waiting, and the words fall from my lips like stones.

So prayed the nymph, nor did she pray in vain,
For she finds him now, as his limbs she pressed,
Growing nearer and nearer to her breast,
Until, piercing each the other's flesh, they run
Together, and incorporate, becoming one.
At last in one face are both their faces joined,
As when the stock and grafted twig combined
Shoot up the same, and wear a common rind.
Both bodies in a single body mix.
A single body with a double sex.

I pull the rubber plug from the drain, and the tub begins to empty, and, in this dream, I dry my hands on a yellow bath towel while I watch the water slipping away, exposing you, like ancient seas retreating to reveal landscapes long concealed by Silurian or Devonian brine.

The boy, thus lost in woman, now surveyed
The river's guilty stream, and thus he prayed.
(He prayed, but also wondered at his softer tone,
Surprised to hear a voice but half his own.)

You brush a strand of coppery hair from my eyes, and kiss me lightly on the bridge of my nose. You have always loved my nose, or so you've frequently professed. When I complain that it is too big or poorly shaped, you have threatened to cut it off and keep it in a tiny wooden box, lined in claret velvet. If I do not appreciate it, you have said, then I should not be permitted to wear so fine a nose, and you would protect it from my scorn.

"Frankly, I've always detected more than an undertone of misogyny in that line," you say, speaking almost so softly as to be whispering, and I wonder whom you are afraid will overhear. "'...a voice but *half* his own?'"

"I don't think that's how it was intended," I reply, staring at the lamp beside our bed, instead of into your skeptical grey-blue eyes.

"The implication is clear," you say. "His voice was diminished in his fusion with the nymph. Not merely altered, and not made greater, but diminished. Ovid paints Hermaphroditus as cursed, as a victim, when he ought to number him among the blessed."

I tell you that it hardly seems so clear cut to me, but there's never any changing your mind.

You parent-Gods, whose heavenly names I bear,
Hear your Hermaphrodite, and grant my prayer;
Oh grant, that whomsoever these streams contain,
If a man he entered, when he may rise again
Supple, unsinewed, and become but half a man!

You place a slip of paper on my belly, just above the navel, and I cannot see what is written there. You have placed it with the words facing down, your handwriting laid against my skin, and I refuse to give you the satisfaction of seeing me reach for it, of knowing I am curious.

"What a little prick," you say. "He's cursed, if you *buy* that line of reasoning, and so he calls upon the wrath of the gods to likewise curse any *other* men who enter the stream, forever. I cannot even begin to see where that makes sense. It's not even proper revenge..." and you trail off, then, turning away from me.

"How old were you?" I ask. "That afternoon in the greenhouse?" The question has never been forbidden, precisely, but I know that it's hardly your favorite topic of discussion.

"What difference does it make?"

"Maybe all the difference in the world."

You take a very deep breath, and sigh, "I was nineteen. A month away from twenty. It was late July. The greenhouse was going wild, by then. No one ever came to tend it anymore, not after my grandfather died."

"That's a shame," I say.

"It was more than a hundred years old by then. The man who designed it had studied under the Belgian architect Alphonse Balat, who designed the Royal Greenhouses of Laeken in the early 1870s. But no one cared, not by then. No one but me, I think. It was like a church, all that glass and iron, those domes, and I would lie there beneath it, safe from the eyes of Heaven."

"It was going wild," I say.

"Isn't that what I just told you?" you ask, more than a hint of impatience in your voice. "Yes, it had been left untended for a long time, all those plants left to grow as best they could without anyone to keep them safe from the winters, or to be sure that the hardier species didn't crowd out and displace the more delicate ones."

"It was July."

"I just fucking *said* that it was July."

I take my eyes off the lamp on the bedside table only long enough to count the owls in the trees, and to see that the moon has climbed higher in the New England sky, and has gone the bright glacial white of the sun off ice. But you're already talking again, in that moment when we are lying together and I am not yet kneeling in the mud beside the pond. You're talking about that day in the greenhouse, fifteen years ago.

135

"I never went back after that. They sealed the place up, chained the doors, and slapped on padlocks. Though, I could have gotten in, if I'd wanted to."

"You're skipping ahead," I say.

"Yes," you reply, "I'm skipping ahead. Are you just trying to piss me off?"

"No, I'm not. It's just that you don't usually skip ahead. I'm sorry," and I imagine, fleetingly, that I *am* genuinely sorry, even if I can now permit myself the luxury of questioning my sincerity. "I never should have brought it up." And then I lie, knowing full well that I am lying, and say, "I'm not sure why I did."

And this is when, perhaps, I see something resting in the shallow pool that has collected at the bottom of the hole that I've dug in the mud. It's larger than a fifty-cent piece, but not as large as a silver dollar (I do not mean to imply that it is a coin). It's disk shaped, and the color of bone, thicker at its center and tapering to a razor-sharp circumference. I reach into the pool, and, with my numb fingers, I lift it out. The polished upper surface glistens in the moonlight. There is some pattern etched into the disk, which puts me in mind of the sort of triskele or triple spiral found in association with many Neolithic and Irish Megalithic sites. I recall it from photographs I have seen of the New Grange passage tomb in County Meath. The disk is slippery, and I slice my thumb open.

"My great grandfather, who had the greenhouse constructed, was especially interested in tree ferns," you continue, without my having prompted you to do so. "And in temperate rainforests, like those in New Zealand and the Pacific Northwest. So, the plants didn't suffer so much from the Rhode Island winters as one might expect. I can still remember some of the Latin names. *Dickinsonia antarctica* – the Tasmanian Tree Fern – that was one of my favorites. And *Cyathea medullaris*, or the Black Tree Fern. The Maori called it *mamaku*."

"It amazes me, that you remember all that."

"Lying there on the flagstones, in the moss and ferns and horsetails, listening to the incessant drone of dragonflies and mosquitoes, and with those gigantic fronds to form a drooping canopy above me, it was easy to pretend."

"To pretend what?"

You're silent for a minute or so, and I kneel in the mud, thinking about Zoeth Howland and the Narragansetts and Sin and Flesh Brook, watching the way the blood from my thumb flows across my palm and encircles my muddy wrist to make a living bracelet before dripping into the hole.

"It might have been the first day of all in there," you say, finally. "It might have been any Carboniferous evening, or a Coal-Forest afternoon. I never wanted to be anywhere else besides the greenhouse, not really. I wanted those days to go on and on, unending. So the violation was not only of my body, but of that sanctuary. It might have been less cruel, if I had simply died."

In the night, my blood is not red, but dark as the ink you scrawl your quotations in, and it could just as well be dripping from the nib of one of your fountain pens as from the torn vein in my thumb.

"Maybe if they had caught the man – " I begin, but you interrupt me.

"There was no man to catch," you say. "It wasn't any man who came to me that day."

"Is that what you told them then? Is that what you told the police?"

"Yes," you answer, turning to face me again, and so I look away from both my bleeding hand and the lamp. Your eyes are no longer blue. They have become the gaping tangerine eyes of an owl, but I don't scream. I detest women who scream. You blink feathery eyelids, and with that beak could so easily part my soul from my skin. As an offering, I give you the last of the story of Hermaphroditus and Salmacis:

The heavenly parents answered him from on high,
Their two-shaped son, the double votary.
Then they gave a secret virtue to the flood,
And tinged its source to make his wishes good.

The bony disk slips from my muck- and blood-slicked grip, and falls with a small splash into the pool, there in the hole I have made for your planting. I don't reach for it again, knowing that I'm not meant to. It has what it needed from me, and I require nothing more of it.

"You're hanging back," you say, laying your head on my shoulder, fingering my nipples until they are both erect. "Holding out. Why is that? Do you resent my gift to you as much as Hermaphroditus resented the gift that the daughter of Zeus gave to him?"

"I don't know what you mean," I say, closing my eyes, wishing there were nothing I had to feel but your touch.

"You do. You know *exactly* what I mean. It's not the owls, or the moon, and it's not the grave. It's not even the drowning that matters. It's what came later, and tonight you've dreamt everything and anything but that."

"You never did have tact. Well, none to speak of," I whisper and shut my eyes, which only results in my opening them in some other, less-traveled corridor of this turning netherward spire. The place I have been trying, all along, not to see, the night I have resisted visiting; it hardly matters if what I view here ever truly took place or not, in an intrinsic, objective sense. We'll let that question stand unanswered for the time being, as pausing to address it would only mislead and distort.

Another night, a night late in spring when the moon is only a slender, waning crescent, and the fields north of the Old Bulgarmarsh Road in Tiverton have yet to sprout. I have been back alone many times now, and this is not returning to the scene of the crime, as much as it is returning to the scene of the consequences of the crime. Though, I think, you would insist there has been no crime committed. I only acted as an extension of your will, in accordance with your desires. I was only ever the instrument of your suicide. And on this night, I go down to the banks of Sin and Flesh Brook alone, following it south to the swampy place where it meets the nameless pond.

Tonight, there are no owls. But the whippoorwills cry like lost children.

I follow a narrow, uneven dirt path that has become familiar as my face in a mirror, and that must have only been a deer trail before I found it. Stepping through the briars and skunk cabbages and the high cattails, then just past the gnarled and rotting trunk of a dead hemlock tree, I can find this spot in my sleep. The mud is deep here, and already I am in up to my ankles. I never bother with shoes on these pilgrimages, no matter the weather; they would only be ruined. I have worn a loose, sleaveless dress you made for me, a simple floral cotton print, and no jacket, despite the cool of the evening. Neither did I see the need for undergarments. This is each and every night I have ever made the trip. But always it is the *first* time, and always I swear a futile promise that it will be my last. No one who has joined the Heleads has need of *my* meager devotion, and maybe, I think, it's only (at best) an insult to you, my coming here, something that was never a part of your plan. I stand there in the mud, shivering, my ears filled with whippoorwills, my head filled with loss and regret and memories like a millstone around my neck.

"It wasn't any man who came to me that day."

And it will be no woman, nor any mere woman's shade, who comes to me tonight. *Woman* is far too small a word, I think, as you rise from the thick mud, a form already so dimly recollected coalescing from whatever is at hand and from bits of dream and, possibly, your own whimsy. On this dark night, the weeds might almost pass for your black hair, and the marsh slime for the skin you gave up months ago. But it is restless, this temporary body, always shifting, as though too great an effort is required to hold the form, and maybe in the years to come you will grow more skilled in this alchemy. Your face comes and goes, one second a perfected likeness, down to the scar on your left cheek, but it melts, coming apart, dissolving, and only a crude and featureless parody of it remains.

Your wet voice is the primordial voice of all bogs – your tongue and teeth, larynx and palate spun from a weave of sundew and peatlands, fishbone, white cedar, sweet gale, bog rosemary, dragonfly larvae and empty turtle shells, waterlogged carpets of red maple leaves, the scurry of predatory water bugs sewn into a gurgling outwash of crayfish and sphagnum, sedges, cranberries, leatherleaf, and the treacherous, seductive traps of insectivorous pitcher plants. Your shoulders writhe with clots of leeches, like living epaulets, and here and there a frog or small snake has been caught up in the suddenness of your accretion, and they squirm in and out of view, as do the gasping mouths, eyes, and fins of perch and pout and calico bass. There are other things, more fantastical and unlikely components of your being – the creeping, segmented shells of trilobites, perhaps. The whorl of an ammonite's shell. But this might only be my imagination. The weeds hang down your shoulders and back and cover your ass like a mane.

"My gift," you say, and there's a rheumy, squelching sort of a sound as you raise your arms so that I can see what you have hauled up from the bottom of the nameless pond at the end of Sin and Flesh Brook. And I do not have words to describe what you hold in both hands, but I know, instinctively, that is has grown, somehow, from a disk of bone-like matter engraved with triple spirals and anointed, fertilized, awakened by my own blood. It has swelled, ripening, and sprouted countless chitinous spines. On the side turned towards me, there is something akin to a proboscis or snout, and from beneath it spills a wriggling tendril. It shines slickly in the night, twisting and thrashing this way and that, and as I watch, the tendril bifurcates, and where it was at first smooth, it quickly becomes festooned with an assortment of quivering prongs and thorn-like projections. And all these words are a sorry excuse for the sight of the thing, whether I have seen it with my eyes or with nothing but my mind. It is horrifying, and it is sublime, and I have never yet beheld anything else so beautiful.

"It was like a church," you say. "All that glass and iron, those domes, and I would lie there beneath it, safe from the eyes of Heaven, as we are now safe from the eyes of Heaven."

Until, piercing each the other's flesh, they run
Together, and incorporate, becoming one.

I know that I should be afraid, but there is no fear in me, and as that tendril twines about my left thigh (and I am surprised to find its touch is unexpectedly warm), I open myself to it. Which is only opening myself to *you*, and I have done that so many times past counting. And there is a kindly smile on the clay and ooze pretending to be your lips as it enters me, as I welcome that entry. The pain is so small and brief as to hardly bear mentioning here. The busy tendrils, their work complete, withdraw, slipping nosily back inside the prickly mass in your hands.

Here, while young Proserpine, among the maids,
Diverts herself in these delicious shades;
While like a child with busy speed and care

Fecunditatem (Murder Ballad No. 6)

She gathers lilies here, and vi'lets there;
While first to fill her little lap she strives,
Hell's grizzly monarch at the shade arrives...

You come apart as readily as you came together, and the marsh eagerly, jealously, takes you back, reabsorbing all that it has generously leant in order for its guardian spirit and most secret daughter to be, however impermanently, corporeal. And, too, it takes back that thing you held, and I do not wonder if you were this night my lover, or if my lover were the marsh, or that if it were, instead, the tentacles or tendrils of your peculiar oblation. For I know, now, it was *all* these at once, and any division drawn between them must be entirely arbitrary.

And the sun rises, and shining through the drapes it rouses me from all dreams, and I lie still in the bed we no longer share. For a long while, I watch the pattern the morning light makes on the walls, and then my hand strays to my sex, which is no longer precisely what it once was. The swelling lips of my vagina, the purple-red arils embedded in the walls of my cunt that anyone might mistake only for the seeds of the pomegranate that damned Persephone. Only that is blood they leak, not juice, when pressed with a thumbnail. The fruit of our union, and I lie here thinking of your great-grandfather's ruined greenhouse, and what might have visited you there. Slipping a finger into myself, past those maturing seeds, I see your face, and think on all the fenny, verdant ages yet to come.

I Am the Abyss, and I Am Light

1.

There is only a passing, brief glint of panic when the process has reached the point that cognitive integrity is finally, and almost irrevocably, compromised. During all the interminable months of psychological prep and antemorphic therapy, Ttisa was repeatedly trained for this moment, against this moment, and both the *shhakizsa* midwives and her human counselors have taught her meditation techniques for making the transition with as little trauma as possible. But, most importantly, as her mind and the mind of the surrogate suddenly bleed one into the other, a carefully constructed series of posthypnotic images is triggered. And Ttisa finds herself staring down from suborbit at a living planet that might be Earth, and a muddy, winding river that might be the Mississippi, or perhaps the Nile, or the Ganges, or no river that has ever flowed anywhere but across the floodplains of her imagination. She sees that the river has reached the sea, as rivers do, and here is the place where sediment-laden freshwater collides with the brine, where an opaque torrent the color of almonds interfaces with blue-green saltwater. The confluence, and there is nothing here to fear, for gravity drags all rivers oceanward, just as it drags all raindrops from the sky, and then hauls water vapor up again.

The confluence, she thinks. *The meeting of the waters. Encontro das Águas.* And so the surrogate echoes, *The confluence, the meeting of the waters.* It continues, then, finding thoughts that are no longer only Ttisa's thoughts, before she has had time to find them herself. *Or it is only one river meeting another,* they each think *almost* in unison. *In Brazil, they call it Encontro das Águas, where the Rio Negro joins with the upper Amazon. Brown water*

143

and black water, but then, linked thus, they come to the next bead on this chain. Ttisa sits at a table, and having just added cream to a cup of coffee, she watches while the cold white swirls like a tiny galaxy, its spiral arms starting to blend with the steaming void. *Soon,* they think (for now there is near-perfect synchronization) *the coffee will be cooler, or the milk will be warmer. The milk will be darker, or the coffee will have brightened. It can hardly matter which.*

Across the breakfast table, a teacher that Ttisa never actually had says, "Now, Ttisa, tell me, where, exactly, does the galaxy begin and intergalactic space end? Likewise, where does each of this galaxy's constituent solar systems begin and end?"

And the new coconsciousness that is neither precisely Ttisa nor her *shhakizsa* surrogate, but which fully accommodates them both, begins to answer. It very nearly offers the teacher facts and theories from dutifully recollected lectures on the heliopause and solar winds, hydrogen walls and the interstellar medium. But then it stops itself and glances back down at the muted caramel-colored liquid inside the cup, and the mind can no longer distinguish milk from coffee, nor coffee from milk. Strictly speaking, both have ceased to exist in the creation of a third and novel substance.

"In any objective sense, the question you've asked is meaningless," the woman seated at the table across from the teacher construct replies. The woman wears the face that Ttisa once wore, when Ttisa was only herself. It speaks with the same voice Ttisa spoke with, and the coconscious entity immediately recognizes the face's residual utility as a cushion avatar – a useful tool, so long as that likeness is not mistaken for anything possessed of singularity.

"Well said," the teacher smiles. "You're doing much better than anticipated. Shall we continue?"

The avatar thoughtfully sips her coffee, and then she nods to the teacher. "Please," she replies, and the teacher returns her nod and glances back down at his notes, displayed in the flickering tabletop.

"You're doing so well, in fact, there's quite a bit here we can skip over – heterogeneous mixtures, including suspensions and colloids, for example."

"Which brings us to compounds," the avatar says.

"Indeed, it does."

From its vantage point in geospace, the new mind goes back to watching the nameless river as it empties into that unknown marine gulf, and it marvels at the memory of the taste of milk and coffee, simultaneously familiar and exotic. There is a line of dark clouds moving in from the northwest, and soon they will hide the landscape below from view. Lightning sparks and arcs, belying the violence inside those thunderheads, and Ttisa shivers, despite the temperature of the amnion, which is identical to her own. Here, there is a slip, a misstep, and in *this* instant, she *is* almost Ttisa again. Identity and discreteness threaten to reassert themselves, dissolving the compound back into its constituent parts; there is a second (and stronger) flare of panic before the surrogate can react.

Without hesitation, it points to the next bead on the chain. And the teacher looks up from his notes and clears his throat.

"We might call it binary fusion," he says, "taking care to distinguish this bonding process from the binary *fission* commonly witnessed in the prokaryotic organisms of the Sol system. Nothing here of either partner is split away, but only combined to create a third, which mentally subsumes the parents, in a sense, even though the end product does retain two functionally independent bodies."

"Am I dying?" Ttisa asks him. The man scowls and furrows his eyebrows, but she continues. "Is it like Theodore said? Is the surrogate devouring me alive?"

"You already have the requisite knowledge to answer those questions for yourself," the teacher tells her. "I'm not here to cater to a lazy pupil."

The confluence, her surrogate whispers wordlessly, in silent tones as soothing as the sight of that primeval, earthly river, flowing fifty kilometers below. *The meeting of the waters.* Encontro das Águas, *as they say in Brazil.*

"*Encontro das Águas*," she says, and sips her coffee. The teacher smiles, satisfied, and, once again, there is only a single mind, and once again, the face and voice of the woman at the table is only an avatar to ease the crossing, and nothing that is being lost.

2.

Four months earlier, Ttisa Fitzgerald opens her eyes again, because Theodore is still talking to her. Talking at her. Ttisa wants to sleep, not talk. Lately, it seems that *all* she wants to do is sleep, and she knows it's mostly a side effect of the drugs and dendrimer serums, her antemorphic regimen combined with the demands of her psych conditioning schedule. The doctors told her to expect the grogginess, but it still annoys her. Right now, Theodore is also annoying her. He's sitting naked on the bed next to her, talking. He's turned away from her, facing the wall, which is currently displaying a realtime image of the north polar region of the planet below. Seventy years before Ttisa was born, a team of Mars-based astronomers christened The Planet Iota Draconis c. If she were not so tired, and beginning to feel nauseous again, she might find the sight moving – the vast boreal icecaps hiding an arctic sea, a wide desert of frozen water which, even from orbit, is more blue than white. The light of an alien star reflected off a swirl of high-latitude clouds. The network of lights marking the ancient *shhakizsa* city, waiting to receive her in only a few more weeks. It is all surely still as wondrous as the day her transport dropped out of sublight, more than thirty parsecs from Earth, and Ttisa first laid eyes on this new world circling a third-magnitude star. But she's sleepy. And nauseous. And her head is beginning to ache.

"Maybe it would be easier," Theodore says, "if you expected me to stay. It would be easier, I think, if you'd not seemed so... indifferent...when I said I wanted to rotate back next quarter."

"I don't know what you want me to say," Ttisa tells him, because she doesn't, and she's too tired and feels too bad to make something up.

"Do you really think you'll even remember me, after?" he asks ruefully, and yes, she says, trying harder than she wants to sound reassuring.

"Of course, I'll remember you, Theo," and she's said this a hundred times now, if she's said it once. "No memories are lost. None at all."

"And you believe that?"

"I believe the data, yes."

She asks the ship to extinguish the lights in the room, and, immediately, they dim and wink out. Then Ttisa closes her eyes again, because even the soft glow from the image on the wall is painful.

"Memory isn't the same as feeling," Theodore says.

"No, it isn't," she agrees.

"Even if you *do* remember me, there's no reason to think that you'll still want to *be* with me."

"There's no guarantee," she admits. Passing across her lips, the words seem unnaturally heavy, and she imagines them tumbling off her chin and scattering across the sheets. "But you've known that for months now."

"You didn't even ask me to stay," Theodore says.

"It would have been selfish of me to do something like that. It would have been greedy and hypocritical."

Theodore makes a doubtful sort of noise, a scoffing noise. "It *might* have helped me believe that you haven't stopped caring about me, about us," he says.

"Yes, it might have," she says, her heavy, tumbling words sounding impatient with him. "But it would also have been cruel, and I'm *trying*, Theo – "

"You think *this* is kindness?" he asks, interrupting her, and if Ttisa's words have begun to seem heavy, Theo's fall like lead weights. "It would have been kinder if you'd *told* me to go. It would have been kinder if you'd told me we were done and gotten it over."

Neither of them says anything more for a moment, and Ttisa opens her eyes partway, squinting, and trying not to flinch. Theodore is silhouetted against the monitor, the lines of his muscular body eclipsing the planet on the wall. He's five years younger than her, and was born Theodora, but that was simple enough to fix when he was still a teenager and started figuring out that the inside wasn't suited to the outside. He was born on one of the Mars colonies, in the shadow of Ascraeus Mons, and has never set foot on Earth.

"I don't want it to be like this," she says, hardly speaking above a whisper. "I've tried so hard, to make sure that it wouldn't go this way."

"You might have asked me to stay," he replies, and she sighs, wishing she'd managed to get to sleep before Theo came back to their quarters after finishing his shift in Telemetry and Comms. He wouldn't have awakened her. He never does. "If you had, perhaps I would be more convinced of your sincerity."

"Theo, *you* said that you wanted to go home, remember? I assumed, when you said that, you were telling me the truth. If you *were*, it would have been wrong of me to try to manipulate you into staying out here with me. I couldn't do that." The words topple from her lips and roll across the bed; even she doesn't find them particularly convincing.

"When I dream, I see all the others," he says, losing her for a second or two. "I dream of them all the time now. I dream of you, with them."

"You've never *seen* the others, Theo. Neither of us has seen the others."

"Yeah, but that doesn't mean that I don't dream about them, almost every time I sleep. *You* could wind up like that, Ttisa, and you know it."

"It's been almost a decade," she tells him. "Almost ten years since the last attempt, and the advances since then…" but she trails off, feeling sicker and wondering if she's going to vomit.

"No guarantees," Theo says. "Your own words. So let's not pretend, okay? Let's not fucking lie to ourselves or each other about all the ways this thing could go wrong. For all we know, it's going wrong already, all that shit they're pumping into you day after day."

"Theo," she whispers, "I'm sorry, but I *need* to sleep. We'll talk later. I finished with the second-tier posthyps today, and I just need to sleep for a few hours. Please."

"I'm going for a walk," he says, and then tells the ship to close down the image feed. Ttisa opens her eyes, and the wall is only a wall again, and the compartment is much darker than before.

"I'm going for a walk," Theodore tells her a second time. "I need some air. I'll be down in the garden, maybe, if you need me."

"Well, put some clothes on first," she says, and Theo mutters something angry that she can't quite make out. He quickly dresses while she stares into the darkness, and soon she's alone with her torpid, muddled thoughts and the nausea and exhaustion. She rolls over, looking for the fast-fading warm spot Theo left on the mattress. She asks the ship to resume the video feed, same coordinates as before, and Ttisa watches the blue-white planet far below until she drifts down to a fitful, haunted sleep.

3.

In the present life there are two impediments which prevent us from seeing each other's thoughts: the grossness of the body and the inscrutable secrecy of the will. The first impediment will be removed by the Resurrection, but the second will remain, and it is in the angels now. Nevertheless the brightness of the risen body will correspond to the degree of grace and glory in the mind; and so will serve as a medium for one mind to know another.

Thomas Aquinas, *Summa Theologiae,* (1265-1274)

4.

Ttisa asks the ship to provide her with a mirror, and so a moment later it does. She stands alone in the cramped lavatory, gazing back at herself with those bloodshot green eyes squinched half-shut against the light. She's dressed in nothing but the short, drab station-issued smocks. No one can ever seem to agree if they're meant to be a very orange shade of yellow, or a rather yellowish shade of orange. The woman in the mirror looks as though she hasn't slept in days, a week, maybe. Her skin is sallow, and there are perpetual shadows beneath her eyes, like matching bruises. Her lips are pale and badly chapped, and there's still a dark smudge across her septum and upper lip from the latest nose bleed.

"You are a liar, Miss Fitzgerald," she says, and yes, the woman in the mirror agrees.

"You are, indeed, a liar."

"And a very poor liar, at that," her reflection sighs.

"I'm not sure that it matters any longer," Ttisa says very softly. "I honestly don't know why I even bother to lie to him."

"Old habits," the woman in the mirror suggests, and Ttisa nods.

"I *am* leaving him," she says. "I'm leaving everyone and everything, in a sense. Most times, it's all I can manage to remember why."

"Being alone is unbearable," the woman in the mirror reminds her, using Ttisa's mouth and tongue to make the words.

"Yes, it is, isn't it?"

"For those who realize that they're alone, and how completely they are alone, very much so."

"*Only* for those who've realized how completely alone they are."

"Yes," the woman in the mirror concedes. "Ignorance is the best defense."

Ttisa stops talking to herself and watches the mirror in silence for a time. Anyone could be forgiven for thinking that she was sick, sick and likely dying, anyone who got a good look at her. Maybe, that hypothetical anyone might suppose there'd been a malfunction in her slot on the sleeper during the long trip from Sol, or maybe it was only something prosaic, some humdrum malady she'd picked up before leaving Earth. Either way, they would surmise, the outcome will likely be the same. Medicine can only do so much, after all.

"It's nothing that wasn't expected," she whispers, as though she might be overheard.

"No. Nothing yet," the sickly looking woman in the mirror says, qualifying the observation.

Ttisa asks the ship to please get rid of the mirror, and soon the lavatory wall is the same dull, non-reflective grey as any other wall. She sits down on the toilet, because her legs feel weak, and she wonders if Theo came back while she was sleeping. There's no evidence that he did, but it's not impossible. Maybe he stood near the bed and watched while she slept. Perhaps, he sat on the padded bench near the bed and kept an eye on her while she dreamed of a meeting that she's told him repeatedly never took place. Officially, it never did. There's no record of it anywhere in her files, and news of the meeting certainly was not included in any of the press packs. She has often wondered why they took the chance, and has never yet arrived at an entirely satisfactory answer. It might have been the doing of one of the project leaders, one of the dissenters, trying to prove a pet point. Or it might have been the *shhakizsa* who saw to it that the meeting took place, leaving the agency with little choice but to acquiesce. In the end, though, *why* and *how* it happened don't seem particularly important. Only that it did. Whatever doubts Ttisa had before she met the sixth attempt were undone by that encounter.

She stares down at the floor between her bare feet. Her toenails look as if they have each been struck smartly with a mallet or hammer, and she thinks about polishing them to hide the discoloration. Again, it's nothing that wasn't anticipated by the pharmacokinetic profile. Nothing to be worried about.

"Being alone is unbearable," she says again. When she asked the sixth why it had proceeded with the process, even after being presented with evidence that there was insufficient momentum to clear all the requisite psychosomatic barriers, that's the reply that Ttisa received. *Being alone is unbearable.*

The answer had not been spoken, of course, because the sixth was no longer capable of speech, any more than it was able to hear. But it was able to communicate with Ttisa, and with its caretakers, by way of a wetware transference matrix incorporated into the sixth's artificial womb. The vox program possessed a very distinct PanAsian mech accent – a giveaway in the enunciation – hinting at its provenance.

"Yes," Ttisa replied, peering into the murky tank, straining to see clearly through the gelatinous support medium and into the sunken black slits that were the vestigial eyes of the sixth. "I think I understand."

"I had thought that you would," the sixth replied. "I had *hoped* that you would."

And later, one of the project psychiatrists wanted to talk about that part of the exchange. Specifically, he wanted a clearer definition of what the two of them had meant by *alone*. At first, Ttisa was at a loss to explain, and then a rather obvious analogy occurred to her.

"I'm in a bubble," she told the man. "And you are in a bubble, as well. We are each in our own perfectly transparent bubble. I can see you, and you can see me. We can even hear each other perfectly well. In fact, the physics of our bubbles even allow us to touch one another. We could even fuck, if we wished. The bubbles are that flexible. But, regardless, we are *still* trapped inside our respective, inviolable bubbles, and no matter how hard we may try, we can never truly touch one another. We cannot ever fully *know* one another. In my thoughts, I am alone, Doctor, isolated, and so are you. And being alone is unbearable."

Ttisa heard a rumor the psychiatrist resigned from the project, shortly after that interview, and that he was rotated back to Sol following a board inquiry. Whether or not the rumor was true, she never saw him again. And no one else on the project has ever asked about her conversation with the sixth.

"I'm sorry, Theo," Ttisa says. "I'm a goddamn liar." And then she realizes how late it's getting, how she's going to be late for her morning conditioning session if she doesn't stop moping about the lavatory and get dressed. She tugs the drab smock off over her head, lets it slip from her fingers, and then leaves it lying on the floor. There will be time to pick it up later. Later, there will be time to worry about Theo.

5.

"Has it begun?" Ttisa asks. "Has it started." But then she realizes that she's hasn't actually asked the question aloud, and so she doesn't expect an answer. She tries to open her eyes, but finds that she's unable to, and so thinks that she might only be dreaming and struggling to wake up.

And struggling to breathe.

A dream, then, of drowning, perhaps. But, if so, the dream would be little more than a hazy, disarranged recollection, proceeding from a childhood mishap. She was not quite five years old, and had gone with her mother to a public natatorium. There was an artificial waterfall at one end of the pool, and, also, a hidden machine that generated artificial waves, so that swimmers might know what it had been like to swim in the sea, when swimming in the sea was still an option. There was a sandy beach, and plastic sea shells.

Hold it up to your ear and listen, her mother said. *Tell me what you hear.*

"I hear a roaring, mother. I hear a terrible, endless roaring, like a wind blowing between the stars."

There is the sense that she is floating, weightless, but it's not the sickening weightlessness of space travel. Which is, in truth, the sensation of always *falling*. Ttisa knows that she is not falling, though she may well have *fallen*, in some archaic, mythic denotation of the word. Having fallen, then, she floats.

Fiery the Angels rose, & as they rose deep thunder roll'd
Around their shores: indignant burning with the fires of Orc

The dim memory of her feet kicking out and not finding bottom, and indeed there is no bottom now to be found. *And when they pulled you from the pool,* her mother once told her, *you were so pale. I thought that we had lost you.*

I am lost now, mother. I am lost forever and always.

They've found me, and I am lost.

The half dream whirls, like cream in coffee, or muddy freshwater meeting a clear tropical sea.

One of the project biologists is talking, though his voice is muted and seems to be reaching her from some place or some time far away from now and here. It is one of her first sessions, an introduction to *shhakizsa* physiology. In particular, digestion and reproduction, two processes inextricably linked in the life cycle of the aliens. She wants the woman to stop lecturing her. Wants only to drift in this silent nowhere that is not falling, and is not drowning, and is neither cold nor warm.

"Direct comparison with humans, or any other mammal, or, for that matter, with any animal species, is problematic. For example, we can refer to this orifice as a mouth, but it also functions as a vagina and anus. We could call this muscular tube here the esophagus, or cervix, or the colon, but we would not be quite correct in doing so, for their functions are not truly analogous. Is *that* organ there a stomach? A womb? How, you'll ask, could it function as both?"

"They're great ugly brutes, you ask me," Theodore says, then goes back to picking at the meal he's only pretending to eat.

"I don't recall asking you," she replies, and he shrugs. "And I don't see where such a subjective matter as 'beauty' is even relevant here."

Theo stops rearranging the food on his plate and glares at her a moment, and his expression is so complex an interweave of contempt, concern, fear, confusion, and anger, that she could not hope to *begin* to separate one emotion from the others.

"When this thing is over," he says, then pauses to take a deep breath, flaring his nostrils slightly. "*If* you survive it, then you'll be as much one of them as human, yeah?"

"Yes," she replies.

Theo lays his fork down and wipes at his mouth with a napkin. "And I'll say, 'She was a woman, once. She was the most beautiful woman I ever saw, and I loved her.' I'll say, 'You might find that hard to believe, but she *was* a woman, once.'"

"And to whom would you say such things?"

"Who do you think would bother to ask? Anyway, they'll take me for a liar, or a madman, if I dare."

Her mother laughs and shows her how to hold the plastic conch shell to her ear. "Now, dear," she says, "don't you hear the sea inside? Don't you hear the waves against the beach?"

I won't tell her what I hear. This time, I'll keep it all to myself.

The biologist draws Ttisa's attention back to the faintly quivering holographic diagram, a generalized cross section of a *shhakizsa*'s radially symmetric anatomy.

"We can make very rough parallels with some Sol taxa," she says. "Among the Eumetazoa of Earth, for example, I might mention the Ctenophora and Cnidaria, and, to a lesser degree, the echinoderms, especially crinoids. If we look to the hydrothermal biomes of Europa, there is a superficial similarity with the parahydroids and the more familiar Gorgonophores. In all these instances, though, if we look closely enough, the parallels break down, and only serve to demonstrate how truly foreign to our concepts of biophysics and morphology these beings are. They – and most other organisms we've seen from the *shhakizsa* home-world – are without precedent, in our experience, which is presently too bound to a single perspective."

"Ugly fuckers," Theo mutters, and gets up from the table. "You ask me – and I *know* that you never bothered to ask me, Ttisa – this whole goddamn affair is an abomination. It is abominable."

Now the project's chief anthropologist is talking, and Ttisa remembers his name, John Grant, because he was one of the few people selected for the panel that she found likeable. His voice is firm and, yet, somehow lyrical.

"It is imperative," he says, "to understand that, for *shhakizsa* society, this process is nothing short of sacred. It's marriage, copulation, and parenthood combined. It is the most intimate communion between two persons imaginable. There are fifteen different words their priests commonly use when referring to the process, and they all translate, more or less, the same: *unification.*"

"Did he actual call them *persons?*" Theo scoffs, and he turns away from her.

She is floating, and the feeling of suffocation has passed. Her lungs have filled with fluid, and there is no longer any need to breathe. The oxygen she requires will be transferred directly to her bloodstream now. There is no pain, despite the corrosively low pH environment surrounding her, and despite that, by now, various enzymes will have triggered the early stages of epidermal transformation and horizontal gene transfer. The digestive, amniotic fluid is filled with powerful analgesics, and the serums and months of conditioning have insured that her human neurology is receptive to them.

"Doesn't it sound like the sea?" her mother asks, and Ttisa, not yet five years old, shakes her head and sets the conch back down on the white, white sand of the natatorium's fabricated beach.

The six umbilical cords begin to wrap themselves tightly about her, each one attaching to a critical, predetermined site on Ttisa's body by means of razor-sharp beaks composed primarily of chitin and complex cross-linked proteins. One for her throat (entering by way of her mouth), another through her sex, her belly, her rectum, and the base of her spine, and yet another penetrating the medulla oblongata via the foramen magnum.

I am not drowning, she thinks. *I could never drown. I am held fast. Embraced, as I have never been embraced before, and I will not fall again.*

"Has it started?"

"Yes," whispers a voice that is not a voice. "It has started. Rest now. You will need it, farther along."

Theo puts down his tab and squeezes his eyes shut. He rubs at his temples, as though his head aches. "It sounds like rape to me," he says. "No, it sounds much *worse* than rape."

"I wish I could make you understand," she tells him. "I would, if I could."

And around Ttisa, all the wide world has shrunken to this golden lagoon of kindly, flesh-filtered light and transmuting fluids, and the gentle, voiceless reassurances in a tongue she understands without having learned.

For the first time in her life, she is sure that she not falling.

6.

Though she didn't go down to the departure bay in time to say goodbye to Theo (and, for that matter, he didn't come to say goodbye to her), Ttisa did watch him leave. She stood alone on the observation deck, and, with an index finger pressed to the wall, traced the steady, silent path of the ungainly, multi-hulled sleeper as it exited the station and moved away towards the pulsing scarlet ring of the starboard ftl portal. She looked away before the embarkation flash, and when she looked back, the ship that would ferry him home was gone. He was gone. And she knew that she'd never see him again.

She knew that she *should* feel remorse.

And she knew, too, that there should be a profound emptiness inside her, an ache that she would carry for a long time to come. But there was nothing of the sort, and it seemed very silly to counterfeit, or to worry over the absence of emotions that would have only caused her pain.

They've changed me this much already, she thought, still watching the ftl portal as the lateral vector array stopped flashing while the entire circuit powered down. The plasma stream had dissipated, and there was nothing visible through the portal now but stars. She picked out the yellow speck of Arcturus, then pulled her hand back from the wall and stared at her fingertip, instead.

That's it, then. He's away. It is for the best, really. He was so unhappy.

"Sleep tight, my love," she said aloud. "Sleep tight and dream." Then, wondering if this was possibly only another part of the experiment, and, if so, how she'd scored, Ttisa turned and left the observation deck.

7.

This far along in the process, three Sol days and counting, there is no longer any meaningful distinction between her memory and that of the surrogate. "It" clearly recalls kneeling on a white beach and holding a plastic conch to its ear, listening for a phantom sea. "She" remembers, with equal clarity, the towering, crystalline spires buried miles deep, beneath the *shhakizsas'* sprawling polar megalopolis, the quartz lattice of temples erected to long-forgotten gods and demons. "It" recalls a day at the beach, and "she" relives a pilgrimage to an archeological wonder. The rapidly mutating body that was Ttisa Fitzgerald drifts, not falling, safe within the sanctuary that has grown around it, the amniotic cyst that cradles what it has become and what it is still becoming.

The confluence, this new, compounded consciousness thinks again. *The meeting of the waters.* Encontro das Águas.

Milk in coffee.

The cold swirl of stars in near vacuum.

All but one of the surrogate's umbilici has withdrawn, completely resorbed into the host's endometrium. The one that remains is there for no other reason than the carnal pleasure of contact, of masturbation. It has swollen to completely fill the thorny, cilia-lined slit that can no longer be described as a human vagina. The enormous body of the surrogate and the far smaller body of the reborn shiver in unison.

We are whole, it thinks, as the latest in a seemingly ceaseless series of orgasms fades. *This is our gift, the gift we have given to ourself. This wholeness, unfettered by the jail of individuality. Our minds are laid bare, and there can be no mental isolation here, and no secrets.*

Being alone is unbearable, it thinks.

We will never be alone again, it replies. *Even when the cyst ruptures and we divide, we will remain as one.*

Is she still here, watching from somewhere within us? The one who was named Ttisa Fitzgerald? but it knows the answer even before the question has been fully articulated. Nothing has been lost, save the abyss between one consciousness and another.

Hold it up to your ear and listen. Tell me what you hear.

You might have asked me to stay.

And I'll say, "She was a woman, once. She was the most beautiful woman I ever saw, and I loved her." *I'll say*, "You might find that hard to believe, but she *was a woman, once."*

And, if not woman, and if not shhakizsa, *what are we now?* it asks itself. *What is this beast we have become?*

There are many words available with which to answer that question, but they all, each and every one, signify unification. It pauses in the flow of questioning and revelry to examine what has been fashioned from the willing offering of Ttisa Fitzgerald – the reborn child, the holy feast, the marriage consummated. In combined lifetimes, it has beheld precious few things so singular in their loveliness, so unlikely in their realization. That impatient daughter tugs roughly at the remaining umbilicus, snared between her legs. And, pleased at the unprecedented fruits of so painful and perilous a labor – a labor that failed six times previously – the amalgam resumes its ministrations.

8.

It is not from space that I must seek my dignity, but from the government of my thought. I shall have no more if I possess worlds. By space the universe encompasses and swallows me up like an atom; by thought I comprehend the world.

Blaise Pascal (1623-1662), *Pensées*

Dancing With the
Eight of Swords

*I have never seen a greater monster or miracle in
the world than myself.*
Michel Eyquem de Montaigne (1533-1592)

I open my eyes, and She is still sitting in the only chair in this
dingy, dim room. She is still watching me. I must have been
sleeping again. If I ask Her, She will tell me that I was sleeping,
and I can imagine nothing She would gain by lying. There is no
resistance or power left to me, and She is all the world now, so I
cannot fathom why She would lie. I don't ask the question. I *was*
sleeping. I *know* I was sleeping, because in my sleep I dreamed,
and in my dream I was not here, in this dim and dingy room with
its one chair and the harpy who sits there and the bed where I lie
sweating and sick and, I think, always dying. I do not know how
long I've lain here, hurting and dreaming and waking and *wishing*
I were only dying. I think no one is brought here to die. I think I
was brought here to *be*, because of what I have *been* and what I
have *done*. I am a dying (or merely dead) woman who has done so
many things, and it is difficult for me to envision a universe that
does not exact retribution. She sits so near, and Her golden eyes
glint like antique coins in the candlelight. I think it must be
candlelight, as it has that quality possessed by candlelight, though
I cannot actually ever see the candles. You ask me, I have done so
very many inexcusable things, and they come back to me in what I
believe are dreams, as I believe I am now awake. I want to ask Her,

how many rooms like this are there? A hundred? A thousand? Some number nearing infinity? She sees that I am awake, and She smiles. Oh, those teeth. Those teeth that would be the envy of any shark or wolf or hyena or demon. She merely smiles, to see me awake again. "Hello," She says, and I don't reply. Not yet. I shut my eyes again, the dreaming still too fresh and sharp and stinking. I shut my eyes, and so, of course, She wants to know *why* I have shut my eyes. *That I will not see*, I reply, and She laughs, knowing goddamn well that I see, eyes open or closed, either way I see one thing or another. Either way, there is no escape. We come here, to this room, and we do not escape. This is what I think. And then She wants to know my dreams, because She always wants to know my dreams. I tell Her they are mine, and She assures me this is true and that She has no wish to deprive me of them. And I ask, my mouth so dry, my throat so raw that I can only just manage the words, I say, *You know already. Why do you ask me, when you know already?* I imagine She is smiling, still, though I don't open my eyes to see if this is true. "Maybe," She replies, "there was something new. They change, sometimes, our dreams." And yes, She says this as though She *is* a being who dreams, and no, I don't believe this. That She is. "So," She says, "tell me what I know already, as I would hear the words again. They are precious, whether novel or threadbare." For a moment, my mind is filled with curses I will not speak, no, not aloud, for my fury only seems to please Her as much as anything else. Novelty and worn-out memories, truth and falsehoods, pain and pleasure, and I cannot now recall how many times She has sworn to me that I *will* learn to see that there are no such distinctions, not in truth, and She only makes reference to them as a kindness to me. I have been consigned to this dim and dingy room, this Pit, this unending moment, and a thoughtful beast has been sent to watch over me. When I do not reply, She asks if my throat is dry, if it aches, and then, before I reply, She offers me something to drink. But I *know* what will be in the cup She raises to my lips. I know that thick, warm draught. I know too well the taste, that some have said is like iron or old pennies, but I have found it to be neither one. I refuse. I will refuse until I can no longer bear to refuse. "Then, please, tell me," She says, Her patient voice still smiling. I do not open my eyes. But I clear my ragged throat, and *my* voice is hardly more than a whisper. "You know already," I say. And how I do *loathe* the sound of it, my own voice, and how I do wish and have prayed to dark things that She would finally take mercy upon me and rip my throat open and take *away* my voice, take it away forever. But I know She *needs* it, needs me able to speak my confessions. "One of your beautiful ones?" She asks, prompting me. "Is that what it was?" I used to think that She was mocking me, but I know now that She is not. "Yes," I whisper. "One of my beautiful ones." And it's not a lie, as I have learned there is no profit whatsoever in lying to the naked, violet-skinned woman (who is, I know, no woman) who sits in the room's single chair. "I was begging her to be silent. I was begging her, begging her to try *harder* than she was already trying." And from Her chair, the harpy – no, she is no *real* harpy, nothing so simple or familiar; it is only a convenient word – asks me, "*Did* she try? Did she *listen* to you?" I shake my head, because that's easier than saying no, and I squeeze my eyes shut even tighter than before. I understand that She can see what *I* see behind my closed eyelids, that there is no shutting Her out, not ever, no, and it's so completely fucking absurd, the way She makes me put it all into words, watering it down, failing entirely to capture the truth. "One of my beautiful ones," I say. "I can't recall her name." And from Her chair, the violet-skinned beast says, "It doesn't matter. Their names are lost." I nod, because it's true. I *always* stole their names. I always took great care to bury their names long before I ever buried any of their bodies. "I said, 'Please, lie still for me. Lie still and do not breathe.' And I told her that if she could just do that, if she could just do her best, I would give her name back to her when I was done." There is a *sound* then, like water dripping, but it isn't water, no, not here in this dry, dim, and dingy room, and I open my eyes. She's still watching me from Her chair. She's leaning forward very slightly, and Her long hair looks much like the pregnant moments before a thunderstorm. Her eyes are like clusters of pomegranate seeds, and She blinks for me. No, She *only* blinks. Not *for* me. I *want* to look away, as I *always* want to look away, as I *never* want to look away, as I *would* look into Her forever until my soul is burned to soot, were that an option. Maybe, it's an option farther along. She's leaning forward, very slightly, and She says to me, "It is not an unreasonable request. But still, they never could lie still enough, could they? And not a single one of them ever managed to hold her breath even half so long enough." I tell Her, then, that I was not lying to them, that I would have released them afterwards, if they'd just done as I asked. I tell Her this again, again, again, as if I think it matters. I don't know if it's true. It may be that She does. That She knows. She always seems to believe me, but that might simply be part of this game, or pantomime, or dance, or whatever the proper fucking word would be for what it is we are doing in this dim and dingy room, She and I. Our vicious, soft-spoken *pas de deux*, recurring, as once night followed day, or day followed night. She is become the sun and I the moon, or conversely, I am the one who burns, and She only reflects the ghost of my light. "I knew, from the start," I say, not taking my eyes from Her, "that no one would ever believe that. The police, I mean. Or if they *did* believe me, they wouldn't care. It would not *matter* that I gave them all a fair and equal chance to walk away. They didn't *have* to die." And, blinking those red, ripe eyes, She says, "They would all have died anyway, in time. You know that. What matter the day? What matter the conveyance? Life has a single outcome, and the hour of that consequence may as well be sooner as be later." I *want* to ask if these words are meant to console me, or lull me, or if She is, instead, mocking what I say to Her. I don't, though. *I* mocked *Her* once, what strikes me as many ages ago, and, for my insolence, She showed me daylight and green meadows and blue skies, and so I know better now. I hold my tongue, as they say. "Which one was it?" She asks. "Which of your beautiful ones were you dreaming of this time?" And, truthfully, I say that I'm uncertain. One of the blondes, which isn't very helpful, as they were almost always blondes. It was a weakness, though I tried to avoid obvious patterns, it *was* a weakness, the blondes. So, yes, I was dreaming of one of the blondes, begging her not to move, not to speak, not to breathe. I was dreaming of the tub filled with icy water. I was dreaming of her flesh, cold as death, but not *yet* dead. Her heartbeat, pulse, inhalations and exhalations, *all* of it there to spoil the illusion. And I stop, stop relating the dream, and I say, again, I never understood the source of these appetites of mine. That I never *invited* them in. And then She says, her voice so soothing, so sincere, that She knows this, She knows this perfectly well. "Our appetites choose us," She says. "Or, they are given unto us. Or they are curses. Regardless, we are not to be faulted for deigning to accept them." And I say (though I've said it already) that it was one of the blondes, and, yes, I took her name and placed it in the jar where I kept all their names. Once, the jar held a quart of dill pickles, but I had washed it, steamed off the label, scrubbed it clean, and so it was a perfectly fit receptacle to hold the slips of white paper on which I placed the names of my beautiful ones after I stole them away. White slips of paper and blue Pelican ink. I used to know the particular shade of blue, but it's something I have since forgotten. I talk about the tub of icy water, and I talk about the girl's lips going *another* shade of blue, but not blue *enough*. "I told her, I said she must not shiver. No matter what, she must not shiver," I say. "But she *did* shiver, didn't she?" my keeper asks, my keeper, or my warden, or whatever. "After all, the response is involuntary, a reflex triggered during the earliest stages of hypothermia. The body shuddering in a self-defeating attempt to warm itself. There is a portion of the hypothalamus located near the *ventriculus tertius*, and it serves as the motor center responsible for shivering. A valuable adaptation, but also a deadly one. It increases the heat output in endotherms by two- or three-fold, but at such a great cost to the shivering organism." And I've heard all this before, for human morphology and physiology are among the subjects of which She has proven a connoisseur. I never will say, *I know that. I've known that shit since college.* When She is done, I glance at the ceiling. There *is* a ceiling in the dim and dingy room, just as there is a floor, and four walls, and a door, and all these things have never ceased to amaze me in their stark simplicity. "I'm sorry," She says. "Please, continue. You were saying that she did shiver, even though you begged her not to do so." And I nod. "Yes," I reply. "She did. She shivered, and her teeth chattered. I showed her the jar with her name, as I sometimes would do, hoping it would *prove* to her that I had the power to restore her name." Which is true, I did. I held the jar of names in front of her open eyes. "Which," I add, "were hazel green." "But it was to no avail," the harpy says. The gargoyle. The siren. The unspeakably beautiful and violet-skinned beast with its delicate, long fingers. "To no avail," I say, playing Echo to Her Narcissus. "She was so exquisitely pale, and her lips and earlobes and the tips of her fingers were going that soft shade of blue," I say. And from Her chair, She nods and leans closer to the bed and says, "Stage-two hypothermia. Is that when you admitted defeat?" And I tell Her, "Yes, that time. But sometimes, some *other* times, I let it go farther. Sometimes, I was more hopeful, or persistant, than other times, and I could control the anger." So I sit on the bed, and She watches me for a while, and for that time, there are no words exchanged between us. And then I spoil the silence by continuing. "I used glue, *that* time. Ethyl-2 cyanoacrylate. Krazy Glue. Whatever. On her lips and inside her nostrils. I held her lips together and pinched her nostrils shut until it set. I know that I could have made it easier for her. But, I was so very furious. I was so fucking pissed off. I'd shown her the *jar*, and even *that* wasn't enough. There were times I thought of doing that to myself, and being done with it. Using the glue, I mean." She frowns slightly, which She does on occasion, and tells me that my frustration and despair were inevitable, to be expected, and I should not be ashamed. "They failed you," She says. "You did not fail them. Your beautiful ones, you only gave to them what they were unable to manage on their own." And I laugh, without meaning to, and quickly cover my mouth and stare down at the bare, stained mattress. At my naked belly and thighs and legs. I awoke here without clothes, and they have never been offered, but neither is She ever clothed, so it doesn't seem unfair. "It is good to laugh," She tells me, and She tells me not to be repentant if I find humor in Her words, even when She did not intend to imbue them with humor. "Do not cover your pretty mouth," She says, so I let my hand drift back down to my left side. "That's better," She smiles. "Now, when she was dead? What then?" And I take a deep breath, an especially deep breath, and I hold it maybe ten or fifteen seconds. The spent air rushes loudly from my mouth and nose. "There is no dignity in a death like that. It is an ugly way to die. Asphyxiation. But you already *know* that." And, "Of course I do," She says in the most agreeable tone of voice. "When I was done – " I begin, but She interrupts me. "When you were done with *what*?"

She asks me, and now Her tone is somewhat less agreeable. She does not permit me to abridge my divulgences. "What did you do when she'd stopped struggling, when her body had ceased to convulse, once the hypoxia had run its course and she was dead? What did you do then?" And I tell Her that I used my fingers, first, and then my tongue, and when She asks me if it was good, I tell Her no, that it was sublime. And now *She* laughs, and oh, that laugh, that laugh is incalculably more frigid than *any* bath I ever gave my beautiful ones, and it cuts me in a thousand secret, invisible, incorporeal places. She *knows* that, knows it well, and, so, She laughs again. When She is finished laughing, She sits up straighter, and crosses Her thin arms. Watching Her watching me, I'm struck again by how, in the apparent candlelight filling the dim and dingy room, the horns sprouting from either side of Her head appear as though they have been mold-blown from molten glass. An almost entirely opaque glass, tinted aubergine. They coil round and back upon themselves like a ram's horns, or a satyr's, though all other visible evidence paints Her as something female. "Your fingers, and *then* your tongue," She says, so now *I've* become Narcissus. "This was before you placed the corpse in the freezer," and I tell Her yes, that this was before. She wants to know, then, if I went back later, when the body had frozen, and I tell Her, honestly, that part wasn't in my dream. "Regardless, I would know. Did you go back to her, this blonde of yours, after she was frozen?" And risking so much and, in the end, risking hardly anything at all, I say to Her, "You love this." She nods and tells me yes, there is *great* delight for Her in hearing these words spoken, and hearing also the accompanying dissonance inside my mind. "Was there not love in you?" She asks. "Each one of them, were they not your heart's own truest love? Was there even one among that number to whom you were not entirely devoted?" I say She already knows the answer, but then I say, because She needs to hear it *spoken*, then I say, "No, there was not even one of them I did not, in turn, love. I took the same chance for them all. I placed myself in mortal danger for *all* of my beautiful ones, and so I *know* that I loved them. I *hurt*, looking into their eyes, and so I know I loved. I hurt *so* much, and *every* time in the most inaccessible recesses of my being, and so I know, and I *don't* doubt that I did truly love them." Then I hear the faint, discordant music that sometimes drifts through the dim and dingy room, like careless hands on a piano badly in need of tuning. Several times, or more times than several, I have come near to asking Her where the music originates, what it signifies, if it has some purpose. But I never have, and I don't this time. I just wait for it to pass. She never even seems to notice it. "Why did this one go to the freezer?" She asks, though She already knows that answer, too. "Why the freezer, instead of the box? Was the box preoccupied?" And I shake my head, and, as the last jangling strains of the music fade, I say, "No. The box was empty. But there was no need of the box. The glue did the trick. It would have been pointless to place her in the box, to go to the trouble of burying her and having to dig her up again, when she was already dead." And "Yes," She says. "Yes, of course. I shouldn't have asked that question. Of course, it would have been unnecessary and meaningless to place her in the box. And an artist must always conserve her energy. It mustn't be squandered on futile endeavors." I say again, so softly that even I hardly hear myself, "She *was* already dead." She blinks (and it has occurred to me, repeatedly, that if I could only be sufficiently attentive, I would be able to catch a pattern to Her blinking; it must be something not dissimilar to Morse code, the blinking of Her eyes like clusters of ripe pomegranate seeds). She blinks. And She glances at the door. I have never yet seen that door open, but I assume it is more than *trompe-l'œil*, surely. The assumption is baseless, and I freely acknowledge that. What was it that Carl Sagan wrote? "A sad spectacle. If they be inhabited, what a scope for misery and folly. If they be not inhabited, what a waste of space." So, yes, what a sad spectacle is that door. If it is a fake, only paint over plaster, what a waste of space. And if it *is*, in truth, an *actual* door, what a scope for misery and folly. She would say, "It might be hope." And I would remind Her that April is the cruelest month, and She, dutifully, would agree. I'm not guessing. We have played that scene more than once. "Did you hear something?" I ask. "Out there, did you hear something?" She turns back to me, and She asks, "No, dear. Did you?" I tell Her that I didn't. Because I didn't. And She blinks. And She smiles. And Her predatory teeth glint in the candlelight. She asks, "Was she left long in the freezer?"

I answer that, as best I can recollect, she was left two or three days. "Before you took her to the river," She says, "there was more. Your fingers or your tongue? Or both?" And now my head fills up with the vision of the blonde, her flesh gone hard as stone, and, since water ice is, indeed, a mineral, she *was* stone, yes, and she was fossilized, and I'd become Pygmalion inverted. She was not so thoroughly colorless as marble, but the frost that dappled the white, white skin of this Galatea was near enough, I think. "I kissed her frozen lips," I say. "But Aphrodite took no mercy on me." This causes Her to laugh again, and it seems safe for me to laugh, as well, and so I do. "I kissed her lips, even at the risk of thawing them with my scalding breath. I laid my hand on the cairn of her breast." And She blinks and says, "You'd shaved her, yes." It's not a question. "Yes, but that was before the bath. That was always at the beginning." "So she was bare and smooth, as would befit such a sculpture," my custodian, or caretaker, or tormentor says. "Of course," I reply. "And I laid my hand there, between her legs, at her sex, and the cold was *so* cold it seemed almost hot, beneath my palm." Leaning forward again, She asks, beetling her violet brows, "That was all?" I say that yes, that was all. "The ice would not permit me entry, and that was always a *rule*. It was a rule that I never once violated. The ice was *final*, and the ice was not ever to be breeched." "No matter your desire?" "No matter my desire," I tell Her, trying hard not to sound bitter, though I *am*, and though She *knows* I am. I lose count of the masks I wear. The futile lies I tell Her. "I took her to the river, to a deep place below one of the bridges. There are gulls there, sometimes, and cormorants. The sun was almost up, but it is quite a desolate place. Still, I was cautious. Always, I was cautious. They never found me." And then She asks a question that consists of a single word. "Police?" I don't want to answer. I want to close my eyes, and sleep, sleep forever, and dream of my beautiful ones, and of a world beyond the dim and dry and dingy room lit with unseen candles. "Police," I nod. "I never fucked up. Or I never fucked up badly enough that they took note. I'm proud of that. I am." She tells me that I *should* be proud, and now She stands, which She rarely does. She stands, rising to Her full height, which must be seven feet, at least. "You should be proud," She says, repeating

Herself. "You got my attention. Which is why it pains me so, that you avoid the mirrors." No, I've *not* mentioned the mirrors. There are two in the room. When I sit up in the bed, my back to the headboard, facing Her, there is a mirror on my right, and another almost directly in front of me. She continues, staring down at me now. "If I were less understanding of your situation," She says, "I would unquestionably be insulted, as you were insulted by your beautiful ones, each time they refused the gift you offered them." If I explain that I mean no insult, I know that will only be another sort of insult, and so I don't. "I am growing sick of our monotonous jousting," She tells me, without there being a hint of anger in Her voice. "Worse, I am growing disgusted with your delusions. I watched over you so long, dear child, and, you *must* know, that was much more the source of your success than any cleverness of your own devising. The police did not see, because I didn't wish them to see." This is nothing I haven't heard before, though the words pound the air with more force and more ferocity than is usual for Her. "I delivered you here, to me," and I know precisely what She wishes me to recall in this precise moment. The gun that I placed to my temple, and the trigger I did not ever have the nerve to squeeze. The bottle of pills I never swallowed. And, then, the noose, tied expertly with yellow nylon rope, and, as they say, the third time is a charm. "No," She says, speaking louder than before. "No, I *am* now less understanding, and I no longer *care* about your situation. There is too much work to be still done for us to go on like this, me mollifying you, as though you are some lost and pathetic soul, consigned to her own private nook of Hell. As though you do not know. It sickens me, the way you *deny*." And I don't ask what it is She thinks that I am denying. I might, but She bends close and places a hand firmly on either side of my face. She has never been so near, and I have never before noticed the stinging odor of Her breath, like cinnamon and gasoline and chrysanthemums and bleach. I gag, and when I try to turn away, She forces my face in another direction, towards the vanity mirror on my right. "You *will* look," She says. "Or I will take away your eyelids and leave you with no choice in the matter. It is *shameful*, a *disgrace*, for one of *us* to fear its own reflection." And here I am, in the instant that has ever been arriving, ever overdue, and She whispers, "An artist must always conserve her energy. It mustn't be squandered on futile endeavors." And I see that there are *two* demons in the mirror, *two* violet-skinned monsters, *two* sets of pomegranate eyes and aubergine horns. And the four walls melt away, and I see this is because they were never more solid than my guilty, fevered thoughts. "You are so beautiful," She says, "Such terrible beauty. And I will *not* have you believing any longer the lies that men and women tell, the falsehoods that would have you believe you are *not* beautiful and not without your rightful place in this Creation." I start to say something, amazed at the configuration of my own jaws, but She places a forestalling index finger to my orchid lips. "Apologize, and I *will* rip the tongue from out your mouth. You will not apologize ever again. There is no shame remaining." So, I'm silent. I don't explain that I'd only meant to thank her, and that it hadn't even occurred to me to apologize. The walls have fallen away, and the stars go on in all directions, and the Void embraces me. "We've all been changed," She says, "from what we were," and I do not disagree. And in the mirror, now, there is only *one* of us reflected, one of *me*, only a single violet-skinned monster and just a single set of pomegranate eyes and one pair of glassy aubergine horns. And I laugh. I laugh until stars flinch, and dead women sleeping in the mud beds of distant rivers stir uneasily in dreams of dim, dry rooms.

Murder Ballad No. 7

No one knows that she is a fairy lady. No one alive, at least.
No one who is only a human man or woman. In this modern day and this disenchanted era, there are none who might even suspect the simple truth of her. She herself did not know until the age of thirteen and the onset of menarche, when she woke one morning to find the bed sheets stained red, and from the blood of her menstruation had sprung minute sprigs of rye-grass and wild thyme. She wadded the ruined and oddly fecund bedclothes into a heap and hid them beneath bulging plastic bags at the bottom of a trashcan. The garbage men and their rumbling truck came and carried them away, and that night, an unruly procession of goblins and pixies arrived and danced in the flowerbed beneath her windowsill. They trampled the pansies flat, and nibbled the impatiens to ribbons, so that the next morning the woman whom the girl had always believed to be her mother blamed the damage on a neighborhood dog. The next evening, the fairies returned and sang for the girl, who, by proxy of blood, was no longer a girl, and who, of course, had never truly *been* a girl. They serenaded her in their high, reedy voices and played raucous, bawdy songs on petite flutes and lyres and drums no larger than a thumbnail. She sat on the floor and listened, though her heart ached to rush outside and join in their revelry. In the long, last hour before dawn, a hairy little bogie of a man perched himself haphazardly upon the window ledge and, more or less off key, and with no evident heed to the tempo set by the musicians below, he sang:

Fast, fast, through the greenwood speeding
Out in the moonlight bright,
Her fairy raid she is leading,

The dainty Queen so light,
And the baby heir of acres wide
She is carrying away to fairyland.
A changeling is left by the nurse's side
And she in the young heir's place shall stand.

And when his song was done, he whispered to her that this must forever be a secret thing between them, a confidence. Before she could object or even think to ask why, the bogie quickly related to her all the mischief that had been done to people only *suspected* of being changelings. He noted, with an obvious, smug sort of pride, that virtually none of the condemned had actually been born to the Shining Court, for the Sidhe are generally much too cunning to allow the babes they leave in place of stolen human children to be found out.

She listened, only half believing, for her life had been easy and kind, and she was unaccustomed to such awful tales. Besides, they'd all happened a very long time ago, in a more superstitious age, in countries far across the sea. All those suspect infants left out to freeze on cold Welsh and English nights, abandoned on cairns or graves or in ditches, the ones flogged and the others placed on hot shovels and held over the coals. Sometimes, the bogie confided, an unfortunate was fortunate enough that it was only pelted with bits of iron or placed in a dung pile.

The logic was simple, said the bogie. Surely, we'd never allow our offspring to suffer so grievously, and would rush in at once to reclaim those left in the stead of their own wee pink whelps.

And, in case all this was still insufficient to keep her from telling tales and giving away the game, the bogie then assured her that it was not only the very young who'd been tortured and suffered at the hands of priests and "fairy doctors." Consider, he told her, the case of an Irish cooper (and here he had to pause to explain that a *cooper* was one who made wooden barrels and wash tubs) who'd suspected his own wife of being a fairy. She had been stolen, he believed, and an *almost* perfect imposter left behind. Only almost perfect, though, because the cooper claimed his wife was not so pretty, and, besides, the imposter was two inches taller than the woman he'd married. The cooper performed a sadistic rite of exorcism, aided by friends and even the unlucky woman's own cousins. They held her immobile while she was forced to swallow a noxious concoction of milk, piss, and chicken excrement, and then placed her naked body above the hearth fire, instructing her to fly away up the chimney. However, neither torture proved sufficient to banish the pretender and restore the cooper's mortal bride. So, the very next night, and again with the assistance of friends and family, the husband drenched the poor woman in lamp oil and set her ablaze with a hot brand. Her charred corpse was found in a shallow grave barely even a quarter mile from their home, the bogie concluded. He stared a moment, looking down into the girl's eyes, and into all the places *behind* her eyes, to be sure that she'd understood.

When the sun rose, the fairies had all gone away, the revelers and the hairy, admonishing bogie, and many years passed before she saw any of them again. And no one knows that she is a fairy lady. No one alive, at least.

She keeps her secrets well, and in this day and age very few take note of her peculiarities or the way she always smells like a summer afternoon. Her neighbors have no cows to stop giving milk if she strays too near, and no chickens to stop laying. She lives at the edge of a great, glittering city, and the people there are far too busy and concerned with money and taxes, electronic gew-gaws and the price of gasoline, to worry about fairies. Whenever they might pause long enough to bother being afraid of anything, it's likely no more than bankruptcy or old age, cancer or the gay couple who moved in next door or, perhaps, an imam overheard praying the salat on a commuter flight. There is no more time in their lives for fairies and changelings than there is for dragons and wicked witches, and often the fairy lady marvels what good fortune she's had to be a changeling in so cynical and disentranced a time and place.

She lives alone, minding her own affairs, and the worst she ever receives is a suspicious, sidelong glance or a rude whisper on the bus. When she's noticed at all, the busy, preoccupied people merely assume that this strange woman is most likely the victim of some mental illness, and, after all, there are pills, and worthy, tax-deductible charities, and board-certified psychologists, so it is nothing with which they need concern themselves.

But even here, and even now, there are bound to be inconvenient exceptions. And worse yet, exceptional exceptions, who are not content with whatever voguish delusions might presently be permitted to the omnipresent lunatic fringe. Those for whom the lure of crop circles, psychic healing, UFO abduction, ancient pyramids on Mars, intelligent design, and even the comforts of hoary astrology have all proven insufficient, and so they might reach back almost a century, finding, say, the "Cottingley Fairies" hoax more to their tastes than the latest schemes of the Church of Scientology. Frances Griffiths and Elsie Wright posing with their Art-Deco fay clipped from magazine pages, and it hardly matters that, as old women, the perpetrators of the fraud both confessed. Because, clearly, they were *paid* to confess, our inconvenient believer will declare, paid handsomely by unscrupulous television producers and the international conspiracy to hide The Truth.

And this is how it starts, with a single, and distinctly inconvenient, exceptional exception. His name is Howard Groesbeck, and he is a nervous man who lives alone in a shabby apartment and works, ironically, in a convenience store. He will only eat foodstuffs that come in metal cans, and will only drink water that has been bottled in Canada (anywhere in Canada will do; Quebec, Nova Scotia, Manitoba – it's all the same to him). His nights are spent looking at pornography on the internet, and his favorite color is brown. But, what is most important here is that at the tender age of thirteen (coincidence noted), he had the great misfortune to catch sight of a bogle while riding the subway. The bogle in question was wearing a knitted red cap, rather like a yarmulke, and was sitting next to an elderly Asian woman who was entirely too absorbed in her newspaper to notice the bogle. But Howard Groesbeck saw it quite clearly, and it saw him, as well. It winked. Ever since that day, he has been what the Irish cooper who murdered his wife might have called "pixy-led."

He first saw the fairy lady three days before midsummer, when she came into the convenience store to buy a Coke and a foil bag of something salty. In his sight, the glamour was no more than an odd glimmering about her head and shoulders. Where almost anyone else would have seen a pale but smartly dressed woman, with raven hair and sage-green eyes, he saw the changeling daughter of elfin royalty. For him, her eyes blazed so brightly that he almost had to turn away. Her skin had the appearance of the rough bark of an oak tree, except where it was obscured by patches of moss and small blue flowers. Her hair could have been spun at the behest of Rumpelstilzchen himself, and it hung almost down to the floor. When she paid him with a debit card, Howard saw that her ring finger was a third again longer than her middle finger, and that her nails appeared to have been chiseled from obsidian. She caught him staring at her, and though it had never happened before, the fairy lady knew, immediately, that this peculiar man was able, by some quirk of nature or nurture, to see through the magic to the heart of her.

She winked at him, because she didn't know what else to do. If she'd known about the bogle with the red cap, she might have only smiled.

Either way, Howard's fate became, in that instant of mutual recognition, inevitable. Though, one could say, instead, that it had become inevitable many years before, that day on the subway when he was thirteen. He spotted the fairy lady again a week later, coming out of a dry cleaner's only a few blocks from his apartment, and after that, he began to follow her, imagining that he was very clever and stealthy and that she had no idea whatsoever that she was being watched by the skinny, nervous man who'd clocked her at the convenience store. This wasn't the case, of course, and every time that he spotted her (having coffee at a Starbuck's, browsing in an occult bookshop, buying lime Jell-O, a can of sardines, and a bundle of asparagus at the market, standing on a crowded street corner, and so on) was a sighting that she had carefully orchestrated. Only that first was happenstance.

And, in the end – which, from another perspective might rightly be called the beginning – she allowed him to follow her from her apartment to a park at the edge of the city, where manufactured greenspace gave way to the real thing. There was a fairy ring of mushrooms here, a rough circle of fat toadstools, fly agaric, fleshy morels, and tiny white death caps sprouting from the leaf mold, clover, and dandelions. The centipedes often came to this ring to court moths and beetles, and the garden's circumference was tended by seven rabbits and a mole (though all knew well enough to avoid the center). It was late in August, not far from September, and almost twilight. The evening was filled with the chartreuse flicker of fireflies, and with the songs of katydids, interrupted only by a catbird, scolding somewhere in the trees.

> *Ye elves of hills, brooks, standing lakes and groves,*
> *And ye that on the sands with printless foot*
> *Do chase the ebbing Neptune and do fly him*
> *When he comes back; you demi-puppets that*
> *By moonshine do the green sour ringlets make,*
> *Whereof the ewe not bites, and you whose pastime*
> *Is to make midnight mushrooms...*

Howard Groesbeck, who had never read *The Tempest*, stood behind the bole of a maple for a while, thinking himself as good as invisible, certain that the fairy lady did not suspect she'd been followed. He'd found the courage to bring along his digital camera, hoping that it might capture what less exceptional human eyes could not see. Every other time he'd stalked the woman, the camera had remained in the bedroom closet. Now, it hung, forgotten, about his neck, dangling from its nylon strap, as his quarry stepped inside the ring of fungi and began, somewhat matter-of-factly, to undress. He did not guess that she removed her blouse and skirt, her bra and panties, her hose and shoes, *for* him, as that would have necessitated the knowledge that he was not half so clever as he believed himself to be. There is no need of fairy magic when a man's own ego will suffice to lead him astray.

Once she was entirely naked and her clothes folded in a neat bundle on the ground, the fairy lady looked over her shoulder, directly at the maple tree where Howard Groesbeck believed himself to be so shrewdly concealed. She only watched for a moment, allowing sufficient time for doubts to begin forming in his mind, time enough for his mouth to go dry, time for his already racing heart to double its tempo. She could smell the razor surge of adrenaline from where she stood, and she thought, briefly, that he might possibly turn and run. Which, admittedly, would have made the whole affair quite a bit more entertaining, so there was a small disappointment when he stayed put. She cleared her throat and called out his name. Not the name nailed to him at birth, the one he'd been baptized under, but another, secret name that even he had only heard once or twice at the corners of dreams. But he knew it now, and, hearing it, Howard Groesbeck almost wet himself.

"I see no sense hiding," the fairy lady told him. "You've gone to so much trouble, and come all this way into the wood, you shouldn't be cowering behind a tree. Let me see you, please."

He hesitated, but only for a fraction of a second, and then stepped out into the open.

"That's much better," she said, and, smiling, revealed to Howard the translucent, crystalline shards of her teeth.

"I can see you," he whispered, his voice trembling like the last light of the fading day. "I mean, I can see the *real* you. I *know* what you are."

"Yes," she said, and turned about to face him. "It's a relief, truth be told. Don't you think it must be a terribly lonely way to live, the way I do?"

It was something that he'd never paused to consider, a possibility that had never once occurred to him. Howard Groesbeck had imagined that this creature must surely come and go, at a whim, as she pleased, between the mortal world and the Hollow Hills. She must have countless daemon lovers, he'd thought, on more than one occasion. And he had followed her into this wild place at the edge of the park expecting to overhear unspeakable conversations, and hoping to witness her indulgence in profane sexual acts with a veritable bestiary of eldritch beings.

"They left me here, all alone," she said, and, on cue, sighed and glanced down at her bare feet.

"Alone?" he asked, his voice seeming impossibly frail, and he swallowed and licked his lips.

"I've not seen another of my race in almost seventeen years now," she replied. "They don't come to me when I call. And, as you can imagine, the sons and daughters of Eve tend to shy away from me. So, yes, it can get quite lonely at times." She looked up then, her green eyes become searchlights in the gathering gloom.

"Why?" he asked, and he dared to take one step towards the periphery of the circle. "Was it a punishment? Were you banished?"

"Banished," she said, and very nearly laughed. "Perhaps. But I could not say, as I do not know, and I don't hazard to guess the intentions of my Lord Finn Bheara, King of the Daoine Sidhe, and his wise court in the glittering halls beneath the hill of Knockma." It seemed to her that this was precisely the sort of nonsense that the nervous man from the convenience store expected to hear from a fairy changeling, and she congratulated herself for keeping a straight face.

"So, you're alone?" he asked again, as though the matter had not already been plainly stated and settled.

"Not anymore, I'm not," she told him, finding just the right tone for her voice, something that was not *quite* joy, but certainly more than common happiness. "Now I have *you*, don't I?" And no sooner had the words left her tongue, than Howard Groesbeck found himself standing *inside* the circle of mushrooms, close enough to the fairy lady that he could have touched her, if he'd dared. There was no recollection of having walked from the maple to the fairy ring, or of having stepped inside. But, even so, staring into her bottomless green eyes, the confusion struck him as no more than a passing trifle, and he let it go.

She took his right hand in her left, then, and leaned close, kissing him lightly on the lips. He found she tasted of nutmeg and bay. "You are a kindly soul," she said, "to come here and offer me your company so freely." Hearing this, a pair of goblins hiding in a nearby thicket of green briar and blueberries almost spoiled her careful masquerade by snickering and farting and noisily snapping their twiggy fingers together. She ignored them, and, near as she could tell, the man from the convenience store hadn't even heard the commotion.

"I should probably be going," Howard Groesbeck muttered, slurring and speaking the words the way a sleepwalker talks when questioned. "I'm working the late shift tonight."

"They won't mind," she said, "if you stay with me a little longer," and, unexpectedly, Howard found himself agreeing.

"You've told no one else about me?" she asked, and when he said that he hadn't, she knew straight away that he was telling the truth. Indeed, there was so little genuine guile about this man, she thought, it was almost hard to believe he was human born.

"And you told no one you were coming here?" she asked.

"Of course not," Howard told the fairy lady. "They would have laughed at me."

"Yes," she agrees, "I believe they would have," and with that, she plunged the sharpened tines of a shed deer's antler deep into his belly and twisted it sharply, first to one side and then the other. Though she did nothing whatsoever to dull his pain, he didn't so much as flinch. The man from the convenience store stood stock still for the disemboweling, his eyes not drifting from her own. This surprised her, and she gave him another kiss for taking it so well, when surely he *must* have hoped the night would go another way entirely. She cradled him in her arms as his life drained away into the soil to feed the hungry toadstools and the earthworms and a ravenous host of brownies hiding just below the sod. The light in his eyes faded slowly, and he smiled while the fairy lady helped herself to no small portion of his liver. It was a delicacy she'd tasted all too infrequently, and she was grateful to this man for not having struggled. She might even have felt a twinge of regret, were she capable, so peaceful was his face as death folded itself around him.

"Close your eyes," she said, and he did. "Sleep here, and I will visit, from time to time."

There was no need to dig a grave, as so little remained of him when she was done. She left only a scatter of bones, gnawed and broken open to reach the marrow inside. When she'd had her fill, she let the brownies crawl up from their subterranean nests and lick her hair and body clean. Then she dressed, and walked back through the park to the city that has far too many things to worry about to be bothered with fairies. No one knows that she is a fairy lady. No one alive, at least. No one who is only a human man or woman. She returns to him, as she said she would, on the evenings that suit her fancy. She finds a weathered bit of shin bone in amongst the clover, or a scrap of skull that has not yet rotted away, and with it she bids him to rise and draws him forth from the ground there inside the ring of mushrooms, to dance with her beneath the moon and the stars and the lascivious eyes that watch from every corner of the night-bound wood. She gives him a new body woven not from blood and sinew, but from the earth, from roots and bugs and fallen leaves. She shapes his face from clay, trying as best she can to remember its angles, but recalling it less and less as time goes by. She gives him eyes she's stolen from jaybirds, or a stray dog, or settles for two quarters from her coin purse. And never yet has the expression of awe faded from this rough simulacrum of his lost countenance, awe and delight and comprehension.

She kisses his lips, which are usually provided by convenient and agreeable garden slugs. Sometimes, she allows him to peer through the glamour that she guards more closely now, though usually it is only the pale, raven-haired woman with sage-green eyes that the ghost of Howard Groesbeck meets when he awakens. No matter. He knows the fairy woman wears the mask.

Lullaby of Partition
and Reunion

The moments themselves have become threads, and the threads have become tangled as the spool turns, reeling them out. The spool, I see, is time, and the threads are moments thrown free, unwound, and then left to dangle, to fray, to snarl one into the other until the integrity of each individual filament is lost. Together, they become something incoherent, and, yet also, something surpassing the need for mere coherence. We close our eyes, or I only close mine, and here I am trying foolishly to tease a single thread free again. You may as well call this action *memory* as to call it anything else. The spool turns, and days and words, similes and metaphors wrap, hopelessly, one about the other, all but indistinguishable. I can hear you speaking quietly in a sunlit room that smells of the cracked leather of old books, and of crumbling pages, and I think this is the first time that we ever talked. If this is the first time, then it may have all begun with the Norns, and, as you talk, you show me illustrations by Arthur Rackham and Johannes Gehrts and Ludwig Burger. Three woman seated or standing together among the gnarled roots of the World Ash, weaving fate, and you tick off their names one by one, as though I'm listening. I *hear* you, and I do hear you well enough that the moments are captured to then be wound about the spool and then *unwound* and matted into this grand tangle with all the rest. I am hearing the words spilling from your thin lips, but it is hard to think clearly of anything but that bright shimmer of auburn hair, a few strands of which have pulled free of your ponytail and now frame the pale mystery of your face. We sit together in the library, and your eyelids have been stitched shut, though I cannot see that this is proving any sort of inconvenience as you turn the crisp, dry pages and smile for me and breathe out hushed enthusiasm. "We are twined," you say. "We are twined, all of us, but some *twinings* are more intimate than others. We are bound, and there is no unbinding, not in this existence, nor any that may come, or that may already have been." But my fingers pick restlessly at the skein, never leaving well enough alone, and I lose the library and the three ladies and Arthur Rackham. I lose *you*, too, for a moment. It is a dazzling moment, laced with that terrible brittleness that precedes genuine panic. I pull another thread free, rolling it between thumb and forefinger, and *this* one here is a night in Boston, at the Kidder Smith Gallery, after our long, chilling walk in the snow along Newbury Street. There are severe black pedestals to support the tiny sculptures, and you're telling me that you met the artist when you were in Tokyo last year. I know that you have never been to Tokyo, but I like the sound of the lie, so I don't contradict you. "They are beautiful," you say, and this *is* true. The dolls have been sculpted from polymer clays, and a very few have been cast in bronze. Not one of these manufactured women is more than seven inches tall. On each black pedestal there are two figurines, although that is not precisely true. On each black pedestal stand two figurines caught in the act of becoming one. Unless the eye and mind assumes the process is one of unbecoming, and then they have been caught in the process of division. You're talking, in whispers, about Eve and the *Midrash Rabbah*, the first man and woman created as a single hermaphroditic organism, and I point out that these figurines are all female. You laugh, and we move along to the next black pillar and the next fusing or dividing pair. "Did you ever imagine that you had a twin," you say, leaning close and whispering directly into my left ear. "Only, something happened, and your twin was lost." I'd never told you that, and it makes me angry for a second or two, hearing you say those things aloud, as though, somehow, you've stolen secret thoughts when I was distracted by these tiny women. "Does it frighten you?" and I allow your question to fill the space between us, unanswered, forcing you to continue. "Fear of disillusion, or assimilation? Becoming less or more than what you presently are?" I bend close to have a better look at the sculpture, not replying right away. I don't want you to think that I'm easy. I don't want to turn and see smug satisfaction in your eyes, to have guessed so much (though, I might have confessed it all, and then forgotten; I am certainly open to that possibility). The two tiny women have skin that is the color of the skin of an unripe apricot. The woman on the left has black hair, while the woman of the right has hair so fair it makes me think, again, of the snow piling up outside the gallery. They lean towards one another, hands on hips, hands on shoulders, but it is impossible to discern precisely where one ends and the other begins. Fingers have sunken into malleable flesh, or fingers have yet to manifest. The foreheads of the two women touch, and here, too, they are one, and white hair and crow-black hair is as snarled as all these moments that have become tangled threads. The two women, leaning together, bring to mind the letter A, and I almost tell you this. But you're talking again, having apparently decided that no response to your questions are presently forthcoming. "They remind me of the letter A," you say, speaking a little louder now, and I nod and gaze down at the sculpture. I've only just begun to comprehend – at this moment, within the weave of this strand – what has been set in motion, and so your words are more startling than they ought to be. I fail to grasp the inappropriateness of my anger and the sense of violation. I want to raise my hands and search my scalp for the window you must have put there in my sleep. It would be smooth, glass or Lucite, skillfully hidden, invisible unless one goes looking for it, a window into all my thoughts. "They spent time together in a sensory deprivation tank," you tell me, and I realize I must be farther along this thread than I'd thought, because I'm not sure who you mean. I ask, and you reply, "The sculptor and her lover. That's how this phase of her work began, this systematic deconstruction of individuality. So, they *are* fusing." I want to touch the tiny women in front of me, thinking that perhaps my groping fingers could find answers and points of contact undetectable by my eyes alone. "Her lover," you say, "a woman from Copenhagen, a painter, she had a sort of nervous breakdown, afterwards." And then, by unspoken agreement, we move along down that narrow white space, the gallery's throat, to the next pair. On the wall above and behind the sculpture is a small white card printed with the words, "The Love of Souls." I read it aloud, and you inform me that the title was possibly borrowed from a painting by a Belgian symbolist named Jean Deville. "He founded *Le Salon d'Art Idealiste*," you continue, knowing that I lack your knowledge of art history, and so *also* knowing that this means next to nothing to me. I want to accuse you of showing off and lingering on trivia, but I know better. No strand emerging from off the spool is genuinely trivial. So, instead, I stand and stare at "The Love of Souls," and you stand so close behind me I can feel the heat from your body. Or I only imagine that I can. I am fairly certain, though, that the two figurines on the pedestal before me are meant to represent the same two persons as those on the previous pedestal. The black-haired woman and the fair, and I wish I knew what the artist and her girlfriend look like. I wish I knew their faces. How literal has the sculptor been, in working through the aftermath of the experiences you have described? Thinking this, I feel suddenly like a voyeur, and I am sure that you see me blush, even though your eyelids are still sewn shut. On the pedestal there is a crow and a white dove, or a lump of coal to contrast with freshly fallen snow. Simple comparisons spring to mind (you have, on more than a single occasion, chided my fondness for metaphor, calling it an intellectual crutch, and I suspect you are correct). Two women, sitting now back to back, though, in truth, they share a single back. A single spine, bifurcating at the neck, affording each her own set of cervical vertebrae. The fair woman's head is tilted forward at such an angle that her chin almost rests against the intersection of her clavicles and manubrium. In contrast, the dark-haired woman's head is raised, as if gazing at the snowy night sky hidden by the gallery ceiling. The fair woman's legs are splayed open in an immodest V, revealing her vagina, while her companion's legs are pulled up close to her chest, her arms wrapped around them, fingers linked. "I don't think I like seeing these," I say. "I think I am not meant to see them." You apologize for having dragged me out into the storm, and then for suggesting the installation, and I say no, you couldn't have known that these pieces would make me uncomfortable. "Anyway, that's the proper function of art, isn't it?" I ask you. "To unsettle us?" and I force my eyes to loiter on these Lilliputian figures, Siamese twins by different mothers. "I don't pretend to know the proper function of art," you say, but there is only the faintest bit of derision in your voice, just enough to make me wish that I'd said something else, instead. The spool turns, and the threads become so hopelessly tangled I sincerely wish that I were able to stop picking at them and simply accept the fact of this unsightly mess. I pull one that seems dyed a sort of indigo, and this is the night we first made love, then got stinking drunk on Pernod Anise. This is your cluttered loft, only a few blocks from Harvard Square. We lie together on the floor, and I'm telling you about the time I used a needle and thread to sew the fingers and thumb of my left hand together, sliding the needle all but painlessly into and through the uppermost layers of skin. I thought you would laugh, but you don't. I'm *never* very good at making you laugh, even when we're drunk and stupid from sex. "It didn't hurt," I say, and you reply, "Would that have made any difference?" I release the indigo thread, and, in its place, choose one the color of lichens or dead moss. I only tug very, very gently, hoping for no more than a glimpse, a glimpse at most, but I really should know better. I tug gently, but quite a lot of the green thread comes free of the tangle. "You'll tell me if I hurt you? You'll use the signal. You have to promise that you will," and I do promise, even if my assurance is a lie. It *should* be painful, and I have, over the months, finally come to comprehend this. What we are seeking, it will not come without discomfort. It isn't meant to. You use surgical thread and a twelve-gauge stainless steel needle, implant grade, and I sit up very straight and watch myself in the bathroom mirror as you work. The latex gloves on your fingers are soon red with my blood. There is more pain than I'd anticipated, as the needle enters and exits, exits and enters, but I don't raise my hand to stop you. I need to *know* this sensation, if there is ever to be any progress towards a goal. And, besides, soon enough the rush of endorphins is making me giddy. We leave my mouth sewn shut for almost five hours. And then you snip the scabby thread with a pair of embroidery scissors. You sterilized them in boiling water and rubbing alcohol, and I have begun to worry that your fear of infection will hold us back. The first words I say when I can speak

again are "Thank you." And you respond, "You're very welcome."
I choose an orange thread now, the gaudy, rich orange of a
tangerine. I choose a tangerine thread from this varicolored
complication, and when I touch it, you're asking me again if I ever
suspected I'd have a twin, someone who was lost, someone I only
almost remember, but sometimes seem to miss more than I can
endure. "Isn't that a fairly common neurosis?" I ask. "Like
thinking that you were adopted, but your parents kept it from
you?" I stare at you a moment. And *in* this moment, you are the
most beautiful woman I have ever seen. No, you are the most
beautiful *person*. "The sense that something is missing," you say,
prompting me. "That something has been *stolen*." I nod, and
speaking hardly louder than a whisper, I reply, "And I have always
felt alone. There's never been a time when I haven't felt alone,
except..." But I don't finish the sentence, and you don't push me.
You change the subject, as you often do upon realizing how near
you've come to the truth. "My mother cried for a week when she
learned I was a lesbian," you say, and it makes me laugh, because
my mother never shed a tear, but said only that she'd always known
I was a mistake. "She actually *said* that, a mistake?" you ask. "She
said worse," I tell you. I select a new thread, one that is almost the
same shade of brown as your eyes, and I loop it snugly about my
index finger. The spool turns, though there is no spool, reeling
out these moments I have chosen to interpret as threads. Here we
are having coffee, and I wish that I could recollect the name of the
café. There is nothing at all remarkable about this thread, and so I
treasure it, but almost immediately move along to another. "No,"
you say. "I'm not shitting you, this is truly bizarre," and you stare
out the window above my bed at a different thunderstorm than
the one we watched, or will watch, from the nameless café. Beads
of rain streak the glass, and when the thunderclaps are loud
enough, the pane rattles in its aluminum frame. "You remember
that I said the girlfriend had some sort of nervous breakdown,
right?" And so I know you're talking about the sculptor whose
tiny women we saw on display at the Kidder Smith Gallery the
previous January. "Yes," I answer. "I remember." There's a flash of
lightning, reflected on your face and the walls, and you wait for
the thunder to come and go before continuing. "She became

utterly obsessed," you say. "After that business in the sensory
deprivation tank, she became obsessed with the thought that her
lover was in fact her twin *sister*, and not only that. She believed
that they'd been conjoined at birth and surgically separated
thereafter. She saw the figurines, the same ones that we saw, and
she took this as a sort of confirmation, that the sculptor knew, as
well." I believe that you meant to deliver this story as though it
were a joke, an anecdote so weird that I would be forced to laugh,
but already the tone of your voice has changed. We are still three
weeks away from the night you sew my lips together, but you know
well enough what's coming. It began with your questions, after
all. Yours were the prying fingers, there at the start, and I'm quite
certain I'd have remained silent, otherwise. That's not blame, by
the way, because there is no blame in me. It's just that these threads
and moments are become so tangled now, I'd at least like to try to
be clear about my feelings. "Obsessed," I say, and you nod and tell
me that while the sculptor slept, the girlfriend used Krazy glue to
fuse their bodies together. She smeared it on their legs and chest,
their breasts and bellies, even the palms of their hands. She
managed to glue the left side of her face to the right side of her
partner's face. A friend found them the next morning, and called
an ambulance. I don't ask what procedure or solvent was required
to separate the two, or how the girlfriend accomplished all this
without waking her victim, but you add that the sculptor has
obtained a restraining order, though she isn't pressing criminal
charges. "How very kind of her," I say, and the sarcasm and
bitterness in my voice takes me aback. I'm not sure you even caught
it. It was only a small bitterness, after all, like a hint of unsweetened
chocolate or citrus zest. And I release the thread, so that the
moment dissolves, which is not at all the same as its being forgotten.
I cannot presently explain the difference, so you must take my
word that the two things are not the same. You *must* take my
word, as *I* must pick at this weave with nails chewed down to the
quick. My cuticles bleed more often than not. This next thread is
as grey as raw oysters, and almost as slippery. Even when I hold it
tightly as I may, it slithers through my fingers. I am holding a
photostat of my birth certificate, which, if I admit its authenticity,
denies the dreams and nightmares that began when I was still a

child, and the loneliness that began sometime shortly thereafter. I don't hold it very long. It slips away, as mere facts always slip away when truth is what we're after. The spool turns like a spiral galaxy, like a Ferris wheel, like the moon going round the Earth to swaddle it in months and tides and other real or imagined lunar rhythms. That thread has left my fingers slick and sticky, and I fumble for any purchase among the labors of Urðr, Verðandi, and Skuld. "You keep picking like this, it's never going to heal," you laugh, then open antique books and show me pictures of those three maidens, watering the gnarled roots of Yggdrasill or busy at their spinning. "You say that as if I have a choice," I reply, and you don't answer me. I clutch at a moment, or a strand, stained as red as pomegranates, and as the strand comes free of the rest, I recognize this particular day and this particular place and this particular memory. You would interject here, hastening to add that it is hardly more than a figment from some restless night's struggle between my conscious and unconscious mind. You know I don't want Freud or Jung, but you'd persist. This thread has countless duplicates, and so I've lost count of how often I've described it to you. Invariably, you scowl and sigh and look away. "I am only seeking wholeness," I whisper. "Reunification, and an end to this goddamned quarantine. *That's* the source of the dream." And you say something appropriately disapproving, perhaps even as mild as "Wishful thinking." We do not argue. You are not angry. You are filled with all the same desires and emptinesses as am I; you have said that many, many times. It is only in how we might seek resolution, or even the *hope* of resolution, that we differ. "Yes, it's a dream," I admit. "But it's a *true* dream," and I know you aren't about to contradict me, even though my eagerness makes you uncomfortable. So: here, below the ever-weaving Norns and the silver spindle of Heaven, my arms are filled to overflowing with this motley of moments that have been transmuted into innumerable threads. You lean back against the nest of pillows and the cast-iron headboard and listen while I talk. You don't interrupt, just as I have not interrupted you when you've put your own dreams into words. I offer a silent prayer to a god I don't believe in that you won't cry this time, but I know you probably will. And then I say that we were lying here, on this same bed, and when I lay my hand upon your waist the distinction between the two was lost. We'd become as malleable, as pliant, as clay, and my palm and fingers vanished painlessly. You leaned forward then, and you were smiling the bright way you smile whenever you are truly, genuinely happy, and I see that as our nipples brushed, that flesh was also merged. No, not clay, I tell you, not clay, but waxworks. Somehow, we have been cut apart and molded into this masquerade of two, but finally that error is being put right. You press your forehead to mine, so that I melt into you, or you melt into me, not unlike the sculpture of the fair woman and the dark-haired woman, the one that reminded me of the letter A. Our frontal lobes flow together, and so our minds begin to commingle and the need for speech is gone. I say that I was afraid, and that the fear surprised me, but then it passed and I could not even recall why I'd been frightened. You pressed your hips and groin to mine. All melds together – pubic hair, labia, our clits, the bones of our pelvises, skin and fat and a host of muscles: *adductor magnus, adductor longus, adductor brevis, illiacus,* the *tensor fascia latæ,* etc. and etc. Nerves are fused, and, simultaneously, in perfect unison, we share a sensation that transcends any orgasm. I cry out, while you bite your lip and remain silent. You are kind, listening, not to point out that I have ceased to describe the dream in past tense, but have begun relating it as though it is occurring *as* I speak. And then you kiss me, and our lips fuse, and now we are one, and now we are whole, a closed system, an odd sort of Ouroboros, the perfected Gemini, freed finally from the tyranny of all former segregations. Except, I remark, that our tongues remain independent, and yours moves playfully across the roof of my mouth. I fall silent, and from your nest of pillows, you run your fingers through my hair and say that it is a pretty dream, an exquisite fairy tale. There's not a trace of condescension in your voice. "No one would ever separate us," you say, "not ever again." And, having reached the end of my dream, I lie as still as I can, listening to the soothing cadence of your heartbeat, and listening also to the clock ticking on the bedside table and hearing traffic down on the street. I remind you that you'll be late for work if you don't get dressed soon, and the pomegranate thread pulls free of my grip, eager to rejoin the tangle. I start to reach for another strand, then hesitate, and for a time that might be very long or the most minute fraction of a second, I try to contemplate the whole. This *tapestry*. That is, if only it were a little more ordered. And lying here, in the fading warmth left on the cotton sheets by your departed body, I acknowledge the present futility of grasping the totality that is You and Me and Us. I settle for my tawdry threads, uncoiling, which I finger like the worn beads of a rosary. Tonight, you have promised that you'll use the needle again, and so the day stretching out before me seems as wide as an ocean, or a desert, or the sky.

Derma Sutra (1891)

And further, by these, my son, be admonished:
of making many books there is no end; and
much study is a weariness of the flesh.

Ecclesiastes 12:12 (King James Version)

Following the 40ᵗʰ Parallel of Latitude across the western frontiers, trace a straight line over any cartographer's labors, and the buff-colored plains and cottonwood groves lead directly, inevitably, to this coal-smoke and cog-grind metropolis kneeling at the craggy feet of the Front Range of the Chippewans. And, by night, from her high garret windows overlooking the Littleton Row stockyards, this tall, pale woman watches the city, the wavering gaslights and the orange hellfire of half a hundred great Bessemer converters. Though many of the people of Cherry Creek – both the citizens and those only passing through, the white men and red Indians and negroes and coolies – have seen her, there are none here who know her name, for never has she *worn* a name – at least not the sort bestowed by mortal men. She was old millenia before the cacophony of this clattering, modern Industrious Age, and she suspects that she will still be watching when this age is done and consigned to history and the *next* age begins. She peers out through heavy velvet draperies, pressing her face to the glass and wishing, as often she wishes, for even the briefest glimpse of the stars and moon veiled by the unending smokestack exhalations of smog and steam. Whatever beliefs the city might tout on Founder's Day and hold dear regarding purpose, commerce, and progress, *she* knows better, that this perpetual cloud has been erected so that humanity might at last lose sight of, and forget, its insignificance before the glittering Vault of Heaven.

There is a noise behind her, a small sound, as of someone stirring fitfully in troubled dreams, and she turns away from the tall windows. Without her hand to hold them apart, the cranberry drapes swing closed again, and so her world contracts down to only the garret and the bed and her guest tangled in the sheets. There is no gaslight permitted here, but only the kinder illumination of a few beeswax candles, and the nameless woman smiles to see her guest is waking. The woman on the bed was, until quite recently, the nearest thing she had to an adversary, because some are not content to let secrets remain secrets, or have so lost themselves in cul-de-sac delusions of right and wrong, fanciful dichotomies of good and evil, that they stray, finally, into the arms of that very thing they would strive to avoid. Or defeat. In her time, the woman lying here, sweating and tangled in the sheets, has styled herself a holy warrior, a crusader, and has imagined in this arrogance that the night and all its inhabitants feared her even as they might fear the morning or a cold iron spike, a hawthorn stake or the glint of a silver blade.

And, to be sure, it cannot be gainsaid that the guest has done some mean bit of mischief with those hands. Once, she used a tincture of strychnine and nightshade to poison a German horologist she thought to be a werewolf. He wasn't. She has, on innumerable occasions, exhumed the blameless dead and rolled them over to lie face down in their coffins, then pierced their lifeless hearts with spears. Ten years ago, she made her way to East Azerbaijan and a necropolis deep beneath the city of Tabriz. There she found and shattered a clay tablet dating back almost five centuries to the reign of Shah Ismail I, believing, without a doubt, that she would thereby bind a powerful and renowned demon. Instead, she set free that selfsame being, and then watched helplessly as it brought plague and madness and slow death to town after town, village after village. And somehow, even *then*, her faith in her own rectitude did not waver; indeed, she only grew that much more zealous, more determined to seek out and exterminate all those she deemed unwholesome and malign.

In Boston, Philadelphia, and then New Amsterdam, she founded chapters of an occult and esoteric society devoted unwaveringly to her cause. Thereafter, she was no more a lone fanatic, but a commander of many likeminded fools and psychopathics, true believers and aspiring martyrs. So it was, at last, that her depredations could no longer be ignored. An example would have to be made, the sort of example that needs be made but once. A message that would instill futility and despair in even in the unquestioning, impassioned minds of such a self-proclaimed "Army of Light." There was a lottery – which is another story – to determine to whom would fall the responsibility of sending this message, and the nameless woman from Cherry Creek won the honor.

"I thought you would sleep another night away," she says, smiling a guileless smile, and goes to stand beside the bed. "Can you hear me, Miss? Or are you still lost and wandering in dreams?" Her guest only moans the softest moan for a response, and the pale woman glances to the slate-topped bedside table cluttered with its assortment of laudanum bottles and morphine-tainted syringes.

"I know too well the sweet, forgetful lure of sleep," she tells her guest, her prize, this fallen prophet from the East. "But we cannot ever surrender ourselves wholly to the kindly embrace of Lord Hypnos and his Oneiroi, lest we forsake all that we are when waking. And *you*, Miss, you would be forsaking so very, very much, for such great hopes ride upon your shoulders."

Her guest's eyelids flutter, almost opening, and the pale, nameless woman bends close to wipe away a string of spittle from her guest's lips and chin. "Wake up," she says, speaking now more firmly than before. "For the moment, dear Tess, the time for sleeping is over and done. It will come again, soon enough, but first..." And, with that, the tall, pale woman lightly slaps her guest's face, and the woman gasps and opens wide her drowsy brown eyes. For a time, there's room in her eyes for only confusion and the haze of the narcotics, only the disorientation and surprise of one waking from a long quiescence to unaccustomed surroundings.

The garret fills up with a slow, dull whir, the windy drone of propellers as one of the big airships comes in low overhead, making its final approach to the Arapahoe Station dirigible terminal. The nameless woman gazes towards the peaked ceiling, then back to her guest, and she smiles, revealing recurved incisors and hooked eyeteeth grown as sharp as some anatomist's dissecting tool. She sits down on the edge of the bed and waits patiently for the racket to fade. The odd sense of stillness that follows has always intrigued her, the illusion that the passing airships leave a great silence, like a wake of calm spilled forth from the drive shafts turning the screws, from those anthracite-fueled engines. In fact, of course, it only, briefly, makes the usual din from the stockyards and the city's background soundscape appear inconsequential by comparison.

She slaps the woman named Tess again, somewhat harder than before, and this time the blow elicits more than a gasp. The guest raises her right hand to shield her face and fend off further attacks. "Please," she begs, though her mouth and tongue are so dry, so disused from her long sleep, that her voice is hardly more than a raw whisper.

"Please?" the nameless woman asks, feigning quite a bit more surprise than she actually feels. A creature such as she does not long survive without gaining considerable skill at the breaking and disassembly of even the most resilient of wills. "I was not aware you were acquainted with so base a word as *please*. How...unlikely... that the formidable and righteous Stephanie Brockett would actually have need of *please*. And, what's more, should lower herself to speak it to the likes of *me*."

"Mock me..." the guest begins, then trails off, her mouth too parched to complete the thought. The nameless woman offers her a glass of tepid water, and holds it to her lips while Tess Brockett manages to swallow a few small mouthfuls. Then the glass is taken away and returned to the table with the needles and vials and laudanum bottles, and the nameless woman uses her long white fingers to gently brush strands of Tess' greying russet hair from her drug- and sleep-addled face.

"How long has it been?" she asks.

"Why? Does it feel as though it has been very long?" the nameless woman replies, still smiling. And, after a second, she adds, "No longer than was necessary."

Tess Brockett's left hand strays to her bare right breast, and the nameless woman laughs.

"Don't you bother worrying about *that*. And don't you flatter yourself, either. Your heart still ticks regular as good clockwork. It was never your life I wanted, dear."

"Then what…what *have* you stolen?" the guest croaks, the zealot, this lottery prize spread out on folds of fine Irish linen the color of frost. "What *have* you taken?"

The nameless woman stops fussing with Tess Brockett's hair and makes a greater show of looking offended than is strictly necessary. "Why, nothing," she replies. "I have taken nothing at all from you. In point of fact, I have gone to some conspicuous lengths to *give* you something for your troubles. Recompense, you might say, remuneration for your time, which I well know is valuable."

And there is another moment or two or three as the nameless woman's words lie bitter upon the mind of Tess Brockett, a few heartbeats before she finally permits her eyes to stray from the creature's derisive face and glances down at her own naked body and what has been made of it. The elaborate tapestry she has become, her skin tattooed with glyphs from the darkest arts of ancient races, with incantations written in Mycenaean Greek and various other Proto-Hellenic languages, power and spite bound in at least a score of forgotten or rarely uttered tongues. Indeed, it seems that hardly an inch of her has been spared, and in many places the tattooed characters have somehow been layered one upon another with such exquisite skill that there has been no blurring together or loss of any of their crucial definition.

"It's what you came for, is it not?" the nameless woman asks, wondering now if Tess Brocket will scream, or if, perhaps, the sight of herself transformed and permanently scarred with these blasphemies has so undone her sanity that she will never scream again. "The unexpurgated text of *De Vermiis Mysteriis*, if not the book itself, which I have kept safe for so many long lives of man," and then she reads aloud a passage worked into the skin just below Tess' navel – "*Tibi, magnum Innominandum, signa stellarum nigrarum et bufaniformis Sadoquae sigilim.*" The words drip poisonously from her claret tongue, as though the organ were fashioned to that end alone, and now there is another sound from the sky, and one may fancy that vast and leathery wings have begun to beat at the sulphurous, furnace-stained clouds.

"That has always seemed to my ears such poetry," the name-less woman says, when the beating of those wings has faded away to no more than loathsome echoes. "One marvels at the rever-ence of its author, to have worked so hard at the cadences, when a cruder syntax would no doubt have sufficed. Old Tsathoggua and his ilk have never struck me as the sort of deities to have such pretty sentiments lavished upon them. But, then, maybe the subtleties of their glory are lost on me." She lays a hand on Tess Brockett's belly, hiding away the passage she has just spoken, and several others, as well.

Her guest's thin lips are trembling almost uncontrollably now, and only by a tremendous dint of will does she retain the lucidity required to speak to the one who has done this unspeakable thing to her, who has marked not only her flesh, but the very roots of her soul.

"Not enough," she says, "to simply kill me and be done with it," and this earns another toothsome smile from the nameless, pale woman.

"No, no, *no*. That would have been such a terrible waste of opportunity, don't you *see*? Which isn't to say there were not a few deaths involved. The three Chinamen I hired to do the work, for example. I could not very well suffer them to live, not after having each read so much of the grimoire. Not to mention a few of the choicer *Sathlattae* from the fabled *Cthäat Aquadingen*, which I am well enough aware you have also long sought to destroy. You don't allow ordinary *men* to read and copy, and possibly commit to memory, such precious, potent lines and then send them back out into the world. That would have been careless, and I have been trusted not to be careless with this matter, Miss."

"Trusted," Tess Brockett murmurs, and the nameless woman is pleased to hear the rapid fraying of that voice, and knows that those who charged her with this duty will not be disappointed.

"Most certainly," she says. "Never, I think, have I won any more solemn task than your own transformation. Any common diabolist or would-be necromancer may mumble a few unholy words, can wield such crude instruments as knives or hot brands to kill and maim and unhorse purity. But there's no art to be found there. No, these undertakings require painstaking consideration,

and patience, too, if one is to so entirely corrupt the flesh and..."
and she pauses, drawing it out, lending a touch more drama,
searching for the least sincere turn of phrase. "...well, one as previously *unsullied* as yourself."

Tess Brockett's eyes drift from her tattooed flesh, and back to
the smiling countenance of the nameless woman.

"I do not dare to ever waste irony, Miss," she says. "Not
irony so perfectly sublime as this," and now the hand laid upon
Tess' belly moves a few inches nearer the carefully shaved cleft of
her sex. Even that secret recess of her body has not been spared
this desecration, and the spiraling, meandering patterns of text
worked into her by the slain artisans create the impression that
her vagina is bleeding maledictions. Though most of the tattoos
covering her body have been executed in shades of grey and black,
blues and greens, a sanguine assortment of reds have been used
between her legs.

"Please," Tess whispers. "Please don't."

"There's that word again," the nameless woman says, and she
does not withdraw her hand. "I truly think it's a sort of disappointment, Miss, hearing that word from your lips. I wonder, when you
burned that house in Nueva España, you and your merry band of
firebugs, when you painted the skies above San Agustín with the
glow of that particular funeral pyre, did the women you...what's
the word? purified...beg as *you* beg now?"

Tess Brockett does not take her eyes away from the woman's
hand, which has settled there upon her crotch like some strange
white insect. "They were *not* women," Tess protests.

"Really now, were they *not*? Did they not also have hearts and
loves and hopes, feelings and souls and desires all of their very own?"

"They were *witches*," Tess Brockett replies, beginning to
shiver at the woman's icy touch, and perhaps also at the horror of
her own fate. "They were not – "

" – spreading their legs for the right gods?" the nameless
woman asks, interrupting her.

Tess struggles to find the requisite volition to shut her eyes,
so no matter what she has to feel, what she has to hear, or know is
true, at least she'll not have to see what has been done, what is still
being done as the creature begins massaging the button of her clit

with one cold index finger. But it's not there to find, that volition. It's been stripped away along with everything else, that strength, and so she watches.

"Witches," she says again. "The concubines of demons, a den of murderesses, tribades…"

"Tribades," the nameless woman sighs, the word leaking from ashen lips, those two syllables almost as boreal as her touch. "Does that get you wet, Miss, thinking on the pleasures they took from one another, needing the cock of no man to find ecstasy?" The nameless woman's eyes glint iridescent hues of crimson and gold in the candlelight as she speaks. "Tell me plain, Tess, why is it you have never married, being the virtuous, proper woman you are? Why is there no *Mister* for thee, Miss?"

Tess grits her teeth together that they will not begin to chatter and click as the stinging chill spreading out from the nameless woman's fingers works its way through muscle, bone, and sinew.

"Just never had the time to settle yourself down, I suppose," the nameless woman says, and she smiles (flashing those teeth again) and slips a finger over the moistened folds of Tess' tattooed labia. "Seems to me, though, an institution sacred as the holy union twixt a man and a woman, seems to *me*, Miss, even our saintly latter-day Jehanne d'Arc should not be deprived of so hallowed an honor. Or has the right man not come along? Could be, you drove a stake in his chest, or sent him off to rot in some Union or English prison. Or…" and the finger pauses, momentarily lingering at the fragile folds of Tess Brockett's maidenhead. "…could it be, the right *man* is no man at all? Maybe, this night, we'll find out."

Stiffening, Tess replies, "There *will* come a day of judgment, beast, a day of final reckoning, even for you." And then she tries to begin reciting a prayer, a desperate petition for intervention and rescue, but she finds it is as though the words written upon her skin have wiped the stanzas of supplication from her memory.

"Will there be, indeed?" the pale and nameless woman asks, and with that, her intruding finger roughly tears and pushes aside the hymen, drawing blood and pain that pales in comparison to the glacial cold filling whatever remains of the woman who was once Tess Brockett. And the nameless woman finds the blood only eases her entry into that long neglected vestibule. "And what, then, of *you*? How will your angry, little god greet its most faithful servant, when it sees the abomination she has allowed herself to be fashioned into? Are you certain there is that much mercy inside your god, that much *compassion* for a poor, broken being whose very existence will now open doorways to insanity and agony and realms of unimaginable chaos?"

"What...?" Tess Brockett begins, then stops, her heart racing, pounding inside its osseous cage of ribs, her breath coming up short now as that finger explores the walls of her sex. "Beast," she gasps, shuddering, "What...would you *ever* know...of compassion?"

"A fair enough inquiry," the nameless woman replies, but then, rather than answering the question, leans down and begins lapping at Tess Brockett, an oddly prickling tongue greedily licking away blood from the torn hymen, along with the salty, pungent wine of vaginal fluids – the living elixir of sebum, sweat, cervical mucus, oviductal secretions, the liquors of the Skene's and Bartholin's glands, urea and squalene, lactic and acetic acids, pyridine, vinous aldehyde, and the juices leaking directly from the delicate membranes of the vagina. The nameless woman is a gourmand, a glutton, a connoisseur of *all* the flavors of female and male, and her prize's horror and repulsion at being so dined upon only enhances its already eloquent sapidity.

The nameless woman drinks long, and she drinks deep, and before she is sated, her teeth have drawn more blood than was afforded by a torn hymen, and Tess Brockett lies weeping and moaning, wracked by the violence of orgasms that transcend and negate any simple, human delectation. The air trapped inside the garret is pummeled again and again by her cries, delirious screams wrung so readily from out her dry larynx and her vocal cords that have lain still for so many days. And, too, the atmosphere below that roof brightens and dims, but not by any guttering of the beeswax pillars and tapers. Indescribable colors seep from the tattoos, glimmers of the nethermost extremes of the spectrum and so alien to the eyes of earthly beings, but colors none the less, and, moreover, colors that Tess' transformation has somehow disposed her to perceive. The incantations rise from her skin and twirl and swoop and coil into infinitely complex spirals, and, between her screams, she can hear the chanting of fiendish supplicants borne on interstellar breezes across incalculable gulfs of distance, time, and nonspacial, nontemporal dimensions.

In the minutes or hours that follow, as the dizzying heights and depths of Tess' euphoria, awe, revulsion, and shock gradually diminish to only an incidental roar behind her eyes, the nameless woman sits crouched there between her thighs. They might make a fitting portrait to hang on the wall of some Libertine's private brothelry, or the altar of those hidden cults that, even in this age of science and machines, worship at the feet of Dionysus or Discordia or kneel before the memory of the monstrous Great Old Ones. Or they might make a thing to be worshipped themselves. The nameless woman kneads creams and unguents into Tess' tattooed skin, and later, she'll explain to her prize how this skin must now be cared for, lest the ink begin to fade and the energies bound therein become uncontrollable. She felt that fleeting instant when the zealot fell and the crusader came to understand that she now numbered among the ranks of the *bête noires* she once hunted with such an insatiable fervor and such perfect conviction.

By the slowest of slow degrees, the nameless woman feels Tess Brockett rising up through strata of dream and delirium, her consciousness returning, and as it comes, expanding like a bubble of mephitic gas nearing the surface of a stagnant mere. What wakes is not what fell to sleep, if one can rightly call such a pell-mell, tumbling descent anything as prosaic as sleep. What wakes in the candlelit garret at the edge of the Littleton Row stockyards in Cherry Creek is a *novel* being, one who's been so exquisitely reforged that only the most general sort of resemblance to its former self remains. What wakes is unfathomable, and broken, and aroused to new purpose. The nameless woman knows that, in time, it will cast aside the name of Tess Brockett to choose another, or, like herself, this new incarnation will realize that it exists now beyond the necessity or appropriateness of human appellations.

What wakes opens eyes gone black as a collier's fingernails, black as bitumen, and the pale and nameless woman smiles her razor smile and blesses this daughter with a few lines recalled from a book of William Blake. "What the hammer?" she asks. "What the chain? In what furnace was thy brain? What the anvil? What dread grasp, dare its deadly terrors clasp?"

It watches the nameless woman for a time before it speaks with this voice could that still could pass for that of Tess Brockett, at least among undiscerning mortal ears or ears untrained to detect atrocity. The nameless woman sees clearly how this makes her triumph all the greater, for certainly it means that many more fools who will not know what has become of their shining knight errant until it is far too late for them to avoid the calamity to be visited upon them.

"*Maintenant vous savez?*" she asks the lovely creature coiled inside the husk of Tess Brockett. "*Pourquoi je ne vous a pas tué?*" Of the more recently devised tongues of man, the nameless woman has always found French the one most suited to victory, and to passion.

"*Je fais,*" it answers, that which is no longer the aging, embittered virgin kidnapped two weeks ago from the platform of the South Platte railroad depot by two Portuguese thugs in the employ of the nameless woman. Both the men are dead now, murdered – like the Chinese tattoo artists – by her own hands and then fed to a sty of convenient and insatiable sows. "But," this living embodiment of two profane books says, "I would hear *you* say it, for the timbre of your voice is unending revelation."

"Very well then, Miss," the nameless woman replies, but first she leans forward to once more kiss the cunt of this flawed and flawless vessel. Even that taste has been altered in the metamorphosis, and she wonders how many men – and women – will die from a single sip of the caustic nectar that now flows from between those southerly lips. "You have surely earned for thyself an indulgence or two."

The woman who was Tess Brockett laughs, and the shadows beyond the reach of the candlelight flinch.

"By your hand," the nameless woman says, "or, rather, by the hand of who you *were* before this fortuitous deliverance, many beyond reckoning have been dispatched. Those the world of piety and hypocrisy name wicked – shape shifters, strigoi, ghouls, blood drinkers, goblins and a host of fairy folk, the Children of Cain and the descendents of the Nephilim, all manner of sorcerers and practitioners of arts and alchemies deemed obscene by those who look to the Four Marks of the Church for their direction."

Another Gesellschaft zur Förderung der Luftschiffahrt dirigible passes over head, this one departing Cherry Creek and bound for the lush green lands beyond the parched plains, bound for the bustling cities of the East; the nameless woman waits until the noise of its turbines and props have faded to a distant, thrumming bumble before she continues.

"It's not that you weren't efficient," she says, "so long as your goal was merely the elimination of what you hated. But, in a more vital sense, your efficiency was an inexcusably wasteful means to your end. You chose – or could not see clear enough to *have* a choice – not to acknowledge that what can be slaughtered can also be converted. More work, true, I'll not deny thee that. And always some inherent risk that the conversion might not take, and so you'd have to kill your quarry, anyway. But to not even *try*, Miss, to ignore even the possibility…if you ask me, there is no true evil in all this sorry world more insidious than waste. Indeed, *all* evil may be deemed wasteful acts."

And as she listens, the tattoos clothing the vessel that held Tess Brockett have begun their writhing, coruscating dance again, and the nameless woman wonders how long it will be before their bearer has learned to marshal them to her bidding.

"Now, I could have killed you. Though that was neither my wish nor the undertaking with which I was cumbered. Your death would have been the merest flick of a wrist, or the pricking of my teeth upon thine previously frail throat. But in such an easy deed would have lain no glory and no genuine accomplishment. Most importantly, no *perversion*. She who lived as my enemy would have died as my enemy, and while an inconvenience would have been removed from my path and the paths of those whom I serve, and who serve me, there is a sense in which she would have won the contest. You know these things, of course, and you comprehend the truth of my words to the very core of your pneuma."

"I do, yes," Not-Tess replies, this sliver of the void wrapped all in passages transcribed both from necromancer Ludwig Prinn's *De Vermiis Mysteriis* and the equally direful *Cthäat Aquadingen* of some unknown Fourth-Century Germanic wizard, the sheath of her soul inscribed with calligraphy and runes, ideograms and eldritch symbols from Semitic, Gothic, Egyptian, Oriental, Arabian, and Persian *musteria*. "Never break what I can bend," she tells the nameless woman still sitting in the space between her legs.

"*Molto buon, il mio amore*," the nameless woman laughs, because of those various and recently contrived languages, she has always found Italian best suited to congratulatory pronouncements. "It may seem like a very simple lesson, like child's play, but look what was required for *you* to finally learn it. Any man or woman may exterminate. I can imagine few efforts that are, in the main, more effortless."

And staring into the glistening black eyes of her Creation, this delicate, indestructible Construct she will soon send out into the wide, wide world, the pale and nameless woman recalls seeing, only twenty years prior, flocks of passenger pigeons fully three miles from end to end, blotting out the sun above the plains, their wings bringing premature twilight to a noonday sky. Now, it is rare to see even a score of the birds at once. And, too, she recalls the vanished herds of shaggy bison, and a captive dodo she once saw in a private menagerie in Utrecht in 1628.

"Extermination does not now, nor will it *ever*, constitute our reason for being here," she says softly, but firmly, admiring the translucent blue-green ribbons of Minoan rising lazily from the breasts of her prize, whirling upwards towards the transverse beams bracing the garret ceiling, born aloft by the breath of their own being. "Let the idiot sons and daughters of Epimetheus pull triggers and crush skulls between stones and set fire to their own. Let *us* mold and configure and frame. Let us only wash across the weary shingles of this waning civilization, and, grain by grain, wear it back to silt and slime. But first, my love, let us *twist* it in our likeness."

"I know now that it was not revenge," says the prize, "what you did to..." And here she pauses, rethinking her words before continuing. "The way you have raveled me and rewoven the skein of my existence."

"Oh, make no mistake, there was, to be sure, a touch of retribution in mine work," the nameless woman says and winks a red and golden eye. "I took my fair share of gratification to see the hunter made the hunted, the slayer slain, the dedicated enemy of depravity and teratism made ruined and inimical to all that which she once protected."

"Then, it was merely justice."

"Perhaps," the nameless woman replies, "if there be such a thing as justice for the damned."

And then, as the vessel before her delights at its own grim emanations – those misty, spinning scraps of thaumaturgy and conjuration – the nameless woman lies down with that which is already quickly forgetting why it ever bothered to be Tess Brockett. What remains of the waning night is filled with the repeated congress of their twining, hungry bodies. Intercourses too refined and furious, too vast and altogether fateful, to ever be called lovemaking. They devour one another, and are each consumed. They revel in the outrageous excesses of their mutual and individual aberrations. And, finally, as the jealous sun rises above the prairie and illuminates the scrubby Chippewan foothills, the two of them find in sleep the soothing umbra that will shield them all through the scalding indifference of the coming day.

The Thousand-and-Third Tale
of Scheherazade

"I never much cared for those stories," the changeling woman says, staring out at all the fresh snow blanketing the rooftops and streets and the stingy front yards of Federal Hill. The January storm that began just after sunset is finally starting to taper off, and the woman sits at the little table by the window, cleaning her guns and watching the large, wet flakes spiraling down through the orange-white glow of the streetlights. The lean young man whom she has taken as her odalisque is lying naked on the narrow bed, not far away from her. In the room there are only three pieces of furniture: the little table where the woman cleans her guns, the narrow bed where the man lies wrapped in a dingy patchwork quilt, and the creaky wooden chair in which the woman is seated. The only light comes from the window and a small desk lamp sitting on the floor near the foot of the bed. The lamp has a stained-glass shade, but the shade is cracked and so dusty that it's hard to make out any sort of pattern or the particular tints of the glass. The oyster-colored walls are bare, save for a single framed tintype photograph hung above the headboard. Neither the man nor the changeling woman know the provenance of the photograph, and it might have been hanging here since long before either of them were born. It shows a nude woman standing in some sort of washtub or basin, a very large python cradled in her arms, and someone has written the names Biancabella and Samaritana across the bottom of the tintype in sepia ink.

"They're marvelous tales," the young man says very quietly, not precisely contradicting her. All things considered, the changeling woman is not unkind, at least not to him. Tonight, for instance, she brought him a pint bottle of Jacquin's ginger-flavored brandy. She opened it after they fucked, and now he's pleasantly drunk, and grateful for the gift, which has helped to push back the cold air and the raw sound of the wind blowing hard around the eaves of the terrible old house on Federal Hill.

"After all the trouble they've caused you," she mutters and shakes her head. The woman wets a bit of fabric with forty-weight Remington bore cleaner, then uses a metal rod to work the cloth back and forth through the barrel of the revolver. She does this several times, then stops and stares at him.

He smiles and stares back, and she wonders, not for the first time, if the things he knows and the months he's spent in the stables might have unhinged his mind. Not many last as long as he's lasted, the men and women kept downstairs, inside the filthy cages built into the subbasement of the old house.

For more than two centuries now, this place has served as a refuge for the Children of the Cuckoo, those stolen as infants and raised up in the warrens below College Hill to labor and officiate for the Hounds of Cain, to walk abroad in the day-lit world where the ghouls dare not venture. Those trained to see to the Hounds' more prosaic concerns, and to make certain that their secrets *remain* secret. To kill, or only maim, or perhaps merely intimidate, as necessary. In all the city, it is only within the walls of *this* house that the changelings are safe from the watchful eyes of their taskmasters. There is no other sanctuary afforded them, no other place where they may do as they please without fear of recrimination.

"It's not such an awful price to pay," he says, "not for the privilege of knowing, beyond any shadow of a doubt, that there are still such wonders among us."

"I'm never going to figure you out," she sighs, and glances at the window again, the window and the subsiding storm, the snow and the heavy winter night crouched above Providence.

"No," he agrees. "I don't think you ever will. Now, do you want to hear the story or not?"

"You didn't grow up on that crap. It's not the same for you as it is for me."

"You haven't answered my question," he tells her, and considers having another sip from the bottle of brandy. It's still more than half full, and sitting on a corner of the little table just beyond the edge of the bed.

"I think, maybe, that's because it's disguising another question altogether, and I'd *prefer* to answer the one that you're *really* asking me." And then she goes back to working on the revolver.

"Fine," the young man says, and reaches for the bottle. "Would you please *allow* me to tell you the story?" He sits up and unscrews the plastic cap, then tilts the pint to his lips. She laughs again, and nods her head.

"And the truth shall set you free," the changeling woman says, selecting the brass bore brush from her tools.

"You probably meant that to be ironic," he says, twisting the cap back onto the bottle of brandy and returning the bottle to it place on the table. "But I don't take it that way. Finding those books, reading what I read, having *seen* what I've *seen*, it truly *has* set me free."

She puts down the bore brush and goes back to watching the snow. "It very nearly got you killed," she says. "But, the Hounds took pity, or what they consider pity. So, instead, you live in filth, in a pen, like an animal. Instead, you're a slave and a whore."

"Yes," he replies. "I do. I am. But that doesn't change what I know, nor in any way lessen the sublimity of the knowledge. What has become of me, it's only the *price* of the knowledge."

"I still don't know why they didn't just kill you outright," she sighs.

"I have no idea," he says. "Perhaps we don't give them enough credit."

The changeling woman laughs, shaking her head again, and she reaches for the ginger brandy. "Yeah, sure. They're sweet as you please, given half the chance. Sweet as strawberry rhubarb pie. Regular fucking teddy bears, and here *we* are, the two of us, living proof."

"Here we *are*, regardless, and that's more than I expected. May I please tell you the story now. It really is one of the very best, in my opinion."

"They're just stories," she says, "though it's beyond me how you remember them all. You couldn't have had the *Red Book* all that long before they caught on."

"It's one of my favorites, this story."

"I already told you I'd listen, but it better not be 'The Fisherman and the Djinn' again, or 'Gulnare of the Sea,' or any of that silly shit about Ali Baba or Sinbad the Sailor."

"It isn't any of those," he assures her, lying down on his back and staring up at the water stains and cracks in the ceiling.

"And nothing about Esmeribetheda and the damn grey witches."

"It's not," he says.

"I've already told you, I have to be out of here and on my way down to Warwick by three, so you best keep that in mind." She takes a long, hot swallow from the bottle, then wipes her mouth and rubs at her eyes, trying, and failing, to remember the last time that she got a full night's – or day's – sleep.

"I will," he says.

"Then get on with it," she tells him, and twists the cap tightly back onto the bottle.

"It's one of the stories that Scheherazade relates to Shahryar and Dinazade, but one that didn't make it into Burton's *The Book of the Thousand Nights and a Night*, or into any of the earlier European translations. I suspect it was originally imported into the *Red Book of Riyadh* from another source, possibly the Persian *Isíhtsöornot* or from the writing of Abd-al-Hazred, though I was never able to confirm this, mind you. It's possible – "

"Just the story, please," she cuts in, trying not to sound annoyed, but sounding annoyed, anyway.

He apologizes and keeps his eyes trained on the ceiling, on the ruined plaster and paint above the bed. He was a scholar, once, and, to him, the origins of the tales are almost as fascinating as the tales themselves; he has trouble remembering that not everyone share's his enthusiasm.

"I'm listening," she says, prompting him. "The clock's ticking," (even though there is no clock in the room, and she doesn't wear a wristwatch).

And so, his head and belly warm from the brandy, and the howling wind seeming not so close and not so cold, the young man begins his story with the usual preamble. Scheherazade whispering the opening lines of a story to her sister; the King awakening, and at once captivated by what he hears; the Queen consort informing Shahryar, regretfully, that the sun was rising, and so her beheading would mean that she'd be unable to conclude the tale; and, finally, the King granting yet another stay of execution, so that he might hear the remainder of her cliffhanger.

"You *think* the silly bastard would see through her maneuvers, sooner or later," the changeling woman says. She's gone back to cleaning her revolver. "No one ever bothers to point out what an idiot this Sassanid 'king of kings' must have been."

"Most don't even remember that he *is* Sassanid, and therefore Zoroastrian, instead of Muslim."

"That's because most don't give two shits," she replies, then turns her attention to the revolver's extractor assembly.

He agrees this is true, and then resumes his story.

"This was, of course, long, long before the war between the Ghûl and the other races of the Djinn – the Ifrit, the Sila, and the Marid. In those days, the men of the desert still looked upon all the Djinn as gods, though they'd already learned to fear the night shades, the Ghûl, and guarded their children and the graves of their dead against them. Among all the fates that might befall the soul of a man or woman, to have one's corpse stolen and then devoured by the Ghûl was counted as one of the most gruesome and tragic conceivable. It was thought by many that to be so consumed would mean that the deceased would be taken from the cold sleep of *barzakh*, never to meet with the angels Nakir and Munkar, and so never be interrogated and prepared for Paradise.

"It was thought that the Ghûl, the night shades, were also shape shifters. It was said that they were especially fond of appearing in the form of hyenas, but that they could also come as scorpions, vipers, and even vultures."

"Are you entirely certain that you're not making this up?" the changeling woman asks, without pausing in her work or even glancing at the young man.

"I'm not," he replies. "Not making this up, I mean. Why?"

"Because I know the tales of the *Red Book*, backwards and forwards, as well as any warren rat, and this is the first I've heard about hyenas and vultures and shape shifting, *that's* why."

"Have you ever read from the book yourself? Have you ever even held a copy in your hands?" There's no challenge in these questions, as the young man has long since learned not to impugn his captors; rather, there's only curiosity, and curiosity is the only thing the changeling woman hears.

"Of course I haven't," she replies. "It's forbidden. We learn the book, what we are told we need to know of it, from the ghouls."

He's silent a moment, listening to the rumble of a snow plow passing by somewhere not far away, and the young man considers the glamours that keep the terrible old house on Federal Hill, and its inhabitants and prisoners, hidden in plain view.

"I'm telling you what I read," he says, and when she doesn't argue, he goes back to the story.

"In those days, there lived a woman to whom Allah had gifted seven sons. Naturally, she was very grateful for them, and yet, regardless, she still desired with all her heart to bear a daughter. So she asked this of Allah, that she might give birth to a baby girl.

"And soon afterwards, she was walking alone through a marketplace, this woman with seven sons. When she saw a mound of white goat cheese, she was so moved by the sight so that she exclaimed, "My Lord Allah! Give me, I entreat thee, a daughter every bit as white and fair and beautiful as this goats' cheese, and I will call her Ijbeyneh.

"Allah heard her prayer, and very soon she was sent an exceedingly beautiful girl, with skin as fair as goat-milk cheese, a daughter with the delicate throat of a gazelle, with blue eyes like blazing sapphires, and hair as black as pitch. The woman kept her word, and the girl was named Ijbeyneh. Everyone in the village who chanced to look upon her loved her at once and without reservation, with the exception of the daughters of her mother's sisters, her cousins, and *they* were very jealous."

"She was *named* after goat cheese?" the changeling woman asks, and she glares at the man on the bed, naked and wrapped in the threadbare patchwork quilt.

"That's what the *Red Book* says," he replies. "That's what I read there."

She laughs, and shakes her head skeptically, then tells him to continue.

"So, when she was seven, Ijbeyneh begged her jealous cousins to please take her with them on one of their walks in the forest. The girl was innocent and had no inkling of her cousins' true feelings for her. They often went deep into the forest, to pick the fruit and berries there, and came back with tales of the marvels they saw. Anyway, the cousins agreed, much to the girl's delight, and Ijbeyneh went with them. The day passed quickly, and when she'd filled her *tarbi'ah* with ripe berries – "

"Wait, what?" the changeling woman interrupts, and she sets aside the revolver's extractor assembly and the worn-out tooth brush she's been using to clean it. "She filled her *what* with berries?"

"Her *tarbi'ah*," the man answers patiently. "It a traditional linen veil, still worn, for example, by Palestinian women."

The changeling nods and stares out the single window in the room, and she frowns when she sees that it's snowing hard again. "You can bet the roads are going to be a bitch," she says.

Then, when a minute or two has passed, and she hasn't said anything more, the lean young man asks her if he can please go on with the story.

"Sure," she replies, wondering if she should call the Bailiff and suggest that maybe the drive to Warwick, and what she has to do there, could be postponed until the roads are clear.

"As I was saying," the man on the bed continues, "Ijbeyneh left her berries at the base of a tree and, on her own, wandered off to pick the wildflowers growing between the enormous sycamore figs. But, later, when she returned, she found that her *tarbi'ah* was filled with ugly, poisonous berries, instead of the delicious, sweet ones she'd worked so hard to gather. Also, her jealous cousins were gone, and she was left alone in the forest. She wandered through the hills, calling out to them, but no one and nothing answered her calls, except for the birds and a few buzzing insects. Finally, when Ijbeyneh tried to find her way home again, she discovered that she'd strayed from the trail, and she quickly became disoriented and lost in the forest.

"When the sun had set, a fearsome Ghûl woman crept up from a cave and came upon her. Surely, the ghoul would have devoured Ijbeyneh, but, as the child was Allah's gift to her mother, she was protected, after a fashion. Instead of eating the girl, the ghoul found her heart was filled with pity for her. And, seeing the ghoul, Ijbeyneh cried out, 'Oh, my Aunt! Please tell me which way my cousins have gone! And which way is home!' The ghoul answered her, 'I don't know, Beloved, but come back and live with me, at least until your cousins return for you.'

"Ijbeyneh agreed, and the ghulah took her to a cave near the very summit of the mountain. There, the child became a shepherdess, and, as the years passed – for her cousins never did come back – the Ghûl grew extremely fond of her. Every night, when the ghoul woman hunted in the forest, and in the rocky desert beyond the forest, she brought only her choicest kills back to the girl. The ghulah would not ever eat until after the girl had eaten. And in a hundred other ways, the Djinn tried to make Ijbeyneh happy and her life a comfortable one. For her, fine silks and ointments were stolen from caravans bound for the city, and for her. too, the ghoul woman found precious stones deep in the cave and polished them for Ijbeyneh to wear. In many ways, as the months came and went, the fair child grew in habit very much like her mistress, learning, for example, to eat the flesh of men and woman taken from the village graves that the ghoul sometimes robbed.

"But, despite the ghulah's best and most determined efforts, despite her love and constant attentions, the girl was not ever happy there on the mountain. Often, she wept for her home and her parents, and she cursed her jealous, traitorous cousins. Meanwhile, in the village, all the many white doves belonging to her father, which Ijbeyneh had fed and tended before she was lost, longed endlessly for the missing daughter's return. They did not coo, as they once had. And whenever they flew, their eyes searched all the wide land for any sign of her. In time, a day came when the doves espied the girl, there on the mountainside, minding the ghulah's flock. Even though she was now a young woman, they recognized her immediately, and they went straight away to Ijbeyneh, lighting on the ground all about her, and showed their joy at having found her alive and well."

"This is starting to sound more like something you looted from Charles Perrault or the Brothers Grimm," the changeling woman says. She presses a thumb gently to the pistol's extractor rod, and begins to clean the underside of the assembly.

"I assure you that I didn't," the young man tells her. "But, if you wish for me to stop – "

"I didn't fucking *say* that, now did I?"

"No, you didn't."

"Whatever and whoever you were before," the woman says, "you are *now* a whore, a whore who doesn't even get paid for his services, a whore whom I could kill and no one would even bother to ask why. So don't second-guess me, or presume what I do and don't want. Just finish the damned story."

The man nods. This is nothing he hasn't heard before, from her lips and from the lips of others. These are words that have become casual, that have long since lost their sting and become no more to him than any other truism: crows are black, water's wet, fire burns, and he's a slave in the service of the changelings, completely at their mercy, and will be until the day they at last have no use for him.

"Should I remind you I don't have all night," the woman mutters, trying to scrub away an especially stubborn and all-but inaccessible bit of grime. "The doves found the girl named after goat cheese, and then what?"

The young man rolls over on his right side, rolling towards the changeling woman, and he reaches for the bottle of brandy. The bed springs squeak loudly. "When she saw them," he says, "Ijbeyneh wept with delight, and she commanded them, 'O ye doves of my mother and of my father, go to them and tell them that their daughter, the dear one, keeps sheep in the high meadows of the mountain. Let them know I have not perished.' And, at once, they flew back to the village.

"Now, years before, the jealous cousins had claimed that the girl had been lost in the forest, though sometimes they told the story so that she'd been set upon by jackals, or a lion, and eaten alive. Her father and her brothers, her uncles and many other men from the village, had searched the hills for her. Her mother took the blame upon herself, weeping endlessly and declaring that this was Allah's curse upon her for not having been content with seven sons."

The lean young man pauses to sip from the rim of the bottle of brandy, and for a moment he watches the changeling clean her gun. The wind is blowing so hard now that even the liquor cannot keep a shiver at bay, and he wraps himself tighter in the frayed quilt.

"As I said, the doves had stopped cooing, when they were no longer cared for by Ijbeyneh. However, after they found her on the mountain, their disposition suddenly changed. The birds ceased to mourn, and became lively again. What's more, it seemed as though they were endeavoring to communicate something to their keepers. A neighbor, struck by the very odd behavior of the doves, convinced Ijbeyneh's father he should learn which way the birds flew every day. He did this, and when he was sure, he gathered together the brothers and the uncles and all those in the village who still adored the fair girl, and, together, this band followed the doves deep into the mountains and up to the high grazing meadows.

"But it had never been Ijbeyneh's intention to be rescued. She'd only wished to have her parents know that she'd not died. In the year's since the Djinn had taken her in, the girl had grown to love the ghulah, and had even consented to become the night shade's concubine. Her home was no longer her father's house, or the safety of the village, but the wild mountainside and the grotto where the ghulah, whom she still called Aunt, pampered her and taught her dark secrets unknown to the sons and daughters of Allah."

"Stop," the changeling woman says, and she puts down the gun and the oily scrap of linen she'd been scrubbing at it with. She turns in her chair and glowers at the young man, who does as he's been told, and is now having another sip of the ginger brandy.

"You said that the ghulah had *failed* to make her happy. But *now* you're saying that they're lovers, and that goat-cheese girl doesn't want to be rescued and go home to mamma and papa?"

The young man nods his head and again screws the cap back onto the pint bottle. "Yes," he says. "You're right. But the contradiction is present in the *Red Book of Riyadh*. I'm only repeating it. It's possible that Ijbeyneh had a change of heart somewhere along the way that the original author failed to note, or that whoever transcribed the story from an older text simply got it wrong. At any rate, I *am* telling the tale just as the book records it. But, if you'd prefer, I'll gladly backtrack and tell it so that the narrative is more consistent."

The changeling woman scowls and sighs and tells him no, just get on with it, and so he does.

"When Ijbeyneh saw the men coming up the mountain, she knew, of course, that she'd made a dire mistake speaking with the doves as she had. She understood that the ghulah would either destroy her father and brothers and uncles – whom she did still care for – or else *they* would succeed in killing her beloved Djinn. Wishing to forestall any such bloodshed, Ijbeyneh abandoned her sheep and raced back to the cave where her Aunt was sleeping. She woke the ghoul in time to warn her that men from the village had learned, somehow, that the fair daughter of the woman with seven sons still lived, and now these men were quickly approaching."

"Had learned *somehow*," the changeling woman mutters. "Lying little cunt."

"A lie of omission, at most," the young man says. "But, regardless, her Aunt told her that, rather than confront the men, there was another way out of the grotto. Or, more precisely, there was a boulder that when rolled back would reveal stairs cut into the limestone, leading down into a great cavern, where an underground lake lapped at subterranean shores. The ghulah said there was a boat there that would ferry them to safety, to the hidden realm of the Ghûl, which no man would ever find.

"You can well imagine Ijbeyneh's profound relief upon hearing this, for she'd already resigned herself to either a violent death fighting at the side of her mistress, or to watching as the men from her family were slaughtered, and then having little choice but to do what was expected of her and dine upon their remains."

"Poor baby," the changeling woman laughs. Satisfied that the revolver's extractor assembly is clean, she goes to work brushing out the cylinder.

"Her Aunt told her to get what few belongings she wished to carry with them, though Ijbeyneh protested that there wasn't time. The ghulah woman kissed her and told her not to worry, that men were, by nature, slow to find the things they sought, and, since there were so many caves in the mountainside, it was unlikely these men would hit upon the one they were looking for right off.

Reluctantly, still convinced they should not be wasting time, the girl gathered up some of the gems that her Aunt had given her, and some of her favorite silks, a crocodile's tooth, the dagger she'd carved from a vizier's shin bone, and a few other things. She bundled them together inside a piece of camel hide while the ghulah crouched in the mouth of the cave and kept watch for the men.

"When she was done, the ghulah led her deeper into the grotto than Ijbeyneh had ever gone before. And just as she heard the triumphant shouts of her own father and her seven brothers, who had discovered the entry to the ghulah's cave, the girl and the Djinn reached the immense boulder concealing the path down to the secret sea below the hills. The ghulah, fearing now that they *had* indeed tarried too long, shoved against the stone with all her might, only to discover that it wouldn't budge."

The changeling woman's cell phone rings, then, and she sets the revolver down and makes an annoyed, dismissive motion with her left hand, silencing the young man on the bed. He rolls back over on his back and resumes his examination of the plaster ceiling while she talks to whoever's on the other end. The call lasts less than a minute, and when it's done, the woman sits staring out the window, cursing the snow.

"You have to go now," the young man says.

"Yeah, I have to go now. That was fucking Pentecost. I'll have someone take you back down to the stables. You can have whatever's left of the brandy. I'll tell them not to take it from you."

"Thank you," he says, keeping his eyes on the ceiling, wishing he could have spent the whole night Above, wishing she'd have stayed in bed after they made love, instead of insisting that she needed to clean the revolver.

He lies still, listening to the January wind, and doesn't talk while she hastily reassembles the gun. There's one crack in the plaster that leads all the way from the top of the doorframe, across the ceiling, to the wall above the headboard, and it reminds him of a river glimpsed from orbit, wending its way along a wide desert plain.

"So..." the changeling woman says, "what happened? Did they get away? Or did goat-cheese girl's father catch up with them?"

"It's complicated," he replies.

"Is it now?"

"Very much so," he says. "A shame I don't have time to finish the story. Maybe…"

"…next time?" she asks, and spares the young man a sidewise glance. "You are really *not* going to tell me how it all ends, are you?"

"I fear that rushing it would spoil the tale," the young man says, "and all I have left to me are these stories. Surely, you understand."

"Fine. If that's the way you want to play, Scheherazade, and if we're *both* lucky enough to live through another goddamn day."

"Just keep your head down," he whispers, trying not to think about the stables below the terrible old house, or whatever it is the changeling woman will do before dawn. "And I'll do the same, to the best of my abilities."

And five minutes later, when she's gone out into the snowy, windy night, he lies alone on the bed with his bottle of ginger-flavored brandy and tries to get a few minutes sleep, there in the relative warmth and comfort of the shabby room, before they come to take him downstairs again.

The Belated Burial

Mere puppets they, who come and go
At bidding of vast formless things...
                    Edgar Allan Poe

Brylee did object to the casket, and also to the hole in the frozen earth. She did object, in a hesitant, deferential sort of way.
But, as they say, her protestations fell upon deaf ears, even though
Miss Josephine fully acknowledged that none of it was necessary.
"It will do you good," the vampire said, and, too, she said, "One
day you'll understand, when you are older." And, she added,
"There is far too little respect for tradition these days." Brylee
came near to begging, at the end, but she's not a stupid girl, and
she knew that, likely as not, begging would only annoy the vampire and make the whole affair that much more unpleasant. Being
buried when one is fully conscious and keenly aware of the con-
fines of her narrow house and the stink of cemetery soil, these
things are terrible, but, as she has learned, there is always something incalculably worse than the very worst thing that she can
imagine. Miss Josephine has had centuries to perfect the stepwise
procession from Paradise to Purgatory to the lowest levels of an
infinitely descending Hell, and she wears her acumen and exper-
tise where it may be seen by all, and especially where it may be seen
by her lovers (whether they are living, dead, or somewhere in
between). So, yes, Brylee objected, but only the halfhearted, token
objection permitted by her station. And then she did as she was
bidden. She dressed in the funerary gown from one of her mistress' steamer trunks, the dress, all indecent, immaculate white

lace and silk taffeta; it smells of cedar and moth balls. Amid the palest chrysanthemums and lilies, babies breath and albino roses, she lay down in the black-lacquered casket, which is hardly more than a simple pine box, and she did not move. She did not make a sound. Not breathing was, of course, the simplest part. Miss Josephine laid a heavy gold coin on each of her eyelids before the mourners began to arrive, that she would have something to give the ferryman. "She was so young," one of the vampires said, the one named Addie Goodwin. "Your sorrow must be inconsolable," said another, the man whom they all call simply Signior Garzarek, who came all the way from New York for the mock-somber ceremony in the ancient yellow house on Benefit Street. "It was an easy death," Miss Josephine told him, struggling to hold back tears her atrophied ducts could never actually manufacture. "She went in her sleep, the poor dear." And there was the sound of weeping, so Brylee knew that not *all* the mourners gathered by Miss Josephine were dead. An antique gramophone played "Be Thou My Vision" again and again and again, and there was a eulogy, delivered by an unfamiliar, stuttering voice. And then, before the lid was finally placed on the black casket and nailed firmly down, Miss Josephine laid a single *red* rose across Brylee's folded hands. The vampire leaned close, and she whispered, "You are exquisite, my dear. You are superb. Sleep tight." When the casket was lifted off its marble pedestal by the pallbearers, Brylee fought back a sudden wave of panic that threatened to get the better of her. She came very near to screaming, and that would have ruined everything. That would have undone all her mistress' painstaking theater and pretense, and only the knowledge that there is always something worse kept her silent as she was carried out to the waiting hearse. *No harm can come to me*, she reminded herself again and again and again. *I am dead, and what harm can possibly come from these silly games. I am dead almost a month now, and the grave can surely hold no horror for me anymore.* "One night and one day," her mistress had promised, "and not an hour longer. You can do that, sweetheart. The time will fly by, you'll see." Brylee had not been told to which cemetery she would be delivered, so it might be the Old North Burial Ground in Providence, or some place as far away as Westerly, or even Stonington Cemetery in Connecticut. The hearse ride was longer than she expected, but maybe it circled blocks and doubled back, so maybe it didn't go very far at all from the yellow house on Benefit Street. She lay still with the gold coins on her eyes and the rose gripped now in her hands, and the words to "Be Thou My Vision" repeating again and again behind her eyelids, which Miss Josephine had sewn shut for the occasion, just in case. *Be Thou my battle Shield, Sword for the fight; Be Thou my Dignity, Thou my Delight; Thou my soul's Shelter, Thou my high Tower: Raise Thou me heavenward, O Power of my power.* Neither death nor undeath had done very much to shatter Brylee's atheistic convictions, so these words held within them no possible comfort. They seemed, at best, a cruel, mocking chorus, childish taunts she would carry with her down into the cold dirt. *Riches I heed not, nor man's empty praise, Thou mine Inheritance, now and always: Thou and Thou only, first in my heart, High King of Heaven, my Treasure Thou art.* "You are fortunate," Miss Josephine told her when Brylee made the aforementioned objections. "When it was my time to go into the ground, I was wrapped in only a cotton winding cloth, with a little myrrh and frankincense, then buried beneath a dozen feet of Egyptian sand. I was forbidden to rise for a full month, and could always hear the jackals and vultures close at hand, pawing and pecking for a scrap of carrion. There was a sandstorm, and a dozen feet became almost a hundred overnight. And when my time below had passed, no one came for me. I was left to dig myself free." Which is to say, again, that the most appalling situation can always become so much more appalling, and the lesson has not been lost on Brylee. She suffered the ride to the unknown cemetery in perfect silence. She made no utterance as the pine casket was lowered into the waiting grave, nor when the raw wound in the January landscape was filled in again by men with shovels and the more efficient bucket of a noisy, chugging skid loader. She was silent as silent ever dared to be, while the earth rained loudly down upon the lid of her casket. But she did flinch, and her sharp teeth pierced her lower lip, half expecting the lid to collapse at any moment, splintered by the weight of all that dirt (though she knew well enough there are steel reinforcements to prevent such a mishap). In the darkness, she grew almost as taut as any genuine corpse bound by the shackles of *rigor mortis*, and she tasted her own blood. Or, rather, the stolen blood that she pretended was her own. In the hour of twilight, before the funeral service, when she was still half awake at best, Miss Josephine had brought a gift to her. "Because it is such a special day," the vampire said, then gently laid the banquet on the bed next to Brylee. The girl's hair was almost the same color as the black-lacquered casket, and Miss Josephine had only taken the smallest sip from her, just enough that she wouldn't struggle and ruin Brylee's last meal before the grave. "It's very kind of you," she told her mistress and pantomimed a grateful smile, though, in truth she was much too nervous to be very hungry; she would not be so impolite as to *say* so. "Do you know her name," Brylee asked. Miss Josephine made a sour sort of face, and asked her what possible difference a name would make, one way or the other. Brylee did not ask the question a second time. Instead, her tongue flicked across the wound that had already been made in the girl's throat. Brylee's incisors and eye teeth made a wider insult of Miss Josephine's kiss, parting skin and fascia, the protective sheets of platysma and sternocleidomastoid muscle, to reveal the pulsing ecstasy of the carotid artery. She'd paid close attention to the anatomy lessons that she'd been sent down to the Hounds to learn, and she knew well enough to avoid the less-healthful, deoxygenated blood of the jugular. And for a short time, to Brylee's surprise, the joy of the nameless girl's fading life rushing into her was enough to take her mind off everything that was to come. When she was finished, when the heart had ceased pumping and little remained but a pale husk, Miss Josephine made her sit up, and she cleaned Brylee's blood-smeared face with a black silk handkerchief imported from France more than a hundred years before. Then her mistress kissed her, licking the last few stains from her face, and they lay together for a time, with the dead girl's body growing cold between them. Miss Josephine's delicate hands wandered lazily across Brylee's body, the vampire's fingernails dancing like animated shards of glass; she spoke of other funerals, other burials, and she spoke of resurrection, too. "There is not a surrender to the clay," she said, "without a concomitant rebirth. We do not lie down, but that we rise when our sleep is done." And these were pretty words, to be sure, as were the prayers she muttered to forgotten deities while her sharp fingers strayed and wandered and found their way inside Brylee. But when the last clod of frozen soil has been shoved rudely back into place, and she can no longer discern the noise of either men or their machines, when all that has *passed* in the preceeding few hours dissolves into a seemingly timeless *present*, the beauty of words is overthrown. Here there is a growing silence, and an absence of light that she knows would not be the least bit lessened if stitches did not prevent the opening of her eyelids. This is the truth lurking in back of all the ceremony. This is the simple and inviolable negation of the tomb. Brylee laughs very softly, for no ears but her own, and then she whispers, more quietly still, "Out – out are the lights – out all! And over each quivering form, the curtain, a funeral pall, comes down with the rush of a storm..." But she trails off, leaving the stanza unfinished. It would be a grand joke, if uttered by Miss Josephine, or Signior Garzarek, but from Brylee's lips, in this box and in this hole, the words tumble senselessly back upon themselves. She stops before they choke her. They lie like ashes and mold upon her tongue. And so she is quiet, and very, very still, because she has been assured it will be only one night and one day before the hour of her exhumation. She can do that much, surely, and when it is over and she's once again safe in the arms of her mistress, even the suggestion that her current situation held some minor species of dread will seem patently absurd. There is nothing here to fear, and even the bitter cold is not a hardship to one such as herself. She is safe inside her shell, and has but to wait, and waiting is the only genuine trial here to be endured. She thinks to speed the end of her interment by busying her mind, because, as Miss Josephine has said, it is *only* an undisciplined mind that can pose any possible threat while she is below. Brylee licks her dry lips, and she begins counting backwards from one-hundred thousand, for she can not conceive any more mundane task. With luck, she will bore herself to sleep, and not wake until the men return with their shovels. She says the numbers aloud, laying each one with the same meticulous care a brick mason might go about his work. And in this manner, time passes, even if she is not precisely aware of its passage. She stops thinking about the underside of the casket's lid, mere inches from her face, and all the weight bearing down upon the wood. She does not dwell on how little unfilled space there is to her left or her right. It hardly matters that she is unable to sit up, or roll over on her side, or bend her knees, and she does not succumb to morbid, irrational fears of suffocation. Dead lungs have no need of air. She counts, and counts, and, soon enough, her voice becomes a calming metronome. "And when you return," Miss Josephine said the night before, "when you are given back to me, delivered from that underworld like Proserpine or, more appropriately, like cruel and wanton Ishtar – when we are so soon reunited, you will never again be called upon to prove yourself. There will only be the long red sea of eternity." And recalling these words, Brylee loses count somewhere after forty-five thousand, and, full in the knowledge of her own recklessness, she listens. Her lips are stilled, and there is no longer the distraction of her voice. There is the sound of the wild January wind, but muffled by her tomb into the most indistinct threnody. Here would be the living hammer of her heartbeat, if her heart still beat. If she still lived. Here would be her hitching breath, perhaps. But her body has been rendered all but inert by the ministrations of her ravenous lover. So, the silence is profound, and for some period of time that passes without being measured, Brylee lies listening to *almost* nothing at all. In this slumberous white month, even the worms and beetles do not stir, and the moles and voles and millipedes are as monstrously serene as the surface of the moon. With no forethought, no intention to do anything of the sort, Brylee raises her right hand, the pads of her fingers brushing the lid above her, wood sanded almost completely smooth. Having found that barrier, touching it, she immediately withdraws her hand. And then, as she begins to feel the dry folds of that alarm she promised her mistress *and* promised herself would not overtake her, she here's a *new* sound. Very far away, at first, or so it seems, and she is reminded of a discarded life, standing on a subway platform station as a train rumbled towards the terminal. Though, whatever thing is the author of *this* approaching tumult would put any subway train to shame. Over minutes or hours, the distant rumble becomes a not-so-distant boom, as of summer thunder, and, at last, a roar. And it cannot be so very far below her, this passing demon, which seems to roll on forever, dragging itself through an unsuspected burrow gnawed in the rotten bedrock below the cemetery. But even now, Brylee does not scream. If she screams, it might hear, and she imagines it moving restlessly, never-sleeping, a labyrinthine circuit running from one graveyard to the next, listening for anything that is, by some accident, not yet dead. In times past, it must have been more often sated than in this faultless age of embalming. She squeezes her eyes shut as tightly as she may (though the stitches forbid any chance of them opening), and remembers something Miss Josephine said when they lay together in bed with the devoured girl's cadaver in between. Brylee was lost in the bliss that follows feeding, and the bliss of her mistresses hands upon her, upon her and within her. "Perhaps, down there, you will even be so fortunate as to hear his coming and going about his incessant, immemorial rounds," and in the haze of pleasure she'd not thought to ask the identity of this possible august visitor, a name nor any other manner of appellation. Around her pine box, the world shudders, and all the prayers she offers up in the all-but-endless pandemonium are shameless, bald-faced lies. But, it passes her by, this innominate leviathan, and either she was unnoticed or nothing it desired. Or, possibly, Brylee was only meant to bear blind witness to its coming and going. No offering trussed up pretty and left helpless within an inverted altar. Some time that she can only mark as later, the ground around and below her is silent and still again, and whatever came so awfully near would seem only a dream, if she did not, by heretofore unsuspected instincts, know otherwise. Brylee lies in the black-lacquered casket, and she is silent, and she is still, and she waits, permitting no thoughts now but her mistress' beloved face and recollections of wide and star-dappled skies stretched out forever above them.

The Bone's Prayer

The sea pronounces something, over and over,
in a hoarse whisper; I cannot quite make it out.
Annie Dillard

1.

She has been walking the beach all afternoon, which isn't unusual for days when she cannot write. And there have been several dry days now in a row, one following wordlessly after the next. A mute procession of empty hours, or, worse still, a procession of hours spent carefully composing sentences and paragraphs that briefly deceive her into thinking that the drought has finally passed. But then she reads back over the pages, and the prose thuds and clangs artlessly against itself, or it leads off somewhere she has not the time or the skill or the inclination to follow. She has deadlines, and bills, and the expectations of readers, and all these things must be factored into the question of whether a productive hour is, indeed, productive.

It becomes intolerable, the mute procession and the false starts, the cigarettes and coffee and all those books silently watching her from their places on the shelves that line her office. And, so, she eventually, inevitably, goes to the beach, which is not so very far away, hardly an hour's drive south from the city. She goes to the beach, and she tries very hard not to think of what isn't getting written. She tries only to hear the waves, the gulls and cormorants, the wind, tries to take in so much of the sand and the sky and the blue-green sea that there is no room remaining for her anxieties.

And sometimes it even works.

Today is a Saturday near the end of winter, and there are violent gusts off the sound that bite straight through her gloves and her long wool coat. Gusts that have twice now almost managed to dislodge the fleece-lined cap with flaps to keep her ears warm. Thick clouds the color of Wedgwood china hide the sun and threaten snow. But, thanks to the inclement weather, she has the beach all to herself, and that more than makes up for the discomfort. This solitude, like the breathy rhythm of the surf, and the smell of the incoming tide, is a balm. She begins at Moonstone Beach and walks the mile or so south and west to the scatter of abandoned summer cottages at Greenhill Point. Then she walks back, following the narrow strip of beach stretching between Block Island Sound and the low dunes dividing the beach from Trustom Pond.

The estuary is frozen solid, and when she climbs the dunes and stares out across the ice, there are flocks of mallards there, and Canadian geese, and a few swans wandering disconsolately about, looking lost. In the summer, the land around the salt pond is a verdant tangle of dog roses, poison ivy, greenbriers, and goldenrod. But now it is ringed by a homogenous brown snarl, and the only sign of green anywhere in this landscape are a few spruce trees and red cedars, dotting the southern edge of the forest to the north.

She turns back towards the sea and the cobble-strewn sand. It doesn't seem to her that the sea changes its hues with the season. Today, it wears the same restless shade of celadon that it wears in June, quickly darkening to a Persian blue where the water begins to grow deep, only a little ways out from shore. Ever shifting, never still, it is her only constant, nonetheless. It is her comfort, the sight of the sea, even in a month as bleak and dead as this.

She begins gathering a handful of pebbles, meaning to carry them back towards the dunes and find a dry place to sit, hopefully somewhere out of the worst of the wind. This beach is somewhat famous for the pebbles that fetch up here from submerged outcroppings of igneous stone, earth that was the molten-hot core of a mountain range millions of years before the coming of the dinosaurs. Here and there among the polished lumps of granite are the milky white moonstones that give the beach its name. She used to collect them, until she had a hundred or so, and they lost their novelty. There are also strands of kelp and bladderwrack, the claws and carapaces and jointed legs of dismembered crabs and lobsters, an occasional mermaid's purse – all the usual detritus. In the summer months, there would be added to this an assortment of human jetsam – water bottles, beer cans, stray flip flops, styrofoam cups, and all manner of plastic refuse – the thoughtless filth that people leave behind. And this is another reason that she prefers the beach in winter.

She has selected six pebbles, and is looking for a seventh (having decided she would choose seven and only seven), when she spots a small, peculiar stone. It's shaped like a teardrop, and is the color of pea soup. The stone glistens wetly in the dim afternoon light, and she can clearly see that there are markings etched deeply into its smooth surface. One of them looks a bit like a left-facing swastika, and another reminds her of a Greek *ichthus*. For a moment, the stone strikes her as something repulsive, like coming upon a rotting fish or a discarded prophylactic, and she draws her hand back. But that first impression quickly passes, and soon she's at a loss even to account for it. It is some manner of remarkable artifact, whether very old or newly crafted, and she adds it to the six pebbles in her hand before turning once more towards the frozen expanse of Trustom Pond.

2.

It's Friday evening, two days after her trip from Providence to the beach. Usually, she looks forward to Friday's, because on Friday nights Sammie almost always stops by after work. Sammie is the closest thing she has to a close friend, and, from time to time, they've been lovers, as well. The writer, whose name is Edith (though that isn't the name that appears on the covers of her novels), is not an outgoing person. Crowds make her nervous, and she avoids bars and nightclubs, and even dreads trips to the market. She orders everything she can off the internet – clothing, books, CDs, DVDs, electronics – because she hates malls and shopping centers. She hates the thought of being seen. To her knowledge, psychiatrists have yet to coin a term for people who have a morbid fear of being looked at, but she figures *antisocial* is accurate enough. However, most times, she enjoys having Sammie around, and Sammie never gets angry when Edith needs to be left alone for a week or two.

They've been mistaken for sisters, despite the fact that they really don't look very much alike. Sammie is two or three inches taller and has striking jet-black hair just beginning to show strands of grey. Edith's hair in an unremarkable dishwater blonde. Sammie's eyes are a bright hazel green, and Edith's are a dull brown. Sammie has delicate hands and the long, tapered fingers of a pianist, and Edith's hands are thick, her fingers stubby. She keeps her nails chewed down to the quick, and there are nicotine stains on her skin. Sammie quit smoking years ago, before they met.

"Well, it was just lying there on the sand," Edith says. "And it really doesn't look all that old."

"It's a rock," Sammie replies, still peering at the peculiar greenish stone, holding it up to the lamp on the table next to Edith's bed. "What do you mean, it doesn't look old? All rocks look old to me."

"The carving, I mean," Edith replies, trying to decide if she really wants another of the stale madeleines that Sammie brought with her; they taste faintly of lemon extract, and are shaped like scallop shells. "I mean the *carving* in the rock looks fresh. If it had been rolling around in the ocean for any time at all the edges would be worn smooth by now."

"I think it's soapstone," Sammie says, and turns the pebble over and over, examining the marks on it. "But I don't think you find soapstone around here."

"Like I was saying, I figure someone bought it in a shop somewhere and lost it. Maybe it was their lucky charm. Or maybe it didn't mean anything much to them."

"It feels funny," Sammie says, and before Edith can ask her to explain what she means, Sammie adds, "Slippery. Oily. Slick. You know?"

"I haven't noticed that," Edith says, although she has. The lie surprises her, and she can't imagine why she didn't just admit that she's also noticed the slithery sensation she gets whenever she holds the stone for more than a minute or two.

"You should show it to someone. A geologist or an archeologist or someone who knows about this stuff."

"I honestly don't think it's very old," Edith replies, and decides against a fourth madeleine. Instead, she lights a cigarette and thinks about going to the kitchen for a beer. "If I took it to an archeologist, they'd probably tell me the thing was bought for five bucks in a souvenir shop in Misquamicut."

"I really don't like the way it feels," Sammie says.

"Then put it down."

"Is that supposed to be a Jesus fish?" Sammie asks, pointing to the symbol that reminded Edith of an *ichthus*.

"Sort of looks like one," Edith replies.

"And *this* one, this one right here," Sammie says and taps the nail of her index finger against the stone. "That looks like astrology, the symbol for Neptune."

"I thought it was a trident, or a pitchfork," Edith sighs, wishing Sammie would put the stone away so they could talk about something else, almost anything else at all. The stone makes her uneasy, and three times in two days she's almost thrown it into the trash, so she wouldn't have to think about it or look at it anymore. "Can we please talk about something else for a while? You've been gawking at that awful thing for half an hour now."

Sammie turns her head, looking away from the stone, looking over her left shoulder at Edith. She's frowning slightly, and her neatly waxed eyebrows are furrowed.

"You *asked* me what I thought of it," she says, sounding more defensive than annoyed, more confused than angry. "*You're* the one who started this."

"It's not like I *meant* to find it, you know."

"It's not like you had to bring it home, either."

Sammie watches her a moment or two longer, then turns back to the tear-shaped stone.

"This one is a sun cross," she says, indicating another of the symbols. "Here, the cross held inside a circle. It's something else you see in astrology, the sign for the earth."

"I never knew you were into horoscopes," Edith says, and she takes a long drag on her cigarette and holds the smoke in her lungs until she begins to feel dizzy. Then she exhales through her nostrils.

"Why does it bother you?" Sammie asks.

"I never said it did."

"You just called it 'that awful thing,' didn't you?"

"I'm going to get a beer," Edith tells her. "Do you want one, as long as I'm up."

"Sure," Sammie says and nods, not looking away from the stone. "I'd love a beer, as long as you're up."

Edith stands and pulls her bathrobe closed, tugging roughly at the terrycloth belt. The robe is a buttery yellow, and has small blue ducks printed on it. "You can have it if you want it," she tells Sammie, who frowns softly, then sets the stone down on the bedside table.

"No," she replies. "It's yours. You found it, so you should keep it. Besides, it's a hell of a lot more interesting than most of the junk you haul back from the shore. At least this time the house doesn't smell like dead fish and seaweed. But I still say you should find an archeologist to take a look at it. Might turn out to be something rare."

"Perhaps," Edith says. "But I was just thinking, maybe it wasn't lost. Maybe someone got rid of it on purpose."

"Anything's possible."

"I'm afraid all I have is Heineken," Edith says, nodding towards the kitchen.

"Heineken's fine by me. Moocher's can't be choosers."

"I meant to get something else, because I know you don't like Heineken. But I haven't been to the store in a few days."

"The Heineken's fine, really. I promise."

Edith manages the ghost of a smile, then goes to the kitchen, leaving Sammie (whose birth name is Samantha, but everyone knows better than to call her that) alone in the bedroom with the peculiar greenish stone. Neither of them mentions it again that night, and later, for the first time in almost three weeks, they make love.

3.

"Well, first off, continents don't just *sink*," Edith says, and she's beginning to suspect that she might only be dreaming. She's sitting on the closed toilet lid in her tiny bathroom, and Sammie is standing up in the claw-foot tub. Sammie was the one who started talking about Atlantis, and then Mu, and Madame Blavatsky's Lemuria.

"And I read about another one," she says. "When I was a kid, I found a book in the library, *Mysteries of the Sea*, or something like that, maybe one of those *Time-Life* series. One of the stories was about a ship finding an uncharted island somewhere in the South Pacific, back in the twenties, I think. They found an island, complete with the ruins of a gigantic city, but then the whole thing sank in an earthquake. Islands can sink, right?" she asks.

"Not overnight," Edith says, more interested in watching Sammie bathe than all this nonsense about lost worlds.

"What about Krakatoa? Or Santorini?"

"Those were both volcanic eruptions. And the islands didn't sink, they exploded. *Boom*," and Edith makes a violent motion in the air with her right hand. "For that matter, neither was completely submerged."

"Sometimes you talk like a scientist," Sammie says, and she stares down at the water in the cast-iron tub.

"Are you saying I'm pedantic?"

"No, I'm not saying that. It's kind of sexy, actually. Big brains get me wet."

There's a sudden fluttering noise in the hallway, and Edith looks in that direction. The bathroom door is standing half open, but the hallway's too dark to see whatever might have made the sound.

"Okay," Sammie continues, "so maybe, instead, there have been cities that never sank, because the things that built them never lived on land. Or maybe they lived on land a long time ago, but then returned to the water. You know, like whales and dolphins."

Edith frowns and turns back to the tub. "You're sort of just making this up as you go along, aren't you?"

"Does that matter?" Sammie asks her.

"Whales don't build cities," Edith says, and there's a finality in her voice that *should* have been sufficient to steer the conversation in another direction. But when Sammie's been drinking and gets something in her head, she can go on about it for hours.

"Whales sing songs," she says. "And maybe if we were able to understand those songs, we'd know about whoever built the cities."

Edith frowns at her, trying not to think about the fluttering noise from the hall. "If we could understand those songs," she says, "I suspect we'd mostly hear about horny whales, or which sort of krill tastes the best."

"Maybe," Sammie replies, and then she shrugs her narrow shoulders. "But the whales *would* know about the cities. Especially sperm whales, because they dive so deep and all."

"You're still working from an *a priori* assumption that the cities have ever existed. You're trying to find evidence to solve an imaginary problem."

Sammie holds up the greenish stone from the beach, then, as if it offers some refutation, or maybe she thinks Edith has forgotten it. In the light from the fluorescent bulb above the sink, the stone looks greasy. Sammie's fingers look greasy, too, as if something has seeped out of the rock and stained her hands.

I really don't like the way it feels.

"It's just something one of the summer people dropped," Edith says, wondering why Sammie didn't leave the stone lying on the table beside the bed, why she's in the tub with it. "The thing was probably made on an Indian Reservation in Arizona, or in China or something. It's just a piece of junk."

"Can't you hear it?" Sammie asks her. "If you listen very closely, it's singing. Not the same song that whales sing, but it's singing, all the same."

"Stones don't sing," Edith says, "no matter what someone's carved on them. I don't hear anything at all."

Sammie looks mildly disappointed, and she shrugs again. "Well, I hear it. I've been hearing it all night. It's almost a lamentation. A dirge. And I don't just hear it, Edith, I can *feel* it. In my bones, I can feel it."

"Really, I don't know what you mean," Edith says, and before she can add, *and I don't* care, *either*, Sammie is already talking again.

"My body hears the song. Every *cell* in my body hears the song, and it's like they want to answer. It's a song the ocean sings, that the ocean has always *been* singing. But, suddenly, my body remembers it, from a very, very long time ago, I think. Back when there were still only fish, maybe, and nothing had crawled out to live on the land."

"You were making more sense with Atlantis and the theosophists," Edith sighs. She sits there on the toilet, staring at the greasy-looking stone in Sammie's greasy-looking hands. The rock's surface is iridescent, and it shimmers with a riot of colors, a rainbow film on an oil-slick mud puddle, or the nacreous lining of an abalone shell. Sammie's hands have become iridescent, as well, and she's saying something about inherited memories, the collective unconscious, somatic and genetic recollection, and Edith wants to ask her, *Now who sounds like a scientist?* But she doesn't.

"We don't know what's down there," Sammie says. "Not really. I read somewhere that we know more about the surface of the moon than about the deep sea. Did you even know that? Do you know about the Marianas Trench? It's so deep, Edith, that if you were to set Mount Everest at the bottom, there would still be more than a mile of water covering the mountaintop."

"Yes, I know a little about the Marianas Trench," Edith replies, trying to be patient without trying to *sound* like she's having to try to be patient. And that's when Sammie stops rolling the tear-shaped stone between her fingers and quickly slips it down to the clean-shaven space between her legs and into her vagina. There's no time for Edith to try to stop her.

"Do you think that was such a good idea?" she asks. Sammie only smiles back, a furtive sort of smile, and doesn't answer the question. But she finally sits down in the tub, and Edith sees that where only a few moments before the water was clear and clean, now it has become murky, and dark strands of kelp float on the surface. There's a sharp crust of tiny barnacles clinging to the white enamel, and she opens her mouth to tell Sammie to be careful, that they're sharp, and she could cut herself. But then the fluttering noise comes from the hallway again, louder than before, and, hearing it, she's afraid to say anything at all.

"It's a message in a bottle," Sammie whispers. "Or those golden phonograph records they sent off on the *Voyager* probes. Messages like that, no one ever expects to get an answer, but we keep sending them off, anyway."

"I don't hear anything," Edith lies.

"Then I suggest you should try listening more closely. It's the most beautiful song I've ever heard. And it's taken so terribly long to get here."

Edith shuts her eyes and smells the ocean, and she smells an evaporating tide pool trapped between rime-scarred boulders, and a salt-marsh mudflat, and all the soft, pale creatures that live in the briny ooze, and, last of all, the sweet hint of pink dog roses in the air. She keeps her eyes shut tightly, straining not to hear the strange, unpleasant commotion in the hallway, which sounds nothing at all like any music she's ever heard. And, for a hopeful moment, Edith begins to believe she's waking up, before the dream abruptly drops away beneath her feet, the dream and the tile floor of the bathroom, and she understands that the water's only getting deeper.

4.

There are dreams that stack in tiers, like a gaily frosted birthday cake, and, too, there are dreams that sit nested snuggly one within the other, the way that Russian matryoshka dolls may be opened to reveal a dizzying regression of inner dolls. Edith cannot say if *this* dream is falling into itself, or merely progressing from tier to tier, whether up or down. She is sitting on the sand among the cobbles at Moonstone Beach, listening to the surf. Above her, the sky is low and looks like curdled milk. In her right hand, she's holding a stick that the retreating tide left stranded, and all about her, she's traced the designs from the peculiar greenish stone. They form a sort of mandala, and she sits at its center. If asked, she could not say whether the circle is meant to contain her, or to protect her. Possibly, it's meant to do both. Possibly, it is insufficient for either task.

The wind is the half-heard voice of the beach, or the voice of the sea. Behind her, it rattles the dry reeds at the edge of

Trustom Pond, and before her, it whips the crests of the breakers into a fine spray.

There is something else there with her, tucked in amongst the sand and the cobbles and the symbols she's traced on the shore. Something that desperately needs to be seen, and that would have her gaze upon nothing else. But she doesn't look at it, not yet. She will *not* look at it until she can no longer bear the pain that comes from averting her eyes.

Only a few moments ago, Sammie was standing somewhere behind her, standing very near, and talking about the January thirteen winters before, when a tank barge and a tug ran aground here. The barge spilled more than eight hundred thousand gallons of toxic heating oil into the sea and onto the beach. The name of the barge was *North Cape*, and the tug was named *Scandia*, and, during a storm, they'd run afoul of the rocks in the shallows just offshore. Both Trustom and Card ponds were contaminated by the spill, and the beach was littered with the corpses of tens of millions of poisoned sea birds, lobsters, surf clams, and starfish.

"It was a massacre," Sammie said, before she stopped talking. There was an unmistakable trace of bitterness in her voice, Edith thought. "She doesn't forget these things. Maybe people do. Maybe the birds come back and the lobsters come back, and no one tells tourists what happened here, but the *sea* remembers."

Edith asked her if that was why the song from the stone is a dirge, if it laments all the creatures killed in the oil spill. But Sammie said no, that the stone was made to keep the memory of a far more appalling day, one that predated the coming of man and was now otherwise lost to the mind of the world.

"Why are we here?" Edith asked.

"Because you would not hear the song," Sammie replied. She said nothing else after that, and Edith assumes she's alone now, sitting here alone on Moonstone Beach, buffeted by the icy wind and doing her best not to see the thing half buried in the sand only a foot or so away. She understands perfectly well that she's fighting a losing battle.

I will close my eyes, she thinks. *I can't see anything with my eyes shut. I'll close my eyes, and keep them closed until I wake up.*

But shutting her eyes only releases the next doll in the stack, so to speak, and Edith finds herself adrift in an all-but-impenetrable blackness, a blackness that is almost absolute. She recalls, clearly, standing and walking out into Block Island Sound, recalls the freezing saltwater lapping at her ankles, and then her knees, recalls it rushing up her nostrils and down her throat, searing her lungs as she sank. But she was *not* drowned, and maybe that was the magic of the carved stone at work, and maybe it was some other magic, entirely. The currents carried her away from land and into the Atlantic, ferrying her north and east past Cape Cod, and at last she'd left the sheer bluffs of the continental shelf behind. Far below her, hidden in veils of perpetual night, lie flat abyssal plains of clay and silt and diatomaceous slime. She is suspended above them, unable to fall any farther, and yet incapable of ever again rising to the surface.

All around her – over and below and on every side – indistinct shapes come and go. Some are very small, a parade of eyeless fish and curious squid, jellies and other bathypelagic creatures that she knows no names for. Others, though, move by like enormous, half-glimpsed phantoms, and she can only guess at their identity. Some are surely whales, and probably also enormous deepwater sharks and cephalopods. But others are indescribable, and plainly much too vast to be any manner of cetacean or squid. Occasionally, she reaches out a hand, and her fingers glide over that alien flesh as it rushes by in the gloom. Sometimes, it seems smooth as any silk, and other times, rough as sandpaper. The haunted, endless night is *filled* with phantoms, *And I am just one more,* she thinks. *They must wonder at me, too, at what I am, at where so strange a beast could have come from.*

And the next leviathan glares back at her with a bulging ebony eye the size of a dinner plate. There's no pupil in that eye, nor evidence of an iris, nothing to mar such an unfathomable countenance. And then the eye is gone, replaced by a flank adorned with huge photophores, each one glowing with a gentle pale-blue light. The sight delights her, and she extends a hand to stroke the thing as it moves past. And Edith clearly sees the thin, translucent webbing that's grown between her own fingers, and the long hooked claws that have replaced the nails she chews to nubs. In the muted blue light cast by the bioluminescent creature, she sees that there are fine scales dappling the backs of both her hands, and they shimmer dully, reminding her of the oily, prismatic stone.

Edith opens her eyes, and she is once more merely sitting within the mandala that she's drawn on Moonstone Beach, thirteen years after the wreck of the *North Cape*. She's still clutching the piece of driftwood and shivering in the wind. She looks over her shoulder, hoping to find Sammie there, but sees at once that she's still alone.

"Sam, I don't *know* what I'm *meant* to be listening for," she says, almost shouting to hear herself over the wind. "I don't *know* what it is, but I *am* listening."

When there's no reply, she isn't disappointed or surprised, because she understood well enough that she *wouldn't* be answered. Any answer she needs is right here before her, held within a crab-gnawed and gull-pecked anatomy, that misshapen mound of rotting flesh coughed up by whatever indifferent gods or goddesses or genderless deities call the globe's ocean their domain.

In the sand before her is a slit, and at first she thinks it is no more than some depression fashioned with her own busy fingers. She leans towards it, and now the wind is speaking, though she cannot say that the words are meant for her ears. She cannot say they are meant for any ears, at all:

There are stories that have no proper beginning. Stories for which no convenient, familiar "Once upon a time..." praeambulum exists. They may, for instance, be contained within larger stories, interwoven with the finest of gradations, and so setting them apart is a necessarily arbitrary undertaking. Let us say, then, that this story is of that species. Where it truly began is not where we will start its telling, for to attempt such a thing would require a patience and the requisite time for infinite regression. I may say that the sea had a daughter, though she has spent every day of her life on dry land. At once, the tumult of a hundred questions about how such a thing ever came to be will spring to mind. What is the nature of the sea's womb? With what or whom did she or he have congress to find himself or herself with child? What of the midwife? What is the gestation time of all the oceans of the world, or its sperm count, when considered as a single being? And, while we're at it, which *being, and from* which *pantheon, do I mean when I say "the sea"? Am I speaking of the incestuous union of Oceanus and his sister Tethys? Do I mean to say Poseidon, or Neptune, Ægir and Rán, or Susanoo of the Shinto, or Arnapkapfaaluk of the Inuit?*

I mean only to say the sea.

The sea had a daughter, but she was orphaned. She grew up in a city of men, a city at the mouths of two rivers that flowed down into a wide bay, fed by other rivers and dotted by more than thirty rocky, weathered islands. Here she was a child, and then a young woman. Here, she thought, she would grow to be an old woman. She'd never desired to travel, and had never ventured very far inland. She had seen photographs of mountain ranges, and read descriptions of the world's great deserts, and that was sufficient.

Edith places the tip of one index finger into the nearer end of the slit in the sand. Except it is not merely sand, though there is something of quartz granules and mica flakes and dark specks of feldspar in its composition. *It is flesh crafted from sand*, she thinks, *or sand painstakingly crafted from flesh.* The gross physiology is self evident now, the *labia magora* and *labia minor*, the *glans clitoris* and clitoral hood. It weeps, or simply secretes, something not so different from sea foam. And lying within it is the teardrop-shaped stone that Sammie slipped inside herself while standing in the tub.

Do you think that was such a good idea?

It's a message in a bottle. Messages like that, no one ever expects to get an answer, but we keep sending them off, anyway.

And Edith removes the stone from the slit in the sand, which then immediately closes, leaving behind no trace that it was ever actually there. She stares at the spot for a moment, comprehending, and then she flings the stone into the sea. There's no splash; the waves take it back without any sound and without so much as a ripple.

The circuit has been closed, she thinks, though the metaphor strikes her as not entirely appropriate.

She looks to the sky, and sees birds wheeling against the curdled clouds. The dream pushes her back into wakefulness, then, and, for a while, Edith lies still, squinting at the half-light of dawn and listening to a woman sobbing softly somewhere in the room.

5.

When Edith was seven years old, she saw a mermaid. One summer's day, she'd gone on a picnic with the aunt and uncle who raised her (after the death of her parents), to the rocky shore below Beavertail Lighthouse on Conanicut Island. There are tidal pools there, deep and gaping clefts opened between tilted beds of slate and phyllite, and in one of them she saw the mermaid. It rose, suddenly, towards the surface, as if lunging towards her. What most surprised her child's mind was how little it resembled any of the mermaids she'd seen in movies and storybooks, in that it was not a pretty girl with the tail of a fish. Still, she recognized it at once for what it was, if only because there was nothing else it could have been. Also, she was surprised that it seemed so hungry. The mermaid never broke the surface of the pool, but floated just beneath that turbulent, glistening membrane dividing one world from the other.

I may say that the sea had a daughter, though she has spent every day of her life on dry land.

The mermaid watched her for a while, and Edith watched the mermaid. It had black eyes, eyes like holes poked into the night sky, and did not seem to have eyelids of any sort. At least, Edith never saw it blink. And then, as abruptly as it had risen, the mermaid sank back into the deep cleft in the rock, leaving behind nothing for a seven-year-old girl to stare at but the sloshing surface of the pool. Later, she told her aunt and uncle what she'd seen, and they both smiled and laughed (though not unkindly) and explained that it had only been a harbor seal, *not* a mermaid.

When they got back home that evening, her uncle even showed her a color picture of a harbor seal in one of his encyclopedias. It made Edith think of a fat dog that had learned to live in the ocean, and looked nothing whatsoever like the mermaid that had watched her. But she didn't say this to her uncle, because she'd begun to suspect that it was somehow *wrong* to see mermaids, and that any time you saw one, you were expected to agree that what you'd really seen was a harbor seal, instead. Which is what she did. Her aunt and uncle surely had enough trouble without her seeing mermaids that she shouldn't see.

A week later, they had her baptized again.

Her uncle nailed her bedroom window shut.

Her aunt made her say the Lord's Prayer every night before bed, and also sewed sprigs of dried wormwood into her clothes.

And they never went back down to the rocky place below the lighthouse at Beavertail, and always thereafter had their picnics far from the sea.

6.

Edith does not doubt that she's now awake, any more than, a moment before she opened her eyes, she doubted that she was still dreaming. This is not the next tier, nor merely the next painted wooden doll in the matryoshka's stack. This is the world of her waking, conscious mind, and this time she will not deny that for the sake of sanity or convenience. There has always been too much of lies about her, too much pretend. When her eyes have grown accustomed to the early morning light, she sits up in bed. Sammie is still crying, somewhere in the room, somewhere very close by, and as soon as Edith sits up, she sees her crouching naked on the hardwood floor near the foot of the bed. All around her, the floor is wet. She has her back turned to Edith, and her head is bowed so that her black hair hangs down to the pine floorboards. Edith glances immediately to the little table beside the bed, but the peculiar tear-shaped pebble from Moonstone Beach is gone. She knew that it would be, but she looked anyway. The air in the room smells like a fish market.

Sammie, or the thing that now occupies the place in this universe where Sammie used to be, has stopped sobbing and has begun a ragged sort of trilling chant in no language that Edith knows or thinks she's ever heard. It sounds much more like the winter wind, and like waves rolling against sand, and the screech of herring gulls, than it sounds like human speech. Edith opens her mouth and almost calls out to Sammie, but then she stops herself. The thing on the floor probably wouldn't answer to that name, anyway. And she'd rather not use any of the names to which it might respond.

Its skin is the same murky pea green as the vanished stone, and bears all the same marks that were carved into the stone. All the same wounds, each pregnant with significance and connotations that Edith has only just begun to grasp. There is a pentacle – or something almost like a pentacle – cut deeply into each of Sammie's shoulders, and a vertical line of left-facing swastikas decorates the length of her spine. Wherever this new flesh has been sliced open, it leaks a greasy black substance that must be blood. Below the swastikas, there is the symbol that reminded them both of a Greek *ichthus*, centered just above Sammie's ass. Edith cannot help but wonder if Sammie was reborn with these wounds already in place, like birth marks, or if they came later, not so differently than the stigmata of Catholic saints. Or if maybe they're self inflicted, and Edith remembers her own hands in the dream, the sharp claws where her nails had been. In the end, it hardly matters how the marks came to be; the meaning is the same, either way.

Do you think that was such a good idea?

It's a message in a bottle. No one ever expects to get an answer, but we keep sending them off...

"When you're ready," Edith says, almost whispering, "I'll be right here. There's no hurry. I know how long you've been waiting." Then she lies back down, and turns to face the wall.

A Canvas for Incoherent Arts

No matter how fast light travels, it finds the dark-
ness has always got there first, and is waiting for it.
Terry Pratchett

The game is ours, or so we like to imagine. We cannot, of
course, ever know for certain that the game is our own inven-
tion. Indeed, whenever either of us pauses to consider the matter,
we both must readily admit how exceedingly unlikely it is that we
are the first to have conceived so simple and obvious a diversion.
I would say *simple* and *obvious*; you would say *inherently elegant*.
You would say the genius of the game *resides* in its elegance. I
wouldn't disagree, but I have never had your way with words. For
that matter, I have never had your way with darkness. I understand, full well, that I'm the student, struggling to keep pace. I
also understand this amuses you, that you always have the edge,
that the advantage is always yours.

And, so, in this space we have set aside for the game, I'm
the one who finds herself cuffed to the stainless-steel ring bolt set
deep into the old masonry. There is a length of chain connecting
the steel bolt to a D-ring, fastened securely to the padded leather
wrist restraints I wear. It's not uncomfortable, and the chain is
long enough that I can stand, and even move as far as the center
of the room. There's nothing in the room, except the ring bolt
and the chain and the cuffs that hold me. And you, of course. The
walls and ceiling and even the floor have all been painted the same
matte black, four heavy coats on every surface. The one window
has been boarded over, and we have seen to it that no light can leak

in around the door. We are thorough, and have insured that, once a new round of the game begins, no illumination enters the room from any source whatsoever.

There *is* a single, naked 60-watt bulb screwed into a socket mounted on the high ceiling, but it can only be switched on from the hallway outside the black room. Once, on a whim, you left me alone in the room for three hours with that bulb burning starkly overhead. On several occasions, you've left me alone in the room, and for extended periods of time, but only that *once* with the light shining. Somehow, the light made being alone in there much worse. Held at bay, the darkness pregnant in every plane and angle of that space seemed far more threatful. Perhaps, I imagined it was conscious and resented the light holding it back, much the same way a hungry lion or jaguar might resent a roaring fire. And, as you have repeatedly reminded me, imagination is the necessary catalyst or reagent, if the room is to become anything *more* than merely an empty room painted black.

You are fond of a line from *Hamlet*, and how it applies to our game and to our black arena or theatre.

...there is nothing either good or bad, but thinking makes it so.

And *this* night might well be any other night when we've chosen to play, which is not to say that our game has become repetitious or monotonous. Accepting the inviolable blackness as a given, as square one, there is an almost infinite number of permutations that might follow. I am alone in the room, cuffed to the chain fastened to the ring bolt driven into bricks and mortar, and I have absolutely no way of knowing what will happen next. Usually (but not always), you leave me for a time with only the dark for company. It might be five minutes, or thirty, or an hour. I have no way of knowing. You've referred to this as the prelude, and the overture, and also described it as "a palate cleanser." Oh, and there's another line of verse you're fond of quoting, this one from Milton, and I find it applicable to the customary waiting period that comes before the game begins in earnest.

The mind is its own place, and in itself, can make heaven of Hell, and a hell of Heaven.

I lie naked on the hard floor, and when you're ready, you'll open the door and slip inside. And, usually, that's the last I'll get of light until the game is done, the muted rectangle from the doorway, creating and framing your silhouette. And even this is not a constant, as you have devised many clever techniques of altering the shade and the quality of light from the hall beyond the room, and also of altering what I might see of your profile. Once in a while, I'll miss your entrance altogether. My face will be turned away from the door, my eyes will be shut, or my light-starved optic nerves will have become preoccupied with nonexistent patterns that appear to dart and swoop about me. You are especially pleased whenever this happens, when my usual disadvantage is increased by an extra element of surprise.

But, to my credit, I have never yet screamed. You've told me that *if* I ever scream, we might stop playing the game.

"What would even be the point in continuing after that," you've said. "Once I've heard you scream, I mean. It's a sort of threshold, and once it's been crossed, I don't really see much to be gained by crossing it again."

I took these words to heart, and, so far, they have been sufficient to stop me from screaming or crying out in any other way, regardless what might happen in the black room. I cannot bear the thought of our game coming to an end. And I don't need to be warned twice.

I lie here on the floor, and the door opens, and then the door closes again. This is one of the times when I happen to be turned towards it, and so I catch the light from the hallway, which has a reddish hue tonight. It's dim, but still bright enough that my pupils ache after all that dark. I squint into the murky red light and see your silhouette, though something about the proportion of your head to your shoulders is wrong. Before I have a chance to figure it out, how exactly you've managed to change your appearance, the door closes again, and the lock clicks loudly as the deadbolt slides into place, and the greater darkness returns.

Long minutes pass, and you haven't said a word. Upon entering, your footsteps were almost impossible to detect. This is another part of the game that varies wildly. Sometimes, your feet are loud against the floor, and sometimes they're muffled and virtually inaudible. Sometimes, you tiptoe with bare feet, and sometimes you brazenly stomp about in hard-soled shoes with sharp stiletto heels. Tonight, you are at your most noiseless, silent as the most accomplished sneak thief, and I don't even bother hazarding a guess as to where you're sitting or standing, kneeling or crouching, at how near or far from me you might be.

I lie very still, and I wait. Time passes, though I have no way of reckoning how much or how little of it comes and goes. I think perhaps I can hear you breathing, somewhere in front of me, but I can't be sure. I close my eyes when motes of nonexistent light begin to dance before them, though that doesn't really help very much.

I close my eyes, and I wait.

And, finally, I begin to wonder if maybe you've mastered some new bit of legerdemain, and have slipped out without my having seen or heard you go. It may be, I think, that I am alone in the black room, and the thought brings a sudden and inexplicable wave of panic. You would surely deem that an *elegant* new strategy, and give yourself a gold star for being so clever. I open my eyes again, thinking perhaps I might have dozed off, that I may have lain here asleep, surrounded by nothing at all but the smothering, absolute darkness. That's happened before. And then, as if you can now count telepathy among your arts, you whisper my name. You only whisper, but in this silent black room that we have fashioned, a whisper can be a thunderclap, and it startles me so badly there's a rush of adrenaline that leaves my heart pounding, and I feel sick and even more disoriented.

"Not getting bored, I hope," you say, still whispering. You're in fine form tonight, and your voice betrays not even the slightest hint of your gender or age, and no trace of emotion, either. It could be anyone's voice, or the voice of no one, at all. And you've long since learned to pitch it in such a way that I'm incapable of knowing from which direction it's coming, so those five words, those six stingy syllables, are no help whatsoever in revealing where you are.

"I'm not bored," I reply, not bothering to whisper, and then I clear my dry throat and struggle to sit upright.

"How can I be sure?" you ask. There's still no trace of *you* in your voice, and it occurs to me (as it has on other nights) that maybe you've found someone to act as your surrogate, that I might be in the black room with a complete stranger, or a close friend, or with the most casual of acquaintances.

"I don't know," I answer truthfully. "I don't know how you can be sure, how I'm supposed to convince you."

"But I assume you *do* understand that it poses a problem, my uncertainty?"

"Yes," I say. "Yes, obviously, of course." And then there's a soft sound, and I can't quite seem to find the language to describe it. A *soft* sound. The best I can do is say that it puts me in mind of someone punching a pillow. But that's not right, not really. It's a much softer sound than that. It seems to have come from somewhere on my left.

"If you *have* grown bored," you continue, "then the solution is self-evident, wouldn't you think?"

"But I'm *not* bored," I tell you again, trying very hard to imbue the words with conviction, though I'm beginning to grow impatient, and maybe a little angry, too. I *know* this is merely some fresh tactic you've devised to throw me off my guard, and I know also that it's my place to play along and see where it's leading. On some level, I don't doubt these things. On another, there is an unfamiliar irritation growing inside me, as whatever expectations I might have had, and whatever desires, whatever tensions, are defused by these unexpected questions.

"Well, you don't seem particularly enthusiastic," you say, and there's a laugh. A high, cold laugh. But I'm almost certain that it's not *you* laughing. Indeed, I'm fairly sure that the laughter began a second or two before you finished speaking.

"Who else is in the room with us?" I ask, and I realize that I'm sweating.

"It's not your place to question," you remind me. "Right now, the *only* thing you should be concerned with is making me believe that you're not bored."

We have a safeword, of course, but I've never yet used it. I've never even come close. But now, I mouth it silently, my tongue and lips forming its exact shape. The irritation I felt a few moments earlier has become, instead, a ballooning anxiety, and there's an unaccustomed confusion in me, as well. One half the object of our game has always been to frighten me, and there have been plenty of occasions when I've been left rattled for hours afterwards. Once or twice, you've scared me badly enough that I've actually pissed myself. Once, I even vomited. But we've both counted this as evidence of *success*, of that genius arising from what you've labeled the game's *inherent elegance.* You are here, in this black room, to scare me, and I am here to be scared.

"Maybe," you say, "the problem is that *I'm* bored, dear. And, maybe, the solution isn't to stop playing, but simply to stop playing with *you.*" And this time, you sound exactly like you, and I think that must be intended to be as menacing as what you're saying. I can't doubt that I'm hearing these things from your lips; I can only doubt whether or not you mean them.

I sit there, sweating, my pulse racing, waiting for the laugh I heard before, but this time it doesn't come.

"Do you think you could find someone else who'd play?" I ask, though my throat is almost too parched to speak. "By your rules, I mean?"

"Dear, what if I already have?" you reply, your voice louder than before.

A stinging drop of sweat runs across my forehead and into my right eye. If my hands were free, I could wipe it away. If my hands were free, I could release myself from the chain attached to the ring bolt set into the room's wall. I could stand up and walk to the door...

"It would be a damned shame, if that's the case" you say, whispering again, and once more affecting that ageless, sexless tone. And this is when I feel the blade at my throat, pressed firmly into the soft nook beneath my chin. It isn't cold, the steel, not like I would have expected it to be, if I'd been expecting it. Maybe it's a small knife, or possibly a straight razor; it's impossible for me to tell which. "We've had such a very, very good time, haven't we?"

"Yes," I tell you, and lick my dry lips. "We've had a wonderful time."

From somewhere near the door, the laughter comes again, but I stay perfectly still, because there's no way of knowing how sharp the blade you're holding is. Maybe, it's so dull it wouldn't slice hot butter. Or maybe, it's sharp enough that any sudden movement of my head to one side or the other would be sufficient to break the skin. Or open an artery.

"This is what I want," you whisper. "I want you to sit here and think about everything I've said. I want you to sit here, and be perfectly, completely quiet until I come back for you. Do you think you can manage that?"

I don't dare nod, so I tell you yes, even though I'm not sure if I should speak, either. I say yes, and you tell me I'm a such good girl, and that you're proud of me, and then you take the blade away from my throat and kiss me gently on the cheek.

"I'll be back later," you say. "I'll be back later, and maybe we'll play a little more."

You cross the room to the door, and I can hear the soles of your bare feet against the painted wood, faint, but clearly audible.

"Remember what I just told you. Not a peep," and you turn the deadbolt, unlocking the door. When it opens, the silhouette against the red glow from the hallway is only your silhouette, undisguised and immediately recognizable. I understand you want to admit no reasonable doubt that you're leaving. You pull the door closed behind you, and the unblemished darkness returns. I try not to dwell on the laughter that couldn't have been yours, or the fact that no one followed you out. Instead, I lie back down and shut my eyes again. And here, in the black room at the center of this game that I have always imagined is ours, and *only* ours, I wait for you to come back for me.

The Peril of Liberated Objects, or The Voyeur's Seduction

Arabella Hopestill can no longer recall, precisely, where or when she acquired the ancient red book. She remembers only that the day was very, very hot, so she assumes it was during the summer, or possibly early autumn. It was a hot day, and the air stank of dust and mothballs and her own sour sweat, and oftentimes she thinks that there were many *other* books involved. It seems, sometimes, there was a sort of necessary trial to gain this treasure, the task of choosing this *one* book from among hundreds or thousands of others. But the truth, which she has not yet even begun to suspect, is that the book acquired *her*, as has always been, and ever shall be, its way. In the millennium since it escaped the dreamlands, it has only once, briefly, been bound by the will of a human being, and, in the end, that man paid dearly for the privilege and the insult.

But Arabella Hopestill knows nothing of the red book's captivity at the hands of that forgotten Italian astrologer and alchemist – now five-hundred years dead and buried in the catacombs beneath Palermo – any more than she knows of the book's origins in the onyx seaport of Inquanok, below the towering, polished walls of the Temple of the Elder Ones. She does not know of the inhuman priests who there guarded it in lightless subterranean chambers. Or of the accident or miscalculation that allowed it to slip, at last, from their watchful gaze and be carried across the sea to Celephaïs in Ooth-Nargai, and from there, in time to the basalt towers of Dylath-Leen, and on to Nir and Ulthar, and across the green plains bordering the River Skai. Araballa will never guess at the dire pact that allowed the nameless red book to find its way past the priests Nasht and Kaman-Thah in the cavern of flame, then up the seventy steps to the waking world. These things are secrets the book has hidden from all prying eyes and minds, that it might never be delivered back into the hands of its keepers in the Temple of the Elder Ones.

Arabella knows only that she can no longer bear to live without the book. Even the thought of someday losing it brings cold sweats and sleepless nights. She has spent too many years in its company, and is terrified at the prospect of her life devoid of the unspeakable, perverse revelations it readily surrenders whenever she takes it down from its place on a particularly high shelf and opens the red leather covers. The paper is brittle, and gone the yellowish brown of fossil ivory. There is no title page, for the book was never named. There is no author, for it needed none. Indeed, there's not a single written word to be found anywhere inside the volume. It is not a book of letters, but a book of images. One does not simply read the red book. Rather, *it* reads the fondest nightmares and most repressed appetites of those who gaze into it, and subsequently shows them what they have always longed to see (even though they may never have been conscious of these longings). In this way, it might fairly be said to be as much a mirror as a book, and Arabella Hopestill, lost and alone and content for the first time in her life, has become a devotee to its endless reflections.

She has little use of any other looking glass, having been convinced when still a young woman that she was too plain to be of interest to any lover, far too humdrum and dim-witted to attract a suitor of any stripe, and hopelessly beyond even the most remote chance for marriage. "Hardly fit for whoring, this one," a comely man said to her, the same year she turned twenty. He told her that, spoke those six words, then laughed, and whatever atrophied stub of dignity and self worth had managed to survive the first two decades of her life was entirely consumed in that instant.

The book has become her lover, or so she sometimes pretends. The book has become all she will ever need.

This evening in August, Arabella lays the book on a table near an open window, so that she can feel and smell the cool salt breeze blowing in off the harbor. There's no light in the room but the feeble glow of the moon (two nights past the first quarter), getting in through that window. She's learned that the book is at its most forthcoming when kept away from the harsh glare of electric bulbs, and that even candlelight can mute the visions it offers up. She opens it at random, seeking no particular page, and there's a faint whistling sort of noise, as though she has unsealed a vacuum, but it only lasts a moment. Then the room is quiet, save the sound of the traffic on the street below, muffled voices from the apartment next door, the songs of night birds, and the eager pounding of her own caged heart.

"Show me," she whispers. "Show me something I haven't seen before. Show me something new, and something awful."

And, immediately, the book obliges, as it always does. The blank page on Arabella's right goes suddenly sooty and strangely translucent. She has the distinct impression that some inner, half-concealed luminosity is struggling to tear itself free of the paper, something caught for unknown eons between the covers like a wasp sealed in a lump of amber. If it *is* a struggle, and not merely an overture before the curtain rises, it never lasts long, and seconds later she's gazing into and *through* the red book, at a small meadow surrounded on all sides by spruces and oaks grown so lofty their uppermost boughs seem to rasp at the exposed belly of the sky. Across the green meadow, violet blooms of columbine compete with anemones and starry yellow flowers that Arabella doesn't recognize. There's a wide brook winding through the meadow, and its banks are muddy and crowded with reeds, starwort, and watercrowfoot. Here and there, the brook ripples and furls as it glides smoothly over a barely submerged outcropping of stone.

"Something *awful*," she says again, as though possibly, the book misunderstood the first time.

And then she sees the unicorn and the maiden, not far from the brook. They must surely have been there all along, but, somehow, she didn't see them before. The woman is very young, and her dress, which hangs from her in shreds, seems to have been woven of golden thread, the way the tatters shine beneath the bright sun falling across the meadow. Even the muddy spatters do not seem to diminish the gleam of that golden dress. The woman is down on her hands and knees, and her long auburn hair hides her face from view. She seems to grip the earth as if she's afraid of falling. Not down, for surely she cannot fall any farther down, but up, into the wide sky sprawling blue and vacant and hungry above the meadow. Her fingers are sunk deep into the mud.

"Yes," Arabella whispers. "Thank you. Yes." She once dreamed this scene, many years ago, though she has no recollection of the dream. The book knows all the dreams of men, and of many other beings, besides, and vomits them forth whenever it sees fit.

This unicorn is a *true* unicorn, not merely a white mare with a horn sprouting from its skull. In equal measure it resembles a billy-goat, or a doe, or some fabulous species of white antelope, as much as it resembles any horse. Its restless tail is very like that of a lion, and the spiraling horn that is its namesake could have been plucked from the upper left maxilla of a bull narwhal. It stands over the woman, snorting and stamping at the muddy ground with its cloven hooves. It's prodigious cock is almost the same exact shade of red as the leather in which the book is bound. The unicorn bares its teeth, and when it snorts, steam seems to billow from its flaring nostrils.

So, this is the scene being played out upon the page for Arabella, the fallen woman trampled beneath the feet of an angry, rutting unicorn. And Arabella looks as closely as she can, squinting to note each and every detail, no matter how terrible or minute or seemingly inconsequential, drinking it all in, for she's learned that the book never gives up the same vision twice. And this is one she knows she'll want to savor again and again and again.

The unicorn bows its shaggy head, and with that gleaming horn, tears away what's left of the golden dress. With another swipe of the horn, it leaves a deep gash in the pale flesh of the woman's lower back. She screams, in pain and fear, and then the unicorn mounts her. She tries to struggle free, to shake the beast off and crawl towards the brook. But thick roots and vines burst from the mire and twine themselves tightly about her wrists and ankles and throat, as though Nature herself has conspired against the maiden, or, Arabella thinks, as though the unicorn commands all green and growing things. The woman screams again when the creature enters her.

Arabella licks at her thin, dry lips and grips the edges of the table by the open window.

And in the dreamlands, past the seventy steps and through the wild, enchanted fungal woods that lie just beyond the Gate of Deeper Slumber, past the River Skai and the narrow, cobbled streets of Ulthar and across the shimmering sea in the onyx city of Celephaïs, the priests within the sixteen-sided Temple of the Elder Ones pause in their prayers. Even after so many centuries, they have not lost all connection to the nameless red book, and in those hours when it works its deceits in the waking world, they bleed a foul, caustic ichor from their palms and the bottoms of their feet. Far below the Temple, in the catacombs that once imprisoned the tome, one among their number has been chained in its place, as a constant reminder of their inexcusable failure. This unfortunate, become a sort of willing surrogate, bears the greater part of their conjunction with the escaped book. The martyr's tongue was cut out, that he might never utter the fell apparitions the book reveals to those waking women and men who, like Arabella Hopestill, have become catalysts for its depredations. What the chained priest bleeds is not to be described.

Arabella stares *into* the page, while the red book stares into her, and by way of its immemorial sorceries she feels every bit of the maiden's hurt and terror and humiliation, her outrage and despair. But Arabella Hopestill *also* is given access to all the sensations and sentiments of the unicorn. She tastes the violated woman's blood upon its tongue, and grows drunk with waves of triumph and boundless cruelty that infects all immortal beings. She perceives the unicorn's every violent thrust, but is no less the victim than the rapist, no more the ravager than she is the ravaged, broken maiden. And she would have it no other way. The experiences the book bequeaths to her would be incomplete and entirely unsatisfying were she given only one half of any of its tableaus (or, in other, more elaborate cases, were she given only a third, or a fifth, or one fiftieth).

Arabella shudders and comes, even as the unicorn comes. She finds the strength to glance away from the page for a moment, trembling and listening to a mockingbird running through its repertoire of borrowed songs. Its impossible to be sure if the bird is in that meadow within the book, or somewhere just outside the open window. The breeze through the window reeks of the exhaust of passing automobiles, and Arabella realizes that she's bitten her tongue hard enough that it's bleeding. With an unsteady hand, she wipes blood and spittle from her lips and chin, and laughs nervously. Already, the ecstasy is fading quickly from her mind and body, as are the torments visited upon the maiden, those vales of anguish and degradation she has known now as though they were her own. Arabella looks back to the book, and already the page is growing murky around the edges.

"As long as I live," she whispers, "I will guard you. As long as I live, I will keep you safe."

At the edge of the brook, the maiden lies shattered, a wreck of meat and golden cloth. Her green-brown eyes are not lifeless, but they seem as empty as the glass eyes of a porcelain doll. The roots that held her have retreated back into the muck.

"As long as I live," Arabella whispers.

The unicorn uses one cloven forefoot to roll the woman over onto her back, and then stands perfectly still for a moment, motionless and white as a figurine carved from alabaster or bone. And then it turns and walks, unhurried towards the shelter of the towering oaks and spruces. Arabella knows everything the beast knows, and the unicorn is quite entirely certain that the woman lying in the mud will bear it a daughter, and that the child will come shortly after the first winter snowfalls smother the meadow and the brook has frozen over.

And then the page is only a blank and brittle page again, and, with trembling hands, Arabella Hopestill closes the red book and sits watching the cars coming and going on the street below her apartment.

Far down in the dreamlands, the hands and feet of the priests who kneel inside the Temple of the Elder Ones cease to display that vile stigmata, and the sacrifice chained far below them finally stops fighting against his unbreakable bonds. As the sun rises over the ebony towers of Inquanok, pushing the night away, that madman slips away into the nightmares that visit the inhabitants of this land, and dreams his bitter, splintered dreams within dreams.

Pickman's Other Model (1929)

1.

I have never been much for the movies, preferring, instead, to take my entertainment in the theater, always favoring living actors over those flickering, garish ghosts magnified and splashed across the walls of dark and smoky rooms at twenty-four frames per second. I've never seemed able to get past the knowledge that the apparent motion is merely an optical illusion, a clever procession of still images streaming past my eye at such a rate of speed that I only perceive motion where none actually exists. But in the months before I finally met Vera Endecott, I found myself drawn with increasing regularity to the Boston movie houses, despite this longstanding reservation.

I had been shocked to my core by Thurber's suicide, though, with the unavailing curse of hindsight, it's something I should certainly have had the presence of mind to have seen coming. Thurber was an infantryman during the war – *La Guerre por la Civilisation*, as he so often called it. He was at the Battle of Saint-Mihiel when Pershing failed in his campaign to seize Metz from the Germans, and he survived only to see the atrocities at the Battle of the Argonne Forest less than two weeks later. When he returned home from France early in 1819, Thurber was hardly more than a fading, nervous echo of the man I'd first met during our college years at the Rhode Island School of Design, and, on those increasingly rare occasions when we met and spoke, more often than not our conversations turned from painting and sculpture and matters of aesthetics to the things he'd seen in the muddy trenches and ruined cities of Europe.

And then there was his dogged fascination with that sick bastard Richard Upton Pickman, an obsession that would lead quickly to what I took to be no less than a sort of psychoneurotic fixation on the man and the blasphemies he committed to canvas. When, two years ago, Pickman vanished from the squalor of his North End "studio," never to be seen again, this fixation only worsened, until Thurber finally came to me with an incredible, nightmarish tale which, at the time, I could only dismiss as the ravings of a mind left unhinged by the bloodshed and madness and countless wartime horrors he'd witnessed along the banks of the Meuse River and then in the wilds of the Argonne Forest.

But I am not the man I was then, that evening we sat together in a dingy tavern near Faneuil Hall (I don't recall the name of the place, as it wasn't one of my usual haunts). Even as William Thurber was changed by the war and by whatever it is he may have experienced in the company of Pickman, so too have I been changed, and changed *utterly*, first by Thurber's sudden death at his own hands and then by a film actress named Vera Endecott. I do not believe that I have yet lost possession of my mental faculties, and if asked, I would attest before a judge of law that my mind remains sound, if quite shaken. But I cannot now see the world around me the way I once did, for having beheld certain things there can be no return to the unprofaned state of innocence or grace that prevailed before those sights. There can be no return to the sacred cradle of Eden, for the gates are guarded by the flaming swords of cherubim, and the mind may not – excepting in merciful cases of shock and hysterical amnesia – simply forget the weird and dismaying revelations visited upon men and women who choose to ask forbidden questions. And I would be lying if I were to claim that I failed to comprehend, to suspect, that the path I was setting myself upon when I began my investigations following Thurber's inquest and funeral would lead me where they have. I knew, or I knew well enough. I am not yet so degraded that I am beyond taking responsibility for my own actions and the consequences of those actions.

Thurber and I used to argue about the validity of first-person narration as an effective literary device, him defending it and me calling into question the believability of such stories, doubting both the motivation of their fictional authors and the ability of those character narrators to accurately recall with such perfect clarity and detail specific conversations and the order of events during times of great stress and even personal danger. This is probably not so very different from my difficulty appreciating a moving picture because I am aware it is *not*, in fact, a moving picture. I suspect it points to some conscious unwillingness or unconscious inability, on my part, to effect what Coleridge dubbed the "suspension of disbelief." And now I sit down to write my *own* account, though I attest there is not a word of *intentional* fiction to it, and I certainly have no plans of ever seeking its publication. Nonetheless, it will undoubtedly be filled with inaccuracies following from the objections to a first-person recital that I have already belabored above. What I am putting down here is my best attempt to recall the events preceding and surrounding the murder of Vera Endecott, and it should be read as such.

It is my story, presented with such meager corroborative documentation as I am here able to provide. It is some small part of her story, as well, and over it hang the phantoms of Pickman and Thurber. In all honesty, already I begin to doubt that setting any of it down will achieve the remedy which I so desperately desire – the dampening of damnable memory, the lessening of the hold that those memories have upon me, and, if I am most lucky, the ability to sleep in dark rooms once again and an end to any number of phobias which have come to plague me. Too late do I understand poor Thurber's morbid fear of cellars and subway tunnels, and to that I can add my own fears, whether they might ever be proven rational or not. "I guess you won't wonder now why I have to steer clear of subways and cellars," he said to me that day in the tavern. I *did* wonder, of course, at that and at the sanity of a dear and trusted friend. But, in this matter, at least, I have long since ceased to wonder.

The first time I saw Vera Endecott on the "big screen," it was only a supporting part in Josef von Sternberg's *A Woman of the Sea*, at the Exeter Street Theater. But that was not the first time I saw Vera Endecott.

2.

I first encountered the name and face of the actress while sorting through William's papers, which I'd been asked to do by the only surviving member of his immediate family, Ellen Thurber, an older sister. I found myself faced with no small or simple task, as the close, rather shabby room he'd taken on Hope Street in Providence after leaving Boston was littered with a veritable bedlam of correspondence, typescripts, journals, and unfinished compositions, including the monograph on weird art that had played such a considerable role in his taking up with Richard Pickman three years prior. I was only mildly surprised to discover, in the midst of this disarray, a number of Pickman's sketches, all of them either charcoal or pen and ink. Their presence among Thurber's effects seemed rather incongruous, given how completely terrified of the man he'd professed to having become. And even more so given his claim to have destroyed the one piece of evidence that could support the incredible tale of what he purported to have heard and seen and taken away from Pickman's cellar studio.

It was a hot day, so late into July that it was very nearly August. When I came across the sketches, seven of them tucked inside a cardboard portfolio case, I carried them across the room and spread the lot out upon the narrow, swaybacked bed occupying one corner. I had a decent enough familiarity with the man's work, and I must confess that what I'd seen of it had never struck me quiet so profoundly as it had Thurber. Yes, to be sure, Pickman was possessed of a great and singular talent, and I suppose someone unaccustomed to images of the diabolic, the alien or monstrous, would find them disturbing and unpleasant to look upon. I always credited his success at capturing the weird largely to his intentional juxtaposition of phantasmagoric subject matter with a starkly, painstakingly realistic style. Thurber also noted this, and, indeed, had devoted almost a full chapter of his unfinished monograph to an examination of Pickman's technique.

I sat down on the bed to study the sketches, and the mattress springs complained loudly beneath my weight, leading me to wonder yet again why my friend had taken such mean accommodations when he certainly could have afforded better. At any rate, glancing over the drawings, they struck me, for the most part, as nothing particularly remarkable, and I assumed that they must have been gifts from Pickman, or that Thurber might even have paid him some small sum for them. Two I recognized as studies for one of the paintings mentioned that day in the Chatham Street tavern, the one titled *The Lesson*, in which the artist had sought to depict a number of his subhuman, doglike ghouls instructing a young child (a *changeling*, Thurber had supposed) in their practice of necrophagy. Another was a rather hasty sketch of what I took to be some of the statelier monuments in Copp's Hill Burying Ground, and there were also a couple of rather slapdash renderings of hunched gargoyle-like creatures.

But it was the last two pieces from the folio that caught and held my attention. Both were very accomplished nudes, more finished than any of the other sketches, and given the subject matter, I might have doubted they had come from Pickman's hand had it not been for his signature at the bottom of each. There was nothing that could have been deemed pornographic about either, and considering their provenance, this surprised me, as well. Of the portion of Richard Pickman's *oeuvre* that I'd seen for myself, I'd not once found any testament to an interest in the female form, and there had even been whispers in the Art Club that he was a homosexual. But there were so many rumors traded about the man in the days leading up to his disappearance, many of them plainly spurious, that I'd never given the subject much thought. Regardless of his own sexual inclinations, these two studies were imbued with an appreciation and familiarity with a woman's body that seemed unlikely to have been gleaned entirely from academic exercises or mooched from the work of other, less-eccentric artists.

As I inspected the nudes, thinking that these two pieces, at least, might bring a few dollars to help Thurber's sister cover the unexpected expenses incurred by her brother's death, as well as his outstanding debts, my eyes were drawn to a bundle of magazine and newspaper clippings that had also been stored inside the portfolio. There were a goodly number of them, and I guessed then, and still suppose, that Thurber had employed a clipping bureau. About half of them were write-ups of gallery showings that had included Pickman's work, mostly spanning the years from 1921 to 1925, before he'd been so ostracized that opportunities for public showings had dried up. But the remainder appeared to have been culled largely from tabloids, sheetlets, and magazines such as *Photoplay* and *the New York Evening Graphic*, and every one of the articles was either devoted to or made mention of a Massachusetts-born actress named Vera Marie Endecott. There were, among these clippings, a number of photographs of the woman, and her likeness to the woman who'd modeled for the two Pickman nudes was unmistakable.

There was something quite distinct about her high cheek-bones, the angle of her nose, an undeniable hardness to her countenance despite her starlet's beauty and "sex appeal." Later, I would come to recognize some commonality between her face and those of such movie "vamps" and *femme fatales* as Theda Bara, Eva Galli, Musidora, and, in particular, Pola Negri. But, as best as I can now recollect, my first impression of Vera Endecott, untainted by film personae (though undoubtedly colored by the association of the clippings with the work of Richard Pickman, there among the belongings of a suicide) was of a woman whose loveliness might merely be a glamour concealing some truer, feral face. It was an admittedly odd impression, and I sat in the sweltering boarding-house room, as the sun slid slowly towards dusk, reading each of the articles, and then reading some over again. I suspected they must surely contain, somewhere, evidence that the woman in the sketches was, indeed, the same woman who'd gotten her start in the movie studios of Long Island and New Jersey, before the industry moved west to California.

For the most part, the clippings were no more than the usual sort of picture-show gossip, innuendo, and sensationalism. But, here and there, someone, presumably Thurber himself, had under-lined various passages with a red pencil, and when those lines were considered together, removed from the context of their accompanying articles, a curious pattern could be discerned. At least, such a pattern might be imagined by a reader who was either *searching* for it, and so predisposed to discovering it whether it truly existed or not, or by someone, like myself, coming to these collected scraps of yellow journalism under such circumstances and such an atmosphere of dread as may urge the reader to draw parallels where, objectively, there are none to be found. I believed, that summer afternoon, that Thurber's *idée fixe* with Richard Pickman had led him to piece together an absurdly macabre set of notions regarding this woman, and that I, still grieving the loss of a close friend and surrounded as I was by the disorder of that friend's unfulfilled life's work, had done nothing but uncover another of Thurber's delusions.

The woman known to moviegoers as Vera Endecott had been sired into an admittedly peculiar family from the North Shore region of Massachusetts, and she'd undoubtedly taken steps to hide her heritage, adopting a stage name shortly after her arrival in Fort Lee in February of 1922. She'd also invented a new history for herself, claiming to hail not from rural Essex County, but from Boston's Beacon Hill. However, as early as '24, shortly after landing her first substantial role – an appearance in Biograph Studios' *Sky Below the Lake* – a number of popular columnists had begun printing their suspicions about her professed background. The banker she'd claimed as her father could not be found, and it proved a straightforward enough matter to demonstrate that she'd never attended the Winsor School for girls. By '25, after starring in Robert G. Vignola's *The Horse Winter*, a reporter for *The New York Evening Graphic* claimed Endecott's actual father was a man named Iscariot Howard Snow, the owner of several Cape Anne granite quarries. His wife, Make-peace, had come either from Salem or Marblehead, and had died in 1902 while giving birth to their only daughter, whose name was not Vera, but Lillian Margaret. There was no evidence in any of the clippings that the actress had ever denied or even responded to any of these allegations, despite the fact that the Snows, and Iscariot Snow, in particular, had a distinctly unsavory reputation in and around Ipswich. Despite the family's wealth and prominence in local business, it was notoriously secretive, and there was no want for back-fence talk concerning sorcery and witchcraft, incest and even cannibalism. In 1899, Make-peace Snow had also borne twin sons, Aldous and Edward, though Edward had been a stillbirth.

But it was a clipping from *Kidder's Weekly Art News* (March 27th, 1925), a publication I was well enough acquainted with, that first tied the actress to Richard Pickman. A "Miss Vera Endecott of Manhattan" was listed among those in attendance at the premiere of an exhibition that had included a couple of Pickman's less provocative paintings, though no mention was made of her celebrity. Thurber had circled her name with his red pencil and drawn two exclamation points beside it. By the time I came across the article, twilight had descended upon Hope Street, and I was having trouble reading. I briefly considered the old gas lamp near the bed, but then, staring into the shadows gathering amongst the clutter and threadbare furniture of the seedy little room, I was gripped by a sudden, vague apprehension – by what, even now, I am reluctant to name *fear*. I returned the clippings and the seven sketches to the folio, tucked it under my arm and quickly retrieved my hat from a table buried beneath a typewriter, an assortment of paper and library books, unwashed dishes and empty soda bottles. A few minutes later, I was outside again and clear of the building, standing beneath a streetlight, staring up at the two darkened windows opening into the room where, a week before, William Thurber had put the barrel of a revolver in his mouth and pulled the trigger.

3.

I have just awakened from another of my nightmares, which become ever more vivid and frequent, ever more appalling, often permitting me no more than one or two hours sleep each night. I'm sitting at my writing desk, watching as the sky begins to go the grey-violet of false dawn, listening to the clock ticking like some giant wind-up insect perched upon the mantle. But my mind is still lodged firmly in a dream of the musty private screening room near Harvard Square, operated by a small circle of aficionados of grotesque cinema, the room where first I saw "moving" images of the daughter of Iscariot Snow.

I'd learned of the group from an acquaintance in acquisitions at the Museum of Fine Arts, who'd told me it met irregularly, rarely more than once every three months, to view and discuss such fanciful and morbid fare as Benjamin Christensen's *Häxen*, Rupert Julian's *The Phantom of the Opera*, Murnau's *Nosferatu – Eine Symphonie des Grauens*, and Todd Browning's *London After Midnight*. These titles and the names of their directors meant very little to me, since, as I have already noted, I've never been much for the movies. This was in August, only a couple of weeks after I'd returned to Boston from Providence, having set Thurber's affairs in order as best I could. I still prefer not to consider what unfortunate caprice of fate aligned my discovery of Pickman's sketches of Vera Endecott and Thurber's interest in her with the group's screening of what, in my opinion, was a profane and a deservedly unheard-of film. Made sometime in 1923 or '24, I was informed that it had achieved infamy following the director's death (another suicide). All the film's financiers remained unknown, and it seemed that production had never proceeded beyond the incomplete rough cut I saw that night.

However, I did not sit down here to write out a dry account of my discovery of this untitled, unfinished film, but rather to try and capture something of the dream that is already breaking into hazy scraps and shreds. Like Perseus, who dared to view the face of the Gorgon Medusa only indirectly, as a reflection in his bronze shield, so I seem bound and determined to reflect upon these events, and even my own nightmares, as obliquely as I may. I have always despised cowardice, and yet, looking back over these pages, there seems in it something undeniably cowardly. It does not matter that I intend that no one else shall ever read this. Unless I write honestly, there is hardly any reason in writing it at all. If this is a ghost story (and, increasingly, it feels that way to me), then let it *be* a ghost story, and not this rambling reminiscence.

In the dream, I am sitting in a wooden folding chair in that dark room, lit only by the single shaft of light spilling forth from the projectionist's booth. And the wall in front of me has become a window, looking out upon or into another world, one devoid of sound and almost all color, its palette limited to a spectrum of somber blacks and dazzling whites and innumerable shades of grey. Around me, the others who have come to see smoke their cigars and cigarettes, and they mutter among themselves. I cannot make out anything they say, but, then, I'm not trying particularly hard. I cannot look away from that that silent, grisaille scene, and little else truly occupies my mind.

"Now, do you understand?" Thurber asks from his seat next to mine, and maybe I nod, and maybe I even whisper some hushed affirmation or another. But I do *not* take my eyes from the screen long enough to glimpse his face. There is too much there I might miss, were I to dare look away, even for an instant, and, moreover, I have no desire to gaze upon the face of a dead man. Thurber says nothing else for a time, apparently content that I have found my way to this place, to witness for myself some fraction of what drove him, at last, to the very end of madness.

She is there on the screen – Vera Endecott, Lillian Margaret Snow – standing at the edge of a rocky pool. She is as naked as in Pickman's sketches of her, and is positioned, at first, with her back to the camera. The gnarled roots and branches of what might be ancient willow trees bend low over the pool, their whip-like branches brushing the surface and moving gracefully to and fro, disturbed by the same breeze that ruffles the actress' short, bob-cut hair. And though there appears to be nothing the least bit sinister about this scene, it at once inspires in me the same sort of awe and uneasiness as Doré's engravings for *Orlando Furioso* and the *Divine Comedy*. There is about the tableau a sense of intense foreboding and anticipation, and I wonder what subtle, clever cues have been placed just so that this seemingly idyllic view would be interpreted with such grim expectancy.

And then I realize that the actress is holding in her right hand some manner of phial, and she tilts it just enough that the contents, a thick and pitchy liquid, drips into the pool. Concentric ripples spread slowly across the water, much *too* slowly, I'm convinced, to have followed from any earthly physics, and so I dismiss it as merely trick photography. When the phial is empty, or has, at least, ceased to taint the pool (and I am quite sure that it *has* been tainted), the woman kneels in the mud and weeds at the water's edge. From somewhere overhead, there in the room with me, comes a sound like the wings of startled pigeons taking flight, and the actress half turns towards the audience, as if she has also somehow heard the commotion. The fluttering racket quickly subsides, and once more there is only the mechanical noise from the projector and the whispering of the men and women crowded into the musty room. Onscreen, the actress turns back to the pool, but not before I am certain that her face is the same one from the clippings I found in Thurber's room, the same one sketched by the hand of Richard Upton Pickman. The phial slips from her fingers, falling into the water, and this time there are no ripples whatsoever. No splash. Nothing.

Here, the image flickers before the screen goes blinding white, and I think, for a moment, that the filmstrip has, mercifully, jumped one sprocket or another, so maybe I'll not have to see the rest. But then she's back, the woman and the pool and the willows, playing out frame by frame by frame. She kneels at the edge of the pool, and I think of Narcissus pining for Echo or his lost twin, of jealous Circe poisoning the spring where Scylla bathed, and of Tennyson's cursed Shalott, and, too, again I think of Perseus and Medusa. I am not seeing the thing itself, but only some dim, misguiding counterpart, and my mind grasps for analogies and signification and points of reference.

On the screen, Vera Endecott, or Lillian Margaret Snow – one or the other, the two who were always only one – leans forward and dips her hand into the pool. And again, there are no ripples to mar its smooth obsidian surface. The woman in the film is speaking now, her lips moving deliberately, making no sound whatsoever, and I can hear nothing but the mumbling, smoky room and the sputtering projector. And this is when I realize that the willows are not precisely willows at all, but that those twisted trunks and limbs and roots are actually the entwined human bodies of both sexes, their skin perfectly mimicking the scaly bark of a willow. I understand that these are no wood nymphs, no daughters of Hamadryas and Oxylus. These are prisoners, or condemned souls bound eternally for their sins, and for a time I can only stare in wonder at the confusion of arms and legs, hips and breasts and faces marked by untold ages of the ceaseless agony of this contortion and transformation. I want to turn and ask the others if they see what I see, and how the deception has been accomplished, for surely these people know more of the prosaic magic of filmmaking that do I. Worst of all, the bodies have not been rendered entirely inert, but writhe ever so slightly, helping the wind to stir the long, leafy branches first this way, then that.

Then my eye is drawn back to the pool, which has begun to steam, a grey-white mist rising languidly from off the water (if it *is* still water). The actress leans yet farther out over the strangely quiescent mere, and I find myself eager to look away. Whatever being the cameraman has caught her in the act of summoning or appeasing, I do not want to *see*, do not want to *know* it's daemonic physiognomy. Her lips continue to move, and her hands stir the waters that remain smooth as glass, betraying no evidence that they have been disturbed in any way.

At Rhegium she arrives; the ocean braves,
And treads with unwet feet the boiling waves...

But desire is not enough, nor trepidation, and I do *not* look away, either because I have been bewitched along with all those others who have come to see her, or because some deeper, more disquisitive facet of my being has taken command and is willing to risk damnation in the seeking into this mystery.

"It is only a moving picture," dead Thurber reminds me from his seat beside mine. "Whatever else she would say, you must never forget it is only a dream."

And I want to reply, "Is that what happened to you, dear William? Did you forget it was never anything more than a dream and find yourself unable to waken to lucidity and life?" But I do not say a word, and Thurber does not say anything more.

But yet she knows not, who it is she fears;
In vain she offers from herself to run,
And drags about her what she strives to shun.

"Brilliant," whispers a woman in the darkness at my back, and "Sublime," mumbles what sounds to be a very old man. My eyes do not stray from the screen. The actress has stopped stirring the pool, has withdrawn her hand from the water, but still she kneels there, staring at the sooty stain it has left on her fingers and palm and wrist. *Maybe*, I think, *that is what she came for, that mark, that she will be known*, though my dreaming mind does not presume to guess what or whom she would have recognize her by such a bruise or blotch. She reaches into the reeds and moss and produces a black-handled dagger, which she then holds high above her head, as though making an offering to unseen gods, before she uses the glinting blade to slice open the hand she previously offered to the waters. And I think perhaps I understand, finally, and the phial and the stirring of the pool were only some preparatory wizardry before presenting this far more precious alms or expiation. As her blood drips to spatter and *roll* across the surface of the pool like drops of mercury striking a solid tabletop, something has begun to take shape, assembling itself from those concealed depths, and, even without sound, it is plain enough that the willows have begun to scream and to sway as though in the grip of a hurricane wind. I think, perhaps, it is a mouth, of sorts, coalescing before the prostrate form of Vera Endecott or Lillian Margaret Snow, a mouth or a vagina or a blind and lidless eye, or some organ that may serve as all three. I debate each of these possibilities, in turn.

Five minutes ago, almost, I lay my pen aside, and I have just finished reading back over, aloud, what I have written, as false dawn gave way to sunrise and the first uncomforting light of a new October day. But before I return these pages to the folio containing Pickman's sketches and Thurber's clippings and go on about the business that the morning demands of me, I would confess that what I have dreamed and what I have recorded here are not what I saw that afternoon in the screening room near Harvard Square. Neither is it entirely the nightmare that woke me and sent me stumbling to my desk. Too much of the dream deserted me, even as I rushed to get it all down, and the dreams are never exactly, and sometimes not even remotely, what I saw projected on that wall, that deceiving stream of still images conspiring to suggest animation. This is another point I always tried to make with Thurber, and which he never would accept, the fact of the inevitability of unreliable narrators. I have not lied; I would not say that. But none of this is any nearer to the truth than any other fairy tale.

4.

After the days I spent in the boarding house in Providence, trying to bring some semblance of order to the chaos of Thurber's interrupted life, I began accumulating my own files on Vera Endecott, spending several days in August drawing upon the holdings of the Boston Athenaeum, Public Library, and the Widener Library at Harvard. It was not difficult to piece together the story of the actress' rise to stardom and the scandal that led to her descent into obscurity and alcoholism late in 1927, not so very long before Thurber came to me with his wild tale of Pickman and subterranean ghouls. What was much more difficult to trace was her movement through certain theosophical and occult societies, from Manhattan to Los Angeles, circles to which Richard Upton Pickman was, himself, no stranger.

In January '27, after being placed under contract to Paramount Pictures the previous spring, and during production of a film adaptation of Margaret Kennedy's novel, *The Constant Nymph*, rumors began surfacing in the tabloids that Vera Endecott was drinking heavily and, possibly, using heroin. However, these allegations appear at first to have caused her no more alarm or damage to her film career than the earlier discovery that she was, in fact, Lillian Snow, or the public airing of her disreputable North Shore roots. Then, on May 3rd, she was arrested in what was, at first, reported as merely a raid on a speakeasy somewhere along Durand Drive, at an address in the steep, scrubby canyons above Los Angeles, not far from the Lake Hollywood Reservoir and Mulholland Highway. A few days later, after Endecott's release on bail, queerer accounts of the events of that night began to surface, and by the 7th, articles in the *Van Nuys Call*, *Los Angeles Times*, and the *Herald-Express* were describing the gathering on Durand Drive not as a speakeasy, but as everything from a "witches' Sabbat" to "a decadent, sacrilegious, orgiastic rite of witchcraft and homosexuality."

But the final, damning development came when reporters discovered that one of the many women found that night in the company of Vera Endecott, a Mexican prostitute named Ariadna Delgado, had been taken immediately to Queen of Angels-Hollywood Presbyterian, comatose and suffering from multiple stab wounds to her torso, breasts, and face. Delgado died on the morning of May 4th, without ever having regained consciousness. A second "victim" or "participant" (depending on the newspaper), a young and unsuccessful screenwriter listed only as Joseph E. Chapman, was placed in the psychopathic ward of LA County General Hospital following the arrests.

Though there appear to have been attempts to keep the incident quiet by both studio lawyers and also, perhaps, members of the Los Angeles Police Department, Endecott was arrested a second time on May 10th, and charged with multiple counts of rape, sodomy, second-degree murder, kidnapping, and solicitation. Accounts of the specific charges brought vary from one source to another, but regardless, Endecott was granted and made bail a second time on

May 11th, and four days later, the office of Los Angeles District Attorney Asa Keyes abruptly and rather inexplicably asked for a dismissal of all charges against the actress, a motion granted in an equally inexplicable move by the Superior Court of California, Los Angeles County (it bears mentioning, of course, that District Attorney Keyes was, himself, soon thereafter indicted for conspiracy to receive bribes, and is presently awaiting trial). So, eight days after her initial arrest at the residence on Durand Drive, Vera Endecott was a free woman, and, by late May, she had returned to Manhattan, after her contract with Paramount was terminated.

Scattered throughout the newspaper and tabloid coverage of the affair are numerous details which take on a greater significance in light of her connection with Richard Pickman. For one, some reporters made mention of "an obscene idol" and "a repellent statuette carved from something like greenish soapstone" recovered from the crime scene, a statue which one of the arresting officer's is purported to have described as a "crouching, dog-like beast." One article listed the item as having been examined by a local (unnamed) archaeologist, who was supposedly baffled at it origins and cultural affinities. The house on Durand Drive was, and may still be, owned by a man named Beauchamp who'd spent time in the company of Aleister Crowley during his four-year visit to America (1914-1918), and who had connections with a number of hermetic and theurgical organizations. And finally, the screenwriter Joseph Chapman drowned himself in the Pacific somewhere near Malibu only a few months ago, shortly after being discharged from the hospital. The one short article I could locate regarding his death made mention of his part in the "notorious Durand Drive incident" and printed a short passage reputed to have come from the suicide note. It reads, in part, as follows:

Oh God, how does a man forget, deliberately and wholly and forever, once he has glimpsed such sights as I have had the misfortune to have seen? The awful things we did and permitted to be done that night, the events we set in motion, how do I lay my culpability aside? Truthfully, I cannot and am no longer able to fight through day after day of trying. The Endecotte [sic] woman is back East somewhere, I hear, and I hope to hell she gets what's coming to her. I burned the abominable painting she gave me, but I feel no cleaner, no less foul, for having done so. There is nothing left of me but the putrescence we invited. I cannot do this anymore.

Am I correct in surmising, then, that Vera Endecott made a gift of one of Pickman's paintings to the unfortunate Joseph Chapman, and that it played some role in his madness and death? If so, how many others received such gifts from her, and how many of those canvases yet survive so many thousands of miles from the dank cellar studio near Battery Street where Pickman created them? It's not something I like to dwell upon.

After Endecott's reported return to Manhattan, I failed to find any printed record of her whereabouts or doings until October of that year, shortly after Pickman's disappearance and my meeting with Thurber in the tavern near Faneuil Hall. It's only a passing mention from a society column in the *New York Herald Tribune*, that "the actress Vera Endecott" was among those in attendance at the unveiling of a new display of Sumerian, Hittite, and Babylonian antiquities at the Metropolitan Museum of Art.

What is it I am trying to accomplish with this catalog of dates and death and misfortune, calamity and crime? Among Thurber's books, I found a copy of Charles Hoyt Fort's *The Book of the Damned* (Boni and Liveright; New York, December 1, 1919). I'm not even sure why I took it away with me, and having read it, I find the man's writings almost hysterically belligerent and constantly prone to intentional obfuscation and misdirection. Oh, and wouldn't that contentious bastard love to have a go at this tryst with "the damned"? My point here is that I'm forced to admit that these last few pages bear a marked and annoying similarity to much of Fort's first book (I have not read his second, *New Lands*, nor do I propose ever to do so). Fort wrote of his intention to present a collection of data which had been excluded by science (*id est*, "damned"):

> *Battalions of the accursed, captained by pallid data that I have exhumed, will march. You'll read them – or they'll march. Some of them livid and some of them fiery and some of them rotten.*

Some of them are corpses, skeletons, mummies, twitching, tottering, animated by companions that have been damned alive. There are giants that will walk by, though sound asleep. There are things that are theorems and things that are rags: they'll go by like Euclid arm in arm with the spirit of anarchy. Here and there will flit little harlots. Many are clowns. But many are of the highest respectability. Some are assassins. There are pale stenches and gaunt superstitions and mere shadows and lively malices: whims and amiabilities. The naïve and the pedantic and the bizarre and the grotesque and the sincere and the insincere, the profound and the puerile.

And I think I have accomplished nothing more *than* this, in my recounting of Endecott's rise and fall, drawing attention to some of the more melodramatic and vulgar parts of a story that is, in the main, hardly more remarkable than numerous other Hollywood scandals. But also, Fort would laugh at my own "pallid data," I am sure, my pathetic grasping at straws, as though I might make this all seem perfectly reasonable by selectively quoting newspapers and police reports, straining to preserve the fraying infrastructure of my rational mind. It's time to lay these dubious, slipshod attempts at scholarship aside. There are enough Forts in the world already, enough crackpots and *provocateurs* and intellectual heretics without my joining their ranks. The files I have assembled will be attached to this document, all my "Battalions of the accursed," and if anyone should ever have cause to read this, they may make of those appendices what they will. It's time to tell the truth, as best I am able, and be done with this.

5.

It is true that I attended a screening of a film, featuring Vera Endecott, in a musty little room near Harvard Square. And that it still haunts my dreams. But as noted above, the dreams rarely are anything like an accurate replaying of what I saw that night. There was no black pool, no willow trees stitched together from human bodies, no venomous phial emptied upon the waters. Those are the embellishments of my dreaming, subconscious mind. I could fill several journals with such nightmares.

What I *did* see, only two months ago now, and one month before I finally met the woman for myself, was little more than a grisly, but strangely mundane, scene. It might have only been a test reel, or perhaps 17,000 or so frames, some twelve minutes, give or take, excised from a far longer film. All in all, it was little but than a blatantly pornographic pastiche of the widely circulated 1918 publicity stills of Theda Bara lying in various risqué poses with a human skeleton (for J. Edward Gordon's *Salomé*).

The print was in very poor condition, and the projectionist had to stop twice to splice the film back together after it broke. The daughter of Iscariot Snow, known to most of the world as Vera Endecott, lay naked upon a stone floor with a skeleton. However, the human skull had been replaced with what I assumed then (and still believe) to have been a plaster or papier-mâché "skull" that more closely resembled that of some malformed, macrocephalic dog. The wall or backdrop behind her was a stark matte-grey, and the scene seemed to me purposefully under-lit in an attempt to bring more atmosphere to a shoddy production. The skeleton (and its ersatz skull) were wired together, and Endecott caressed all the osseous angles of its arms and legs and lavished kisses upon its lip-less mouth, before masturbating, first with the bones of its right hand, and then by rubbing herself against the crest of an ilium.

The reactions from the others who'd come to see the film that night ranged from bored silence to rapt attention to laughter. My own reaction was, for the most part, merely disgust and embarrassment to be counted among that audience. I overheard, when the lights came back up, that the can containing the reel bore two titles, *The Necrophile* and *The Hound's Daughter*, and also bore two dates – 1923 and 1924. Later, from someone who had a passing acquaintance with Richard Pickman, I would hear a rumor that he'd worked on scenarios for a filmmaker, possibly Bernard Natan, the prominent Franco-Romanian director of "blue movies," who recently acquired Pathé and merged it with his own studio, Rapid Film. I cannot confirm or deny this, but certainly, I imagine what I saw that evening would have delighted Pickman no end.

However, what has lodged that night so firmly in my mind, and what I believe is the genuine author of those among my nightmares featuring Endecott in an endless parade of nonexistent horrific films transpired only in the final few seconds of the film. Indeed, it came and went so quickly, the projectionist was asked by a number of those present to rewind and play the ending over four times, in an effort to ascertain whether we'd seen what we *thought* we had seen.

Her lust apparently satiated, the actress lay down with her skeletal lover, one arm about its empty ribcage, and closed her kohl-smudged eyes. And in that last instant, before the film ended, a shadow appeared, something passing slowly between the set and the camera's light source. Even after five viewings, I can only describe that shade as having put me in mind of some hulking figure, something considerably farther down the evolutionary ladder than Piltdown or Java man. And it was generally agreed among those seated in that close and musty room that the shadow was possessed of an odd sort of snout or muzzle, suggestive of the prognathous jaw and face of the fake skull wired to the skeleton.

There, then. *That* is what I actually saw that evening, as best I now can remember it. Which leaves me with only a single piece of this story left to tell, the night I finally met the woman who called herself Vera Endecott.

6.

"Disappointed? Not quite what you were expecting?" she asked, smiling a distasteful, wry sort of smile, and I think I might have nodded in reply. She appeared at least a decade older than her twenty-seven years, looking like a woman who had survived one rather tumultuous life already and had, perhaps, started in upon a second. There were fine lines at the corners of her eyes and mouth, the bruised circles below her eyes that spoke of chronic insomnia and drug abuse, and, if I'm not mistaken, a premature hint of silver in her bobbed black hair. What *had* I anticipated? It's hard to say now, after the fact, but I was surprised by her height, and by her irises, which were a striking shade of grey. At once, they reminded me of the sea, of fog and breakers and granite cobbles polished perfectly smooth by ages in the surf. The Greeks said that the goddess Athena had "sea-grey" eyes, and I wonder what they would have thought of the eyes of Lillian Snow.

"I have not been well," she confided, making the divulgence sound almost like a *mea culpa*, and those stony eyes glanced towards a chair in the foyer of my flat. I apologized for not having already asked her in, for having kept her standing in the hallway. I led her to the davenport sofa in the tiny parlor off my studio, and she thanked me. She asked for whiskey or gin, and then laughed at me when I told her I was a teetotaler. When I offered her tea, she declined.

"A painter who doesn't *drink*?" she asked. "No wonder I've never heard of you."

I believe that I mumbled something then about the Eighteenth Amendment and the Volstead Act, which earned from her an expression of commingled disbelief and contempt. She told me that was strike two, and if it turned out that I didn't smoke, either, she was leaving, as my claim to be an artist would have been proven a bald-faced lie, and she'd know I'd lured her to my apartment under false pretenses. But I offered her a cigarette, one of the *brun* Gitanes I first developed a taste for in college, and at that she seemed to relax somewhat. I lit her cigarette, and she leaned back on the sofa, still smiling that wry smile, watching me with her sea-grey eyes, her thin face wreathed in gauzy veils of smoke. She wore a yellow felt cloche that didn't exactly match her burgundy silk chemise, and I noticed there was a run in her left stocking.

"You knew Richard Upton Pickman," I said, blundering much too quickly to the point, and, immediately, her expression turned somewhat suspicious. She said nothing for almost a full minute, just sat there smoking and staring back at me, and I silently cursed my impatience and lack of tact. But then the smile returned, and she laughed softly and nodded.

"Wow," she said. "There's a name I haven't heard in a while. But, yeah, sure, I knew the son of a bitch. So, what are you? Another of his protégés, or maybe just one of the three-letter-men he liked to keep handy?"

"Then it's true Pickman was light on his feet?" I asked.

She laughed again, and this time there was an unmistakable edge of derision there. She took another long drag on her cigarette, exhaled, and squinted at me through the smoke.

"Mister, I have yet to meet the beast – male, female, or anything in between – that degenerate fuck wouldn't have screwed, given half a chance." She paused, here, tapping ash onto the floorboards. "So, if you're *not* a fag, just what *are* you? A kike, maybe? You sort of *look* like a kike."

"No," I replied. "I'm not Jewish. My parents were Roman Catholic, but me, I'm not much of anything, I'm afraid, but a painter you've never heard of."

"Are you?"

"Am I what, Miss Endecott?"

"Afraid," she said, smoke leaking from her nostrils. "And do *not* dare start in calling me 'Miss Endecott.' It makes me sound like a goddamned schoolteacher or something equally wretched."

"So, these days, do you prefer Vera?" I asked, pushing my luck. "Or Lillian?"

"How about Lily?" she smiled, completely nonplussed, so far as I could tell, as though these were all only lines from some script she'd spent the last week rehearsing.

"Very well, Lily," I said, moving the glass ashtray on the table closer to her. She scowled at it, as though I were offering her a platter of some perfectly odious foodstuff and expecting her to eat, but she stopped tapping her ash on my floor.

"Why am I here?" she demanded, commanding an answer without raising her voice. "Why have you gone to so much trouble to see me?"

"It wasn't as difficult as all that," I replied, not yet ready to answer her question, wanting to stretch this meeting out a little longer and understanding, expecting, that she'd likely leave as soon as she had what I'd invited her there to give her. In truth, it had been quite a lot of trouble, beginning with a telephone call to her former agent, and then proceeding through half a dozen increasingly disreputable and uncooperative contacts. Two I'd had to bribe, and one I'd had to coerce with a number of hollow threats involving nonexistent contacts in the Boston Police

Department. But, when all was said and done, my diligence had paid off, because here she sat before me, the two of us, alone, just me and the woman who'd been a movie star and who had played some role in Thurber's breakdown, who'd posed for Pickman and almost certainly done murder on a spring night in Hollywood. Here was the woman who could answer questions I did not have the nerve to ask, who knew what had cast the shadow I'd seen in that dingy pornographic film. Or, at least, here was all that remained of her.

"There aren't many left who would have bothered," she said, gazing down at the smoldering tip-end of her Gitane.

"Well, I have always been a somewhat persistent sort of fellow," I told her, and she smiled again. It was an oddly bestial smile that reminded me of one of my earliest impressions of her – that oppressive summer's day, now more than two months past, studying a handful of old clippings in the Hope Street boarding house. That her human face was nothing more than a mask or fairy glamour conjured to hide the truth of her from the world.

"How did you meet him?" I asked, and she stubbed out her cigarette in the ashtray.

"Who? How did I meet *who*?" She furrowed her brow and glanced nervously towards the parlor window, which faces east, towards the harbor.

"I'm sorry," I replied. "Pickman. How is it that you came to know Richard Pickman?"

"Some people would say that you have very unhealthy interests, Mr. Blackman," she said, her peculiarly carnivorous smile quickly fading, taking with it any implied menace. In its stead, there was only this destitute, used-up husk of a woman.

"And surely they've said the same of you, many, many times, Lily. I've read all about Durand Drive and the Delgado woman."

"Of course, you have," she sighed, not taking her eyes from the window. "I'd have expected nothing less from a persistent fellow such as you."

"How did you meet Richard Pickman?" I asked for the third time.

"Does it make a difference? That was so very long ago. Years and *years* ago. He's dead – "

"No body was ever found."

And, here, she looked from the window to me, and all those unexpected lines on her face seemed to have abruptly deepened; she might well have been twenty-seven, by birth, but no one would have argued if she laid claim to forty.

"The man is dead," she said flatly. "And if by chance he's *not*, well, we should all be fortunate enough to find our heart's desire, whatever it might be." Then she went back to staring at the window, and, for a minute or two, neither of us said anything more.

"You told me that you have the sketches," she said, finally. "Was that a lie, just to get me up here?"

"No, I have them. Two of them, anyway," and I reached for the folio beside my chair and untied the string holding it closed. "I don't know, of course, how many you might have posed for. There were more?"

"More than two," she replied, almost whispering now.

"Lily, you still haven't answered my question."

"And you *are* a persistent fellow."

"Yes," I assured her, taking the two nudes from the stack and holding them up for her to see, but not yet touch. She studied them a moment, her face remaining slack and dispassionate, as if the sight of them elicited no memories at all.

"He needed a model," she said, turning back to the window and the blue October sky. "I was up from New York, staying with a friend who'd met him at a gallery or lecture or something of the sort. My friend knew that he was looking for models, and I needed the money."

I glanced at the two charcoal sketches again, at the curve of those full hips, the round, firm buttocks, and the tail – a crooked, malformed thing sprouting from the base of the coccyx and reaching halfway to the bend of the subject's knees. As I have said, Pickman had a flare for realism, and his eye for human anatomy was almost as uncanny as the ghouls and demons he painted. I pointed to one of the sketches, to the tail.

"That isn't artistic license, is it?"

She did not look back to the two drawings, but simply, slowly, shook her head. "I had the surgery done in Jersey, back in '21," she said.

"Why did you wait so long, Lily? It's my understanding that such a defect is usually corrected at birth, or shortly thereafter."

And she almost smiled that smile again, that hungry, savage smile, but it died, incomplete, on her lips.

"My father, he has his own ideas about such things," she said quietly. "He was always so proud, you see, that his daughter's body was blessed with evidence of her heritage. It made him very happy."

"Your heritage..." I began, but Lily Snow held up her left hand, silencing me.

"I believe, sir, I've answered enough questions for one afternoon. Especially given that you have only the pair, and that you did not tell me that was the case when we spoke."

Reluctantly, I nodded and passed both the sketches to her. She took them, thanked me, and stood up, brushing at a bit of lint or dust on her burgundy chemise. I told her that I regretted that the others were not in my possession, that it had not even occurred to me she would have posed for more than these two. The last part was a lie, of course, as I knew Pickman would surely have made as many studies as possible when presented with so unusual a body.

"I can show myself out," she informed me when I started to get up from my chair. "And you will not disturb me again, not ever."

"No," I agreed. "Not ever. You have my word."

"You're lying sons of bitches, the whole lot of you," she said, and with that, the living ghost of Vera Endecott turned and left the parlor. A few seconds later, I heard the door open and slam shut again, and I sat there in the wan light of a fading day, looking at what grim traces remained in Thurber's folio.

7. (October 24th, 1929)

This is the last of it. Just a few more words, and I will be done. I know now that having attempted to trap these terrible events, I have not managed to trap them at all, but merely given them some new, clearer focus.

Four days ago, on the morning of October 20th, a body was discovered dangling from the trunk of an oak growing near the center of King's Chapel Burial Ground. According to newspaper accounts, the corpse was suspended a full seventeen feet off the ground, bound round about the waist and chest with interwoven lengths of jute rope and baling wire. The woman was identified as a former actress, Vera Endecott, *née* Lillian Margaret Snow, and much was made of her notoriety and her unsuccessful attempt to conceal connections to the wealthy but secretive and ill-rumored Snows of Ipswich, Massachusetts. Her body had been stripped of all clothing, disemboweled, her throat cut, and her tongue removed. He lips had been sewn shut with cat-gut stitches. About her neck hung a wooden placard, on which one word had been written in what is believed to be the dead woman's own blood: *apostate.*

This morning, I almost burned Thurber's folio, along with all my files. I went so far as to carry them to hearth, but then my resolve faltered, and I just sat on the floor, staring at the clippings and Pickman's sketches. I'm not sure what stayed my hand, beyond the suspicion that destroying these papers would not save my life. If they want me dead, then dead I'll be. I've gone too far down this road to spare myself by trying to annihilate the physical evidence of my investigation.

I will place this manuscript, and all the related documents I have gathered, in my safety deposit box, and then I will try to return to the life I was living before Thurber's death. But I cannot forget a line from the suicide note of the screenwriter, Joseph Chapman – *how does a man forget, deliberately and wholly and forever, once he has glimpsed such sights.* How, indeed. And, too, I cannot forget that woman's eyes, that stony, sea-tumbled shade of grey. Or a rough shadow glimpsed in the final moments of a film that might have been made in 1923 or 1924, that may have been titled *The Hounds Daughter* or *The Necrophile.*

I know the dreams will not desert me, not now nor at some future time, but I pray for such fortune as to have seen the last of the waking horrors that my foolish, prying mind has called forth.

At the Gate of Deeper Slumber

05.

It would be easier if I were only watching her die. But I know that I'm witnessing something far worse, a transition that will not conclude with the finality and peaceful oblivion of death. She's alone inside the wide circle we prepared with a paste of white chalk and pig's blood, and I've sworn to Suzanne that I'll never dare cross its terrible circumference, no matter what I might see or hear, and no matter what she may say. She is alone in there with the metal box and what it contains, and I am alone out here, with all the world about me. It only *seems* as though the world has gone away. It only seems that the entire universe has somehow contracted down to a space no farther across than the diameter of her circle. It would be easier, perhaps, if this dwindling of the cosmos *were* more than an illusion.

Two women, alone together, at the end of all that ever was and will ever be.

That would be easier.

Suzanne lies shivering on her left side, her eyes following me as I use the stub of a charcoal pencil to retrace the ring of protective runes and symbols about the periphery of the circle. I've lost track now of how many times I've drawn them on the hardwood floor. I draw them, and the wood absorbs them, or they evaporate, or simply cease to be. I can't say which; it hardly matters. I can only keep watch and restore them each time the thing inside the box, the shining thing trapped inside the circle with Suzanne, takes them away.

I am trying to think of it as nothing more insidious than an infection – a virus or bacterium – this force slowly devouring and transfiguring her. But that's a lie, a bald-faced lie, and I've never been a very good liar.

"Is it morning?" she asks, her voice hardly more than a raw whisper. I look up at the tall windows, at the summer sun streaming in, but the daylight seems far away and completely inconsequential. I know the thing inside the box is preventing the light from entering our circle, and that there's only darkness for Suzanne. I saw it very briefly, before she pushed me away. I saw it, and, what's more, I *felt* it, that black that would put even the perpetual night at the bottom of the deepest ocean trench to shame.

"Yes, it is," I reply. "It's a beautiful day. The sky is blue. There are no clouds, and the sky is blue."

"Nothing's getting past me," she says, and then I nod and go back to drawing on the floorboards. I want to say more, want to tell her anything reassuring, anything that's comforting, but, like I said, I'm a shitty liar. And Suzanne has moved forever beyond reassurances and comfort. She makes a hurtful sound that's almost like crying, and I try hard not to look. I've seen too much already, and every new glimpse only weakens my resolve. I can't possibly help her. No one and nothing can. And I can't run away and leave the circle untended, anymore than I could leave Suzanne more alone than she is already. So, I grit my teeth and scribble at the varnished wood with my bit of charcoal pencil. The room is hot, and a rivulet of sweat runs down my forehead, into my left eye; I try to blink it away.

"I know the names of the messenger," she mutters hoarsely, and I think it's a miracle she can still talk after what the thing in the box has done with her lips and teeth and tongue. I wouldn't exactly call that seeping hole in her face a mouth, not anymore. "The Black Pharaoh, I know all the names he's ever worn."

"Well, do me just one goddamn favor," I tell her, and I know I'm being selfish. "Do us *both* a favor, and keep them to yourself."

"He so loves to hear his names spoken aloud by living beings," Suzanne whispers. There's a wet, shuddering sound from inside the circle, and she's silent again. But there's no mercy in her silence. I think there's no mercy remaining, or, more likely, mercy was only ever a fairy tale we told ourselves to get from one minute to the next. At the edge of this circle, in the presence of the thing not quite held inside that box, all our cherished illusions ravel and diminish. This, I suspect, is why the charcoal symbols on the floor dissolve almost as quickly as I can draw them. They were never *more* than symbols, never anything more vital than wishful thinking. Benevolent gods have not bequeathed us any safeguard against the void, and all our desperate sorceries have conjured only impotent figments.

I *know* this, as surely as I know that the glistening trapezohedral engine inside the box is corrupting and reshaping her to suit the needs of whatever made it, however many innumerable eons ago. It is an open window, and some abomination on the other side is gazing through it into her, even as she is gazing across those unfathomable gulfs of time and space into the watcher on the other side.

From the open box Suzanne fished out of a rocky tidal pool, I can hear the pipes playing again, and also the frantic, careless footfalls of the dancers who swoop and careen and howl before the throne of Chaos. Bleeding from all the symmetrically staggered kite-faces of the shining trapezohedron, I clearly hear that toneless, monotonous music. It would be so easy, I think, to join Suzanne. Easy *and* just. This is the most wicked deed in all my life, allowing her to face the abyss alone.

And I finally raise my head and look directly at her for the first time in hours, and, in this moment, I understand that I am exactly the same sort of coward as Perseus, only braving the countenance of Medusa secondhand, and that Suzanne has become a warrior's polished shield.

03.

We're lying together in bed. I kiss her, and she tastes like the sea. Or maybe it's only the smell from the shop below her tiny, cluttered apartment on Wickenden Street, the place that sells tropical fish and aquariums, that I'm mistaking for the taste of her. But that's never happened before. Too many things are happening that have never happened before. For example, I look into her eyes, and for a moment I'm unable to find *her* in her eyes. For that moment, I see nothing that could ever be confused with humanity. And then she blinks, and smiles, and Suzanne's eyes are only Suzanne again.

"It's under the bed," she says, though I haven't asked where she's keeping the box from the tide pool.

"Couldn't you think of some other place to keep it? Someplace that *isn't* under the bed?"

"It doesn't bother you, does it?" she asks, still smiling, and I believe she's only pretending to sound surprised. Of course, it bothers me, just the thought of the metal box and its contents stashed in the shadows and dust beneath us. It bothers me that it was there while I made love to her, and that I didn't know. It bothers me that we didn't leave it where she found it almost a week ago, washed up among the rocks, stranded with the kelp and crabs below the lighthouse.

"Yeah, as a matter of fact, it makes me a little nervous," I admit, reluctantly, and Suzanne laughs and nuzzles my naked breasts. Her lips brush across my left nipple, and I flinch. I can't say *why*, not exactly. Only that there is some unexpected and almost painful sensation from that brief contact, something that causes me to flinch. I cannot describe it, except by contradictory analogies. It feels like a static shock. It feels like an ice cube pressed against my skin. It feels sharp and hot, like the needle of a tattoo gun.

She looks up at me and frowns.

"It's just a strange old box," she says.

"Well, there must be some other place in the apartment where you can keep it, besides under the bed." I'm trying not to appear unreasonable. After all, it's not my apartment, or my bed. But if her expression is any indication, I'm not doing a very good job.

"Sure," Suzanne says, raising herself on one elbow and staring at me. "If it upsets you that much, I'll move it. I can stash it on top of the bookcase, or in the bottom of the closet. You want to pick which?"

"The closet seems like a pretty good idea," I reply, and she sighs and nods her head.

"Don't think I've ever seen you spooked like this," she says, getting out of bed and pulling on her bathrobe. It's the one I gave her last Christmas, dark red sateen with white roses. She doesn't cinch the belt or tie it, but lets the robe hang open.

"So, are you disappointed?" I ask her, watching Suzanne as she stoops to retrieve the box from beneath the bed. "Maybe having second thoughts?"

"No, I'm most definitely *not* having second thoughts. It's just, you always try to come on so butch and all, and now you're creeped out by an old box."

"Yeah, well, it's a fucking creepy old box," I say, "and you *know* it's fucking creepy." Then she stands again, holding it in both her hands. It isn't at all heavy. I know that because I'm the one who carried it from the tide pool back to her car. The whitish-yellow metal gleams dully in the glow from the lamp on the bedside table. The hinged lid and each side of the box has been stamped or engraved with bas-relief images, worn and dented now, but still plainly discernable. I think the designs are meant to depict living creatures, but they put me in mind of nothing so much as the biomechanoid monstrosities of H. R. Giger's paintings and sculptures. I don't like looking at the box's grotesqueries, and yet I find it very hard to look away. Giger's work has always had this same morbid affect on me.

Suzanne carries the box across the small bedroom and opens the closet door, then stands staring for a moment at the disarray of clothing jammed inside.

"You're saying it doesn't make you uncomfortable?" I ask. "Not even a little bitty bit?" She shrugs, and sets the box down on the floor. Then Suzanne begins excavating a hole in her dirty laundry, making a space large enough that the metal box can sit on the closet floor. She tosses a pair of jeans over her shoulder, and they land not far from the foot of the bed, the legs splayed in different directions.

"I want to know what it is," she tells me. "I want to know what it is, and where it came from, and who made it, and why."

"You don't want very much, do you?"

"Only the moon," she laughs again. "And don't you go telling me how curiosity killed the cat. I never met a cat yet who would have been better off without curiosity."

"I wasn't going to say that."

"Good," she says, and out comes a great wad of panties and T-shirts and more jeans. "But, if you swear you won't freak out, there is something weird. I made some rubbings of the box this afternoon. One from each side."

I roll over on my back and stare at the ceiling, wishing that I had a cigarette, that Suzanne hadn't convinced me to quit. "Something weird," I say, like a wary echo.

"Well, the box has six sides, right, like most boxes. I mean, it's basically a hollow cube. And I used one sheet of paper for each side. But, and here's where it gets weird, when I was finished, I had eight rubbings on eight sheets of paper. I didn't even realize that I was *making* eight rubbings, not until it was over."

"You lost track and did two of the sides twice," I suggest, but my mouth has gone dry, and there's gooseflesh on my arms. I doubt I sound anything like convincing.

"Sure, I thought of that, right off. But when I compared the rubbings, they were all different. And when I tried to match them all up with the images on the box, I could only find six. On the box, I mean."

I sit up and stare at her. Suzanne has her back to me. She's just placed the box inside the closet, and is busy piling dirty clothes in on top of it.

"And *then*, after that, you put it beneath the bed?" I ask.

"It's only a box," she says again and shuts the closet door. "I'm sure I'll figure it all out later. Weird shit like that happens, you know? But you can't let it go and freak you out. When I was a little girl, I was sure I'd seen a sea monster, but, turned out, it was only a seal."

I lie there, staring up at the ceiling, trying not to think about the box or the shining thing inside, and unable to think of anything else. In a minute or two, she comes back to bed.

04.

It's almost dark, and I'm watching something on television when Suzanne gets back from Salem. I reach for the remote, press a button, and the screen instantly goes black. She's complaining about the traffic between Boston and Providence, and about

Boston drivers, in general. I sip at the glass of cheap Scotch I've been nursing for the last half hour. All the ice has melted, and the sides of the tumbler are slick with beads of condensation. I try not to notice the oddly intimate way she's holding the box, and I'm grateful when she sets it down on the kitchen counter. I'm grateful when she's no longer *touching* it.

"Well, that wasn't altogether unprofitable," Suzanne says, and then sits down on one of the barstools at the counter. There are three of them, the cushions upholstered in some sort of shiny red vinyl fabric embedded with flakes of gold glitter. I want to call it Naugahyde, but I'm not sure that's right. Suzanne found the stools cheap at the Salvation Army over on Pitman Street. Here and there, the upholstery is marred by cigarette burns.

"I thought you'd be back sooner."

"Like I said, all the fucking traffic," she reminds me, then produces a manila folder from her pea-green laptop bag. She lays the folder on the countertop and taps it twice with her right index finger.

"So, what'd you find out?" I ask, and Suzanne taps the folder a third time, and answers me with a question of her own.

"Ever heard of the Church of Starry Wisdom?"

"Wasn't that one of Aleister Crowley's little clubs?" I ask, and watch the blank television screen.

"No, it isn't. Or wasn't. Whichever." I hear her open the folder, but I don't turn around. "This was way before Crowley's time. Near as anyone can tell, the order was founded by an egyptologist and occultist named Enoch Bowen, sometime around 1844. At least, in May of that year he came back from a dig on the east bank of the Nile, at a site near Thebes. The following July, he bought an abandoned Free-Will Baptist sanctuary on Federal Hill, and started the Church of Starry Wisdom."

"Never heard of it," I tell her.

"Neither had I. But that's not too surprising. Whatever Bowen and his followers were up to, seems it didn't sit too well with the locals. By December 1844, ministers in Providence were denouncing the Starry Wisdom. Four years later, there were rumors of blood sacrifices, devil worship, that kind of thing. Various sordid scandals and hostilities ensued. Though by

1863, there appear to have been at least two hundred people in Bowen's congregation. And sometime in 1876, Thomas Doyle, who was the mayor of Providence at the time, stepped in and the church was summarily shut down. After that, Professor Bowen and most of his followers left Providence, it seems. There are rumors of the Starry Wisdom cult reemerging in other places. First in Chicago, then, near the end of the 19th Century, somewhere in Yorkshire."

The way she's talking, Suzanne reminds me of someone reading a book report to her high-school classmates.

"Colorful story," I say, and take another sip of the lukewarm Scotch. "But what's any of this got to do with your box and its bauble?"

"Just about everything," Suzanne replies, her tone growing exasperated, and I glance at her over my shoulder. She looks tired, tired but excited. Jittery. On edge. She forces a smile for me, and continues.

"Look, now you're being dense on purpose," she says. "When Bowen returned from Egypt in 1844, he brought back an artifact he discovered during an excavation there. A carving or stone or cartouche. This artifact, which is only ever referred to as 'the Shining Trapezohedron,' was supposed to be some sort of magical gateway. Bowen and his cohorts thought they could use it to talk to ancient Egyptian gods, or maybe gods older than the Egyptians. Babylonian. Sumerian. I don't know. That part's not clear, exactly who or what they were worshipping. But the artifact was used to summon them. In return for blood offerings and profane sexual rites – the usual crap – the Starry Wisdom cult believed these gods would offer up all the hidden secrets of the universe."

I turn back towards the television, and consider switching it on again.

"You're not believing a word of this, are you?" she asks.

"Not especially," I reply.

"It isn't like I'm making it up. I have photocopies of contemporary newspaper accounts – "

"I didn't *say* I think you're making it up. That's not what I meant. That's not what I said."

"That's sure what it *sounded* like," Suzanne sighs, and god, I hate it when she sulks. I finish the Scotch, and set the empty glass on the floor beside the futon.

"So, you're saying the thing in your peculiar yellow box, that it's Bowen's Shining Trapezohedron?"

"Yeah, that's what I'm saying."

"But wouldn't the cultists have hauled their holy of holies away with them when they fled Providence?"

"If you're not going to take this seriously, I'm going to stop right now, okay?"

I close my eyes. I'm beginning to get a headache, that dull, faint throb winding itself up tight and jagged somewhere directly behind my eyes.

"I have to be at work in half an hour," I say. "I traded shifts with that new guy. The restaurant will be packed wall to wall tonight, and I'm not looking forward to it, that's all. I'm not trying to be a bitch. It just seems strange, that these Starry Wisdom fruitcakes wouldn't have taken their sacred relic with them when they left."

"It seemed strange to me, too," Suzanne says, and the tone of her voice has become hard and defensive, all the enthusiasm drained away. "But the church building was still standing in the thirties, and even that long after the Starry Wisdom left Providence, people on Federal Hill were scared to death of the place. In 1935, a painter named Robert Blake broke in – "

"Robert Blake?" I ask, opening my eyes again. "Like the guy who played Baretta?"

"Yeah, like the guy who played Baretta. He apparently broke into the abandoned church and found the trapezohedron on an altar in the steeple." I hear her turn a page. "He was from Milwaukee, but was staying near Brown, someplace on College Street close to the John Hay Library. And he died there, not long after he broke into the church. Struck by lightning in his apartment, if you can believe that."

"This is what you drove all the way to Salem to find out?" I ask. "This is what Tirzah told you?"

"Yeah, but it's not exactly a secret. These articles, they're mostly from the *Providence Journal*. I just never heard of any of it.

I guess it's not the sort of stuff you learn in history class. Anyway, showing the box to Tirzah was *your* idea."

And yeah, that part's true. We met Tirzah a few years back, during a lesbian-only retreat out on the Cape. But that's another story. She runs a witchcraft shop in Salem, reads Tarot cards for tourists, etc. & etc. "She's undoubtedly the weirdest person we know," I say. "It made sense, letting her see it. So...Baretta steals this thing, and gets struck by lightning."

"I wish you wouldn't drink before work," Suzanne says.

"And I wish you'd left that damned box where you found it. If wishes were horses..." There's a drawn out few moments of quiet then, as if neither of us knows our next line and we're waiting on a helpful prompt from backstage.

"At any rate," she says, finally breaking the silence. "One of the men who investigated Blake's death, a doctor named Ambrose Dexter, found the stone among the dead man's effects. He chartered a fishing boat in Newport, and dropped the metal box into Narragansett Bay, somewhere off Castle Hill. That's the deepest part of the bay, you know. There in the Eastern Passage, between Newport and Beavertail."

"No," I say. "No, I didn't know that. But I *do* know I'm gonna be late if I don't get dressed and get out of here. We'll talk about this later." I stand, feeling dizzy, unsure if it's from the Scotch or the nascent headache, or maybe a bit of both. I look at Suzanne, who's still staring at the contents of the manila folder, and I point at the dented metal box on the counter. "You should just get rid of it," I tell her. "Hell, sell the thing on eBay. I'm sure some freak would pay a pretty penny for it."

She looks up and glares at me. "Jesus. You don't *sell* something like this on eBay. Whether or not Enoch Bowen was a lunatic, it has historical significance."

"Fine," I tell her. "Whatever. Then give it to a museum." Suzanne shakes her head, and goes back to reading the sheaf of photocopied pages.

"I found it," she whispers. "It's mine to do with as I please." And I don't disagree. I'm not in the mood for arguments, especially not one I know I'll lose.

01.

"Hey! I think I've found something," Suzanne shouts. The waves slamming against the rocks and the wind off the bay obscure her voice so that I can only just make out the words. I'm lying on the blanket we've spread out over a relatively flat place among the tilted, contorted beds of slate and phyllite. I'm lying there with my eyes shut, the sun too warm on my face, shining straight through my eyelids and making me sleepy. I don't want to get up. If I get up to see whatever it is she's found, I'll have to bring the blanket along, or it'll blow away.

"Come see!" she shouts.

"Bring it *to* me!" I shout back without bothering to open my eyes. Often, it seems that Suzanne and I love the rugged coast around the old Beavertail Lighthouse for entirely different reasons. I come here to get away from the city, for the smells and sounds of the sea. And she comes for the flotsam and jetsam, for whatever she can find dead or dying in the tide pools. Her apartment is littered with the garbage she's brought back from the edge of the sea. Shells and bones, weathered shards of Wedgwood china, unusually shaped pieces of driftwood, rounded pebbles and cobbles, fishing lures, rusted and unrecognizable pieces of machinery, a page from a Chinese newspaper, a ruined lobster pot. You could decorate a good-sized chowder house with all the junk Suzanne's scavenged from beaches up and down Rhode Island and Massachusetts, Maine and Nova Scotia. She has more jars of beach glass than I've ever bothered to count.

"It's *big*!" she calls out. "Get off your lazy ass and come look!"

I open my eyes, squinting at the afternoon light, and I see now that there's a herring gull standing only a few feet away, watching me. It cocks its head to one side, and its pale irises seem simultaneously startled and filled with questions. I make a shooing motion with my hands, and the bird squawks, then spreads its grey wings and the wind seems to snatch it away.

"Hold your horses," I say, not shouting, though, not really caring whether Suzanne's heard me or not. I stand and wad the blanket into a tight bundle, tucking it under my right arm. I'd thought that her voice was coming from somewhere to the south, but I soon spot her ten or fifteen yards north of me, kneeling on the smooth, dark shale next to one of the deeper pools of seawater left behind by the retreating tide. Her head is bowed slightly, her hands clasped in front of her, and I think she looks like someone praying to the bay. Then she turns towards me and points at something in the water. By the time I reach the edge of the pool, she's already pulled it out onto the rocks, along with a rubbery, fat tangle of kelp and bladderwrack. The box gleams dully in the sun.

"What is it?" she asks me, and I tell her I have no idea. I stand there, gazing down at the yellow-white metal and the slippery knot of seaweed tangled around it. There are intricate, spiraling images worked into the gleaming surface of the box, and seeing them, the first word that comes to mind is *unwholesome*. Whatever the artist was trying to depict in these bas-reliefs, from life or only her or his imagination, it was unwholesome.

"I can't figure out how it opens," Suzanne says, sounding puzzled and chewing thoughtfully at her lower lip. She pulls away the strands of seaweed. "There are hinges, *here* and *here*, but no sign of a latch. I'm not even sure I can tell where the top and bottom parts fit together. I can't find the seam. Is that gold, what it's made from? Maybe white gold?"

And I want to say, *Put it back, Suzanne. For god's sake, put it back. Don't touch it.* I want to ask why she can't see the obvious *unwholesomeness* of it. But I don't, and then she presses her right thumb into a very subtle depression on the front of the box and it opens with an audible pop, easy as you please. She laughs, like a child delighted at having gotten all the sides of a Rubik's Cube to match up.

Suzanne lifts the lid, and at first, all I can see in there is darkness, such an entirely complete darkness that my eyes are useless against it, and I have the distinct and disquieting impression that sunlight is unable to penetrate that umbral space.

"Shut it," I say, but she doesn't seem to have heard me. She doesn't close the box, or tell me that I'm being silly. Instead, Suzanne reaches *into* that inviolable blackness, and I'm absolutely *certain* that she's going to scream, and when she pulls her arm back, all that will be left is the bloody, spurting stump of her wrist. I'll scream, too, as if in reply, as if in empathic agony.

She lifts something out of the box, and it also gleams beneath the sun.

"A crystal," she says. "Some kind of crystal." I feel sick, just looking at it. The same way I get nauseous on the deck of a listing boat, I feel sick when I look at the thing from the metal box. But, nonetheless, I *do* look at it. I *don't* turn away. Its glassy, kite-shaped facets are vaguely iridescent, and I'm having a lot of trouble figuring out what color it is, if, indeed, it's any *one* color. At first, it appears to be greenish black, like an overripe avocado's skin. But I catch hints of crimson, too, then hints of violet, and *then* the whole things glimmers a very deep cobalt blue. Suzanne holds it up, turning it this way and that so that I can get a better view. There's an ugly, greasy quality to the light flashing off its perfectly delineated, four-sided faces.

"Put it back, please," I say, speaking very softly. "Put it back inside." Suzanne stares at me a second or two, then nods and does as I've asked. She closes the metal box, and there's another pop when it shuts. I sit with her, at the edge of the tide pool, with the box between us. The pool is full of tiny mussels and the whorled shells of periwinkle snails, with seaweed and small, scuttling crabs. The rock beneath the water is scabbed with sharp barnacles.

There was never any discussion about whether we'd keep the box or leave it there. Never any question. When she's ready to go, I carry it for her, and it weighs a lot less than I expected.

02.

And now I sit down to write about the dream, the dream I have the night after we find Enoch Bowen's trapezohedron. It's the same dream I have when I can no longer stay awake to draw vigilant runes around the binding circle where Suzanne lies, the circle and the star, the flaming, all-seeing eye and the shattered wreck of her. I can no longer take solace in a clock face or the track of the sun or moon across the sky. I am not contained in any single moment, and the assumed order of the world is lost on me. I've heard the piping flutes, and the drums, and the lumbering foot-falls of titan gods who've danced away the eons of their exile. I've felt the precious safety net of time falling away. There's only now. This moment, which I may call past or present or future. Suzanne sleeps peacefully beside me, and she's whole, but she also lies broken and transformed within the Elder Sign carefully chalked upon the floor of her apartment. I've torn the story apart, no longer able to perceive the illusion of chronology, and I've haphazardly strewn the scenes, just as Suzanne has been torn, and as she's been strewn. I rearrange and lie. I present the gorgon's face reflected in a polished shield, and I will never be even half so strong as I'd need to be to tell the full, vicious truth of it. I'm amazed to have made it this far. I come to confess, but can at best drop hints and innuendo. Suzanne was the sacrifice, not me. It was Suzanne who swallowed the pomegranate seeds. Ask her.

Surely some revelation is at hand...

I used to think so.

All our roughest beasts have come and gone, slouching past, and now wait together impatiently at the threshold of what we, in our cherished ignorance, have named a *universe*. We see inconvenient shards of truth in dream, perhaps, or in the contents of a metal box coughed up by the sea.

I shouldn't tarry, or digress. There is too little coherence remaining within me to squander even an ounce. *This* is the dream. The rest is hardly better than window dressing. Quit stalling and spit it out; the ocean has obliged, and now it's my turn:

Suzanne and I are walking along a sandy beach, not the rocks at Beavertail, and the summer sun beats mercilessly down on the bloated corpses of innumerable thousands of crabs and huge lobsters and dead fish that have been tossed ashore by the waves. Haddock and cod, flounder and striped bass, tautog and weakfish and pollock. I ask her if it was a red tide did this, and she asks me if there's ever been any other sort. The air is far too foul and heavy and hot to breathe, and I'm relieved when she turns away from the Atlantic and towards the low dunes. There's a narrow, winding trail, almost overgrown by dog roses and poison ivy, and it leads to the old church on Federal Hill. I remember that the church was demolished decades ago, all its derelict secrets become anonymous landfill. But in the dream, the shrine of the Starry Wisdom has been restored, or it has never precisely fallen, or we are removed to a time before its destruction. It hardly matters which. No, that's not true. It matters not at all.

Suzanne leads me from the sun-blighted day into night, and into that crumbling antique sanctuary, past the fearful, praying throng that has gathered on its steps, those shriveled old Italian women clutching their onyx and coral rosaries. They spare a hateful peek at me, each and every one in her turn, and the curses that spill from their lips are more befitting witches than good New England Catholics.

"Oh, don't mind them," Suzanne says. "They're bitter, that's all. They can't hear the music. Not a one of them has ever danced, and now they're old and frail and won't ever have the opportunity."

She leads me through silent vales of dust and shadow, and our path is as indirect as this cockeyed, wandering narrative. Together, we wind our way between apparently endless rows of warped and buckled pews, between chiseled marble columns rising around us to shoulder the awful, sagging burden of the church's vaulted roof. Then we move away from the nave, revisiting the vestibule, and she shows me the concealed stairway spiraling up and up and up into the sky. We climb the wooden steps until the moon is only a silver coin far below us.

"Wipe your feet," Suzanne tells me, and I see we've finally reached the top of the stairs and gained the steeple. If this place has ever held a peal of bells to chime the hour and call the faithful to worship, they've been removed. There are four tall lancet windows, painted over so that the daylight might never enter the circular room.

"You should have waited for me below," Suzanne says, and her eyes flash yellow-white in the gloom. "You should have waited on the beach. I can see that now."

I don't reply, and I don't glance back the way we've come. I know it's much too late to retrace that route, and I don't try. There's a ring of seven high-backed chairs arranged about a low stone pillar. And in each chair sits a robed figure, their faces veiled with folds of golden silk. They don't look up when we enter the steeple, but keep their attentions focused on the peculiar metal box sitting on the stone pillar. The box is open. There can be no doubt whatsoever that it's the same box she found in the tide pool, the box Enoch Bowen brought home from Thebes, so I don't have to peer inside to know its contents.

The seven seated figures have begun to chant, and I watch while she undresses, then takes her place before the altar. I watch as a tangible, freezing blackness is disgorged by the box, by the thing *inside* the box. I watch as those hungry tendrils wrap themselves tightly about her, and draw her down, and enter her.

"Yes," she whispers. "I will be the bride. I will be the doorway. I will be the conduit." And there is so much more. I don't doubt that I could write page after page setting down the blasphemous things that I dreamt I saw in the steeple of the rotting church. I could never spend a moment doing anything else, and what remains of my life would be utterly insufficient to record more than a fraction of those depredations. There is no bottom to this dream. Wherever I choose to stop, the point is chosen arbitrarily.

I stand among the dunes, looking out across a dying sea, and watch while clouds gather on the bruised horizon.

The wind is scalding, and I cannot find the sun.

There is another shore, you know, upon the other side.

00.

The afternoon is fading quickly towards dusk, and I sit outside the chalk and blood circle drawn on the floorboards. From time to time, I glance at the sky outside, or at the door leading to the hallway. Or I scrounge the courage to look inside the circle again. But she's gone forever, even the ruin it made of her. She's gone, and the box is gone, and the trapezohedron is gone. There's very little remaining to prove she was ever here. I cannot conceive that one woman's body and soul were possibly enough to appease that hunger. It is all beyond my comprehension.

There is a bloody spot where she lay, blood and bile, and a few lumps of something colorless and translucent that remind me of beached jellyfish. There are scorch marks where the box sat. There's the faint odor of ammonia and charred wood.

"It was a beautiful day," I say, and at first the sound of my own voice startles me. "The sky was blue, Suzanne. There were no clouds, and the sky was blue. I think it will be a beautiful night."

And then, with the heel of my bare palm, I begin to erase the protective circle, and the five-pointed star, and the burning eye.

> We cannot think of a time that is oceanless
> Or of an ocean not littered with wastage
> Or of a future that is not liable
> Like the past, to have no destination.
>   T. S. Eliot, *The Dry Salvages*

Fish Bride (1970)

We lie here together, naked on her sheets which are always damp, no matter the weather, and she's still sleeping. I've lain next to her, watching the long cold sunrise, the walls of this dingy room in this dingy house turning so slowly from charcoal to a hundred successively lighter shades of grey. The weak November morning has a hard time at the window, because the glass was knocked out years ago and she chose as a substitute a sheet of tattered and not-quite-clear plastic she found washed up on the shore now, held in place with mismatched nails and a few thumbtacks. But it deters the worst of the wind and rain and snow, and she says there's nothing out there she wants to see, anyway. I've offered to replace the broken glass, a couple of times I've said that, but it's just another of the hundred or so things that I've promised I would do for her and haven't yet gotten around to doing; she doesn't seem to mind. That's not why she keeps letting me come here. Whatever she wants from me, it isn't handouts and pity and someone to fix her broken windows and leaky ceiling. Which is fortunate, as I've never fixed anything in my whole life. I can't even change a flat tire. I've only ever been the sort of man who does the harm and leaves it for someone else to put right again, or simply sweep beneath a rug where no one will have to notice the damage I've done. So, why should she be any different? And yet, to my knowledge, I've done her no harm so far.

I come down the hill from the village on those interminable nights and afternoons when I can't write and don't feel like getting drunk alone. I leave that other world, that safe and smothering kingdom of clean sheets and typescript, electric lights and indoor plumbing and radio and window frames with windowpanes, and follow the sandy path through gale-stunted trees and stolen, burned-out automobiles, smoldering trash-barrel fires and suspicious, under-lit glances.

They all know I don't belong here with them, all the other men and women who share her squalid existence at the edge of the sea, the ones who have come down and never gone back up the hill again. When I call them her apostles, she gets sullen and angry.

"No," she says, "it's not like that. They're nothing of the sort."

But I understand well enough that's exactly what they are, even if she doesn't want to admit it, either to herself or to me. And so they hold me in contempt, because she's taken me into her bed – me, an interloper who comes and goes, who has some choice in the matter, who has that option because the world beyond these dunes and shanty walls still imagines it has some use for me. One of these nights, I think, her apostles will do murder against me. One of them alone, or all of them together. It may be stones or sticks or an old filleting knife. It may even be a gun. I wouldn't put it past them. They are resourceful, and there's a lot on the line. They'll bury me in the dog roses, or sink me in some deep place among the tide-worn rocks, or carve me up like a fat sow and have themselves a feast. She'll likely join them, if they are bold enough and offer a few scraps of my charred, anonymous flesh to complete the sacrifice. And later, much, much later, she'll remember and miss me, in her sloppy, indifferent way, and wonder whatever became of the man who brought her beer and whiskey, candles and chocolate bars, the man who said he'd fix the window, but never did. She might recall my name, but I wouldn't hold it against her if she doesn't.

"This used to *be* someplace," she's told me time and time again. "Oh, sure, you'd never know it now. But when my mother was a girl, this used to be a town. When I was little, it was still a town. There were dress shops, and a diner, and a jail. There was a public park with a bandshell and a hundred-year-old oak tree. In the summer, there was music in the park, and picnics. There were even churches, *two* of them, one Catholic and one Presbyterian. But then the storm came and took it all away."

And it's true, most of what she says. There was a town here once. A decade's neglect hasn't quite erased all signs of it. She's shown me some of what there's left to see – the stump of a brick chimney, a few broken pilings where the waterfront once stood – and I've asked questions around the village. But people up there don't like to speak openly about this place, or even allow their thoughts to linger on it very long. Every now and then, usually after a burglary or before an election, there's talk of cleaning it up, pulling down these listing, clapboard shacks and chasing away the vagrants and squatters and winos. So far, the talk has come to nothing.

A sudden gust of wind blows in from off the beach, and the sheet of plastic stretched across the window flaps and rustles, and she opens her eyes.

"You're still here," she says, not sounding surprised, merely telling me what I already know. "I was dreaming that you'd gone away and would never come back to me again. I dreamed there was a boat called the *Silver Star*, and it took you away."

"I get seasick," I tell her. "I don't do boats. I haven't been on a boat since I was fifteen."

"Well, you got on this one," she insists, and the dim light filling up the room catches in the facets of her sleepy grey eyes. "You said that you were going to seek your fortune on the Ivory Coast. You had your typewriter, and a suitcase, and you were wearing a brand new suit of worsted wool. I was standing on the dock, watching as the *Silver Star* got smaller and smaller."

"I'm not even sure I know where the Ivory Coast is supposed to be," I say.

"Africa," she replies.

"Well, I know that much, sure. But I don't know *where* in Africa. And it's an awfully big place."

"In the dream, you knew," she assures me, and I don't press the point further. It's her dream, not mine, even if it's not a dream she's actually ever had, even if it's only something she's making up as she goes along. "In the dream," she continues, undaunted, "you had a travel brochure that the ticket agent had given you. It was printed all in color. There was a sort of tree called a bombax tree, with bright red flowers. There were elephants, and a parrot. There were pretty women with skin the color of roasted coffee beans."

"That's quite a brochure," I say, and for a moment I watch the plastic tacked over the window as it rustles in the wind off the bay. "I wish I could have a look at it right now."

"I thought what a warm place it must be, the Ivory Coast," and I glance down at her, at those drowsy eyes watching me. She lifts her right hand from the damp sheets, and patches of iridescent skin shimmer ever so faintly in the morning light. The sun shows through the thin, translucent webbing stretched between her long fingers. Her sharp nails brush gently across my unshaven cheek, and she smiles. Even I don't like to look at those teeth for very long, and I let my eyes wander back to the flapping plastic. The wind is picking up, and I think maybe this might be the day when I finally have to find a hammer, a few ten-penny nails, and enough discarded pine slats to board up the hole in the wall.

"Not much longer before the snow comes," she says, as if she doesn't need to hear me speak to know my thoughts.

"Probably not for a couple of weeks yet," I counter, and she blinks and turns her head towards the window.

In the village, I have a tiny room in a boardinghouse on Darling Street, and I keep a spiral-bound notebook hidden between my mattress and box springs. I've written a lot of things in that book that I shouldn't like any other human being to ever read – secret desires, things I've heard, and read; things she's told me, and things I've come to suspect all on my own. Sometimes, I think it would be wise to keep the notebook better hidden. But it's true that the old woman who owns the place, and who does all the housekeeping herself, is afraid of me, and she never goes into my room. She leaves the clean linen and towels in a stack outside my door. Months ago, I stopped taking my meals with the other lodgers, because the strained silence and fleeting, leery glimpses that attended those breakfasts and dinners only served to give me indigestion. I expect the widow O'Dwyer would ask me to find a room elsewhere, if she weren't so intimidated by me. Or, rather, if she weren't so intimidated by the company I keep.

Outside the shanty, the wind howls like the son of Poseidon, and, for the moment, there's no more talk of the Ivory Coast or dreams or sailing gaily away into the sunset aboard the *Silver Star.*

Much of what I've secretly scribbled there in my notebook concerns that terrible storm that you claim rose up from the sea to steal away the little park and the bandshell, the diner and the jail and the dress shops, the two churches, one Presbyterian and the other Catholic. From what you've said, it must have happened sometime in September of '57 or '58, but I've spent long afternoons in the small public library, carefully pouring over old newspapers and magazines. I can find no evidence of such a tempest making landfall in the autumn of either of those years. What I can verify is that the village once extended down the hill, past the marshes and dunes to the bay, and there was a lively, prosperous waterfront. There was trade with Gloucester and Boston, Nantucket and Newport, and the bay was renowned for its lobsters, fat black sea bass, and teeming shoals of haddock. Then, abruptly, the waterfront was all but abandoned sometime before 1960. In print, I've found hardly more than scant and unsubstantiated speculations to account for it, that exodus, that strange desertion. Talk of overfishing, for instance, and passing comparisons with Cannery Row in faraway California, and the collapse of the Monterey Bay sardine canning industry back on the 1950s. I write down everything I find, no matter how unconvincing, but I permit myself to believe only a very little of it.

"A penny for your thoughts," she says, then shuts her eyes again.

"You haven't got a penny," I reply, trying to ignore the raw, hungry sound of the wind and the constant noise at the window.

"I most certainly do," she tells me, and pretends to scowl and look offended. "I have a few dollars, tucked away. I'm not an indigent."

"Fine, then. I was thinking of Africa," I lie. "I was thinking of palm trees and parrots."

"I don't remember any palm trees in the travel brochure," she says. "But I expect there must be quite a lot of them, regardless."

"Undoubtedly," I agree. I don't say anything else, though, because I think I hear voices, coming from somewhere outside her shack – urgent, muttering voices that reach me despite the wind and the flapping plastic. I can't make out the words, no matter how hard I try. It ought to scare me more than it does. Like I said, one of these nights, they'll do murder against me. One of them alone, or all of them together. Maybe they won't even wait for the conspiring cover of nightfall. Maybe they'll come for me in broad daylight. I begin to suspect my murder would not even be deemed a crime by the people who live in those brightly painted houses up the hill, back beyond the dunes. On the contrary, they might consider it a necessary sacrifice, something to placate the flotsam and jetsam huddling in the ruins along the shore, an oblation of blood and flesh to buy them time.

Seems more likely than not.

"They shouldn't come so near," she says, acknowledging that she too hears the whispering voices. "I'll have a word with them later. They ought to know better."

"They've more business being here than I do," I reply, and she silently watches me for a moment or two. Her grey eyes have gone almost entirely black, and I can no longer distinguish the irises from the pupils.

"They ought to know better," she says again, and this time her tone leaves me no room for argument.

There are tales that I've heard, and bits of dreams I sometimes think I've borrowed – from her or one of her apostles – that I find somewhat more convincing than either newspaper accounts of depleted fish stocks or rumors of a cataclysmic hurricane. There are the spook stories I've overheard, passed between children. There are yarns traded by the half dozen or so grizzled old men who sit outside the filling station near the widow's boardinghouse, who seem possessed of no greater ambition than checkers and hand-rolled cigarettes, cheap gin and gossip. I have begun to believe the truth is not something that was entrusted to the press, but, instead, an ignominy the town has struggled, purposefully, to forget, and which is now recalled dimly or not at all. There is remaining no consensus to be had, but there *are* common threads from which I have woven rough speculation.

Late one night, very near the end of summer or towards the beginning of fall, there was an unusually high tide. It quickly swallowed the granite jetty and the shingle, then broke across the seawall and flooded the streets of the harbor. There was a full moon that night, hanging low and ripe on the eastern horizon, and by its wicked reddish glow men and women saw the things that came slithering and creeping and lurching out of those angry waves. The invaders cast no shadow, or the moonlight shone straight through them, but was somehow oddly distorted. Or, perhaps, what came out of the sea that night glimmered faintly with an eerie phosphorescence of its own.

I know that I'm choosing lurid, loaded words here – *wicked, lurching, hungry, eerie* – hoping, I suppose, to discredit all the cock and bull I've heard, trying to neuter those schoolyard demons. But, in my defence, the children and the old men whom I've overheard were quite a bit less discreet. They have little use, and even less concern, for the sensibilities of people who aren't going to believe them, anyway. In some respects, they're almost as removed as she, as distant and disconnected as the other shanty dwellers here in the rubble at the edge of the bay.

"I would be sorry," she says, "if you were to sail away to Africa."

"I'm not going anywhere. There isn't anywhere I want to go. There isn't anywhere I'd rather be."

She smiles again, and this time I don't allow myself to look away. She has teeth like those of a very small shark, and they glint wet and dark in healthy pink gums. I have often wondered how she manages not to cut her lips or tongue on those teeth, why there are not always trickles of drying blood at the corners of her thin lips. She's bitten into me enough times now. I have ugly crescent scars across my shoulders and chest and upper arms to prove that we are lovers, stigmata to make her apostles hate me that much more.

"It's silly of you to waste good money on a room," she says, changing the course of our conversation. "You could stay here with me. I hate the nights when you're in the village, and I'm alone."

"Or you could go back with me," I reply. It's a familiar sort of futility, this exchange, and we both know our lines by heart, just as we both know the outcome.

"No," she says, her shark's smile fading. "You know that I can't. You know they'd never have me up there," and she nods in the general direction of the town.

And yes, I do know that, but I've never yet told her that I do.

The tide rose up beneath a low red moon and washed across the waterfront. The sturdy wharf was shattered like matchsticks, and boats of various shapes and sizes – dories and jiggers, trollers and Bermuda-rigged schooners – were torn free of their moorings and tossed onto the shivered docks. But there was no storm, no wind, no lashing rain. No thunder and lightning and white spray off the breakers. The air was hot and still that night, and the cloudless sky blazed with the countless pin-prick stars that shine brazenly through the punctured dome of Heaven.

"They say the witch what brought the trouble came from someplace up Amesbury way," I heard one of the old men tell the others, months and months ago. None of his companions replied, neither nodding their heads in agreement, nor voicing dissent. "I heard she made offerings every month, on the night of the new moon, and I heard she had herself a daughter, though I never learned the girl's name. Don't guess it matters, though. And the name of her father, well, ain't nothing I'll ever say aloud."

That night, the cobbled streets and alleyways were fully submerged for long hours. Buildings and houses were lifted clear of their foundations and dashed one against the other. What with no warning of the freakish tide, only a handful of the waterfront's inhabitants managed to escape the deluge and gain the safety of higher ground. More than two hundred souls perished, and for weeks afterwards the corpses of the drowned continued to wash ashore. Many of the bodies were so badly mangled that they could never be placed with a name or a face, and went unclaimed, to be buried in unmarked graves in the village beyond the dunes.

I can no longer hear the whisperers through the thin walls of her shack, so I'll assume that they've gone, or have simply had their say and subsequently fallen silent. Possibly, they're leaning now with their ears pressed close to the corrugated aluminum and rotting clapboard, listening in, hanging on her every syllable, even as my own voice fills them with loathing and jealous spite.

"I'll have a word with them," she tells me for the third time. "You should feel as welcome here as any of us."

The sea swept across the land, and, by the light of that swollen, sanguine moon, grim approximations of humanity moved freely, unimpeded, through the flooded thoroughfares. Sometimes they swam, and sometimes they went about deftly on all fours, and sometimes they shambled clumsily along, as though walking were new to them and not entirely comfortable.

"They weren't men," I overheard a boy explaining to his friends. The boy had ginger-colored hair, and he was nine, maybe ten years old at the most. The children were sitting together at the edge of the weedy vacant lot where a traveling carnival sets up three or four times a year.

"Then were they women?" one of the others asked him.

The boy frowned and gravely shook his head. "No. You're not listening. They weren't women, neither. They weren't *anything* human. But, what I heard said, if you were to take all the stuff gets pulled up in trawler nets – all the hauls of cod and flounder and eel, the dogfish and the skates, the squids and jellyfish and crabs, *all* of it and whatever else you can conjure – if you took those things, still alive and wriggling, and could mush them up together into the shapes of men and women, *that's* exactly what walked out of the bay that night."

"That's not true," a girl said indignantly, and the others stared at her. "That's not true at all. God wouldn't let things like that run loose."

The ginger-haired boy shook his head again. "They got different gods than us, gods no one even knows the names for, and that's who the Amesbury witch was worshipping. Those gods from the bottom of the ocean."

"Well, I think you're a liar," the girl told him. "I think you're a blasphemer *and* a liar, and, also, I think you're just making this up to scare us." And then she stood and stalked away across the weedy lot, leaving the others behind. They all watched her go, and then the ginger-haired boy resumed his tale.

"It gets worse," he said.

A cold rain has started to fall, and the drops hitting the tin roof sound almost exactly like bacon frying in a skillet. She's moved away from me, and is sitting naked at the edge of the bed, her long legs dangling over the side, her right shoulder braced against the rusted iron headboard. I'm still lying on the damp sheets, staring up at the leaky ceiling, waiting for the water tumbling from the sky to find its way inside. She'll set jars and cooking pots beneath the worst of the leaks, but there are far too many to bother with them all.

"I can't stay here forever," she says. It's not the first time, but, I admit, those words always take me by surprise. "It's getting harder being here. Every day, it gets harder on me. I'm so awfully tired, all the time."

I look away from the ceiling, at her throat and the peculiar welts just below the line of her chin. The swellings first appeared a few weeks back, and the skin there has turned dry and scaly, and has taken on a sickly greyish-yellow hue. Sometimes, there are boils, or seeping blisters. When she goes out among the others, she wears the silk scarf I gave her, tied about her neck so that they won't have to see. So they won't ask questions she doesn't want to answer.

"I don't have to go alone," she says, but doesn't turn her head to look at me. "I don't want to leave you here."

"I can't," I say.

"I know," she replies.

And this is how it almost always is. I come down from the village, and we make love, and she tells me her dreams, here in this ramshackle cabin out past the dunes and dog roses and the gale-stunted trees. In her dreams, I am always leaving her behind, buying tickets on tramp steamers or signing on with freighters, sailing away to the Ivory Coast or Portugal or Singapore. I can't begin to recall all the faraway places she's dreamt me leaving her for. Her nightmares have sent me round and round the globe. But the truth is, *she's* the one who's leaving, and soon, before the first snows come.

I know it (though I play her games of transference), and all her apostles know it, too. The ones who have come down from the village and never gone back up the hill again. The vagrants and squatters and winos, the lunatics and true believers, who have turned their backs on the world, but only after it turned its back on them. Destitute and cast away, they found the daughter of the sea, each of them, and the shanty town is dotted with their tawdry, makeshift altars and shrines. She knows precisely what she is to them, even if she won't admit it. She knows that these lost souls have been blinded by the trials and tribulations of their various, sordid lives, and *she* is the soothing darkness they've found. She is the only genuine balm they've ever known against the cruel glare of the sun and the moon, which are the unblinking eyes of the gods of all mankind.

She sits there, at the edge of the bed. She is always alone, no matter how near we are, no matter how many apostles crowd around and eavesdrop and plot my demise. She stares at the flapping sheet of plastic tacked up where the windowpane used to be, and I go back to watching the ceiling. A single drop of rainwater gets through the layers of tin and tarpaper shingles and lands on my exposed belly.

She laughs softly. She doesn't laugh very often anymore, and I shut my eyes and listen to the rain.

"You can really have no notion how delightful it will be, when they take us up and throw us, with the lobsters, out to sea," she whispers, and then laughs again.

I take the bait, because I almost always take the bait.

"But the snail replied 'Too far, too far!' and gave a look askance," I say, quoting Lewis Carroll, and she doesn't laugh. She starts to scratch at the welts below her chin, then stops herself.

"In the halls of my mother," she says, "there is such silence, such absolute and immemorial peace. In that hallowed place, the mind can be still. There is serenity, finally, and an end to all sickness and fear." She pauses, and looks at the floor, at the careless scatter of empty tin cans and empty bottles and bones picked clean. "But," she continues, "it will be lonely down there, without you. It will be something even worse than lonely."

I don't reply, and in a moment, she gets to her feet and goes to stand by the door.

"But She Also Lies Broken and Transformed": An Afterword

In nova fert animus mutatas dicere formas corpora. My spirit moves me to tell of bodies changed into new forms. So begins Ovid's *Metamorphoses*, the monumental braiding of Greek myth into Latin epic which in its time came in second only to Vergil's *Aeneid* as the preeminent poem of the classical world; its continuing influence through the medieval and Renaissance periods into the modern day is incalculable. If you know the stories of Echo and Narcissus, or Arachne the weaver, or Daphne who escaped from lust-struck Apollo to become the laurel tree, or Pygmalion who carved himself a lover of ivory that warmed to flesh in his embrace, you have Ovid and his *mutatas formas*, his changed shapes, to thank for it.

Caitlín R. Kiernan sings of the *changing*. Again and again throughout these stories, their subjects (or objects) are reshaped in ways both figurative and fleshly: from wolves, into doorways, into states of becoming which have no fixed end, no aetiological resolution. The transitions can be as simple as the consent which makes the difference of a sacrifice or the snap of a shutter which preserves a moment of intimacy as art. Some entail only a shift of understanding: the recognition by practical Cala Weatherall of "The Melusine (1898)" that she hungers for more in her world than the clear laws of mathematics and a bed untroubled by men. Some are achievable only through the completion of complex sequences of action: the comprehensive medical-sociological modifications of "I Am the Abyss and I am the Light," the title ritual of "The Belated Burial." No one leaves any of these stories as they entered, if only in awareness of that fact.

In some, the act of transformation accompanies an identifiable narrative motive. The nameless young man of "Rappaccini's Dragon (Murder Ballad No. 5)" makes himself a poisoned garden in order to avenge the death of his twin brother; he is at once mastermind, decoy, and murder weapon, Vindice playing the venom-smeared skull. (All revenge tragedies are metamorphoses. The bereaved become the reavers: Benjamin Barker into Sweeney Todd, Beatrix Kiddo into The Bride. The agent of their conversion, an absorption into the habits and movements of another as attentive and limerent as love.) The narrator of "Dancing with the Eight of Swords" derives pleasure from the serial murder of her "beautiful ones," a process which involves the application of cold and cyanoacrylate and renders its recipients "sculpture." The storyteller of "The Thousand-and-Third Tale of Scheherazade" imitates his namesake in order to prolong his life, already so altered by his captivity among the changelings of Federal Hill that any move he makes to retain it feels less like self-preservation than volunteering for further uncertainty. Change in these cases is a means to an end, the byproduct of a process oriented elsewhere; that it occurs is not inconsequential, but neither was it the primary drive. More often, though, change is its own *raison d'être*. The one piece of horror in this book is the lead story, where a wolf robbed of her pelt like a selkie of its skin discovers she cannot reclaim it; she can possess the physical object of fur and hide, but she will still die locked in this insufficient human body, diminished from what she once was. Other characters strain to become more than they are, or to experience as closely as possible that which is. As much as sex or food or breathing, the impulse to be *other* is, in Kiernan's fiction, an essential and justified desire.

The word is used advisedly. Ovid's explorations of identity through its loss or alteration are not solely sexual in theme or focus, but his most memorable stories are those impelled by love or desire, especially the transgressive or ambiguous which implicitly question the limits by which the normal is defined – the incestuous obsessions of Myrrha and Byblis, the genderbending romance of Iphis and Ianthe, the infamous, fatal passion of Pasiphae for her bull. The twenty-five stories reprinted here under the heading of "Weird Romance" were originally published in *Sirenia Digest*, whose subtitle until February 2010 was *A Monthly Journal of the [Weird and] Weirdly Erotic.* Some of the most striking images in this collection are of sexual congress, fundamentally presented *as* a transgressive act – stepping beyond the boundaries, an appropriately polymorphous definition as it applies to anything from simple kink to the transfiguring or annihilating communion of which the human sexual act is posited as a pale, striving reflection:

> "The surgeon – the cannibal surgeon – lays aside her clamps and scalpel, and she stares deeply into her lover's one remaining eye. All the universe is cradled within that eye, which is the soft green of moss after a spring rain. And she says, 'No, I cannot take your voice away.' Before her confused lover can respond, the cannibal says to her, 'I see now that there is more to me than appetite, and more to you than the capacity for surrender. Already, I have taken more than I deserve, and I will take no more, not now or ever.'"
>
> – "The Bed of Appetite"

> When the sleek purplish tip of the hidden organ or appendage emerges from the folds of her labia, there are audible gasps from the audience. The girl encircles it with her left thumb and middle finger, and the spotlight glimmers wetly off that taut iridescent shaft. But before the watchers can mistake her for some common hermaphrodite, the head of the shaft swells slightly and the foreskin opens to reveal minute rows of needle-like teeth. At least, they look more like teeth than anything else, and so the girl has always *thought* of them as teeth.
>
> – "Untitled Grotesque"

> She reaches down to the thatch of the bound woman's pubic hair, and easily slips the detached finger into her – blood making such an excellent lubricant – then

works it in and out, in and out, time after time after time.
— "Concerning Attrition and Severance"

She starts to take the melusine's hand, recalling again details of her vivid dreams – the wordless embraces in lightless, submerged halls formed of coral and the carved ribs of leviathans. Already, she knows the taste of the melusine's thin pink lips, the feel of those vicious teeth upon her skin, the unspeakable pleasure of the faerie's mouth and hands and those appendages for which men have not ever devised names upon her and probing deeply within her.
— "The Melusine (1898)"

And now my head fills up with the vision of the blonde, her flesh gone hard as stone, and, since water ice is, indeed, a mineral, she *was* stone, yes, and she was fossilized, and I'd become Pygmalion inverted. She was not so thoroughly colorless as marble, but the frost that dappled the white, white skin of this Galatea was near enough, I think. "I kissed her frozen lips," I say. "But Aphrodite took no mercy on me."
— "Dancing with the Eight of Swords"

And then you kiss me, and our lips fuse, and now we are one, and now we are whole, a closed system, an odd sort of Ouroboros, the perfected Gemini.
— "Lullaby of Partition and Reunion"

Edith places the tip of one index finger into the nearer end of the slit in the sand. Except it is not merely sand, though there is something of quartz granules and mica flakes and dark specks of feldspar in its composition. *It is flesh crafted from sand*, she thinks, *or sand painstakingly crafted from flesh*. The gross physiology is self-evident now, the *labia majora* and *labia minora*, the *glans clitoridis* and clitoral hood. It weeps, or simply secretes, something not so different from sea foam. And lying within it

is the teardrop-shaped stone that Sammie slipped inside
herself while standing in the tub.

– "The Bone's Prayer"

She's gone, and the box is gone, and the trapezohedron is gone. There's very little remaining to prove she
was ever here. I cannot conceive that one woman's body
and soul were possibly enough to appease that hunger. It
is all beyond my comprehension.

– "At the Gate of Deeper Slumber"

This is more than metamorphosis as the external manifestation
of sexual knowledge or the means of its achievement, the frisson
of the strange or the reassurance of self-image by counterexample.
This is an eroticism of metamorphosis itself, where the capabilities
of the human body to be augmented/deformed/replaced/
reconceived are as powerfully charged as whatever uses that newly
altered body might afterward be put to, where the small responsive
properties of clit or cock or nipple are merely intimations of the
greater pliability of the world in which Kiernan's characters make
their assignations and play their parts. There is a reason the sea
moves through so many of these stories, the parent and original
of their fluid, uncontainable nature. (*Protean*: from Proteus, the
Old Man of the Sea, the primordial sea-god whom Menelaos in
the *Odyssey* must grasp and hold fast while he shifts from seal to
lion to serpent, even to the unsentient shapes of water or tree;
he will prophesy, but only to one who does not let him go. In
none of Kiernan's stories can the otherworld be held where
it does not deign to remain.) It has no final form, no fixity.
All is in flux. So we rarely see interactions between two simply
human beings, unless one of them is in the process of becoming
otherwise; the vectors of change are themselves subject to it, like
the sea-assimilated siren-vampire of "Flotsam" or the marsh-
lover of "Fecunditatum," who was once a woman in her great-
grandfather's greenhouse and now plants seeds of her own within
the narrator's welcoming flesh. Sometimes there are catalysts,
stimulants – a bony disk, an old metal box, an instrument fallen
from the sky, a peculiar greenish stone – but these objects, too,

rarely keep the shapes in which they were (or allowed themselves to be, since the distinction of in-animate, much like the division between the terrible and the transcendent, is so permeable in these stories as to be nearly meaningless) discovered. In one of the gentlest stories, "Beatification," we observe the protagonist in the last stages of her preparation for a ritual feast in honor of Mother Hydra (the Lovecraftian sea-figure Kiernan has most made her own, another casual transformation) at the hands of a "pretty eunuch." The shaving, the anointing with spiced oils, the stuffing with "peeled garlic gloves and whole yellow chanterelles, diced shiitakes, peppercorns, and ripe cranberries" are almost cosmetic adjustments, the taste of her blood "[o]nly an intimation of what is to come." Unstated, she looks forward to her consumption by those who worship through her, their conduit of godhead; what she is becoming is transubstantiation. We do not see the miracle completed, the violet-eyed woman as we knew her finished. Where the story ends, in our minds she is always changing. At the ends of some stories, we do not even know into what.

The *other*. There must be lines drawn somewhere, or the act of crossing them is without meaning. A recurring motif in *Confessions of a Five-Chambered Heart*, appropriate to its genre, is the sexual meeting with something the narrator can neither categorize nor entirely understand, which is both damning and correct. It seduces, sometimes. Sometimes it asks no leave. (Janet held on to Tam Lin while he was changed in her arms to beast after wild beast, a red-hot burning iron last of all: she cannot let go until he is a man in his own mother-naked skin again or the fairy land's hold over him will remain. She was carrying his child, her own body changing. Had she failed, his heart would have been turned to stone within him, his eyes made into knots of tree. Imagine running your fingertips over the wooden eyes of the man you love, the cursed toy of the fairy queen. The fairy lady of "Murder Ballad No. 6" kisses the lips of a man with stranger eyes than these.) Here as in Kiernan's earlier, less explicitly erotic work, there is a terrifying immanence in yielding to something which is incomprehensibly greater than oneself, after which nothing, literally, can ever be the same. Knowledge is a hole in the world into which her characters fall, not because early film history or classical literature or planetary science are valueless disciplines, but because they cannot pertain to the place where words run out. Namelessness, an existence beyond the reductive summations of human taxonomy, in fact seems to designate the most successful kind of metamorphosis.

"A Canvas for Incoherent Arts" at first appears to be the outlier in this table of contents. The title is a nod to the *Salon des Arts Incohérents* of fin-de-siècle Paris, an avant-garde, anti-art movement interested in the deliberate presentation of the irrational, the experimental, and the absurd, a sort of proto-Dada incorporating everything from found art to conceptual art to works of mixed media where the media could include a live rabbit, a painted man, and a moon made of yesterday's bread; given the combination of caprice and strict objective that governs the characters' interactions, it seems an appropriate allusion. There is a striking absence of overt metamorphosis. A woman waits alone in a room; she is left the same way – perhaps – after a brief, disturbing visit from a second party so practiced in camouflaging their physical tells – footsteps, voice, even distance – that s/he appears as anonymous and ominous as the walls of the "black room" within which they observe the rules of their long-played game. There is the possibility that a third person has been introduced into what has heretofore been a private exercise, although it is possible that the narrator is only intended to fear so. This is, after all, the ideal of the game: "You are here, in this black room, to scare me, and I am here to be scared." And yet the title turns out to be literal – nothing in the black room has coherence except the narrator's anxiety, which she *can* name and describe, the adrenaline nausea, the dry throat, the stinging prickle of sweat, the unsettling combination of annoyance and true dread as she is forced to wonder whether the game has finally altered in ways she was not prepared for, despite her anticipatory acceptance of the start conditions: "I am alone in the room…and I have absolutely no way of knowing what will happen next." The "unblemished darkness" has become the sea, without the sea's comforting indifference. Everything may be shifting shape. Everything may *have* no shape. There is nothing in the dark to get hold of, but there is the awful prospect that the dark might reach out and take hold itself. The unknowable, the unnameable.

It is perhaps the most minimalist story in the collection, and the most brutal.

The defining story of the collection, however, may be "Derma Sutra (1891)." In the steam-powered, alternate version of Denver, Colorado known as Cherry Creek, a pure-minded, self-styled monster slayer is defiled so thoroughly and transcendently by a creature known only as "the nameless woman" that she becomes, through the tattooing of her stringently "unsullied" skin with desecrating texts and the sexual invasions of her prey-turned-predator, a monster to rival her midwife-maker. "She felt that fleeting instant when the zealot fell and the crusader came to understand that she now numbered among the ranks of the *bêtes noires* she once hunted with such an insatiable fervor and such perfect conviction...What wakes is unfathomable, and broken, and aroused to new purpose." The act is liberating and appalling: it obliterates "Stephanie Brockett" and awakens in her reforged body something even more unclassifiable than its parent, never even described with the same epithet twice. "[A] *novel* being... the lovely creature coiled inside the husk of Tess Brockett...the living embodiment of two profane books...this flawed and flawless vessel." At one point the nameless woman makes mental reference to "her Creation, this delicate, indestructible Construct" as if in homage to Mary Shelley's Creature, but the style is the closest Kiernan has allowed herself to a pastiche of Lovecraft (describing acts which would no doubt have horrified him). It is also the most clinically and erotically graphic of the stories in this collection, tabulating the chemical makeup of an aroused woman's juices with the same attention it devotes to the geography of Cherry Creek or the listing of real and fictitious texts that have gone into the "vessel"'s tattoos. With the same frankness, the nameless woman explains her rationale for the transformation rather than elimination of Tess Brockett in terms that might stand equally as an apologia for the existence of *Confessions of a Five-Chambered Heart* in all its polyvalence as opposed to the kinds of shape-change signified by the were-leopard boyfriends who populate the shelves of paranormal romance alongside sparkling vampires: "But in such an easy deed would have lain no glory and no genuine accomplishment. Most importantly, no *perversion*."

To pervert, from the Latin *pervertere*: to turn round or turn about, to turn a thing from its rightful course and send it in another direction altogether, now used almost solely in the sexual sense or the sense of ideological distortion. *In quae miracula... verteris?* one of Ovid's characters asks another, mid-transformation – *What astonishing thing are you turning into?* (A dolphin, as it happens. Do not mistreat Dionysos, *virginea puerum...forma, a boy with a maiden's look.*) It is an alterity that would be recognized by more characters than Medon or Tess Brockett, though some of them would also count it a gift. It is the twists and bends the author gives to familiar elements of myth and folklore as they are retold and repurposed in the telling, so that neither mermaids nor harpies nor satyrs can look quite the same when these stories are done with them. And it is a depravity, if it is a depravity, or a release, if it is a release, which is not confined to the turning page. Reader, you have let the writer in. You have allowed her stories to enter you and they must, like any foreign introduction, effect a change. (In the red book of "The Peril of Liberated Objects, or The Voyeur's Seduction," rape is committed by one archetypal figure of innocence on another while the woman reading reaches climax: "She perceives the unicorn's every violent thrust, but is no less the victim than the rapist, no more the ravager than she is the ravaged, broken maiden. And she would have it no other way." Did you read the story? Were you her, too? Is that perverted? Discuss.) At the end of this book, you also lie broken and transformed. Or perhaps you are admiring your tattoos. Either way, Caitlín R. Kiernan has changed you, and like all the best metamorphoses, it is not over yet.

It is that sinister enchantment which derives from a profound evil that is kept at just the right distance from us so that we may experience both our love and our fear of it in one sweeping sensation.

Thomas Ligotti, "Nethescurial" (1991)

The preceding stories first appeared in *Sirenia Digest*, Issues Nos. 23-41, October 2007-May 2009. The author would like to thank all the people who have made, and continue to make, the *Digest* possible, beginning with the subscribers, and including William K. Schafer, Vince Locke, Kathryn Pollnac, Jacob Garbe, Gordon Duke, Sonya Taaffe, and Geoffrey H. Goodwin. You guys *still* keep the wolves at bay.

"Subterraneous" and "Fecunditatum (Murder Ballad No. 6)" originally appeared as "Untitled 31" and "Untitled 33," respectively. "Murder Ballad No. 7" originally appeared as "Murder Ballad No. 6." Also, the Elder Sign as depicted in "At the Gate of Deeper Slumber" follows August Derleth's version, and for that I apologize to the memory of Lovecraft.

About the Author

Trained as a vertebrate paleontologist, Caitlín R. Kiernan did not turn to fiction writing until 1992. Since then, she has published eight novels – *The Five of Cups, Silk, Threshold, Low Red Moon, Murder of Angels, Daughter of Hounds, The Red Tree*, and, most recently, *The Drowning Girl: A Memoir*. Her short fiction has been collected in *Tales of Pain and Wonder*; *Wrong Things* (with Poppy Z. Brite); *From Weird and Distant Shores*; the World Fantasy Award-nominated *Alabaster* and *To Charles Fort, With Love*; and *A is for Alien*. She has also published a short sf novel, *The Dry Salvages*, and two volumes of erotica, *Frog Toes and Tentacles* and *Tales from the Woeful Platypus*. She has scripted graphic novels for DC Vertigo, including thirty-eight issues of *The Dreaming* and the mini-series *The Girl Who Would Be Death* and *Bast: Eternity Game*. In 2012, she will return to comics with *Alabaster* (Dark Horse). Her many chapbooks have included *Trilobite: The Writing of Threshold, The Merewife*, and *The Black Alphabet*. In 2011, Subterranean Press released a retrospective of her early work, *Two Worlds and In Between: The Best of Caitlín R. Kiernan (Volume One)*. She recently completed her next novel, *Blood Oranges*.